THUG LIFE: E~

"I'm goin' to the bat~
He stood and began walking towards the men's room. His route took him past Mario, who was still chuckling with his boys about Shade's sisters. However, just as he drew even that nigga, Shade quickly spun towards him, slipping a hand under Mario's chin and pulling his head back, while at the same time placing a steak knife at the fool's throat.

Mario and his idiotic friends immediately went silent. They had been so busy guffawing that they hadn't even noticed Shade take the knife from his set of cutlery when he stood up. But they damn sure noticed it now.

Mario gulped and then slowly lifted his hands, palms out – a gesture that was intended to tell his friends not to do anything stupid while simultaneously keeping his hands where Shade could see them.

"Do not mistake me for somebody who gives a fuck about consequences," Shade hissed, leaning close to Mario's ear. "I'll stab you in the neck in the middle of this fuckin' restaurant, and post a video of that shit online, unnastand?"

Mario nodded – or rather, nodded as best he could with his head pulled back and throat exposed.

"Good," Shade said. "Now listen, 'cause I'm only gone say this shit once. You can say whatever the fuck you want about *me*. I don't give a shit. In fact, I'm one of the few muhfuckas on the planet who'll let niggas get away with talkin' shit 'bout my momma. Again, I don't give a fuck. But if you *ever* mention my sistas again, I'm gonna do shit to you that's so fucked up, they gone need a new branch of science to describe it."

With that he tossed the knife onto the table, at the same time roughly shoving Mario on the side of the head. He then walked out of the restaurant, feeling Mario's eyes on his back like daggers the entire time.

THUG LIFE: EMANCIPATED

THUG LIFE: EMANCIPATED

By

Nirvana Blaque

THUG LIFE: EMANCIPATED

This book is published by Fat Boy Publishing.

ISBN: 978-1-937666-60-6

Printed in the U.S.A.

THUG LIFE: EMANCIPATED

ACKNOWLEDGMENTS

I would like to thank the following for their help with this book: GOD, as always, for HIS grace and mercy, and my family, who are always there for me.

THUG LIFE: EMANCIPATED

Thank you for purchasing this book! If you enjoyed it, please feel free to leave a review on the site from which it was purchased.

Also, if you would like to be notified when I release new books, please subscribe to my mailing list via the following link: http://eepurl.com/gShzML

Finally, for those who may be interested, I have included my blog and social media info:

Blog: https://nirvanablaque.blogspot.com/

Facebook: https://www.facebook.com/nirvana.black.3597

Twitter: https://twitter.com/BlaqueNirvana

PROLOGUE

"What da fuck is this?" Shade asked, looking around.

"It' a fuckin' gold mine, like I told you," replied Sneak, proudly surveying the room they were in.

Shade gave his companion a reproachful look, then turned his attention back to their surroundings.

They were currently in a room in the subbasement of a dilapidated – actually condemned *– high-rise. The place was pitch black, but they were able to see courtesy of a couple of headlamps that Shade always kept in his tool bag. The light from the headlamps revealed the room where they found themselves to be filled with lots of piping and all kinds of machinery: HVAC equipment, water heaters, air handlers, and so on.*

"It's not a gold mine, you stupid nigga," Shade admonished. "It's just an old-ass mechanical room. It's how they controlled heat, water and all that shit when people used to live here."

"Well, whatever it is, there's a lotta fuckin' metal in here," Sneak said. "And that gotta be worth sommin'."

"It ain't worth shit," Shade countered.

Sneak shook his head. "Naw, man. I saw this report on the news sayin' steel and shit is worth like hundreds-a-dollahs a ton."

Shade looked at him in exasperation. "So?"

"So this like findin' a fuckin' treasure chest!" Sneak muttered excitedly.

"Nigga, how much you thank a ton is?"

"I don't know," Sneak admitted with a shrug. "Like two or three pounds?"

"Try two thousand."

Sneak's eyes went wide. "What?"

"Yeah, nigga. A ton is two thousand pounds. Yo ass shudda paid mo' attention in math class. Besides, if you could get that much for metal, niggas all through the hood wouldn't be lettin' cars just sit there and rust in they front yard. They'd sell them bitches."

Sneak looked down sheepishly. "I guess that make sense."

"No need to guess. Fact is, steel is cheap, muhfucka – you can get a ton for a few bills. So this ain't no payday. Shit… When you said you found sommin' in here you needed help with, I thought we was talkin' 'bout a fuckin' safe or sommin', not a damn boiler room."

As he spoke, Shade thought about how he'd come to be involved in this shit.

Basically, the building they were in had been condemned for years and was slated for demolition in about a week. In a bout of inspiration, Sneak had decided to go through the place and see if there was anything inside worth taking. Normally it would have been an utter waste of time; after years of dilapidation the place had been used as everything from a crack den to a hangout for teen degenerates. That being the case, it had been picked pretty clean.

That said, Sneak had a gift for finding things that other people overlooked. It was pretty much how he got his nickname: he picked up on shit that would sneak by other muhfuckas. In this instance, he'd come across an area in the basement where the ceiling had collapsed, leaving a large pile of debris against one wall. In sorting through it, he'd come to realize that there was a door behind the rubble, which led to the mechanical room. Excited by his discovery, he'd then offered Shade part of what he would only describe as a "massive payday," but without giving any details.

Now that he was here, tool bag and all, Shade was having a tough time not getting pissed.

"Anyway," Shade finally droned. "Thanks for wastin' my fuckin' time – 'specially on a Friday night."

"Hold up," Sneak said. "There's gotta be sommin' in here worth takin'."

"I told you, nigga – steel is fuckin' cheap. So's iron and most other metal you gonna find in here."

"Okay, but what about copper? Some of this shit look like it might be copper, and I remember that's more expensive that steel."

"Yeah, it is," Shade admitted with a nod. *"At least yo ass was halfway payin' attention to that news report."*

"Well, let's see what copper we can get outta here."

"It ain't worth it," Shade insisted.

"It's gotta be worth somin',*"* Sneak insisted. *"I see junkies tryin' to sell that shit to scrapyards all the time."*

"A junkie will sell his own momma for one hit off a pipe," Shade said. However, noting that Sneak still seemed taken with the copper idea, he went on. *"Look, copper usually go for three, maybe four bucks a pound on the open market. You gone be sellin' to a scrapyard, so you talkin' 'bout bein' paid maybe half that at best, but most likely it'll be less — say, one-fifty. That mean hauling a hundred pounds of copper outta here is only gonna get you 'round a hundred and fifty dollahs."*

"One-fifty?" Sneak echoed disbelievingly. *"Seriously?"*

"Yeah, nigga," Shade stressed. *"There's a reason I don't do this kinda shit. It makes for a shit payday. Now let's step."*

"Wait," Sneak said softly. *"Can we do it — the copper, I mean?"*

"What da fuck?" Shade blurted out *"You deaf, nigga? This shit ain't worth the time or the effort."*

"It is to me,*"* Sneak admitted.

"Then get some other nigga to help you with it."

"It'll take time to find somebody else who know how to take pipes and shit loose and won't try to cheat me. Plus, by the time I get somebody, the damn crackheads will have found this place and stripped it clean."

"This buildin's a fuckin' deathtrap," Shade shot back. *"Even the junkies know that, which is why nobody in they right mind will come up in this bitch. We lucky this muhfucka ain't collapsed on toppa us. We'll just designate this shit a life lesson and call it a day."*

"I can't," Sneak insisted. *"I need the money. And you owe me."*

Shade frowned. He really didn't want to put in a bunch of time and effort taking out a shitload of pipe that would sell for less than he'd earn working a shift at a fast food joint. But Sneak was right – the dude had done him a solid in the recent past, so Shade owed him.

"A'ight," Shade grumbled, acquiescing, "But don't thank that this shit gone become a habit."

****

It took Shade maybe an hour to get a decent amount of copper – roughly fifty pounds. The problem was that the building was old and there was lots of rust and corrosion. Sneak, of course, was no help whatsoever. He was sixteen – the same age as Shade – but had dropped out of school after ninth grade. Thus, he had little in the way of practical knowledge and even less in the way of useful skills, other than a talent for occasionally finding shit.

Shade, on the other hand, had had a grandfather who pretty much served as the neighborhood handyman. He'd been able to fix everything from plumbing to electrical to automobiles, and he'd passed that knowledge on to his grandson. More to the point, fixing shit was pretty much how Shade formally earned money, although those repairman skills also came in useful at times like this.

"Okay, I thank that's all we can get for now," Shade finally said as he shoved a piece of pipe into a duffel bag Sneak had brought. "Let's get the fuck outta here."

"Don't seem like much," Sneak mumbled disappointedly.

"Yo ass gonna feel different after luggin' that shit five blocks to the car."

"Ain't you gone carry it part of the way?"

"Nigga, I got my tool bag, plus I just did all the work. So far, you ain't done shit to earn more than a finder's fee."

"A'ight, a'ight," Sneak conceded. "I'll carry it."

Rather than say anything, Shade merely grunted in irritation and began heading towards the exit. Sneak slung the bag of pipe onto his back with a slight groan, and then followed.

THUG LIFE: EMANCIPATED

As they trudged back up to the ground floor, Shade carefully watched his step. As he had already noted, the fucking building was falling apart (it was condemned for a reason), and the last thing he needed was to roll an ankle on some debris or have the floor collapse under him. He also still had his work gloves on; he'd not only worn them when removing the pipe from the mechanical room, but had actually had them on since the moment they stepped inside the place. It was probably overkill, but he didn't see the need to risk infection by accidentally cutting his hand on a rusty stairwell railing, jabbing a finger on a nail sticking out of a wall, or any other shit like that. As if in confirmation of this, he suddenly heard Sneak yelp behind him.

"Ouch!" Sneak hissed.

They were currently in a first floor hallway, and in the gloom and silence of the deserted building, Sneak's painful cry – although low and muted – sounded like a grenade going off to Shade.

"What is it?" he asked, keeping his voice to a whisper as he turned to his rear.

"Stubbed my toe on sommin'. Hurts like a muhfucka."

Glancing at the floor, Shade saw what he assumed was the culprit: a large cinderblock.

"Look nigga, you wearin' that headlamp for a reason," he admonished. "Use it."

Sneak nodded. "A'ight, I'll–"

"Shhh!" Shade suddenly hissed, cutting him off. He listened for a second, and then heard the noise he'd picked up a second ago: a grunt or cough of some sort.

"Turn yo headlamp off," he ordered.

Sneak let out a frustrated groan. "But you just said–"

"Turn it off!" Shade grumbled, trying to keep his voice down as he reached up and turned his own headlamp off. A moment later, his companion followed suit.

"What is it?" Sneak asked.

"Somebody in here with us," Shade stated. "Come on."

"But I can't see shit," Sneak protested.

Shade massaged his temples in aggravation for a moment, then said, "Hold out ya hand."

He felt more than saw Sneak comply. Taking the outthrust hand, Shade placed it on his shoulder. He then turned back around and said over his shoulder, "Stay close and be quiet." He then began heading towards the exit again.

With the headlamps off, their pace was practically glacial, but it couldn't be helped. The lights would have made them easy targets for whoever was in the building with them. However, as they continued walking, the sound Shade had earlier began to get louder and become more distinct. Moreover, it also seemed to be accompanied by something akin to a person clapping their hands. After hearing it for a few minutes, he suddenly had a very good idea of what was going.

He was proven right a minute or so later when they rounded a corner and saw a soft light coming from a doorway farther down the corridor. Still staying quiet, they crept closer, with Shade noting the noises getting louder. Right before they got to the doorway in question, Shade halted and turned to Sneak.

There was enough light coming from the doorway for them to see each other, and Shade noted a look of befuddlement on Sneak's face. Ignoring it, Shade put a finger up to his lips, indicating silence. Sneak, still looking nonplussed, nodded.

Shade turned and began swiftly, but quietly, walking past the doorway the light was coming from. However, he couldn't resist glancing into the room's interior – and he saw exactly what he had expected. Still, he never stopped moving. The same couldn't be said of his companion.

Human nature being what it is, Sneak was compelled to look into the room as well. But instead of just glancing in and continuing on as Shade he had done, he stopped and stared. In truth, he practically froze in place.

Sensing that Sneak was no longer keeping up, Shade looked over his shoulder and saw him standing in the doorway, transfixed. Unlike Shade, Sneak apparently hadn't figured out what the noises were in advance, and seeing it had caught him off guard. Shade was about to walk back and try to quietly pull him away when Sneak suddenly did something totally fucking unexpected.

"Hey!" Sneak shouted into the room. "Hey you fuckin' faggots! I see you, and I'm gonna tell everybody!"

What da fuck???!!! Shade thought. Here they were trespassing, breaking-and-entering, burgling, committing larceny and a dozen other crimes… The last thing they needed was somebody being able to put them at the scene. But that dumbass Sneak didn't seem to realize that. (Not to mention the fact that what they'd seen was enough to make most niggas want to shut them up permanently.)

Suddenly furious, Shade raced back towards Sneak. Concurrently, he heard something akin to clothes rustling, and a deep voice said, "Get that lil' nigga."

Sneak still just stood there, not seeming to understand that shit was about to go down. Shade grabbed him by the scruff of the neck and damn near dragged his ass away from the doorway. It seemed to break whatever spell Sneak was under, and Shade let him go. He then switched on his headlamp and started to run, the pounding of footsteps behind letting him know Sneak was running as well.

Shade hadn't gone more than a few steps before a sound like a thunderclap boomed in the hallway. Wincing, Shade instinctively ducked his head; at the same time, something slammed into the upper portion of the hallway a few feet ahead of him, chipping the drywall.

Gunshot, he immediately said to himself. He also instinctively understood that – as narrow as the hallway was – whoever was shooting at them wouldn't miss many more times. (It also didn't help that his headlamp was on, but he'd be fumbling around in the dark without it.)

Desperate, Shade flung himself at a nearby door as another shot rang out, forcefully flinging it open as he dashed inside, followed by Sneak.

They were in a stairwell. Without wasting a moment, Shade began dashing up the stairs, stealthily mouthing, "Come on!" over his shoulder.

A few seconds later, he was at the door for the next floor but found it chained shut. Shade mentally groaned, but started running up to the next floor, with Sneak hot on his heels. It was chained as well. Even worse, he heard voices below them.

"They musta come in here," said a gravelly voice, and Shade saw illumination from some type of electric lantern – a device he'd seen when he'd first passed the men in the room on the first floor. A moment later, he heard footsteps pounding up the stairs.

Shit! he muttered to himself, then he and Sneak dashed up to the next floor – not wasting any effort on trying to be quiet – only to find it fettered as well. The same was true of the floor above.

It wasn't until they reached the sixth floor that they found the door leading from the stairwell to be unchained.

Or the chains were cut off, Shade mentally concluded as they exited the stairwell and began dashing down the sixth-floor hallway. As with the rest of the building, it was pitch black except for the light from Shade's headlamp. Likewise, there was more evidence of why this place was condemned: there were gaping holes in the walls, water was dripping from the ceiling in spots, and there was a strong smell of mildew throughout the place. Last but not least, the floor was warped and uneven in spots.

These were all things that Shade merely noted in passing. His main objective was to put enough distance between them and their pursuers to effectuate an escape of some sort. So focused was he on that notion that he almost made a fatal error.

He was at a point where the warped floor appeared to rise up like a speedbump of sorts, then he practically skidded to a halt as he realized that there was nothing on the other side. Or rather, a good portion of the floor on the other side of the little bump had fallen away – completely collapsed from all appearances. (And from what Shade could see, the same was true of the floor below.) Basically, the warped shape of the floor combined with the minimal amount of light created an optical illusion, making it appear that the hallway was intact until you got right up on it.

The gap in the floor was about fifteen feet wide, with the hallway continuing on the other side. Eyeing the distance, Shade quickly assessed that, with a running start, he could probably jump across – but not with his tool bag. The same was true of Sneak, who – amazingly – was still carrying the bag holding the copper pipe. (Personally, Shade would have dropped that shit a long time ago, but apparently Sneak really did need the money.)

The creak of hinges brought Shade back to himself as he noted that their pursuers had stepped out into the hallway, the light from their lantern making them easy to spot. He hastily reached up to turn off his headlamp, but it was too late. They had been spotted.

"Get 'em!" he heard the gravelly voice say.

A moment later, the sound of gunfire rang out again and Shade ducked. A second later, two things happened almost simultaneously. First, he heard a loud clatter as Sneak dropped the bag of piping and staggered into him. At the same time, Shade saw the electric lantern that their pursuers were carrying hit the floor and go sliding a few feet to the side. By virtue of its illumination, he then saw one of their pursuers slowly rising from a prone position on the floor.

Shade immediately realized what had happened. The uneven floor had tripped one of the niggas chasing them – the one holding the lantern – and sent him sprawling. At that juncture, he also understood something else from an odd wheezing sound that was coming from right next to him: Sneak had been shot.

Knowing that they only had a few seconds, Shade grabbed Sneak and essentially dragged him in the direction of a doorway that he'd seen earlier. He had to feel around for a few moments to locate it, then hustled them inside. At that point he let Sneak flop down to the floor, his back to one of the walls of whatever room they were in.

Shade couldn't tell how bad Sneak was injured, but at the moment had a tough time feeling sorry for him. The stupid muhfucka had basically called out some other niggas for being gay. That kind of shit don't fly in the hood – a muhfucka will cut your heart out for just implying that he might be a rump-rider. Everybody knows that. Sneak damn well should have known it. If a nigga is open and notorious about being gay, he'd be at home fucking his boyfriend in a bed with feather

9

down pillows and thousand-count sheets — not pounding his ass in a condemned building that a stiff breeze could knock over. Now, because of Sneak's inability to keep his fucking mouth closed and turn a blind eye to some shit that was none of his business, they were probably going to die.

"You a'ight?" Shade heard one of the niggas in the hallway ask.

"Yeah," said the other one, "but I'm real pissed now. Wait 'til we find these muhfuckas."

Shade didn't like the sound of that, but they were pretty much trapped. Fumbling around in the dark would get them nowhere fast, but he didn't dare turn his headlamp on.

Hmmm, he thought as an idea suddenly occurred to him.

Feeling for Sneak's head, he found his friend's headlamp and took it off. Peeking out the doorway, he saw one of the niggas in the hallway bending down to pick up the lantern. Knowing that he had no time to waste, Shade leaned out into the hallway, then quickly switch on the headlamp and tossed it — in as straight a line as he could — across the gap in the hallway to the other side.

"There they go!" shouted one of the niggas in the hallway as Shade ducked back inside the room.

Footsteps came pounding down the corridor, and one of the niggas chasing them said, laughingly, "I think one of 'em fell. Hurry up, Glen!"

"No, man — wait…" muttered the other one.

"Come on," said his buddy. "They still — Ahhh!"

"Babe!" screamed the other nigga — Glen — as his boyfriend's yelp seemed to diminish in volume before being abruptly cut off.

Peeking out the doorway, Shade noted Glen standing near the edge of the collapsed floor, holding the lamp in one hand and a gun in the other. He was staring down into the space where his boyfriend had fallen. Shade couldn't really see his face, but the nigga's body language said volumes. And then Glen himself spoke.

10

"*You muhfuckas!*" *He snapped, looking around wildly. "I'm gone kill you!*"

He then began firing randomly into the darkness. Shade flung himself down, lying prone on the floor a few feet from where Sneak was still slumped against the wall. It felt like he lay there forever, but was probably no more than fifteen or twenty seconds – enough time for Glen to empty his clip. Glen, however, was so focused on shooting his quarry that he didn't even seem to notice that he was out of ammo. He just continued squeezing the trigger.

Knowing that the man's gun was empty, Shade now felt he had a chance. More importantly, he had the germ of an idea.

When Glen had been firing, the muzzle flash had provided enough light for Shade to spy something in the hallway that he'd forgotten about: the bag full of copper piping. Now that the man's gun was empty, Shade chose to act on a sudden inspiration.

Dashing into the hallway, he headed to where he'd seen the bag of piping. Not bothering with trying to find the handles, he picked the bag up and flung it at Glen, who was plainly visibly because of the lamp he still held. The bag struck him in the torso, eliciting a slight grunt from the man. However, its momentum pushed him backwards – and over the edge of the collapsed hallway. Unlike his boyfriend, however, Glen went over without a sound. A few seconds later Shade heard a metallic clink as the bag of copper – and presumably Glen – struck the bottom.

THUG LIFE: EMANCIPATED

Chapter 1

"What da fuck, Nissa?" Shade yelled at his sister. "You s'pose to been watchin' her ass!"

"You try keepin' an eye on a crack hoe," Nissa retorted. "You blink, and dem bitches gone."

Shade groaned in frustration. He was pissed at his sister, but she had a point. A fucking crackhead could look like they were out of it and damn near unconscious one second, then the next them muhfuckas juiced up like somebody put a damn long-lasting battery in their back. And the crack hoe in question – their mother Gin – ran hot-and-cold like that all the time.

That said, Gin wasn't a crack hoe, per se. Truth be told, she would do drugs of any and every stripe: crack, weed, smack... She was an equal-opportunity junkie, ready to smoke, snort, or shoot up anything likely to provide her next high (although, to be frank, crack did seem to be her drug of choice).

Under normal circumstances, Shade wouldn't give a fuck where their mother had vanished to, and cared even less about when – or if – she planned on coming back. The problem was that every now and then, like today, they needed her strung-out ass to be in position, and right now she wasn't.

"Look, I'm sorry," Nissa said, interrupting Kane's reverie.

"Don't worry 'bout it," Shade said, his sister's apology alleviating his anger to a large degree.

They were currently in the living room of their home – a three-bedroom, one-bath bungalow that had been home to their family for three generations now. It had been bought by their maternal grandparents about forty years earlier – before the neighborhood went completely to shit. Now it was just another house in the hood, although maintained better than most.

"Well," Shade finally droned, "I gotta go find her. In case you forgot, we got Child Protective Services comin' by soon."

Nissa groaned and rolled her eyes. "I hate that CPS bitch."

Shade nodded. "I know, but we don't need to give her no excuse to flex her muscles – 'less you want her to break us up and ship us all off to different foster homes."

"Naw," his sister mumbled, shaking her head.

"Good, now what time Cherry gettin' home?"

"She should be here any minute," Nissa stated. "She know to come straight home from the bus today."

Shade simply nodded. Their little sister was the sweetest kid on the planet – never gave any one any problems at home, school, wherever. She'd come straight home, just like she'd been told.

"A'ight, I'm gone go find Gin," Shade declared, and began walking towards the front door. A moment later, he was gone.

****

He found Gin, as expected, at a nearby crack den. It was close enough that he probably could have walked there, but since time was of the essence, he had driven their car – a ten-year-old black sedan that had belonged to their grandfather.

The crack house in question was one residence in a long section of row houses, most of which had been boarded up. It was actually the third place that Shade checked, but – other than location – there was barely anything to distinguish it from the other two spots he'd hit.

First of all, like crack houses everywhere, the place was full of junkies. Most were lying around looking lethargic or completely passed out. A couple, however, had glanced up when he came in, but – after satisfying themselves that he wasn't a cop or some other threat – went back into whatever fucking dreamworld they lived in when high.

Next, it was filthy. There was trash everywhere: beer bottles, smashed furniture, old boxes of takeout that were moldy and rancid…even used condoms. (That last made Shade aware of a couple overtly fucking in a corner of the room. He was happy to see that the woman wasn't Gin, although it wouldn't have been the first time he'd caught her in *flagrante dilecto*.)

Finally, the place stank like a muhfucka. It smelled like an elephant had taken a shit in there, vomited, and then died. But it was nothing but the rank and putrid smell of unwashed masses in close proximity. Basically, when you got hooked on shit like crack, hygiene was one of the first things to go.

Eventually he found his mother in a back room, sitting on the floor with her back to the wall, eyes half-closed. She was snuggled up next to some nigga with a nappy-ass afro who had an arm around her.

Shade didn't say anything – just grabbed Gin by the elbow and hauled her ass to her feet. She didn't offer any resistance; she barely seemed to notice he was there. The nigga she'd been next to, however, was a different story. Gin being pulled away from him seemed to trigger something in his drug-addled brain, and he suddenly stood up as Shade began dragging Gin out the room.

"Hey!" shouted the crackhead who'd been next to Gin, causing Shade to spin around. "Where you takin' her?"

Shade looked him up and down for a second. The guy was a lot taller than he looked sitting; he stood at least a head above Shade – maybe six-six – but was also rail thin. In fact, he was damn near emaciated, and looked like a stiff breeze would send him bouncing along like a tumbleweed.

"I said, where you takin' her?" the man repeated.

"How da fuck is that yo bizness?" Shade shot back.

"I gave her a hit off my pipe," the guy explained. "She said if I did, she'd…"

He trailed off as Shade eyed him evilly.

"What, nigga?" Shade demanded. "What exactly was my *momma* s'pose to do for yo black ass?"

"Yo momma?" the tall nigga repeated a little nervously, and Shade saw that he was practically toothless. It was a pointed reminder that he didn't need to get into a scrape with a fucking crackhead.

First of all, as his grandfather had always noted, pounding the shit out of a crackhead was damn near inhumane most of the time.

"Like beating up a baby who's handicapped and retarded," his granddaddy had been fond of stating.

Secondly, as the missing teeth reminded him, a lot of these muhfuckas were seriously diseased. Hygiene might be the first thing to go when it came to junkies, but health was a close second (and usually related to personal sanitation in some way). They had everything from damn cholera to scabies to hoof-and-mouth disease. Punching one of these fools out wasn't worth the risk of getting a cut on your hand or something.

As luck would have it, the nigga facing Shade backed down, saying, "It's cool. She don't owe me nuthin'."

Shade simply glared at the man for a second, then – still holding Gin by the elbow – marched her towards the door.

THUG LIFE: EMANCIPATED

Chapter 2

"We back," Shade shouted as he and Gin walked through the front door. Nissa came out the kitchen, followed by their younger sister Cherry.

Nissa looked their mother up and down for a second, her disapproval evident as she stepped closer. "*You* gone have to get her in the shower."

"Huh?" her brother muttered, perplexed. "I'm the one went out and found her."

"Yeah, but I don't feel like fightin' with her ass," Nissa declared. "She act like soap and water is fuckin' battery acid whenever you try to bathe her – she be scratchin' and clawin' to get out."

"Well, I cleaned her ass up last time," Shade noted. Nissa didn't deny that, but made it clear that she wasn't in the mood to deal with making their mother presentable at the moment.

From there, the argument then went back and forth, with Shade and Nissa each stating why the other should be the one to get their mother washed up. On her part, Gin acted like they weren't even there. She was still in her own world, same as she'd been since Shade found her, and seemingly ignored the bickering between her two oldest kids.

Shade and Nissa had been squabbling for about a minute, when an unexpected voice made them both pause.

"I'll do it," Cherry said. Then, without waiting for a response, she stepped forward and grabbed Gin's hand. "Come on, Momma." A moment later, she began leading Gin to the bathroom.

Shade and Nissa merely looked at each other. Basically, their little sister had put them both to shame by volunteering for the task they were trying to foist off on each other. After a couple of seconds, Nissa sighed in resignation, then followed her sister and mother to the bathroom.

THUG LIFE: EMANCIPATED

Chapter 3

While his sisters worked on Gin, Shade spent a few minutes making sure the house was decent: no piles of dirty dishes in the sink, spoiled food in the fridge, and so on. However, he needn't have bothered; he and Nissa normally kept the place pretty clean, and – knowing what was up – his sister had gone the extra mile to make the place spic-and-span. Still, it didn't hurt to double-check. They didn't want that give that hoe from CPS any excuse to claim they were living in squalor or filthy conditions and needed to be removed from the home.

He had just finished inspecting the kitchen when he heard a car pull up into the driveway. He ran to the living room window and peeked out. As expected, it was Mrs. Romano from CPS.

Shade watched for a second as she heaved her bulk from the aged SUV that she drove. Mrs. Romano was five-four but plainly obese – the bitch had to weigh at least three hundred pounds. That said, she was surprisingly spry for someone her size, and (aside from having to occasionally squeeze in behind the wheel of a car) didn't seem to be inhibited by her weight to any large degree.

Shade stepped back from the window and then walked quickly to the bathroom. Sticking his head inside, he noted that his sisters had seemingly finished getting Gin washed up and were in the process of drying her off.

"She here," he announced. "Game faces on."

He then headed back to the living room without waiting for a reply. Marching straight to the front door, he stood by until the bell rang the bell, waited a few seconds, and then opened the door.

"Mrs. Romano," he said with a smile. "Please come in."

"Joshua," the woman replied flatly, calling him by his given name as she stepped inside, carrying a clipboard with a sheaf of paperwork attached. She then walked into the living room as Shade closed the door.

She looked around critically for a moment. "Place looks halfway decent."

"Thank you, ma'am," Shade said politely. "We try."

"Don't thank me yet," she stated. "I still need to look around – make sure you haven't just swept all the trash under a rug or into a closet."

Shade shook his head. "No, ma'am. We wouldn't do that."

"That's what all you peo-," she began, then caught herself. "I mean, everybody says that," she muttered as she tossed her clipboard down onto the coffee table. "Alright, let's start in the kitchen."

"Certainly," Shade said, leading the way.

Once there, Mrs. Romano made a big show of looking in the fridge, cabinets, pantry, etcetera.

Most CPS folks weren't interested in busting families up. They'd make a cursory inspection of the premises, but as long as some muhfucka wasn't sitting at the kitchen table rolling a joint, or they didn't see roaches crawling all over a newborn or a swarm of maggots in the trashcan, they were cool. Unless there were blatantly obvious signs of neglect or abuse, they tried to keep families together.

Mrs. Romano was the fucking opposite of that. If she saw so much as one dead fly on a window sill or a banana in a fruit bowl turning brown, the bitch acted like it was fucking bubonic plague and would be saying she had to get the kids out the home. Of course, that was all just a pretext for what she *really* wanted, and Shade mentally rolled his eyes as he thought about it.

That said, Shade didn't have to let her look through a damn thing. Under CPS rules, Mrs. Romano was required to ask for permission to even open a fucking drawer, and he could always say no. But that would just piss her off, and he really needed to stay on her good side – he didn't need her getting angry at him and then making up some bullshit story about smelling weed in the house, seeing a loaded gun on the table, and so on. Ergo, he politely gave her permission to look through whatever she fucking wanted. As she did, she asked him questions.

"So how are things at school?" she inquired as she looked in the fridge.

"Fine, ma'am," he said truthfully. "Cherry's getting straight A's, while Nissa has all A's and a B in Physics."

"I meant *you*," she clarified as she opened up a carton of milk and put her nose damn near in it and sniffed.

"Straight A's, ma'am."

"And what's your momma up to? She staying clean?"

"Yes, ma'am," Shade declared trying to sound sincere.

"Where is she?" Mrs. Romano asked as she straightened up and closed the refrigerator door.

"In the back. She hasn't been feeling well lately."

"Hmmm," Mrs. Romano droned. "Funny how she's *never* feeling well."

Shade didn't comment, but Mrs. Romano's snide comment was a subtle jab at her suspicion that Gin was probably dope sick. Basically, if they go too long without drugs – in some cases, just a few hours – junkies start to feel violently ill. Thus, if they try to sober up before an important event (like a visit from CPS), junkies will often get sick.

In this case, however, it was quite the opposite. Gin was fucking high, so no risk of her being dope sick. However, it would be great if she looked at least halfway sober, but there was no guarantee it would happen.

"Well, let's see the rest of the house," Mrs. Romano said after another glance around the kitchen. Shade simply nodded and then led the way back into the living room. Just as they got there, his sisters came out the back with Gin between them, wearing a bathrobe and sporting a bandanna around her head, covering her hair. She looked tired and gaunt, but at least she was standing upright and not swaying like she was about to collapse.

Mrs. Romano looked at her for a second, then said, "Nice to see you again, Gin. How you doin'?"

"I'm good," Gin replied, then wiped a finger under her nose and audibly sniffed before adding, "Been feelin' a lil' sick, though."

"Uh-huh," Mrs. Romano muttered in a suspicious tone. "You staying off the drugs?"

"Yeah," Gin assured her with a nod. "I been clean for months."

Shade saw Nissa struggling to keep a straight face, but he had to give Gin credit. Their mother was an unrepentant drug addict and total crackhead (among other things), but she knew how to put her game face on when it counted. That said, Mrs. Romano didn't seem fully convinced and simply stared at her for a few seconds. However, before the silence became too awkward, Nissa softly cleared her throat, drawing their visitor's attention.

"And how have you two girls been?" Mrs. Romano asked, glancing back and forth between Nissa and Cherry.

"Just fine, ma'am," Nissa declared, answering for both of them.

"Good to hear, LaNissa" Mrs. Romano stated, using Nissa's formal name. Turning to Cherry, she asked, "And how have things been at school Cheryl?"

"Just fine," Cherry replied politely.

21

"That's great," Mrs. Romano told her with a gratuitous smile. "And you look so pretty today."

"Thank you," Cherry said, blushing.

"And are those new shoes?"

"No, ma'am," Cherry stated, grinning bashfully.

'Well, I'm surprised," Mrs. Romano declared. "Kids these days always want the latest....what's the word? Kicks?"

"Yes, ma'am," Shade confirmed.

Mrs. Romano nodded. "Take my youngest. She wants a new pair of shoes that cost two hundred dollars. Two hundred! Can you believe that? Two-zero-zero."

"Unbelievable," Gin muttered in commiseration.

"Exactly," Mrs. Romano stated with a nod. "Anyway, let me finish up and get out of your hair."

Chapter 4

It took maybe another fifteen minutes for Mrs. Romano to go through the rest of the house. Fortunately, everything seemed to meet her approval, but Shade expected as much. The only untoward thing that happened was a call that came in on his cell about midway through her inspection.

After glancing at the Caller ID, Shade had answered with a curt, "I'll call you back," before swiftly hanging up.

Looking at him in disapproval, Mrs. Romano had asked, "You got someplace better to be?"

Shade had promptly shaken his head in response. Still, Mrs. Romano had continued giving him the stink eye for a few moments before returning to her scrutiny of their house. Shade was quietly relieved when she finished a few minutes later.

Going back to the living room, they found Gin and Cherry seated on the sofa.

Coming to her feet, Gin looked at Mrs. Romano and said, "Thanks for coming by. It was nice seein' you again."

It was the wrong thing to say – especially in the dismissive tone that Gin used. In essence, you didn't tell Mrs. Romano when she was leaving your house; she told *you*. Even suggesting that her visit was over, as Gin had done, was a cardinal sin that would tick the woman off.

As evidence of this, Mrs. Romano simply frowned at Gin, at the same time seeming to absentmindedly reach into the pocket of a jacket she was wearing. When she withdrew her hand, she was holding a small plastic bag with a sealable opening. In it was a cylindrical container with a screw-on lid that Shade immediately recognized: a drug test kit.

Internally, Shade fought to keep his cool. It was Gin's fucking drug habit that had gotten them into this shit with CPS in the first place. A year earlier she'd been busted for public intoxication, and – even though they only held her ass overnight – she spent the entire time in lockup screaming about how she had to get home to her three minor kids. That had brought Child Protective Services running.

For six months after that, they had gotten weekly visits from CPS. Also, Gin had been required to take a monthly drug test. She undoubtedly would have failed that test every time, but a workaround had been established which alleviated the problem.

For the last six months, the CPS visits had been cut back to monthly. In addition, Gin's drug tests were now randomly administered. More to the point, it had looked like they might escape this time without Gin having to pee into a cup. That is, until she opened her mouth and pissed Mrs. Romano off.

Mrs. Romano was still gripping the drug test and giving Gin a narrow-eyed stare when Nissa stepped from the kitchen.

"I'm sorry," she apologized, handing Mrs. Romano her clipboard. "I had to move it to wipe off the coffee table."

Mrs. Romano let out a slight groan of annoyance before muttering, "That's okay." Taking the clipboard from Nissa with her free hand, she pocketed the drug test with the other – much to Shade's relief.

"So, do I have everything?" Mrs. Romano asked, waggling the clipboard slightly and looking back and forth from Shade to Nissa.

"I think so," Shade answered.

"Great," their visitor replied. "I guess I'll be on my way."

With that, she headed to the door, with Shade and Nissa on her heels.

Once outside, she turned to the two of them and said, "Alright then. See you next month." She then stepped towards her SUV and a moment later was inside.

"How much?" Shade asked softly as he watched Mrs. Romano shift through the papers on the clipboard.

"Two hundred," Nissa muttered under her breath. "That's the amount she was hintin' at, so that's what I gave her."

"You sure it was two bills?"

"Yeah, I put it an envelope at the back of the clipboard, under the papers."

Shade simply gave a subtle nod while continuing to look at Mrs. Romano, who had her head down and was undoubtedly counting the money.

This, of course, was the workaround that they'd found for Gin's drug tests. Basically, from the moment she started working their case, Mrs. Romano had dropped hints that she could be bought, and Shade had picked up on it quickly. Thus, they had worked out a system: Mrs. Romano would leave her clipboard in some open and accessible area whenever she came to visit, and someone – either Shade or Nissa – would slip some money in an envelope under the papers on it. That way, Mrs. Romano never actually asked for anything and never received any cash in hand. In fact, she didn't even witness anything and therefore had deniability if any kind of bribery charge ever arose.

That said, fifty bucks was usually enough to appease her. For that amount of scratch, she'd happily report that any drug test came back clean. However, if she was in a pissy mood or found something she could report, the price might be higher. Or, like today, she might simply drop hints about some upcoming expense.

Like a new pair of kicks, Shade thought.

Mrs. Romano suddenly looked up with a bright smile on her face, a surefire indicator that she was satisfied with the payoff. Shade had only been slightly worried in that regard. Gin's remark could easily have cost them another fifty if Mrs. Romano had decided to insist on the random drug test. Thankfully, the two hundred she was getting had seemingly been enough.

As she started her car, she gave them a big wave, like they were close friends saying goodbye.

"I really do hate that bitch," Nissa grumbled as she and her brother, both smiling, waved back while Mrs. Romano began backing out the driveway. "It would be great if she had some kinda accident."

As she finished speaking, Nissa gave her brother a knowing look. On his part, Shade simply shook his head in disagreement.

"The devil you know," he reminded her. "It's better to deal with the devil you know. The next person might be worse."

With that, they went back inside.

Chapter 5

Once back inside the house, Shade noted that the living room was empty. However, that wasn't surprising. Cherry knew the routine by this point, and had presumably taken their mother to her bedroom to lie down.

"So," Nissa intoned, "how much that two hundred set us back?"

"Enough," Shade admitted. These days, given what he was trying to do on the down low – and what it was costing – they didn't have a dime to spare. The two bills they'd had to give to Mrs. Romano would leave their stash a little low, but it couldn't be helped.

The stash, of course, was a hidden spot where the household cash was kept – hidden because if Gin ever found, it was game over: no money for food, clothes, utilities, etcetera. Shade was typically the only person who contributed to it, but Nissa knew where it was. Thankfully, she didn't abuse the privilege, only getting money from it for necessities, emergencies, and occasionally some spending cash for herself or Cherry (which Shade expected and didn't mind).

"But don't worry about the cash," Shade continued. "I can make it up."

"If you say so," Nissa muttered with a shrug. Then, switching gears, she asked, "Anyway, can I use the car tonight?"

Frowning, Shade shook his head. "Sorry, I need it. Got some errands to run."

"No problem," his sister assured him, nodding her head in understanding but with a melancholy look on her face.

"You sure?" Shade asked.

"Yeah. I just wish sometimes that we'd kept the other one."

Shade simply nodded. The "other one" was a car he'd come into possession of in the recent past – a gift that Shade had received from a cousin as thanks for getting them out of a jam. He had sold it almost immediately, because they had needed the cash. Plus, they already had their grandfather's old car. Technically, Shade owned it, but he tried not to be an asshole about it and had shared it pretty much equally with Nissa since she'd gotten her license. That said, he did occasionally have to pull rank in that regard, like at the present.

"How about tomorrow?" he offered.

Nissa frowned. "Don't you have stuff to do?"

He shrugged. "Most of it's close by. I can hoof it."

"Okay, cool. I just need it for a couple of hours around noon."

"That works," Shade said. "A'ight, I'm outta here."

He then began walking towards the door, pulling out his cell phone to make a call as he did so.

THUG LIFE: EMANCIPATED

Chapter 6

Mr. Willie's backyard was always popping. Willie, a retired truck driver, usually had at least ten people out back on weekdays, and weekends it would be fifty or more. Most of them were middle-aged or older, although the age range generally ran the gamut from early twenties to octogenarians. People generally just stood around shooting the shit, or playing cards or dominoes at some tables set up around the yard.

In addition, Willie had a barbeque pit that seemed to constantly be in use, although it wasn't always Willie doing the cooking; more often than not, one of his visitors would bring the food – a slab of ribs, a bunch of chicken drumsticks, and so on.

All in all, Willie's backyard was one of the places in the hood where people had a tendency to congregate. It was kind of like an outdoor barbershop, but with better food, better entertainment, no hair clippings, and no closing time. And it was in Willie's backyard that Shade found who he was looking for on this particular Friday night: a fat-ass, forty-something nigga called Roderick White.

Willie's backyard was like community property. With people constantly going in and out (especially on weekends), the gate was always open and you didn't have to ask permission to enter. That being the case, Shade just walked into the backyard, then scanned the crowd until he spied Rod, sitting at a table playing dominoes with three other people. Shade made a beeline for him.

Most people in a situation like that might have stepped close to the person they were seeking and waited to be recognized. Shade – having earlier dealt with shit like hunting down Gin and paying Mrs. Romano two bills they didn't have – was already in a piss-poor mood.

"Rod, I need to talk to you," he said without preamble.

Rod cut his eyes momentarily in Shade's direction, then went back to looking at the dominoes in his hand before blandly asking, "What can I do for you, young blood?"

"I need to talk some business wichu," Shade replied. "*Now.*"

The other players, noting Shade's tone, tried to unobtrusively lay their bones on the table while slowly backing their chairs up. Bearing in mind the number of people who frequented Willie's backyard (and the fact that it was in the hood), violence wasn't uncommon. Neither was gunplay.

Apparently noting that shit was serious, Rod laid his dominoes on the table.

"I'll be right back," he said to his fellow players and then stood up. By that time, Shade was already walking away, apparently having assumed Rod would follow (which he did). A few moments later they were out of the backyard, but Shade didn't stop walking until they reached the sidewalk in front of Mr. Willie's house.

"You went to see Taranda Webster today," Shade said in a matter-of-fact voice.

"Yeah, I saw dat hoe," Rod answered. "What about it?"

"First of all, she ain't no hoe. Second, you owe her a hundred bucks."

Rod looked him up and down, seemingly surprised. "So whachu s'pose to be, her pimp?"

"Nigga, as far as you concerned, I'm da fuckin' Secretary of Labor, makin' sure workers ain't gettin' mistreated. All you need to know is that I'm the muhfucka she call when shit like this need to be fixed."

As he spoke, Shade reflected on the fact that it was Taranda who had called him while Mrs. Romano was at his house. At the time, he'd already had an idea of what the call was about. Taranda confirmed it later, when he called her as he was leaving the house: some nigga had stiffed her. Fortunately, it hadn't taken much effort to run Rod down.

"Anyway," Shade continued, "you made a deal with her for a Benjamin, so you in da hole right now."

"Uh-uh," Rod declared, shaking his head. "It was forty, and I gave her that."

"Naw, nigga. You fucked her, and the price was a hundred. You knew that b'foe hand."

"Look, man," Rod muttered in exasperation, "That bitch pussy was whack. Plus, it ain't like I bust some big nut. Forty is all that shit was worth."

"It ain't her fault yo dick too small or too limp to get any friction. Once you put even the tip of that shit inside her, it was a done deal."

Rod suddenly puffed his chest up defiantly. "And if I say I ain't gone pay?"

"Oh, you gone pay, muhfucka," Shade assured him, leaning in. "The question is whether you get to walk away after, or have to be *carried* away."

There was an intensity to Shade's tone and a look in his dark gray eyes that was impossible to ignore. Plus, Shade knew that he looked older than his actual age, which was usually a good thing. People tend to think they can talk kids out of shit or get over on them, but they're less eager to push the envelope with adults. In this instance, Rod decided not to push.

Reaching around to his back pocket, Rod pulled out his wallet, opened it, and began counting out some bills.

"You lucky," Rod inform Shade. "It's Friday and payday – plus I'm on a winnin' streak with the bones – so I'm in a good mood."

As he finished speaking, he held out three twenty-dollar bills, which Shade swiftly took.

"I said a hundred," Shade reminded him.

Rod frowned, giving him a crazy look. "I gave that stank hoe forty, now I'm givin' you sixty. I ain't no math whiz, but that's a hundred."

"It was a hundred when you made the deal with Taranda," Shade confirmed. "But now *I* gotta be compensated for *my* inconvenience."

Rod just stared at him for a moment. Like a lot of people in the hood, he knew Shade more by reputation rather than personal interaction. However, that reputation made it clear that Shade wasn't someone you wanted to cross. Nevertheless, Rod still looked like he wanted to protest – or maybe try teaching Shade a lesson of some sort. Fortunately, common sense prevailed.

Counting out another forty dollars, Rod mumbled, "Man, you one cold muhfucka."

Chapter 7

Taranda was obviously expecting him, because Shade had barely finished knocking before she opened her apartment door.

She was a cute girl, with high cheek bones and pouty lips, and her hair currently done up in a bun. She was wearing an eye-catching teddy that accentuated her shapely, hourglass figure. Noting her wardrobe, Shade wasn't sure she whether she was simply getting ready for bed or expecting someone. Regardless, it was easy to see why men would want to sleep with her (and be willing to pay for it).

Shade held out the cash that he'd taken from Rod, stating, "Here ya go."

"Thanks," Taranda said, taking the money. A moment later, she handed half of it back to him. "For ya trouble."

Shade shook his head. "Naw – keep it."

Taranda tilted her head slightly to the side, giving him an odd look. "You sure?"

"Yeah," Shade confirmed with a nod.

Taranda merely nodded for a moment, her attention focused on the money. She was roughly a year older than Shade and – just like him – was doing whatever it took to try to survive and keep her family together. In her case, it was a younger brother and sister. But with her dad locked up, older brother dead and a mother who'd run off years earlier, shit was obviously hard.

She'd tried her hand at dealing, but got ripped off on the second day – mugged at gunpoint. She'd had to scramble like crazy to pay back her supplier, who had fronted her the product and wasn't the type of nigga to accept excuses. (In truth, Shade always felt that Taranda's supplier had set her up, which would have been far from a surprise.)

She'd followed that up with work as a stripper. She definitely had the body for it, but she couldn't leave her little brother and sister alone every night, and giving all her money to a sitter would defeat the purpose of working in the first place.

Ultimately, she'd settled for earning money on her backside. It gave her a nice chunk of change – enough for her family to live on as well as set some scratch aside – and didn't require a bunch of time. Those were critical for someone in Taranda's position. More importantly, she'd managed to build up a stable of regulars – guys (and in one case, a woman) she saw on a routine basis and who she considered "safe" (meaning that they were unlikely to try any rough shit or stiff her when it was time to pay).

"Anyway," Taranda droned, bringing Shade back to himself, "thanks for your help."

"No problem," Shade insisted. "I take it Rod wasn't a regular."

"A regular *asshole*," she quipped, crossing her arms. "I gave 'im a try on somebody's recommendation – they said his wife had left his ass and he needed some 'female companionship'. But once we were done, the nigga didn't wanna leave, even though I explained the rules up front. Nigga kept sayin' sommin' 'bout a 'second wind'."

Shade chuckled. Taranda charged by the hour, but her services came with a slight corollary: Once you *cum*, you gotta *go*. Didn't matter if it took you five minutes or five seconds; once you shot your load, it was time to get the fuck out. Most niggas respected that, but apparently Rod – thinking he could get it up again in short order – had wanted to get his full hour, and had decided to shortchange Taranda when she ordered him to step. That's when she'd called Shade.

To be clear, he wasn't a pimp. He didn't keep Taranda under his thumb, claw off part of her daily take or any shit like that. He was just a friend – somebody else who knew just how fucking hard it was simply to take care of yourself at their age, let alone other people. So he merely tried to help her out whenever she ran into issues – a favor with no strings attached. (He also did the same for a few other girls in the same position.) Basically, it was the type of thing he'd want someone to do for his sisters if, for some reason, he wasn't around. (Not that his sisters would be turning tricks…)

"So, you wanna come in for a minute?" Taranda asked, looking at him suggestively.

Shade immediately understood what was being offered. Since he wouldn't take the cash, she was proposing recompense in another form. A special way of saying thanks.

He was sorely tempted. It wouldn't have been the first time he had tangled with Taranda in the sheets, and she had mads skills in that department. (In fact, he started getting hard just thinking about it.) But on those other occasions, they had boned because it was what they both wanted; it hadn't been part of a business arrangement with money changing hands, or because one of them felt they owed the other. They had simply wanted to fuck the shit out of each other. The current circumstances were different, though.

He didn't think the sex in and of itself would mean anything to Taranda. She'd told him a while back that tricking was just a job to her, no different than any other; she traded her time and skills for pay – end of story. It was simply what she *did*, not a definition of who she *was*. That said, accepting the invitation she'd just made would make him more like a pimp or a john rather than a friend, which was a line he really didn't want to cross. People did favors for friends; they didn't do shit for johns.

Sighing, he looked at Taranda and said, "I appreciate the offer, but I got plans."

"That's too bad," she said with a wink. "Well, thanks again."

As she finished speaking, she spread her arms and stepped forward giving him a solid hug, which he returned. The teddy might as well have been made of air for all the good it served then, because he felt her nipples – firm and hard – against his chest. His dick throbbed in response, and he fought the impulse to tell her that he changed his mind and would love to come in, drag her into the bedroom by her hair, and fuck her like a caveman.

Instead, he merely stepped back as the hug ended, then said bye before turning and walking away. A second later, he heard the Taranda's apartment door close behind him. At the same time, a tiny voice started screaming in his brain, calling him a fucking moron for turning down both pussy *and* money – especially the latter, considering his current need for funds. And it was with that thought in mind that he pulled out his cell phone and made a call. It was answered on the second ring.

"Mrs. Jamison?" he intoned. "It's Shade. I was wonderin' if you had anythang you needed done around the place tomorrow?"

THUG LIFE: EMANCIPATED

Chapter 8

The next morning got off to what amounted to a late start for Shade, with him waking up around eight o'clock. Years of working alongside his grandfather had made him an early riser, and he usually got up with the sun. However, he'd had a late night, having run some errands after leaving Taranda, so sleeping in on this particular day could be forgiven.

He hurriedly washed up and got dressed. Then, as he headed to the kitchen for breakfast, he heard voices. Recognizing them, he frowned. – or rather, frowned because of *one* of them. When he reached the kitchen a few seconds later, he saw who he expected: Nissa and Cherry sitting at the breakfast table, along with Nissa'a boyfriend, Goose.

Shade gave his sister's beau a hard stare. Goose was seventeen, and by most estimations he really wasn't a bad guy. Like a lot of people in the hood, he did what he had to in order to get by, but had seemingly avoided getting caught up in any hardcore gangster shit. That gave Shade some peace of mind, since it meant there was less chance of Nissa getting caught in some kind of crossfire, or simply being at the wrong place at the wrong time. More importantly, he appeared to genuinely like Nissa and treated her well.

Shade's problem with Goose generally stemmed from the fact that the nigga had no direction in life. He'd be graduating from high school soon – barely, in Shade's opinion – but had no fucking idea what he wanted to do after that or any type of plan: no college, no straight nine-to-five, no going into the military. His main ambition seemed to be continuing to live with his grandmother, who herself subsided on a fixed-income in the form of Social Security. Basically, Goose was the type of nigga a woman would end up having to take care of, instead of the other way around.

"Hey," Nissa droned, getting Shade's attention. "Goose brought us breakfast."

As she spoke, she gestured towards a couple of paper bags on the table. Still frowning, Shade picked one up and reached into it, pulling out what appeared to be some kind of breakfast sandwich – something akin to a sausage biscuit.

"This shit's cold," he stated blandly, glancing at Goose again and then at his sister. Nissa, of course, knew that Shade's comment was really a question: *How long has this nigga been here?*

"Be nice," Nissa admonished. "I was gonna do some cleanin' this weekend, so I asked Goose to come over this mornin' to help me move some furniture and stuff around. I figured you'd be gone by now."

"Yeah, I'm runnin' behind," Shade admitted. "I should get goin'."

"Can you check the toilet before you go?" Cherry suddenly asked. "It's stopped up."

Shade's brow furrowed. "When that happen?"

Cherry shrugged. "This mornin', I guess. It was fine last night."

"Where's Gin?" Shade asked.

"Don't know," Nissa answered. "She took off last night while you were out."

"A'ight," Shade muttered, nodding sagely as he started eating the sausage biscuit. "Well, let me go take care of the toilet, then I'm gone."

He then turned and left, heading back to the bedroom, where his tool bag was. By the time he reached it, the sausage biscuit was gone. He then grabbed his tools and hurried to the bathroom.

****

It only took Shade a few minutes to unclog the toilet. He generally kept things like the plumbing and electrical in their house running without a hitch – something his grandfather had taught him. Occasionally, however, Gin would flush random shit down the toilet: plastic sandwich bags, dirty handkerchiefs, roach clips, and so on. That's why his first thought upon learning about the stopped-up toilet was to ask where she was. Needless to say, the fact that she wasn't presently at home didn't mean she hadn't down something to cause the current problem. (And bearing in mind that his mother had once flushed a dirty needle, he was working with gloves on.) What he actually pulled out of the toilet line, however, was something that first surprised and then angered him.

Trying to contain his fury, Shade marched back to the kitchen, where Goose, Nissa and Cherry were still at the table.

"Goose," Shade began, trying to keep his voice even, "can you help me with sommin' outside for a minute?"

"Ah, sure," Goose replied, plainly surprised, since Shade rarely ever spoke to him without prompting. Nissa however, recognizing her brother's mood, suddenly looked worried but didn't say anything.

As he'd done with Rod the night before, Shade just started walking towards the back door, and Goose followed. A moment later, they were in the back yard, at which juncture Shade actually led them to the side of the house.

Once there, Shade turned and faced Goose, who looked at him expectedly. Rather than say anything, Shade lifted his right hand – which was still gloved – and flicked his wrist in Goose's direction. A moment later, something wet and rubbery hit Goose in the face.

It wasn't hard and didn't hurt, but Goose closed his eyes and flinched instinctively. He then brought a hand up and wiped his face; he blinked, and then his eyes went wide when he saw, on the ground, the item that Shade had hit him with: a used condom.

"What da fuck???!!" he screeched. "Are you crazy?!"

"Naw, nigga," Shade shot back. "You da one crazy, flushin' fuckin' rubbers down my toilet."

"Man, you got that wrong. Me and Nissa ain't even doin' nuthin'."

Shade's eyes narrowed. "You might wanna rethink that last statement."

Goose frowned. "Whachu mean?"

"What I mean is that you the only nigga besides me been 'round here lately. Now, my crackhead momma's in the wind, so that just leaves my two sistas as the only fems in the house. Now if you sayin' you ain't done nuthin' with Nissa, that just leaves our lil' sista Cherry, you, and a used condom. I don't like that math and you shouldn't either, 'cause it mean that shit's 'bout to escalate in a way that's gonna be fuckin' unhealthy for you."

Goose gulped. "Okay, um, maybe Nissa and me–"

"*Maybe?*" Shade interjected incredulously.

"Okay, okay. We, uh, we did so sommin'. We was on the couch, and–"

"Muhfucka, I don't need no details," Shade snapped, cutting him off. Trying to keep his cool, Shade took a deep breath. "Look, I'm responsible for Nissa, but I don't try to control her. She does *what* she wants with *who* she wants, and she's smart enough to be careful."

"Okay, cool," Goose muttered, sounding relieved.

"But you need to unnastand sommin'," Shade continued, with a hard edge to his voice now. "If she get pregnant, you takin' care of that baby."

Goose nodded. "Yeah, dawg – I get where you comin' from."

"Naw, nigga," Shade countered, shaking his head. "This ain't gone be one of them hood situations, where you drop off a pack of diapers every other month then brag to muhfuckas 'bout how you takin' care of yo kid. You payin' for *everythang*."

Goose look confused for a moment. "Whachu mean, 'everythang'?"

"I mean *everythang*, nigga," Shade stressed. "The kid need a new pair of shoes, you buyin' 'em. They got private school tuition, you payin'. They got a class trip to muhfuckin' France, you coughin' up the funds."

Goose looked stunned. It was as if he was hearing something that he had never considered before, something outside the realm of possibility – like being told he had a vagina.

"Basically," Shade continued, "if you knock up my sista, every red cent needed to support that kid is comin' from you – even if I have to harvest yo fuckin' organs to get it."

THUG LIFE: EMANCIPATED

Chapter 9

"Where's Goose?" Nissa asked as Shade came back inside.

"He said he had to go," Shade replied, recalling how Goose had seemed eager to be elsewhere after the comment about his organs getting cut out.

Nissa looked at her brother skeptically. "You ran 'im off, dinchu?"

Shade shrugged. "If he ain't no punk, he'll be back."

"Dammit, Shade," Nissa swore. "I liked him."

"You must have, since you..."

Shade trailed off, suddenly seeming to remember that their little sister was still present, sitting at the table.

"Cherry, give us a minute," he said to her.

"I wanna stay," Cherry whined. "I'm tired of bein' sent out every time you guys mention sex and stuff."

Shade kept his face impassive but turned to Nissa, who shrugged and gave him a *what-do-you-want-me-to-say?* look.

"So can I?" Cherry pleaded.

"Huh?" Shade muttered, coming back to himself.

"Can I stay?"

Shade seemed to consider it, but then shook his head. "Naw – maybe next time."

"That's what you always say," Cherry groused as she got up from the table. "I'm not a lil' kid, ya know."

"I know," Shade noted, talking more to her back as Cherry left the room. Once he was sure she was out of earshot, he turned back to Nissa.

"Do we need to have a talk 'bout you bein' discreet?" he asked.

"She didn't see me and Goose, if that's whachu gettin' at," Nissa stated.

"Then how she know what I was 'bout to comment on?"

"'Cause she ain't stupid," Nissa stated. "You thank she don't know 'bout sex just 'cause we tiptoe 'round the subject when she in the room? Thank about it: when did you and I start learnin' 'bout that shit? When we were maybe six? Seven?"

"Shit," Shade muttered. "You a late bloomer if you in the hood and get to first grade without knowin' 'bout sex."

"Exactly. So Cherry know all 'bout people throwin' down in the bedroom."

"Thanks," Shade muttered sarcastically. "You just made my day."

"Look," Nissa went on, ignoring his comment. "Just 'cause she know what fuckin' is don't mean she stop bein' a sweet kid."

"I know that," he declared. "But I don't want her to—"

"What?" Nissa demanded, cutting him off as she crossed her arms defensively. "Start fuckin' niggas in her teens?"

Rather than immediately reply, Shade gave his sister a steely look. Nissa met his gaze without flinching. A moment later, Shade let out a deep breath.

"I don't judge," he stressed. "You know that. I was just hopin' that Cherry could stay innocent as long as possible."

"We in the fuckin' ghetto," Nissa said flatly. "As somebody once told me, you stop bein' innocent 'round this bitch when you get outta diapers."

Shade chuckled at that, recognizing that those were his words that his sister had just repeated.

"A'ight," Shade conceded. "We can start tryin' to include Cherry in discussions from now on – if it's appropriate."

"Good," Nissa added. "Plus, she know what we be talkin' 'bout anyway."

"True," Shade confirmed with a nod. "Now, gettin' back to the main topic, I thought I told you to tell all these niggas not to flush they rubbers down the toilet."

"Okay, first of all, it ain't a bunch of niggas," Nissa shot back. "There's just the one, and I *did* tell 'im. But I guess maybe he worried 'bout somebody findin' it."

Shade's eyebrows went up in surprise. "That's a fuckin' joke, right? He thank I'm gone go diggin' through the trash, lookin' for used condoms so I'll know if my sista's bonin' some nigga?"

Nissa shrugged. "Anythang's possible."

"Or maybe *I'm* not the one he's worried about findin' it," Shade suggested.

Nissa looked confused for a moment, then burst into laughter.

"Ha!" she barked. "So you sayin' he worried I'm gone fish his used, smelly rubber out the trash so I can go squirt his jizz up in myself? Like he some kind of fuckin' catch who's so wonderful that I wanna trap him by havin' his baby? *That's* a fuckin' joke!"

"Anythang's possible," Shade shot back as his sister giggled wildly.

"Nigga, I'm the one make that muhfucka wear a condom in the first place," Nissa declared. "Flushin' it down the toilet is prolly just his way of bein' defiant."

"Well, he gone have to find another way to express his displeasure," Shade stated, "'cause if I dig another rubber out our toilet, I'm gonna shove that bitch down his throat."

Chapter 10

Shortly after his conversation with Nissa, Shade left. His call to Mrs. Jamison the night before had resulted in him being told to show up bright and early. Thus, at roughly nine a.m., he found himself knocking on the door to the Jamison residence – a two-bedroom, one bath apartment in the projects.

The door was opened by Mr. Jamison. He was in his early thirties and a huge muhfucka – roughly six-five in height and all muscle. Not the kind of nigga you want to get on the wrong side of.

"Hey, Shade," Mr. Jamison said in a deep voice. "Come on in."

Tool bag in hand, Shade walked inside and Mr. Jamison closed the door. He found himself in a modest living room, where four children – roughly between the ages of five and nine – sat on a couch watching cartoons on television.

"Hey, Pumpkin," Mr. Jamison called out towards the back of the apartment. "Shade's here."

"A'ight," answered a feminine voice from a back room.

Mr. Jamison reached towards the rear pocket of the jeans he wore and pulled out his wallet.

"This cover everything you need to do?" he asked, handing Shade a small sheaf of bills.

"Yes, sir," Shade answered, taking the money and putting it in his pocket.

"Cool," Mr. Jamison said with a nod before turning to the kids. "A'ight you lil' monsters, let's go to the park."

Cheering gleefully, the kids jumped up from the couch as their father turned the television off. Their enthusiasm brought a slight smile to Shade's lips, as he remembered a time when he would get just as excited about an outing.

"Y'all have fun," said a nearby voice, and Shade looked up to find Mrs. Jamison standing in the hallway leading to the back of the apartment.

She was a good-looking woman in her late twenties, about five-six with almond-colored skin. She was also completely stacked, with a voluptuous figure that was plainly evident, despite the fact that she currently wore a frumpy-looking bathrobe.

"Ain't you comin', Momma?" asked one of the kids, a little girl.

"Naw, baby," she responded. "I'm not feelin' too well. Plus somebody need to show Shade what he needs to do."

The child looked a little crestfallen, but perked up when Mr. Jamison said something about getting ice cream later. He then kissed his wife on the cheek before hustling the kids to the door. A moment later, it was just Shade and Mrs. Jamison in the apartment.

"You said sommin' 'bout a leak on the phone last night?" Shade inquired.

"Yeah," she said with a knowing smile. "Come on."

She turned and began walking down the hallway, and Shade followed. A moment later she stopped in front of a doorway, which Shade knew from past visits to be the entry to the bathroom.

"The sink?" he asked as he stepped inside.

"Mm-hmm," she droned. She then turned and headed towards her bedroom, which was directly across the hall.

Shade watched her for a moment as she went inside and appeared to close the door behind her, then turned his attention to the task at hand. Setting his tool bag on the floor, he opened up the cabinets beneath the sink and prepared to go to work. However, he had done no more than turn the faucet on when he heard Mrs. Jamison call out.

"Shade, can you come in here for a minute?" she asked.

Rather than respond verbally, Shade merely turned the water off before walking out the bathroom. Mrs. Jamison's voice had seemingly come from her bedroom, and now that he was standing in front of it he noticed that it was cracked open slightly rather than completely closed. He pushed the door open and saw what he expected: Mrs. Jamison lying on the bed completely fucking naked.

Her tits, as always, were magnificent. As large as they were, you'd expect them to sag, but her shit was tight in that regard — titties round and firm. (And to the best of his knowledge, all natural.) Her skin was flawless except for a thin horizontal scar on the lower part of her stomach. Finally, she had hips that were wide but not oversized, and nice, shapely legs.

In one fluid motion, Shade reached down and pulled his shirt up over his head, simultaneously kicking off his shoes. He then stepped quickly to the edge of the bed, near Mrs. Jamison's feet.

Crawling onto the bed, he began to lovingly kiss her inner left thigh, starting just above her knee and moving up. At the same time, he reached out and ran a hand, gently but firmly, across her stomach, sides, and hips. He continued kissing his way up, but just before he got to her vulva he switched and began kissing the other leg, making Mrs. Jamison groan in frustration.

"Fuck this seductive thigh-kissin' shit," she grumbled. "Eat my pussy."

Shade chuckled slightly, then did as told. As he placed his mouth on her pussy she let a little gasp and shuddered slightly, then moaned as he put his tongue and lips to work.

"Oh, yeah," she moaned. "Oh, *fuck* yeah. Eat that pussy, nigga. Eat it. Lap it up like a fuckin' dog. You like it, donchu? Tell me you like that shit."

"Mm-hmm," Shade muttered truthfully in response. He always thought she smelled and tasted wonderful – like strawberries and cream. He was actually thinking he could do this all day as he put his mouth on her clit.

"Right there!" she shouted, arching her back. "Right there! Right *fuckin'* there!"

By this time she had her hand on his head, almost trying to shove his head inside her pussy – like a woman giving birth in reverse. On his part, Shade had his hands underneath her, gripping her ass and lifting it as he continued eating.

"Ah! Ah! Ah!" she croaked almost melodically, sounding as though she couldn't quite catch her breath. Then she shrieked, her legs tightening around Shade's head as she came, shuddering almost convulsively, and then collapsed back onto the bed, breathing hard.

Slowly, Shade began kissing his way up her body, propping himself up with one hand while using the other to squirm out of his pants. In just seconds, he had them off, then used his knees to spread her legs apart. His dick was like a slab of granite at that point, heavy and throbbing as he slid into positon.

"Not yet," she said softly, stroking his head as he began sucking one of her titties. "Tease me with it first."

Gently biting her nipple, Shade complied, using his free hand to grip his dick and do as she directed.

"That's right," she mumbled, eyes closed in ecstasy. "Tease me with that shit. Run the head of that big dick all 'round my pussy lips. Just like that, just like that. Mmmm…that's right. Tease a bitch 'bout what's comin'. Now, slip the head inside – just the head! Mm-hmmm… Now waggle that shit up and down. Oh yeah… Keep doin' that shit for a hot minute. Let a bitch know yo shit is for real hard and she 'bout to get *fucked*. That her pussy 'bout to get stretched *all* the way out."

"Now," she continued, her eyes snapping open, "fuck me."

Shade rammed his dick inside her, making her let out a blissful moan. He then began thrusting repeatedly, starting slowly but steadily increasing the tempo with every plunge – and with her seeming to gasp every time he went balls deep. Her pussy was tight and felt incredible as Shade worked on trying to establish a rhythm; but just as he got to a sustainable pace, she lifted a hip and pushed up from the bed with one arm. Instinctively understanding what she was doing, Shade went with her motion and rolled over, letting her get on top.

She immediately straddled him, and a second later her hips started moving, her pussy sliding up and down the length of his dick. Unlike Shade, however, she didn't waste time with pacing or any shit like that. She just began riding his dick like she was a bandit with a posse hot on her trail.

"Squeeze my titties!" she blurted out suddenly, which was almost redundant since Shade already had his hands on those bad boys. "Squeeze 'em, nigga! Oh yeah, like that! Now slap my ass! Harder! Harder, dammit!"

She kept barking orders like a drill sergeant, and Shade obeyed: sucking the fingers she put into his mouth, rubbing her clit, pinching her nipples hard enough to damn near break them bitches off... Whatever she asked, he did, all the while concentrating like a muhfucka to keep himself under control.

Finally, she stopped giving commands and settled for just trying to take his dick in as hard and fast (and deep) as possible. Then, without warning, she changed her technique, moving her hips in a sort of grinding pattern that – from Shade's perspective – allowed her pussy to get a renewed grip on his dick that was head-spinning.

"Cum now," she muttered, continuing to grind. "Cum now. Cum now."

As he'd done all the way up to that point, Shade did as ordered and released his load, thankful to no longer have to hold back and groaning loudly. As he squirted up in her he felt her shudder again, just like she had when he'd eaten her pussy (and that shit felt incredible as he was cumming). At the same time, she squealed in a high keening voice. Then she collapsed on top of him, completely out of breath.

****

They lay there for a moment, then she slowly rolled off him.

"Oh, *shit*," she said with a smile. "Whenever you get married, that bitch better send me a thank you card for turnin' you into a damn fuckmaster."

"Yes, ma'am," Shade said, smirking.

She stretched towards the side of the bed near her, reaching towards a nearby nightstand. Opening the drawer, she took out a joint and a lighter. A moment later, she had the joint lit and was taking a puff. She then offered it to Shade, who – as always – declined. As she smoked, she absentmindedly ran a finger along the scar on her belly. His attention drawn to it, Shade reached over and touched it.

"My C-section scar," she stated. Then, in a half-pleading voice said, "Don't look at it." However, she didn't make any effort to cover it or move his hand away.

"It's barely noticeable," he assured her.

"Maybe *now*," she admitted, "but it was butt-fuckin' ugly b'foe – all jagged and shit. Wudda scared off any nigga even thankin' 'bout eatin' my pussy."

"You got it fixed?"

"Now exactly," she explained. "The first kid we had, I did it normal – what they call a vaginal delivery. The last three, they did 'em all by C-section. That's when the cut a bitch open and take the baby out."

Shade simply nodded, although he already knew what a C-section was.

"But see," she went on, "when you have more than one C-section, they try to go back in through the same spot, so they done cut me open in that same place three times. For the first two, I musta had shitty doctors caused those muhfuckas sewed me back up like fuckin' Frankenstein – left me with an ugly-ass scar and everythang. Or maybe they was pissed 'cause they always asked if they could tie my tubes, like the world didn't need any mo' Black babies, and I always said 'No.' The last time, though – the doc evidently knew what the hell he was doin' 'cause it's a fuckin' beauty mark compared to what it was b'foe. Guess maybe that was my reward, 'cause when *he* asked 'bout tyin' my tubes I told him to shred them bitches – I was done havin' kids after numba fo'."

As she finished speaking, she tapped the ashes from the joint into an ashtray on the nightstand. She then turned to him, letting her eyes roam for a moment over his well-developed pecs and sculpted abs before reaching out a hand and letting it wander across his torso...across *his* scars.

Unlike her, however, he was less self-conscious about his blemishes, which had come as a result of being shot at a young age. (He'd told her that much previously, but hadn't given any specifics and she had never pried.) Truth be told, he'd had the scars for so long that he rarely even thought about them unless someone pointed them out.

"What time yo husband comin' back?" he asked.

"Not for a while," she answered. "Him and his White boyfriend gone take to the kids to the movies after they leave the park."

51

Shade simply nodded at that. Mr. Jamison had come out a few years back, deciding to be honest about who and what he was. It had come as a bit of a surprise to most people because – in addition to being big and muscular – Mr. Jamison had also done a stint in the Marines and moonlighted as a bouncer. Combine all that shit with fathering a brood of kids, and it was about as masculine as you could get.

Still when you come out the closet like he did, you're bound to get challenged – especially in the hood. However, niggas in the street wised up real quick to the fact that a muhfucka's orientation don't mean he can't put your ass in the dirt. Some fool found that out the hard way about a year earlier – made the mistake of calling Mr. Jamison a fag when he was out with his kids – and to this day that muhfucka was *still* looking for the rest of his teeth.

Surprisingly, however, rather than separate after Mr. Jamison revealed his sexual preference, he and his wife had decided to stay married. As she put it, he was her best friend, and she couldn't imagine not coming home to him every day – plus, they had four kids together. Basically, they were making it work. That said, she still had certain needs ("the occasional deep dickin'," as she put it), which is where Shade came in.

He had actually been doing repairs for the Jamisons for a couple of years. Initially, Mrs. Jamison had seemed to get a kick out of teasing him with double entendres and such whenever he came over to do work for them. To her credit, however, she never actually tried anything sexual with him until after his last birthday, which implied that she knew the law – basically, that the legal age of consent was sixteen.

The first time it happened was shortly after his sixteenth birthday, when he was in the Jamison's kitchen fixing a leak. He was lying on his back on the floor, head and shoulders in the cabinet under the sink while he worked on the pipes. No one was there but him and Mrs. Jamison, and then he unexpectedly felt a hand on his dick. For a brief moment, he'd been worried that it was Mr. Jamison – that he had come in unexpectedly and was now giving in to some primal urge, and Shade had gripped the wrench in his hand in expectation of maybe having to fight that nigga off. But when he lifted his head, he saw that it was actually Mrs. Jamison, and she wasn't wearing a stitch of clothing.

She had his pants unzipped and his dick out in a flash, and then it was in her mouth. It was so unexpected that mentally Shade just froze for a moment; his body, on the other hand, shifted into overdrive, with his dick becoming engorged in about two seconds. And then her mouth really went to work, licking and sucking with first-rate finesse and an intensity so great that Shade shot his load in less than a minute.

He came so explosively that he half expected to see cum gushing from her ears and nose. Amazingly, she didn't spill a single drop. She just swallowed, smiled at him, and then began saying some incredibly raunchy shit that he had only imagined women telling him in his dreams up to that point, all the while continuing to work his dick with her mouth. In no time at all he was hard again. Then she had mounted him and tried to ride his ass into the sunset.

She'd given him a big bonus then – some extra cash that was much-needed, to tell the truth. She'd also let him know in no uncertain terms that he should give her a call if he ever needed to earn a few bucks, and she'd find something for him to do.

He'd taken her up on the offer a few times since then (like at present). It was pretty clear that Mr. Jamison knew what was up, but apparently he and his wife had an understanding in that department. Still, since he was ostensibly supposed to be doing work whenever he came over, Shade always brought his tool bag and was never presumptuous about what was going to happen. Instead, he'd go about his normal routine and prepare to actually work (at least until Mrs. Jamison told him to drop whatever he was doing and come do *her*).

Of course, it had initially seemed odd to Shade that she'd choose to compensate him – or any man – for something he'd willingly do for free.

"The money keeps shit from getting confused," she'd explained one time. "'Cause this ain't a relationship. It's just fuckin', plain and simple."

That was fine with Shade, but was also one of the reasons why he didn't judge girls like Taranda, who earned a living on their backs. Looking down on them would have been hypocritical when he was doing the same thing himself (although on a much more limited basis).

As for why Shade instead of some other nigga, Mrs. Jamison apparently liked younger guys – said they had a lot more energy. There was also the fact that she liked giving orders when she fucked, and most older niggas didn't care for that. Apparently they felt it was a comment on their technique and implied that they didn't know what the fuck they were doing in the bedroom. Shade, however, understood that it was a turn-on for Mrs. Jamison. (In fact, he suspected that some facet of her personality housed a fierce dominatrix who was dying to get out. Thus, he had no problem imagining her wearing a bunch of tight black leather and walking around spanking niggas with a riding crop.)

"So, how much my husband give you?" Mrs. Jamison asked, interrupting Shade's reverie.

He shrugged. "Don't know – didn't count it."

Mrs. Jamison simply nodded and reached towards the ashtray, putting the joint out. She then opened the nightstand drawer again and pulled out a black clutch wallet. Opening it, she pulled out a twenty-dollar-bill and put the wallet back.

"Here," she said, handing him the twenty. "You earned a bonus today."

"Thanks," Shade uttered as he took the cash.

"Don't spend it all in one place," she added jokingly.

"Yes, ma'am."

She frowned slightly at that, then rolled onto her side, facing him, with her head propped up on one hand.

"Look," she stated. "I fuckin' love dirty talk – it just turns me the fuck on. So when we goin' at it, you can say shit like 'Suck my dick, bitch,' and talk all you want 'bout how you gone tear my pussy up and stuff like that. Shit like that just gets me wet. But you keep callin' me 'ma'am' and you gone make me feel old and embarrassed 'bout showing you my titties and puttin' yo dick in my mouth, unnastand?"

"Yes, ma–" Shade began, then caught himself. "I mean, yeah, bitch."

She giggled at that. "Well, a'ight then." She then leaned over, bringing her head towards his groin, saying, "Now, let's see if you got another one in you."

Shade was tempted to argue that he didn't – that their previous bout of fuckin' had drained him. But he quickly realized it would have been a lie, because as she ran her tongue over his balls and began working his shaft with her hand, he felt himself start to stiffen.

THUG LIFE: EMANCIPATED

Chapter 11

It was roughly an hour later when Shade finally left the Jamisons' apartment. He probably could have departed sooner, but – after his second round of fucking with Mrs. Jamison – he actually went through the trouble of checking to make sure they didn't have any leaks. It was his way of making sure they got their money's worth on all fronts.

As he was leaving, tool bag in hand, he noted one of the Jamisons' neighbors in the hallway – a girl around his age, walking towards him carrying a bag of groceries.

She was tall and light-skinned, with a bit of an exotic look. Her facial features were accentuated by high cheek bones and full, pouty lips on which she currently wore a tempting shade of red lipstick. At present, her curly hair was tied in an attractive ponytail, and she was wearing a low-cut blouse that clung to a shapely figure, along with a pair of yoga pants that highlighted firm, toned legs. All in all, she was gorgeous.

Shade recognized her right away as Yoni, the new girl in school. In fact, they had a class together. "New," however, was somewhat of a misnomer since she was actually from the area. Her family had left the city more than a decade earlier and had only recently moved back a few weeks ago.

Still, even if she was only nominally new, Yoni represented just one thing to niggas in the hood: fresh pussy. That meant muhfuckas were lining up for a chance to be the first to tap that ass (and with her face and body, it was a line that stretched around the block). Shade, however, wasn't one of them. He had too much other shit going on. Apparently Yoni did as well, because it was his understanding that she didn't give any of those niggas chasing her the time of day.

She glanced at Shade as they approached each other. There was a knowing look in her eye, and Shade assumed that she expected him – like just about all the other niggas she walked by – to try throwing some game at her.

Not today, he thought. Instead, he simply gave her a short wave and muttered "Hi" as they passed each other.

However, before he'd gone another two steps, he heard her call out to him.

"Hey," she said in his direction, causing him to spin around. "You Shade, right? The one who fixes shit?"

He nodded. "Yeah."

"You got time to look at sommin' for me?"

"Uh, sure."

"Great," she uttered, then turned to what was apparently her apartment door.

She spent a moment unlocking the door, and then hustled inside. Shade, not having been given a direct invite, meandered towards the door – which she'd left open – but didn't enter. A moment later, her face appeared in the doorway.

"I meant *today*, nigga," she grumbled impatiently, at which point Shade hastily stepped inside and she closed the door.

"The kitchen," she muttered, leading the way. Shade quietly followed.

Once there, she tossed the groceries she was carrying onto a counter next to the refrigerator.

"The stove," she said, pointing. "The vent on the hood won't turn on."

Shade merely nodded and stepped to the stove, at which point he immediately flipped the switch on the vent. After confirming that it wouldn't turn on, he flipped the switch back to "off." He then opened up his tool bag and went to work.

****

Yoni first put the groceries in the fridge, then spent her time watching Shade repair the vent. Fortunately, it only took him a few minutes to ascertain the problem, and he didn't think it would take long to fix.

"It's just a loose electrical connection," he explained as he worked. "It's a common problem in this model."

Yoni merely gave a noncommittal grunt in response. On his part, Shade simply continued dealing with the vent. Frankly speaking, he was used to people watching him while he worked. Most muhfuckas in the hood felt if they turned their head for two seconds, you'd rob them blind so they usually kept an eye on you. Over time, however, Shade usually built up enough of a rapport with people that his regular customers grew to trust him.

That obviously wasn't the case with Yoni. In addition, Shade felt her watching him with what felt like more the normal amount of interest. There was an intensity in her gaze that went beyond the usual make-sure-he-don't-steal-some-shit oversight.

Finally she spoke, saying, "You don't recognize me, do you?"

"Yeah," he countered. "We have a class together."

"Naw," she stated, shaking her head. "I guess I misspoke. I meant to ask if you remember me. From when we lived here b'foe."

"Yeah, I do."

"Really?" She asked skeptically.

"Yep."

"Prove it," she practically demanded, crossing her arms.

Shade sighed. "We had kindergarten together with Ms. Bass."

Yoni merely stared at him in surprise for a moment, then muttered, "Damn! You *do* remember."

Shade looked at her with a raised eyebrow. "You thought I was lyin'?"

She shrugged. "Niggas say all kinda shit if they thank it'll hold a bitch attention."

"So what's it mean if I *ain't* tryin' to hold yo attention?"

"Means yo ass is blind," Yoni declared as she put one hand on her hip, which she then thrust out provocatively. "Or gay."

Shade chuckled. "Or maybe I just always tell the truth."

"Yeah, right – and maybe I'm a flyin' monkey," Yoni noted sarcastically. "Anyway, I'm surprised you remember Ms. Bass."

"Ha!" Shade barked. "It's the nice ones you don't remember. The mean ones, you *never* forget."

"She was more than mean. She was a racist bitch who had no business teachin' kids. Remember how she used to make us eat our whole lunch – even if it was sommin' you hated?"

Shade nodded. "Well, in her defense, she said it was 'cause most of us was on free lunch and it was taxes from people like her that paid for our food. So she was gonna make sure we didn't waste it."

"She didn't give a shit 'bout that," Yoni argued. "She just saw a chance to torture a bunch of poor black kids and took it by makin' us eat that slop they used to serve."

"You just mad 'cause she yelled at you for sneezin' on my lunch tray one time."

"I remember. She sent me to the principal's office for that – like I sneezed on your shit on purpose, but it was a accident."

"Well," Shade droned, "it wasn't *exactly* a accident..."

Yoni frowned. "Whachu mean?"

"I didn't like what they were servin' that day, so I acted like I was puttin' some pepper on my food but slung it around kind of freely. That's what made you sneeze. Then I just told Ms. Bass I couldn't finish my food 'cause somebody sneezed on my plate."

"You fuckin' asshole," Yoni growled in faux anger. "You know, I hated you after that for gettin' me in trouble."

"I wasn't tryin' to. I actually didn't even care who sneezed, 'cause – whoever it was – I was just gonna say they sneezed on my plate. You just happened to be next to me that day."

"Lucky me," she uttered mockingly.

"Anyway, I'm done," Shade said, flipping the switch on the vent. Unsurprisingly, it came on. He let it run for a second, then turned it off.

"Cool," Yoni said with a nod. "Now when my no-cookin' daddy burn sommin' up on the stove again, I don't have to worry 'bout the place fillin' up with smoke."

"You safe on that front," Shade declared as he put his tools away. "Oh, I should speak if he's here since–"

"He's out," she interjected somewhat cryptically, her voice making it clear that it wasn't a subject she wanted to talk about. "So what I owe you?"

"Nuthin'," Shade told her. "It's on the house."

Yoni looked at him in surprise. "You sure?"

"Yeah."

"Well, that's nice of you. I wasn't expectin' that."

"Sure you weren't," Shade teased. "Like you not used to niggas doin' stuff for you for free." As he finished speaking, he winked, causing her to smile. "But seriously, let's just consider it payback for gettin' you in trouble with Ms. Bass. Now we even."

"That's cool," she admitted with a nod. "But I wanna give you *sommin'* for your time."

As she spoke, she gave him a coquettish look, at the same intertwining her fingers in front of her and bringing her arms forward in a way that pushed up her ample bosom.

"Naw, uh, that's okay," Shade assured her.

"Well, I'm gonna give you sommin' anyway," Yoni said, moving closer to him. "Sommin' I *know* you gone enjoy."

"Uh…what's that?" Shade asked as she stepped inside his personal space.

Leaning in, she put her lips next to his ear and said in a breathy whisper, "Lunch."

She then burst into laughter.

Chapter 12

Shade tried to stress to Yoni that the joke was on her: it was too early for lunch.

"Like you really thought that's what I was talkin' 'bout," she teased.

"Honestly, I wasn't thinkin' anythang," Shade insisted.

"Nigga, what happened to always tellin' the truth?"

"I am," he insisted.

"Muhfucka, stop lyin'," Yoni said, giggling.

"Seriously, I ain't know what the hell you were talkin' 'bout, so I really didn't have anythang in mind."

"Whatever," Yoni muttered dismissively. "But I was only half jokin'. I do wanna give you lunch. You okay with a sandwich?"

"Yeah, but like I said b'foe, it's a lil' too early for lunch."

"So take it wichu," she suggested as she pulled a loaf bread from a nearby cabinet.

****

He didn't take it with him. Despite his comment about it being too early for lunch, Shade ending up eating the sandwich that Yoni made for him. In fact they ate together, since she made one for herself as well.

Sitting on Yoni's living room couch, they talked as they ate, although the conversation initially consisted mostly of Yoni asking questions about people and things in the neighborhood that had changed while her family had been away. However, she deftly avoided answering when Shade inquired about what her life had been like for the past ten years, preferring to give generic responses to everything.

Eventually, the conversation moved on and they found themselves discussing everything from movies to music. Although she could occasionally be coarse, Shade found Yoni to be smart and funny for the most part. Likewise, she seemed to find him entertaining and witty. More to the point, she didn't seem to be in any rush for him to leave.

At some point, however, Shade realized that he had been talking with Yoni for well over an hour (although it only seemed like five minutes). Thanking her for the sandwich, he reluctantly told her had to go.

"I need to check on my lil' sista," he explained as he retrieved his tool bag.

"Oh, that's so sweet," Yoni droned as she began walking him to the door.

"I guess," Shade commented with a shrug. "Anyway, thanks again for lunch."

"No, thank *you* for fixin' the vent," Yoni countered.

"No problem," Shade assured her.

The two of them then just stood there at the door, staring at one another, each seemingly waiting for the other to say something.

"Oh, do you have a pen and paper?" Shade finally asked.

"Uh, probably," Yoni said, then walked towards the kitchen. Shade thought he heard a couple of drawers open and some things being moved around. A few moments later Yoni came back into the room carrying a pencil and a small notepad.

"Great," Shade said as he took the pencil and started scribbling on the pad. A few seconds later he handed them back to her saying, "Here's my number. Call me if you need anythang else fixed 'round here."

"Sure," Yoni said flatly, tepidly taking the items from him.

"Well, I better get goin'," he said, opening the door and stepping into the hallway. "See ya."

Yoni didn't respond. She simply closed the door behind him.

Shade stood there for a moment, staring at the closed door, wondering if he should knock and—

No, said a voice in his brain. *You got enough shit goin' on at the moment. You don't need a female complicatin' shit even further.*

However, before he could decide whether to heed the voice or not, the door to Yoni's apartment seemed to fly open.

Standing in the doorway, she gave him a stern look and simply stated, "Ask."

Shade frowned. "Huh?"

"Ask me," she said.

"Ask you what?"

Yoni let out a slight sigh of frustration. "Come on – don't be like all these other niggas in the hood, actin' like they too cool to let a woman know they really into her. I mean, I'm the girl here so I shouldn't be makin' the first move, but here I am openin' the door for you" – she gestured towards the doorframe around her – "*literally* openin' the fuckin' door for you. Now *ask.*"

Shade simply stared at her for a moment, then let out a deep breath, "I don't mean to be forward, but can I get yo number?"

"Fuck naw, nigga," Yoni shot back. "Do I look like I date fuckin' repairmen?"

Then she slammed the door.

Shade simply stood there, the little voice screaming *I-told-you-so* in his brain, while hysterical laughter came from the other side of Yoni's door.

Chapter 13

"You know how you can tell when you in the fuckin' projects?" Detective Wade Gummerson asked as he put a stick of chewing gum in his mouth.

It was somewhat of a rhetorical question, but his partner – Detective Ramsey Blanchard – responded anyway. "How, Gummy?"

"Because they always attach some lofty-ass name to all the buildings and community," Gummy explained, "like 'Heights' or 'Manor' or 'Estates.'"

"Hey, I live in *Covington* Estates," said a voice from behind them.

"We know," said Blanchard. "The projects."

Gills, the person behind the two detectives, merely let out a sigh of disgust. He was a twenty-two-year-old hustler who had lived in the hood his entire life, but that didn't mean he liked people talking shit about where he came from. Making a big deal about it, however, would just spur Gummy and Blanchard – two homicide detectives with more than 20 years apiece on the force – to razz him some more.

The three of them were currently in the detectives' unmarked police car, which was parked at present in a little-used alley. The two officers sat in the front seat and Gills was in the back. Of course, being in an unmarked car often didn't mean shit in the hood. If you knew what to look for, they usually weren't that hard to pick out.

"So whachu got for us?" Gummy asked, looking at Gills in the rearview mirror.

"Nuthin'," Gills responded.

"Whachu mean, 'nuthin'?" Blanchard shot back.

"I mean nuthin'," Gills repeated.

"What da fuck, man?" Gummy complained. "You gotta be the worst damn snitch on the planet."

"Hey!" Gills barked angrily. "I ain't no fuckin' snitch!"

"Of course not," Gummy said chummily. "You just a dude who tells the cops everythang they wanna know about his friends, family and loved ones in exchange for money."

"Fuck you, Gummy," Gills uttered. "I'm out this bitch."

"Okay, okay," Blanchard intoned as Gills slid towards one of the rear doors. "You not a snitch. You a 'confidential informant' – maybe the best damn Cee-Eye in the city."

Gills didn't immediately say anything, but after a moment, he slid back towards his original position in the middle of the back seat.

"So now that we done kissin' yo ass," Blanchard continued, "how 'bout you give us some info we can use."

"I already told you clowns," Gills insisted. "Ain't nuthin' on the streets 'bout this shit y'all tryin' to run down."

"Bullshit," Gummy declared. "Niggas on the street always talkin' – even if they don't do it directly. A fuckin' armored car gets robbed, and the next day a broke, jobless muhfucka is out tryin' to buy a new car with cash. A jewelry store gets hit, and suddenly some hoe in the hood is sportin' a rock on her finger the size of basketball."

"In short," Blanchard added, "word about shit always gets out, 'cause muhfuckas on the street is always talkin' – even if they don't do it with they mouth."

"Now, we got what's probably a triple-homicide," Gummy chimed in. "Three dead bodies in an abandoned building. One of 'em shot, and two that maybe got pushed off a ledge. Somebody gotta know *sommin'*."

"All anybody know is the shit they showed on the news," Gills said. "When the fuckin' demolition crew showed to tear the damn buildin' down a few weeks back, they did a final check to make sure wasn't no crackheads or homeless muhfuckas in there, and they found the bodies."

"And that's it?" Blanchard inquired. "Ain't no other chatter about what the fuck happened up in there?"

"If anybody knows, they ain't talkin'," Gills declared.

"Okay, so forget about what actually happened," Gummy said. "What's the word on the street about the muhfuckas who died in there?"

Gills frowned. "Whachu mean?"

"I mean, what were they into?" Gummy explained. "Did they owe somebody money? Did they piss off a drug cartel? Did they rip off the wrong person? What?"

Gills didn't immediately answer. In fact, the silence from the back seat was so prolonged that Blanchard turned around to make sure that nigga hadn't slipped out without them noticing. Gills was still there, brow crinkled in thought.

"Looks like you know sommin' after all," Blanchard stated. "Spill it."

"Look, I don't *know* nuthin'," Gills stressed. "But…"

"But what?" Gummy asked.

Gills let out a deep breath, like this was a subject he didn't care for. "Two of the muhfuckas you askin' 'bout – the two that fell – they were drug dealers. Part of Zerk Simon's crew."

"We know all that," Gummy asserted. "In fact, one of 'em was Glen Simon, the Beserker's lil' brother. The other was a thug on Zerk's payroll named Chris Little."

"Well, rumor on the street says that Glen and Chris had a thang."

Blanchard frowned. "Da fuck that mean?"

"It mean they were fags," Gills explained. "But you didn't hear that from me. That muhfucka Zerk crazy…they don't call him 'Berserker' for nuthin'. No tellin' what he'll do if he find out somebody sayin' his lil' brutha liked dick."

"So whachu tryin' to say?" Blanchard asked. "That maybe this was some kinda love triangle?"

Gills shook his head. "Naw, I'm not sayin'–"

"Hang on," Gummy interjected, suddenly sitting up. "Who's that?"

The person he was speaking of was a young man who had just entered the alley, walking directly in front of their car. He was tall and looked to be in his late teens. He glanced at the car as he went by, momentarily locking eyes with Gummy. The detective noted that the guy had a handsome face and striking gray eyes. He also observed something else that set off alarm bells in his brain.

"That's Shade," Gills said matter-of-factly.

"Shade?" Gummy echoed. "Who's he with?"

Gills frowned. "Whachu mean?"

"Who's he run with?" Gummy explained. "What gang, what crew, what clique?"

Gills shook his head. "Shade don't run with nobody."

"Hmmm," Gummy droned, rubbing his chin in thought. "Alright Gills, get the fuck out. But when we call you again, you better have some fuckin' useful information for us."

"Whatever, man," Gills said, sliding towards one of the rear doors.

"And see what else you can find out about this Shade guy," Gummy tacked on.

Gills grumbled something in response that was hard to understand as he got out and shut the door, but Gummy was barely paying attention.

Recognizing the look on his partner's face, Blanchard asked, "So whachu thinkin'?"

"I'm thinkin' we need to find out more about this Shade character."

"You thank he connected to our case?"

"Don't know," Gummy admitted. "But did you notice anything unusual about him?"

"Like what?"

"He was carrying a tool bag," Gummy stated, which was the thing that had caught his attention earlier.

Chapter 14

Shade left Yoni's apartment building feeling exuberant.

After asking for her number and getting the door slammed in his face, he had simply stood there for a moment, listening to her laugh. After a few seconds, she opened the door, grinning from ear to ear.

"Sorry," she apologized, "but that was too good an opportunity to pass up."

"Well, you lucky I'm still out here."

"Nigga, please," she droned, crossing her arms. "Yo ass wasn't goin' nowhere."

He raised an eyebrow. "Somebody thinks pretty highly of themselves."

"It's not thinkin' highly if it's true," she countered. "Now gimme yo phone."

Shade handed her his cell phone, as requested, and then waited as she tapped some info into his contacts.

"A'ight," she said, giving the phone back. "Now you got my number."

"Cool," Shade said. "Maybe I'll give you a call some time."

"Maybe?" she echoed, giving him a dubious look. "Nigga, you got jokes."

He chuckled at that, and she giggled as well. They then spent another fifteen minutes chatting in the hallway before Shade finally dragged himself away.

He found himself smiling as he reflected on the time he'd spent with Yoni. It was probably the most in-depth conversation he'd had with someone outside his family in a long time. More importantly, it was arguably the most fun he'd ever had with a girl (with his clothes on, that is). In short, he was practically giddy as headed back home, thinking nothing could spoil his mood.

And then he saw the cop.

Deciding to take a shortcut, Shade had gone through a nearby alley, and he was floating so high on cloud nine that he really didn't notice the car at first. When he did, he only casually glanced at it, but when he saw the occupants – especially the guy behind the wheel – his instincts went into overdrive. He only locked eyes with the driver for a second, but everything about the guy screamed "Cop."

Shit! Shade muttered to himself, although he managed to continue walking without breaking stride. Under normal circumstances, he probably would have made the car as an unmarked police vehicle before he even stepped into the alley. As it was, he had barely paid attention to it, and thus had failed to look for the tell-tale signs of a cop car: municipal tags, spotlight on the mirror, emergency lights in the grill or dash, and so on. That being the case, it was simply raw instinct that told him the guy he'd seen was a cop.

Of course, being in the hood, seeing cops wasn't unusual (although most of them were uniformed). But there was something about the one in the driver's seat – the way he had looked at Shade seemed to suggest more than just casual interest. Even worse, Shade felt the man's eyes stay on him as he continued on his way.

Not good, Shade thought as he continued heading home. *Not fuckin' good at all.*

THUG LIFE: EMANCIPATED

Chapter 15

Shade felt relief wash over him as he arrived home, stepped inside, and closed the door. He hadn't realized how tense he'd been, but something about that cop had really put him edge. Again, it wasn't anything tangible – just instinct.

Trying to put the cop out of his mind, he spent a moment looking around the living room, feeling something was out of place. Nissa was obviously gone; the car wasn't outside, and this was around the time when she said she'd be out – most likely at the mall with her chick-clique. That's when it hit him: normally, Cherry would be out here watching television on a Saturday, assuming she didn't have homework or something similar to do. (And he would have gotten a text if she was going out to play with friends.)

Curious, he dropped his tool bag by the door and headed towards the back of the house. As he began walking down the hallway, he heard noise coming from the bathroom. As he drew closer, he saw that the bathroom door was only half-closed. More importantly, he could hear what was being said inside.

"–ta find the vein," Gin was saying.

Already knowing what was happening, Shade pushed the door open wide and stepped inside. Gin looked up as he came in. The lid of the toilet was down and she was sitting on it, looking more strung out than usual. She also had a length of rubber tubing tied around one arm, with Cherry next to her, holding a needle.

"Cherry," Shade said forcefully, trying not to yell. "Go to your room."

Recognizing her brother's mood, Cherry moved to obey, setting the needle she'd been holding on the bathroom counter.

Shade merely glowered at his mother as Cherry went by him, keeping silent until she left and he heard the door to her and Nissa's room shut.

"Da fuck you doin', Gin?" he growled as he walked to the counter and picked up the needle. "I told you I didn't want you doin' this shit 'round here."

"Nigga, who da hell you thank you talkin' to?" Gin demanded. "I'm *yo* momma! You talkin' like you *mine*."

"You ain't nobody's momma," he shot back. "A real mother wouldn't have her daughter shootin' her up. She'd be ashamed to even let her kid see her on this shit, but you not only givin' Cherry a ringside seat, you done made her yo cornerman."

"Fuck you, nigga!" Gin screamed. "You talk like that to the woman that birth you?"

Shade sighed in exasperation. "You need to leave, Gin."

"Muhfucka, you gotta lotta nerve tryin' to throw me out the house I was raised in."

"That's 'cause it's *my* house."

"But it should be *mine*. Daddy shudda left it to *me*!"

"Yeah, well, he didn't," Shade reminded her. "He left it to me, along with the car, the money, and everythang else."

"Only 'cause you tricked him," Gin insisted. "Got him to cut me off. Othawise, he wudda left it all to me."

"No," Shade countered, shaking his head. "'He knew that if he left it to you, the fuckin' crack dealers would own it inside a week and his grandkids would be on the street. That's why he cut you off, Gin – 'cause you were a fuckin' crackhead junkie. You still are."

Gin's eyes narrowed in anger. "Da fuck I ever do to have a hateful bastard like you for a son?"

"Fucked around with some asshole," Shade replied.

Gin shook her head in disbelief. "Can't believe I'm *yo* fuckin' momma."

"That's 'cause you not," Shade declared. "Like I said b'foe, you ain't *nobody's* momma. You just a fuckin' cuckoo bird, layin' yo eggs in other folks' nest – people like yo parents – and expectin' them to raise yo kids."

Gin just stared at him for a moment, and Shade could see all kinds of emotions running through her: anger, disgust, frustration and more.

"Just gimme my shit," she finally said, stomping towards her son and reaching for the needle.

"Fine," Shade muttered. "Take this shit and get out."

She snatched the needle from Shade as he spoke – or snatched it as best she could without jabbing herself – then headed towards the living room (and presumably the front door).

Shade followed, noting how tightly she gripped the needle as she headed to the door. As she opened it, Shade spoke, getting her attention.

"Now this the last time I'm tellin' you," Shade stated. "I realize you a junkie and got a problem, but don't do that shit 'round here again – and especially don't get Cherry mixed up in it."

Gin merely scowled at him for a few seconds, then stomped out and slammed the door behind her.

Chapter 16

After Gin left, Shade locked the door and then went to check on Cherry. He knocked on the bedroom door, then waited until he heard her say "Come in" before stepping inside. She was sitting on her bed reading a book, but stuck a bookmark in it and set it aside.

"You okay?" Shade asked.

She nodded. "I'm fine."

"Good," Shade intoned. "Anyway, I thought we talked 'bout Gin and what you s'posed to do when you see her with needles and stuff like that."

"I know – I'm s'posed to stay away if she's doin' drugs, but she needed help."

Shade shook his head. "Gin was takin' drugs way before you were even born. I doubt she needs yo help stickin' a needle in her arm."

"But she looked like she was havin' trouble, and I know that people can die if air gets in the needle, right?"

Shade walked towards his sister, letting out a deep breath as he did so, then sat down next to her on the bed.

"What you talkin' 'bout is called an 'air embolism,'" He told Cherry. "And yeah, it can kill somebody, but it's not like in the movies where they inject a little bit of air into somebody's IV or sommin' and the person dies. It takes a lot of air for it to be fatal – more than what can fit in those rinky-dink needles Gin be usin'."

"Well, it just looked like there was bubbles in the needle, and I didn't want anythang to happen to her."

"I understand that. But Gin's not yo responsibility. She should be takin' care of *you*, not the other way around."

Shade tried to keep his voice even as he spoke, but failed to keep his tone from reflecting his anger towards Gin. More to the point, Cherry picked up on it.

"You really should be nicer to her," Cherry advised. "She still our momma, and even if she ain't the best one, she the only one we got."

"Nice don't really work with Gin," Shade argued.

"That's only 'cause of the drugs," his sister countered. "You should still try."

Shade just stared at her for a minute, then let out a deep sigh. "A'ight, I'll try to be nice to her from now on."

"Thanks," Cherry said, smiling. She then leaned over and gave him a big hug, which he returned. "I think just bein' nice to her will help Momma a lot."

Shade was tempted to give a snide response, but before he could say anything the doorbell rang.

"I wonder who that is," Cherry muttered, releasing her brother from her embrace.

"Don't know," Shade confessed with a shrug before standing up. "Let's go find out."

With Cherry trailing him, he began walking to the front door. The doorbell rang two more times in quick succession before they got there, indicating that their visitor was impatient.

Hold on, muhfucka, Shade thought, trying not to get agitated as the doorbell was pressed yet again.

Once he got to the door he glanced out the peephole, then frowned in concern.

Turning to Cherry, he fervently whispered. "Go to your room and lock the door. Don't come out until me or Nissa come get you."

Cherry nodded and then dashed towards the rear of the house. Still frowning, Shade opened the door. There were four thuggish-looking niggas standing outside.

One of them – a bald muhfucka sporting a goatee – smiled and said, "Lord Byron requests the honor of your presence."

THUG LIFE: EMANCIPATED

Chapter 17

Le'Andre "Lord" Byron was a mid-level drug dealer – well above the bottom of the food chain, but still a long way from the top. That said, he had managed to amass a decent amount of power in the game, and – among other things – currently ran his own crew.

His nickname, Lord Byron, was derived from the famous Romantic Era poet. Not that Le'Andre knew fuck-all about balladry – that nigga couldn't tell a verse from a stanza. He had simply paid enough attention in the one English class he took to realize that his name resembled that of somebody famous, and – as niggas are wont to do – he made off with that shit, adopting the mantle of "Lord Byron" when he got into the drug game.

All of this flitted through Shade's brain as he sat in the back seat of an SUV with two of the niggas who'd ben at his door sitting on either side of him, and the other two in the front seat. When they had told him why they were there, he had simply grabbed his tool bag and left with them, closing and locking the door behind him.

Presumably they were on their way to Lord Byron's crib – a nine-thousand square foot fixer-upper that Byron had bought the year before (in someone else's name, of course) as part of a tax sale. The property was located at the far edge of the hood, in an area that had once been known as the "Gold Coast" among the city's Black population.

During its heyday, the Gold Coast had been home to professional and upwardly mobile Blacks – doctors, lawyers, educators, and the like. They were arguably the "Talented Tenth" that W.E.B. Du Bois had spoken of back in the day and represented what African Americans were truly capable of achieving. Moreover, their enclave of beautiful homes and spacious yards was a testament to what you could accomplish through dedication and hard work, and as the population of Black professionals grew there was talk of Gold Coast expansion.

Such talk, however, came to an abrupt end after the good white folks on the City Planning Commission got in on the act. It seems that, after careful review, the Commissioners decided that what those uppity "Nigrahs" on the Gold Coast really needed wasn't expansion, but a closer relationship with their downtrodden brethren. Next thing you know, a couple of tenements – soon to be filled with the unemployed and working poor (of the dark-skinned variety) – were zoned for construction right next to the Gold Coast. Property values collapsed and Gold Coast residents fled in droves.

Even with prices depressed, however, Gold Coast homes cost more than what the average person had to spend, which created a unique dilemma: people who could afford the homes didn't want to live in the hood; people who didn't mind living in the hood couldn't afford the homes. At the end of the day, former Gold Coast residents were stuck with houses they couldn't sell, and which costs more than they were worth. In many instances, the owners simply abandoned the homes, allowing the banks to foreclose on them or letting the city take possession for failure to pay the requisite property taxes and auction them off (which is how Lord Byron came to own his current residence). Ultimately, the Gold Coast became something of a ghost town – full of large, empty houses that had mostly been ransacked and vandalized.

Shade was still reflecting on all this when they reached Lord Byron's place, entering a broad circular driveway. As they drew close, Shade took note of the house. It was a two-story Chateau-style home, built to resemble a castle and sat on roughly two acres. Some of the highlights included a porte cochere, a tower and a turret. (There were also a couple of niggas armed with semi-automatic weapons stationed strategically around the perimeter of the house.)

Shade was impressed. He'd been hired to do some work around the house when Lord Byron first bought it, and he remembered it as a dilapidated, graffiti-stained husk. It looked fucking elegant now – almost like new. Shade hated to admit it, but that the nigga Byron had done good.

The SUV stopped in front of a set of ornate double doors with brass knockers. Still carrying his tool bag, Shade and his four-man escort got out, and they swiftly led him inside.

Like the outside of the home, the interior had gotten a makeover. Where there had been rotting wooden floors, there was now fresh tile. Walls that had been permeated with holes had been replastered and painted. A rusting handrail on a winding staircase had been replaced with an eye-catching, wrought iron banister. In short, the place had essentially been restored to its original state, if not improved.

Eventually Shade was led into what he recalled was the master bedroom, and it was there that they found Lord Byron.

He was tall – maybe six-two in height – and handsome, with a dazzling smile that women seemed to love. He was currently dressed in jeans and sneakers, but had decided to forego a shirt, revealing his bare chest and six-pack abs. That said, he did have a royal mantle that he wore draped across his shoulders; it was red and lined with white fur, and hung down to just below his knees. On anyone else, it would have looked like a pimp cape, but on Lord Byron it simply looked natural. In short, he may not have actually had royal or noble blood in his veins, but – if you overlooked the absence of a shirt – he did an excellent job of pulling off the look. (If also didn't hurt that he carried around a two-foot gilded scepter.)

"Shade, my man," he said with a smile as he approached. "Whaddup?"

"You tell me," Shade replied as he stepped forward, giving Lord Byron some dap.

Byron stepped back and spread his arms out in an expansive gesture meant to encompass the room. "So, whachu thank?"

"It's nice," Shade stated, nodding as he looked around. He was about to add that it probably cost a small fortune, then he realized that everything he'd seen, from the tile to the handrails, had probably been boosted form somewhere.

"Nice?' Byron echoed incredulously. "*Nice?* After power washin' the outside and puttin' a new coat of paint on this bitch, all you can say is 'nice'? After I put in hardwood floors, the best you can thank of is 'nice'? After installin' tile, a fuckin island kitchen, and granite countertops, 'nice' is all that comes to mind?"

"Fine – this muhfucka's off the hook," Shade uttered monotonously. "That whachu wanna hear?"

"Damn straight," Byron insisted with a nod.

"Well, if you ever decide to make it a career, you got a future flippin' houses."

Byron actually seemed to contemplate this for a moment, scratching his chin, and then stated, "Now *that's* an idea."

"Anyway," Shade droned, setting his tool bag down, "Whachu need me to work on 'round here?"

"Huh?" Lord Byron muttered, frowning.

"You got sommin' you need a repairman for, right?" Shade asked. "I mean, fo' of yo henchmen show up on my doe'step sayin' you need me, I assume you got sommin' in this bitch need fixin'."

For the first time, Lord Byron seemed to take note of the four niggas who had escorted Shade in. They were still present – apparently on standby in case their boss needed them. Lord Byron let out an exasperated sigh then made a dismissive gesture, at which point the thuggish quartet left, closing the door behind them.

"So all fo' of them muhfuckas showed up atcho' doe'?" Byron asked, to which Shade gave a curt nod in response. "Yeah, that's not exactly what I intended, but it's the result of some shit that happened recently. Basically, I sent a crew out to visit somebody maybe two weeks ago; two of 'em went to the doe' while two stayed in the car. Well, some fine-ass bitch answered the doe' buck naked. Since then, muhfuckas scared of missin' out on sommin', so now all of 'em go to the doe' when they makin' a house call."

"It's called FOMO," Shade told him.

"FOMO?" Byron repeated curiously.

"Means 'Fear of Missin' Out,'" Shade explained. "FOMO. It's when people do shit not 'cause they really want to, but 'cause they scared they gone miss out on sommin'. Like buyin' a lottery ticket. You might think the lottery is a scam, but you pool yo money with neighbors or co-workers to buy tickets together, 'cause you can't stand the thought of them niggas gettin' rich without you."

"FOMO, huh?" Byron said, seeming to weigh the term. "I like that."

"Anyway," Shade intoned, "why you sendin' fo' niggas to get me in the first place? One wouldn't do?"

"The numbas got nothin' to do wichu. They was off handlin' some other business and just scooped you up on the way back."

"So that quartet wasn't intended to intimidate a muhfucka," Shade surmised verbally.

"Were you?" Lord Byron asked. "Intimidated, that is?"

Shade didn't respond. Instead, he merely tilted his head to the side, looking at Byron with a *What-do-you-think?* expression.

Lord Byron laughed. "See? That's why I like yo ass. Most muhfuckas who look out and see fo' thuggish niggas on they porch, they gone take off runnin' out the back."

"How you know I didn't?"

"'Cause niggas who run gotta be dragged in here by my boys, and then they all shakin' and shit, like they fuckin' bones turned to rubber. But you walk in here cool as a muhfuckin' snow cone in a blizzard."

"That a problem?"

"Naw," Byron stressed, shaking his head. "But it make me wonder: how does a nigga yo age get brass balls like that?"

"What da fuck?" Shade growled. "We on Oprah now? We 'bout to talk about our feelins' and shit?"

"Ha ha!" Byron laughed. "See, that's what I'm talkin' 'bout – the way you just man up and say what the fuck's on yo mind. Most muhfuckas too chicken-shit to talk like that to me, even though I'm the nicest nigga around."

"Yeah, right – you Mr. Congeniality," Shade stated sarcastically, which caused Byron to chuckle even more.

Basically, Lord Byron had the ability to be charming and could come off as a nice guy, but Shade knew there was also another side to his personality. In short, the nigga could be utterly ruthless when the situation called for it. You couldn't get as far as he'd gotten in the drug game without that particular character trait, and anyone who thought he was soft because he occasionally seemed affable was in for a rude awakening.

"But back to my original question," Shade continued. "You brought me here, so what's the problem?"

"Honestly, ain't no problem with the house," Byron replied.

"What?" Shade blurted out, almost disbelievingly. "I cancelled other appointments 'cause I thought you had a busted pipe floodin' this bitch, or a loose electrical wire or some shit like that."

Shade wasn't just grandstanding. He'd had other repair jobs on his agenda, and he'd had to call to reschedule those while en route to Byron's crib. He didn't like doing shit like that – it made him come off as unreliable – but tellin' Byron's crew that it was an inopportune time would have been more trouble than it was worth.

Fortunately, Byron seemed to be in an understanding mood. Reaching into a pocket, he pulled out a rolled up wad of cash and peeled off two individual bills, which he then held out. Taking them, Shade couldn't help but note that each was a Benjamin.

"We good now?" Byron asked, then continued without waiting for a response as he put the cash away. "Anyway, the reason I wanted you here is 'cause the house is actually finished. I got a ton of furniture comin' in a little later, but by the end of the day this bitch gone be completely pimped out. That bein' the case, I'm havin' a lil' housewarmin' party tonight. Mostly my crew, but a few outside guests."

"And what – you wanted to personally invite me?" Shade inquired.

"Not exactly," Lord Byron replied. "This party gone be the shizzle, so I was lookin' to line up some world-class talent to come in and entertain."

"Well, I'm flattered you thought of me," Shade deadpanned, "but shakin' my ass in a g-string for a bunch of niggas ain't my thang."

"Damn, nigga," Byron chortled. "I'm gone start callin' yo ass in whenever I need a good laugh. But just in case you serious, it ain't you I'm interested in."

"Good to know. So why you got me here?"

"Word on the street is that you got a solid stable of hoes. Since I got a need for feminine entertainment, I figured we could make a deal."

"You heard wrong," Shade countered. "First of all, it ain't a stable; it's like four girls. Second, they ain't hoes. They just doin' what they gotta do to get by. Lastly, I ain't no pimp. These girls ain't out there walkin' the streets for me. All I do is help'em out from time to time – like when they dealin' with a nigga that don't wanna pay up."

"Style that shit however you want," Byron said. "But it still reads the same, which is that you got a line on some hoes – 'scuse me, some *girls* – that can help make this a real party tonight. And from the way you talkin', it sound like they could use the money."

Shade frowned, then simply asked what he was thinking. "Why me?"

"Huh?" Byron intoned, sounding confused.

"Don't take this the wrong way," Shade explained, "but muhfuckas like you and yo crew is what keep strip joints open. Plus, I heard about yo parties and the women you have at 'em. Bottom line is that you probably got a hundred hoes on speed dial – or niggas who can get'em for you. So what the fuck you need me for?"

"You right," Lord Byron acknowledged with a nod. "Gettin' bitches for a bash ain't no thang – I can have wall-to-wall pussy up in here with one phone call. Chicks that'll come up for the party, do a strip routine, take the boys into a back room or outside for a good time… All that shit. But the truth is that it's always the same ole hoes. It's always the same bitches, wearin' the same outfits, doin' the same fuckin' routines. Or at least it feels like that to me, and the shit's gotten old. I want to kick things off *fresh* in my new crib."

"I get it," Shade said. "You want some new blood to help break in your new place."

"Exactly," Byron chimed in. "So whatchu say?"

Shade contemplated for a moment. "Look man, it's like I told you – these girls don't work for me. I can't commit to anythang for 'em."

"But you can ask, right?"

"I can, but I don't think they right for this party."

"How's that?" Lord Byron asked, frowning.

"'Cause it sound like you lookin' for strippers that are willin' to do some suck-and-fuck on the side. The girls you askin' 'bout don't fit that description. They doin' what they have to do to make it, but it usually don't involve no dance music, strip routines, or any of that shit. They ain't exotic dancers."

"They can take they clothes off, can't they? 'Cause that's all muhfuckas care about. This ain't gone be a bunch of White boys who thank strippin's an art form. It's just some niggas who want bitches to show some tits and ass, so that's all I need 'em to do. And I'm assumin' that if yo girls fuck for money, they won't have a problem with nudity."

"Come on, man – don't bullshit me," Shade urged. "You ask me to bring some girls to yo party that you know make a livin' on they back, then expect me to believe that all you want 'em to do is *strip*?"

"That's all *I'm* hirin' 'em to do," Byron declared. "But if they wanna make arrangements or engage in other transactions with muhfuckas at the party, that's between *them*."

"That brings up another point," Shade noted. "In addition to not being professional *strippers*, these chicks ain't professional *hoes*. They not used to fuckin' dozens of niggas a night or suckin' off an endless parade of musty dicks."

"And they won't have to," Lord Byron assured him. "They ain't gotta do nuthin' they don't wanna do."

"So nobody's gonna raise hell or go apeshit if these girls only fuck two niggas apiece and then say they done spreadin' they legs for the night?"

"They'll miss out on a lot of money, but I personally guarantee that nobody will give them shit about anythang like that."

Shade nodded in understanding, brow creased in thought. Assuming Lord Byron put a decent amount of cash on the table, it was probably a good deal. That said, something about the entire thing felt weird as fuck. There was something going on here that he couldn't quite put his finger on.

"One last thing," Shade said after a few moments. "Like I said b'foe, these ain't professional strippers, so they won't be like those bitches you see on the pole who done all had boob jobs and tummy tucks. They ain't had no work done, so I can't promise that they all gonna have firm tits or tight asses."

"So they not swimsuit models," Lord Byron concluded. "That's fine – I just want some new blood up in here for this muhfuckin' party. I ain't lookin' for perfection, and most of the niggas that show up gone be too drunk to care. All yo girls gone have to do to pacify 'em is a lil' striptease. Long as they can do that, muhfuckas won't care if a bitch got two left arms and her head's on backwards."

Shade was still frowning when Byron got through speaking. The whole thing still felt off, but he couldn't nail down exactly why it rubbed him the wrong way.

"Four grand," Shade finally said. "Half now, the rest when the girls show. *If* they show, I should say, 'cause they may not be interested."

"Yeah, right," Byron muttered as he pulled out the wad of cash again and began peeling off hundreds. "Like they gonna turn down a thousand bucks apiece to prance around naked for a few hours. Or rather, a thousand minus whatever *yo* cut is."

Shade ignored that last comment. "If any of 'em say 'No,' you get that part of the money back."

"Sounds good," Byron stated as he finished counting and held a sheaf of bills out to Shade. "Look man, I know you worried, but nuthin's gone happen to ya girls – I promise. And Lord Byron always keeps his word."

Reaching out to take the money, Shade asked, "You do know who the real Lord Byron was, donchu?"

"Oh yeah," Byron said with a grin. "Old school player – a fuckin' blueblood who had tons of money and got plenty of ass."

"He was a notorious bisexual, infamous for chasin' young men and boys, and for knockin' up his own sister."

Byron's eyebrows went up in surprise for a moment, then he simply shrugged, muttering, "Oh, well – nobody's perfect."

THUG LIFE: EMANCIPATED

Chapter 18

After meeting with Lord Byron, Shade was given a ride home by the same quartet that had picked him up. By that time, Nissa was back, as evidenced by the car parked in the driveway.

Walking inside, he noticed his sisters in the kitchen. They both immediately came towards him.

"You okay?" Nissa asked.

"Yeah," Shade confirmed. "Why you ask?"

"Cherry said she saw you leave with a bunch of knuckleheads."

Shade looked at his youngest sister. "I thought I told you to go to your room."

"And I did," Cherry stated. "But then I thought about sommin' happenin' to you, so I went and peeked out the window."

Shade simply stared at her for a moment. Typically he'd scold her for being disobedient, but he honestly didn't think she'd made a misstep in this instance.

"It's okay," he assured Cherry. "You did the right thang."

Cherry smiled, apparently happy to know her instincts had been correct. Nissa, however, still looked a bit concerned.

"So who was it?" she asked.

"Lord Byron," Shade replied. "He got some kind of hoedown goin' on tonight and wanted to talk to me about providin' entertainment."

"Entertainment?" Nissa echoed, confused.

"Women," he clarified, then glanced at Cherry for a second before continuing. "Girls like Taranda."

"Oh," Nissa muttered. "You think they'll do it?"

"Prolly, based on what he's offerin'," Shade acknowledged. "But I'll give 'em a call and find out."

"Do you think they *should?*" Nissa asked.

"Don't know," Shade admitted with a shrug. "I'm gettin' a weird vibe about this party, though."

Nissa frowned. "Like sommin's gonna go down?"

Shade shook his head. "Naw, nuthin' like that. Just a feelin' that sommin's off."

"Then it probably is," Nissa concluded.

"Maybe," Shade agreed. "But I got some errands I need to run. I'll think on it some mo' while I'm out."

"A'ight," Nissa droned as her brother headed for the door. "Be careful."

THUG LIFE: EMANCIPATED

Chapter 19

In Gummy's opinion, Arthur Lampanelli looked like a cop. That was unsurprising, since Officer Lampanelli was currently in uniform (as was his partner, Barry Shoemaker) and standing outside his patrol car, which was parked in the lot of a grocery store. With Lampanelli, however, the cop look went beyond the clothes. Although in his late forties, he was big and burly – a guy who clearly worked out regularly – and sported a stereotypical policeman's buzz cut. But more than anything else, he exuded an air of authority, which probably made it easy for people to make him as a cop wherever he went, whether in uniform or not.

That said, Lampanelli had a somewhat relaxed demeanor. Despite having a patrol route that included some of the roughest areas of the city (if not the country), he came across as a guy who didn't rattle easily. The same couldn't be said of his partner, Shoemaker, who was obviously new to the force and, judging from the way he constantly glanced about, clearly jittery about the neighborhood he'd been assigned to. Gummy viewed him as the type of cop who was more likely to shoot someone out of nervousness than justification. Truth be told, he'd be something of a liability until he stopped being so skittish, which was probably why he'd been partnered with a veteran officer like Lampanelli.

"So," Blanchard droned, "you know 'im?"

"Who, Shade?" Lampanelli replied. "Sure – real name's Joshua Green. Lives with his mom and two younger sisters, but mom's a junkie."

"The dad?" Gummy inquired.

"Old-school gangster named Zeke Green," Lampanelli answered. "He had some pull in the streets at one point, but been locked, oh, maybe ten years now."

"Damn, Lamp," Blanchard uttered, "You got this much info 'bout everybody on yo beat?"

"What can I say?" Lamp quipped with a grin. "Two decades around here, you pick up a few things. But seriously, I know about Shade because of his grandfather."

"What's *his* story?" Gummy asked.

"Nothing unusual for this part of town," Lamp explained. "Got killed in a drive-by a few years back. You might have heard about it."

Blanchard shook his head. "Wasn't our case."

"Still, it was on the news," Lamp noted.

"Are you fuckin' kiddin'?" Gummy blurted out. "You know how many drive-bys we get in this city? There's probably one happening right now."

Lamp seemed to consider this for a moment, then merely stated, "Touché."

"Was the old guy mixed up in something?" Blanchard asked.

Lamp shook his head. "Nope – just wrong place, wrong time. He basically worked as a neighborhood handyman and was just leaving a job when somebody rode through and shot the place up. He wasn't the target, just collateral damage. Shade was with him when it happened."

"That's fucked up," Gummy noted.

"Tell me about it," Lamp muttered. "Anyway, I was first on the scene. I took him home, then checked up on him a couple of times after that, tried to make sure he and his family were doing okay."

"Were they?" Blanchard asked.

Lamp made a so-so gesture with his hand. "About the best they could with a junkie mom and the only father-figure dead."

Gummy frowned in thought for a moment. "Any idea who did it?"

"Some shitbird named Ed Wiggins," Lamp stated. "Used to call him Evil Ed."

"Never heard of him," Gummy declared. "Did he stand trial?"

Lamp snorted in derision. "Come on, Gummy – you know how this works. There's a big difference between what you *know* and what you can *prove*. Plus, nobody around here will ever testify about shit like that."

"So this Evil Ed just walked?" Blanchard suggested.

"Not exactly," Lamp remarked. "About three weeks after the drive-by, he died."

Gummy raised an eyebrow in surprise. "How?"

"Motorcycle crash," Lamp explained. "He was zipping along the highway one night and just went straight off the road – smashed into a transformer or something."

Gummy seemed to contemplate for a moment. "You think this Shade kid might have had something to do with it?"

"What – the crash?" Lamp muttered, clearly surprised. "No. Like I told you, it was an accident. Why would I think Shade had something to do with it?"

"Just trying to get your assessment of him," Blanchard chimed in.

"Well, in my opinion, he's a good kid," Lamp said. "Pretty much took over where his grandfather left off in terms of being the local handyman. From what I hear, he does good work."

"You ever hear about him being into anything?" Gummy asked. "Gangs? Drugs? Shit like that?"

Lamp was shaking his head before Gummy even finished forming his question. "Naw – never heard about him being mixed up in anything along those lines."

"What about other shit?" Gummy continued. "He got beef with anybody? Maybe owe somebody some money?"

"It would be news to me," Lamp declared.

"What about a girl?" Blanchard suggested. "Any love triangle shit he might be caught up in?"

"Far as I know, his only girlfriend is his tool bag," Lamp noted. "Takes it with him damn near everywhere."

"Well, is there anybody that just picks on him?" Gummy inquired. "A neighborhood bully or somebody like that?"

"Hey, I don't claim to see or know *every*thing," Lamp admitted. "And to be honest, I haven't done much more than say 'Hi' to that kid in a long time. So is it possible that some shit's going on that I don't know about? Abso-fucking-lutely. But nothing like the shit you guys are asking about has reached me."

"So in your opinion, this Shade is squeaky clean," Blanchard surmised.

"Man, you two really have a hard-on for this kid," Shoemaker chirped, speaking for the first time. The other three officers just stared at him, like he was a dog that had learned to speak, but could only spout gibberish.

"Look," Lamp said after a few seconds, "twenty years I walk this beat, now you two want to go after one of the few kids I've seen in all that time who's never been in trouble. Shoemaker may be green, but it sounds like he called this one right. You guys have it in for Shade for some reason."

Gummy seemed to reflect on this for a few moments, then said. "Okay Lamp, you made some valid points, but allow me to show you things through *our* lens. See, Blanchard and I have spent a good chunk of the day calling people at Shade's school: teachers, counselors, and so on – who, by the way, did not like having to spend any part of their Saturday talking to a couple of homicide detectives. You know what we found out?"

"What?" asked Lamp.

"That everyone speaks about Shade the same way you do," Gummy explained. "He's a straight-A student, doesn't cause any problems, never gets into fights, and so on. He's even enrolled in dual-credit courses at a local community college."

"Oh," Blanchard intoned. "And don't forget that he's won a bunch of academic accolades, including an award for reading the most books three years in a row."

"What's your point?" asked Lamp.

"My point is this," Gummy stated. "His old man isn't some street king keeping him protected. He doesn't have some thuggish older brother telling folks in the hood that he's untouchable. He's not in a gang. He's not dealing. He's not a jock. He's not one of the cool kids. He's not in any clubs. He's just a straight-A student taking a bunch of advanced course, and he reads more books than a fucking librarian."

Lamp gave him a confused look. "And that's a problem?"

"The problem," Gummy went on, "is that out in the *'burbs*, all that shit I mentioned is enough to get you labeled a nerd and bullied for life. But in the *hood*? It's like he was hand-crafted by the Almighty for a daily ass-beating. I mean, he's a bully's wet dream – especially around here. He should be collecting wedgies, black eyes and purple nurples like they're gold bullion. But from everything we've heard, none of that shit happens, which begs the question: why doesn't anybody fuck with this kid?"

Lamp looked as though he wanted to respond, but before he could Gummy's cell phone began to ring.

"I gotta take this," Gummy said as he looked at the Caller ID. "Thanks, Lamp. We'll reach out if we need anything else."

Looking at his partner, he then tilted his head towards their car, which was parked just a few feet away. He answered the call as he got into the driver's seat and Blanchard got in on the front passenger side.

"Hey, Max," Gummy said, putting the cell on speaker. "Thanks for callin' me back."

"I'm busy," said a surprisingly feminine voice. "What do you want?"

Gummy gave Blanchard an exasperated look but didn't immediately say anything. Jennifer "Max" Maxwell was the Chief Medical Examiner for the county – a role that kept her pretty busy. Thus, even at the best of times, she had a tendency to be no-nonsense and always tried to get straight to the point. The fact that she was working on a Saturday meant that she'd have even less patience than usual.

"I wanted to ask about that report you did," Gummy said.

"I do a lot of reports," Max shot back. "Can you be more specific?"

"The three bodies found a few weeks back in that condemned building," Gummy replied.

"Gimme a sec," Max said, and in the background Gummy heard the sound of fingers typing on a keyboard, a surefire indicator that Max was at the computer in her office. "You got a file number?"

Gummy looked at Blanchard, who replied with, "Eight-seven-why-dash-two-ex-nine."

There was more keyboard clatter, then Max said, "Got it. Three bodies. One died of gunshot-related wounds, the other two from blunt force trauma consistent with a fall of more than thirty feet. What's your question?"

"For the two that fell, did you get any indication of sexual activity?" Gummy asked.

"That was in the final report," Max stated, sounding slightly frustrated. "Can't you pricks in homicide read?"

"I *did* read it," Gummy countered. "Didn't see anything about that."

"No, what you read was the *preliminary* report," Max shot back. "Not the *final.*"

"Come on, Max," Gummy pleaded. "You know how much fuckin' paperwork we have to deal with on these cases? We shouldn't even have to dick around with a cock-tease like a preliminary report."

"Okay asshole, let me explain to you how this works," Max grumbled. "A fuckin' body comes in, and everybody from the police chief to the D.A. is suddenly ridin' my ass, wantin' to know how the person died so they can figure out if they need to open a homicide investigation. So job one for my department is always figuring out the cause of death. We do that asap and put it in a preliminary report so shitheads in other departments can determine what they want to do next. And while they're busy scratching their balls trying to decide how things should be handled, we go back and finish our work and eventually file a *final* report – which may take a little while because there's always a new corpse coming in, and we have to temporarily put other shit on hold while we figure out *that* cause of death, and so on."

"Alright, we get it," Blanchard blurted out. "It's a vicious fuckin' cycle."

"That it is," Max agreed. "But ultimately we issue a final report in each case. At that point, it would be great if the dumb fucks receiving it would actually read the damn thing. Instead, they mostly just compare the cause of death to the initial report to make sure nothing's changed, but it looks like you two ball sacks didn't even do *that.*"

"Forgetting about what we did or didn't do," Gummy interjected, "can you just answer the question? Was there any indication of sexual activity?"

"Let's see…" Max droned. "It looks like Decedent A, Glen Simon, had minuscule tears around the anus indicative of anal penetration. Anal swab found pre-ejaculate that was a match to Decedent B, Chris Little."

"So they had sex," Blanchard concluded. "Anything to suggest it wasn't consensual?"

"No – there was nothing consistent with sexual assault," Max replied. "No blood or skin under Decedent A's nails, or injuries attributable to anything other than the fall. Plus, an oral swab of Decedent B found traces of semen that matched Decedent A."

"So Chris sucked Glen off, then fucked him," Gummy summed up. "It may not be strictly related to their deaths, but it would have been nice to know that before."

"Hey, shithead," Max grumbled defensively. "In case you weren't listening, my initial focus was determining the cause of death. Now, outside of being impaled and maybe anally probed by aliens, very few people in human history have died from taking it up the ass."

"You speaking from experience there, Max?" Blanchard chided, chuckling.

"Oh yeah," Max replied snidely. "Your wife took it like a champ – said it was nice to finally have at least one hole filled, even if it was her ass. But for some reason, she asked if I could bring a *black* strap-on next time."

"Geez, Max," Blanchard muttered as Gummy burst out laughing. "You kiss your parents with that mouth?"

"Blanchard," Max intoned, "you'd pay good money to know the things I make this mouth do."

"Somehow, I believe that," Blanchard replied with a chortle.

"Anyway," Max droned, "since it's supposed to be my day off, I'd like to wrap up here and try to squeeze in a mani-pedi, or maybe even a fuckin' Brazilian wax job. So if there's nothing else…"

"There is one thing," Gummy said as Max trailed off. "Regarding the third body – the gunshot victim – were there any similar signs of sexual activity like the other two?"

"No," Max confirmed. "Nothing like that."

"So no love triangle," Blanchard surmised.

"Well, the forensic guys filed their supplemental report this morning," Gummy stated, "and it said–"

"Are you fucking kidding me?!" Max interjected angrily. "You'll read the supplemental report of those braindead jerkoffs in Forensics, but you won't read a final report from the M.E.'s office?"

"In all fairness," Gummy retorted, "theirs is – as you yourself just stated – a *supplemental* report, and it was only like a page long. Plus, being supplemental, it only highlighted stuff that wasn't in their original report. Your final report is like fifty fuckin' pages, about twice as long as the preliminary, and repeats a bunch of the same shit. Finally, I *have* to read the stuff from Forensics because those guys process the evidence from the scene – guns, bullets, etcetera – and their report might have new evidence about the crime or point us in the direction of a suspect."

"And did it?" Max asked, sounding frustrated.

"Yeah," Gummy answered. "First of all, the CSI folks found a bag of copper piping at the scene."

"I know all about that," Max told them. "I had to rule those out as cause of death – confirm that nobody used them to knock any of your victims in the head."

"Well, the forensic guys found tool marks on that copper," Gummy continued. "They matched tool marks that were found on a bunch of equipment in a subbasement of the building. The problem is that they didn't find any *tools*. No wrenches. No pipe cutters. No nothing. Which means that…"

"Someone else was there," Max surmised as Gummy trailed off.

"Bingo," chimed in Blanchard. "Damn, Max – you would have made a damn fine detective."

"I'm damn fine, period," Max corrected, causing the two detectives to laugh. "But I got a ton of shit to deal with, so I need to go."

"Understood," Gummy said. "Thanks, Max."

"You want to thank me?" Max asked. "Then don't forget that we're having dinner with my parents this week."

"How can I forget?" Gummy shot back. "You remind me every day."

"Is that a problem?" Max demanded.

"No – I'm looking forward to it with bated breath," Gummy declared sarcastically. "Anyway, should I bring anything?"

"No," Max assured him. "Just don't be late. And don't be an asshole."

Gummy was about to reply that he was never an asshole, but Max had already hung up.

THUG LIFE: EMANCIPATED

Chapter 20

"So," Blanchard droned as Gummy put away his phone. "Sounds like things are gettin' serious between you and the coroner."

"First of all," Gummy retorted, "just havin' dinner with her parents doesn't mean we're gettin' engaged. Second, she's the Chief Medical Examiner, not the coroner."

Blanchard shrugged. "What's the difference?"

"An M.E. is an actual medical doctor who performs autopsies and such. A coroner is usually elected or appointed, and doesn't have to be a doctor. Also, the coroner is typically the person who decides whether a death should be ruled a homicide or not."

"Interesting," Blanchard muttered.

"You wanna know what *I* find interestin'?" Gummy said. "How the fuck you spend over twenty years in homicide and not know this shit?"

"Just lucky, I guess," his partner said, grinning. "But to fair, I've been on the *force* for over twenty years; I've only been doin' homicide for ten. Also, if I remember correctly, the coroner and Chief M.E. have always been the same person."

"True," Gummy stated, acknowledging his partner's point. Historically, the two positons had always been merged, with the same person serving in both capacities. As far as Gummy knew, Max was the first person to turn down an offer to assume the dual roles. (Specifically, she had said that only a "fucking fool" would take on twice the work for a minimal increase in pay.) Bearing all the relevant facts in mind, Blanchard could be forgiven for his lack of knowledge on the subject.

"Anyway," Blanchard intoned, "about that supplemental Forensics report. I don't think I saw that."

"Probably the new email system. Half the shit being sent to me seems to get lost in the ether for a few hours and then randomly pops up in my inbox. Regardless, I printed out a copy of the report and was lookin' it over before I picked you up this mornin'. Check the glove box."

"Anything helpful in it?" Blanchard inquired as he opened the glove compartment.

"Nothing that will get the D.A. excited. The facts are too disjointed – can't fit this shit together in a way that makes sense."

"Come on, Gummy. Figurin' this shit out is half the fun."

Gummy's eyes narrowed. "You got a theory?"

"Maybe."

"Okay, walk me through it."

"Which scenario?"

"All of 'em – includin' the crazy ones."

"Okay, but let's start with the known facts," Blanchard said.

"That's easy enough," Gummy declared. "We got three bodies. Our two cliff jumpers, Simon and Little, and our gunshot victim, uhm…"

"Willam Waddell" Blanchard chimed in. "Known in the hood as Sneak."

"Right...Waddell. Anyway, the M.E.'s report says the time of death is roughly the same for all three. But ballistics and fingerprints on weapons recovered from the scene show that Simon shot Waddell."

"So unless Simon found a way to spring back up into the air after fallin' a couple of stories onto a pile of rubble, he must have shot Waddell before he did his swan dive."

Right," Gummy agreed. "And the evidence indicates that Little fired his gun as well – also at Waddell, we presume – but didn't hit anything."

"Unless you count the wall," Blanchard added.

"Okay, those are the basic facts. So what's your theory?"

"Alright consider this scenario. Little and Simon are lovers, but that shit don't fly when you're a couple of bangers. So, miserable at the thought of not being able to be who there are, they decide that if they can't be together in this world, they'll be together in the next."

"So you're thinkin' suicide pact."

Blanchard shrugged. "Wouldn't be the first time for some shit like that, and maybe they have one last romantic rendezvous before decidin' to end it all."

"What about them shootin' their guns in that abandoned buildin'?"

"Could have been celebratory, like firin' a gun on the Fourth of July or New Years. They're excited that they'll get to be together forever."

"So they decide to go out with a bang, in more ways than one," Gummy summed up. "And how do you explain Waddell?"

"Wrong place, wrong time. Maybe they're not aiming for him; they're just shootin' randomly – don't even know he's there – and a stray bullet hits him."

"What about the bag of copper pipe? And our missin' fourth person?"

Blanchard seemed to consider for a moment, then just murmured. "Who the fuck knows? Maybe some dude was in there stealin' pipe and then came across the bodies. He panics, drops the copper and takes off runnin'."

"Not a terrible theory," Gummy conceded, "except that Waddell's prints were on the bag with the pipe, and said bag was found with Simon and Little."

"Alright, let's scrap the suicide pact and go with Scenario Number Two: murder-suicide."

"I'm listenin'," Gummy told him.

"Well, instead of Simon and Little decidin' to end things together, maybe one of them – let's say Little – has been havin' an affair. He then tells Simon that he's leavin' him for this sweet piece of ass he's been tappin' on the side."

"Meaning Waddell."

"Exactly," Blanchard confirmed. "So Little gives Simon one last pity-fuck, but Simon ain't ready to let go. He pulls a piece on Little, then forces him to call Waddell – has him say he wants to meet up in that condemned buildin'. When Waddell shows, Simon marches the other two upstairs. He then shoots Waddell and ultimately ends up divin' into that chasm in the floor, takin' Little with him."

"That still leaves the copper piping and our fourth person."

"Maybe Waddell showed up early and bumped into someone stealin' some pipe. He takes it from him and chases the guy off. When the rest of his love triangle shows up later, he gets shot for his trouble by a jealous Simon."

"And the pipe?"

Blanchard shrugged. "Maybe Simon – thinkin' it's important to Waddell – takes it as a final 'Fuck you' to his rival before flingin' himself and Little to their deaths."

"So Simon's holdin' a gun in one hand, a shit-ton of copper pipe in the other, and still manages to drag Little over the edge with him? How the fuck does he do that – with his eyelashes?"

"Well," Blanchard intoned, "Simon's got a gun. Maybe he tells Little to jump or get shot."

"You're forgettin' that Little has his own gun, which he fired a couple of times. In fact, he still had bullets left, but Simon didn't. That being the case, seems like *he'd* be the one callin' the shots, not Simon."

"So maybe I got it backwards," Blanchard suggested. "Maybe it was Simon leaving Little for Waddell, and Little's the one who went into a jealous rage."

"And that somehow leads to Simon shootin' the side piece he was leavin' his boyfriend for?" Gummy asked. "That makes sense to you?"

Blanchard seemed to contemplate for a moment, then said, "Okay, so that theory's shit. Let's go to Scenario Number Three."

"Which is?"

"Just straight-up robbery. Waddell and a buddy go into that buildin' to steal some copper. They're on their way out with the goods when Simon and Little somehow get on to them and try to jack 'em. Waddell ends up gettin' shot and his buddy runs off."

Gummy's brow creased as he let his partner's hypothesis roll around in his head for a moment. "That's not bad – certainly better than that love triangle shit. But the problem is that metal's fuckin' cheap, not worth killin' over. If metal was valuable, people wouldn't waste bullets shootin' each other. Hell, they wouldn't even waste the blade on a knife - they'd just stab muhfuckas with wooden chopsticks or sommin'."

"Metal's not valuable?" Blanchard blurted out skeptically. "Try tellin' that to a crackhead. If they think they can sell it, it's worth sommin' to 'em."

"That's different. A junkie's value system is misaligned when it comes to cash. They'll do practically anything for a damn penny. But we're not dealin' with that situation."

"So if not for the pipe, why shoot Waddell?"

"Let's think about that for a second," Gummy remarked. "What are people willin' to kill for?"

You mean in the ghetto?" his partner inquired. "Damn near anything."

"Well, if you get rid of the outliers – like crackheads, and psychos who'll strangle you for coughin' too loud – what is it that people in the hood will kill over?"

"Money, of course,"

"Also drugs, but a lot of the time that's practically the same as money."

"Love."

"Right," Gummy agreed. "There's also their rep."

"Can't forget *that*. Assholes in the hood will pop a cap in you for bad-mouthin' 'em – like sayin' that they're a snitch. Or they like golden showers. Or they're gay."

And just like that, the light bulb came on for both detectives, and for a second they just stared at each other.

"Holy shit!" Blanchard exclaimed a few seconds later. "Little and Simon didn't kill Waddell for the pipe. They'd killed him because he saw 'em."

"Okay, let's run it back one more time," Gummy said. "Waddell and a buddy go into that buildin' to steal some pipe. On their way out, they see Simon and Little doin' the deed – maybe they snuck in there for a quick tryst thinkin' they wouldn't bump into anybody in an abandoned buildin'."

"But they're seen by Waddell and his compadre," Blanchard remarked.

"Right. But the lovebirds don't wanna get outted, so they chase our two pipe thieves through the buildin', endin' up on that floor where Waddell gets shot."

"And our fourth man?"

"He somehow gets the jump on Simon and Little – pushes both of those shitheads over the edge."

"And then what – he just packs it in and goes home?"

"Why not? Ain't shit he can do for Waddell, and he probably figures the other two got what they deserve."

"And the copper they came for?"

"Presumably our mystery man is also the guy who removed the pipe. If he's got that skill set, he's probably worked with metal and knows it ain't worth the trouble. Begs the question of why he'd bother in the first place, but that's a problem for another day. For now, we just assume that after the other three were dead, he grabbed his tools and got the fuck out of Dodge."

"Okay, so what do we know about this guy, other than the fact that he's got some plumbin' skills."

"Based on the evidence, not much," Gummy admitted. "The fuckin' demolition crew, when they went through the buildin', tramped through the whole fuckin' place like they were in a damn gay pride parade. Anything like footprints, shoe impressions and so on got fucked up, tainted or contaminated."

"Well, it's not like they knew it was a crime scene before they found the bodies."

"Still doesn't excuse the fact that they might have given someone a get-out-of-jail-free card."

"And by 'someone' you mean this Shade kid you saw earlier."

"Like I said before, he was carryin' a tool bag. When I saw that, a lot of things kind of clicked into place."

"Or maybe they just *seemed* to click because you'd read that supplemental report earlier and still had some of those facts buzzin' around in your brain."

"Naw," Gummy stressed, shaking his head. "It wasn't just that. There was something else... His expression, his body language, everything. It all said volumes. I *know* he's involved."

Blanchard simply let this soak in for a moment. In truth, it wasn't much to go on. However, there was something to be said for a cop's intuition, and Gummy's instincts were better than most. It wouldn't have been the first time that he had nailed the right suspect with little or no evidence other than a hunch.

"Even if you're right," Blanchard finally said, "good luck gettin' a search warrant based on *that*. It's like sayin' you saw a bank robber drive off in a car, so the next muhfucka you see behind the wheel is a suspect. Plainly speakin', it's pretty fuckin' thin."

"Which is why we tryin' to flesh this shit out," Gummy said.

THUG LIFE: EMANCIPATED

Chapter 21

It was late afternoon when Shade got back to the house. He'd spent part of the time while he was out talking to his "stable," as Lord Byron had put it. In addition to Taranda, there were three other girls in the same line of work that he occasionally helped out: Dumplin', Kay-Kay, and Donna.

Dumplin', as her name implied, was a little on the heavy side – thick and curvy, with ass for days. She was at least a good forty pounds overweight, but what she lacked in terms of a slender form she more than made up for in confidence and élan. She carried herself like she was the finest thing on the planet, and that type of spunk and self-assurance was its own form of sex appeal. In short, men loved her.

Kay-Kay was practically the polar opposite of Dumplin'. She was lithe and lissome, with an athletic figure that she worked hard to maintain. She was also somewhat shy and reserved, which made her current profession something of an odd choice.

Finally, there was Donna, who could only be referred to as a "girl" in a very loose and generic sense. Whereas none of the other three were older than twenty, Donna was pushing up on forty at the very least. However, she was a veteran in the field of prostitution, having begun trickin' at the age of fifteen. That said, she still had a decent body and had maintained her looks, so attracting clients was never a problem, although she considered herself "semi-retired" at present.

Those three, along with Taranda, were on board with going to the party. In light of the money being offered, that was no surprise to Shade – even though he told them he'd be taking twenty percent of the money Byron was paying as his cut. Frankly speaking, however, he had thought Kay-Kay was likely to turn him down. With her personality, he had a difficult time envisioning her entertaining a room full of thugged-out muhfuckas – despite the fact that she regularly had sex for money.

At that juncture, however, he didn't have any more time to mentally debate the subject. It was bound to be a long night, and – after running around all damn day – he needed to rest up beforehand. So, after saying a cursory hello to his sisters (and asking Nissa to wake him in two hours), he went straight to his room and stretched out on the bed. In less than a minute, he was asleep.

****

He woke up famished about thirty seconds before his sister rapped on the door. Following her knock, he called out to let her know he was awake. He then went to the bathroom and quickly freshened up – including taking a shower. Afterwards, he got dressed, throwing on a pair of black cargo pants and a black golf shirt. Next, he headed to the kitchen and made himself a couple of sandwiches.

Nissa joined him at the table, watching him eat for a moment before asking, "You still got a bad vibe 'bout this party?"

"It's not a *bad* vibe," he corrected. "Just a *weird* one. But yeah."

"Still, maybe you should just drop the girls off and pick 'em up later."

Shade shook his head. "I told 'em I'd be there in case muhfuckas started actin' crazy – you know how niggas be when they high or drunk."

"Well, try not to get killed," his sister teased. "We ain't got no extra money to be buryin' yo ass."

Chapter 22

Shade left almost immediately after he finished eating. He had told Taranda and the others that he would pick them up and didn't want to be late.

He went to get Dumplin' first, which was deliberate and by design. Basically, he understood that women sometimes see everything as a status symbol – including who gets to ride in the front seat of a car. More to the point, whoever he picked up first would probably ride shotgun. Given her size, it made sense to have Dumplin' ride in the front seat rather than squeeze into the back with two other people. Ergo, even though it didn't make sense logistically since she lived farthest away, she became Shade's first passenger that evening.

Next, he went to get Taranda. Apparently she was already downstairs waiting, because the minute he called to say he was there she came marching out the building.

Their third stop was to pick up Donna and Kay-Kay, who lived in the same tenement. Needless to say, Shade was a little surprised when Donna showed up and told him Kay-Kay wasn't coming.

"Huh?" he muttered as Donna got in the car. "Why not?"

"She didn't specifically say," Donna admitted as she settled into the back seat with Taranda. "But if I had to guess, I'd say it had to do with *you*."

"Me?" Shade blurted out, his eyebrows going up in surprise. "What the fuck did *I* do?"

"It's more about what you *haven't* done," Donna informed him, giggling. "*Yet.*"

Shade frowned. "What the hell you talkin' 'bout?"

"Ha!" Donna laughed. "You really don't get it do you? Damn, men are dumb."

"Get what?" he asked, starting to get frustrated.

Donna didn't immediately answer, at which point Dumplin' chimed in, saying, "She got the hots for you."

"What?" Shade almost shouted.

"She feenin' for some of that shady dick," Donna explained, grinning. As she spoke, she leaned forward and touched his side, before letting her hand start to glide towards his crotch.

Shade playfully smacked her hand, at which point she snatched it back, laughing.

"You kiddin', right?" he asked.

"No," Donna countered, shaking her head. "And that's why she not comin'. She thank that if you see her slippin' off to earn some cash with a coupla niggas at this party, you ain't never gonna want nuthin' to do with her."

"I don't judge, "Shade stressed. "All of you know that. Plus, I already know what she does. It ain't no secret."

"Well, knowin' it and seein' it are two different thangs," Taranda noted.

Shade spent a moment reflecting on what he'd just been told. In all honesty, he generally had way too much shit going on to be dealing with females. Hell, even when he genuinely connected with a girl – like with Yoni earlier in the day – he typically didn't pursue it. (There was a good chance, however, that Yoni would be the exception to that rule.) Thus, it was more than possible that he could have missed signs of infatuation from Kay-Kay, assuming what he was hearing was true. Regardless, he didn't have time to address it at the moment.

"A'ight," he said after a few moments. "Byron will just have to be satisfied with the three of you. He'll probably be wantin' part of the money back, but that won't affect any of you. That bein' said, I wish Kay-Kay had just told me she didn't wanna do this. I might have been able to line somebody else up."

"Kay prolly just said 'Yes' 'cause she didn't wanna disappoint you," Donna offered. "But just so you know, there's still gonna be fo' of us."

Shade gave her a skeptical look. "How do you figure?"

"When Kay told me she wasn't comin', I reached out to another girl that I thought might be interested," Donna explained. "She's down for the cause."

Shade considered this for a moment, then asked the obvious question. "Who?"

Rather than answer directly, Donna said, "Here she comes now."

As she spoke, Donna pointed with her chin – not in the direction of her own tenement, but towards one across the street. Kane looked in the direction indicated and saw a girl walking in their direction. And then he did a double-take, convinced that his eyes were playing tricks on him.

The girl heading towards them was Yoni.

Chapter 23

"Wait here," Shade said to no one in particular, then scrambled out of the car without waiting for anyone's acknowledgement of his statement.

He made a beeline for Yoni, only casually noting that she was sporting a mid-length jacket that was currently unbuttoned. Yoni saw him approaching, and initially her lips began curving into a smile. Then she saw the look on his face.

"Whachu thank you doin'?" he practically hissed, after glancing towards his car to make sure they were out of earshot.

"Whachu mean?" Yoni demanded.

"This party," he explained. "It ain't for you."

"Oh really?" Yoni quizzed, crossing her arms and giving him a skeptical look.

"Yeah. These niggas are gonna be expectin' a particular type of entertainment."

"Yeah – *female* entertainment. You don't thank I fit the bill?"

As she finished speaking Yoni put her hands on her hips, spreading open her jacket in the process. Under it she wore something like a catholic school-girl outfit: a short plaid skirt that barely came down to her ass-cheeks (which were exposed, courtesy of a thong she wore), along with a matching tie-front crop top with a plunging neckline that made her tits look amazing. Plainly speaking, she looked sexy as fuck, but Shade pushed that thought to the back of his mind.

"It's not just about being female," Shade admonished. "Do you know what these muhfuckas gone expect you to do?"

"All I know is that I need to make some paper," Yoni shot back. "A bitch got bills to pay."

"Yeah, but you don't wanna earn this way," Shade told her. Somewhere in the back of his mind he knew he was being a hypocrite, but at the moment he didn't care.

Yoni angrily looked him up and down for a moment. "Who da fuck you thank you are? You thank one conversation after ten years gave you a read on who I am? Nigga, you don't know me. You don't know if I go to church every Sunday or be up on the pole every night – whether I wear a chastity belt or spread my legs for any nigga who buy me popcorn at the movies. So don't act like you know what I earn or how I earn it. We exchanged phone numbers today, not fuckin' promise rings, so you got no claim on me or what I do."

"I just don't wanna see you do sommin' you gone regret."

"From what I heard, I ain't gotta do nuthin' I don't wanna do. But if I feel like lettin' niggas stick a dick in every hole, then that's what I'm gone do, and if you can't handle that then lose my fuckin' number. Now back the fuck off so I can go get paid."

She then marched angrily past Shade, brushing by him as she headed towards the car. A moment later, Shade followed.

Chapter 24

On the drive to Lord Byron's crib, Shade had Dumplin' pop open the glove compartment. Inside were four wads of rolled-up cash, bound with rubber bands.

Shade made sure each of his passengers got one of the rolls, saying, "That's four bills for each of you, which is five hundred apiece, minus my twenty-percent cut."

Shade paused, waiting to see if he'd get any pushback. When he initially called the girls, he had told everyone upfront what Byron was paying and what his cut would be. Thankfully, none of them had given him any grief over it. Of course, he hadn't talked to Yoni, so his statement was more for her benefit than anyone else. However, from what he could see of her in the rearview mirror, she didn't seem to have a problem with the size of his commission.

With that settled, he went on. "That's actually half of what's due. You get the rest when we get to the party."

"That's what I'm talkin' 'bout," chirped Donna. "Nuthin' a bitch like more than gettin' paid up front."

The others chuckled at that, almost giddy at what was looking to be a great fucking payday.

"Okay, ground rules," Shade continued. "Number one: you bein' paid to strip. That's it. Beyond that, you ain't gotta do anythang you don't wanna do." He made a point of looking at Yoni in the rearview as he said this, but she was busy holding up a compact and doing something with her makeup. "Number two: if you decide you wanna do more than that, you negotiate that price with whatever nigga you dealin' with. Number three: you get in any kind of trouble – nigga starts hasslin' you, gets too grabby, whatever – you shout for me."

All of his passengers generally mumbled in agreement with this.

"What about cell cameras?" Dumplin' asked unexpectedly.

Shade's brow furrowed. "What about 'em?"

"I don't want these niggas snappin' pictures and shit of me shakin' my moneymaker and then postin' it online," Dumplin explained.

"From what I hear, Lord Byron don't allow shit like that," Donna told her.

"He had a problem a lil' while back," Taranda chimed in. "Some muhfucka snuck and took some pics at one of Byron's parties, then tried to use 'em to get some charges against hisself dropped. Since then, Byron treats his parties like you at a strip club – no pictures, videos, and or any shit like that."

"Okay, cool," Dumplin' said in relief. "So what happened to the nigga that took the pics?"

Nobody said anything, which was an answer in and of itself.

THUG LIFE: EMANCIPATED

Chapter 25

When they arrived at Byron's crib, the driveway was full of cars, as was the street leading to it. That being the case, they ended up parking about fifty yards from the house.

As he stepped out the car, Shade grabbed a tactical flashlight from the floor by the driver's seat. It was an item that he normally kept in his tool bag, but had brought along for just-in-case purposes.

By that time, the girls were all out of the car as well. It was already dark out, but from the light of a flickering street lamp above he saw them each adjusting their clothes. Like Yoni, the other three wore mid- or full-length jackets; however, he couldn't quite see what they had on underneath, and hadn't paid too much attention earlier.

"Can I leave my purse in yo car?" Donna asked.

"Better to put it in the trunk," Shade replied. His windows were tinted and he didn't think anyone could see inside, but it was best not to take any chances.

With the girls following him, he walked to the rear of the car and unlocked the trunk. He took a quick look around to make sure no one was watching, then opened it. As he lifted the trunk lid, an interior light came on, giving him his first good view of what the girls were wearing under their jackets.

As with Yoni, the other three sported various versions of stripper outfits. Dumplin', for example, had on fishnet stockings and some kind of plus-size lingerie. Donna was wearing what looked like a cop costume that consisted of black booty shorts with a pair of handcuffs on a belt loop, and a matching zip-up top with a sewn-on badge. (She also had what looked like a policeman's cap tucked under one arm.) Finally, Taranda sported an exotic cage bra and a sexy miniskirt. In essence, it looked like all of the women with him had brought their "A" game from a stripping standpoint.

As that thought pass through Shade's mind, Yoni stepped forward and tossed her purse inside before turning in his direction.

"You can hold my cell?" she asked, speaking to him for the first time since he picked her up. At the same time, he noticed a cell phone in her hand.

"No problem," he assured her as he reached out and took the phone. A moment later, his hand went to one of the cargo pockets on his pants, at which point he lifted the Velcro flap and dropped the phone inside.

Donna and Taranda then followed suit, putting their purses in the trunk and handing their cells to Shade, who promptly pocketed the devices. Everyone then turned their attention to Dumplin', who was clutching her purse like her life depended on it.

Realizing that everyone was staring her, Dumplin' finally explained her apprehension, saying, "If I leave my purse, how am I s'posed to carry any cash I earn?"

"Ha ha!" Donna laughed. "You can tell who the rookie is that ain't never been on the pole."

"Ignore her," Taranda instructed Dumplin'. "You gotta have a garter, see?"

As she spoke, she spread open her jacket and tapped the upper part of her right leg, where there was indeed a thigh garter. At that juncture Shade noticed that both Yoni and Donna sported similar accessories.

"What does that do?" Dumplin' asked.

Taranda sighed, then turned to Shade. "Can you hand me a few bills, to demonstrate?"

Nodding, Shade reached into a pocket. He had some cash folded up in there, which he promptly took out and handed to Taranda.

"Okay, here's what you gotta do," Taranda explained. "First, straighten the cash out." As she spoke, she unfolded the bills she had gotten from Shade, eventually holding them in her hand at their full length.

"Then you tuck it into your garter," she continued, pulling the garter away from her skin and sliding the bills behind it. Then she let the garter snap back into place at roughly the center point of the cash before folding the bills over.

"Now you have to secure it," Taranda stated, taking a rubber band that Shade had noticed earlier from her left wrist. (In fact she had several of them there, as did Donna and Yoni.)

Looping the rubber band around the cash three times, she said, "You wanna make sure the rubber band is good and tight 'round the money. And then – voilà."

Taranda stood up straight; the money stayed attached to her garter. "Now no one can take it without you noticin'," she told Dumplin'. To demonstrate, she tugged on the cash, which also pulled on the garter (and presumably created some type of feeling or sensation that the person wearing the garter was sure to notice).

Dumplin', who had paid rapt attention during the demonstration, simply nodded but still looked a little unsure as Taranda handed Shade his cash back.

"I didn't bring a garter, though," she finally admitted. "Or rubber bands."

No one said anything for a moment. It was blatantly obvious that none of the other girls had brought extras. They probably hadn't even thought about it.

"Can't I just keep my purse with me?" Dumplin' finally asked of no one in particular.

"When's the last time you saw a stripper strutting around with a purse during her act?" Donna asked. "And if you set that bitch to the side while you dance, everythang in there gonna be gone when you pick it up again."

119

Dumpklin' looked almost despondent at this, and it wasn't hard for Shade to figure out why. Clearly, she needed the money from this party badly (not that the other three didn't), and she didn't feel comfortable not having it close by or on her person.

"Give it to me," he finally said.

Dumplin' gave him an odd look. "Huh?"

"Your purse," he explained. "Give it to me. I'll hold it for you durin' the party. Then you can just brang cash as you earn it and tuck it inside."

"You sure?" Dumplin' asked nervously.

"It's not a problem," Shade insisted, closing the trunk. A moment later, still looking unsure, Dumplin' handed him her purse.

"A'ight," Donna intoned. "Now that that's settled, let's go make this money."

With that, they began walking towards Byron's mansion. Looking in that direction, Shade noted a couple of floodlights around the grounds that highlighted both the scale of the residence and its artistic design. In brief, the place was just as impressive at night as during the day.

"Is that where we goin'?" Dumplin' asked, slightly in awe.

"Yeah," Shade said.

"Damn," Donna muttered. "That place is – ahhh!"

Donna screeched as one leg seemed to slide out from under her. She probably would have fallen if Shade hadn't put out a hand to steady her.

"This fuckin' road!" she swore as she regained her balance. "It's full of damn holes and shit!"

"Nobody lived out here for a long time," Shade observed, "so the city didn't worry about maintainin' the streets 'til recently. Plus, it's practically in the hood so it wasn't a high priority."

"That's fucked up," Taranda noted.

"It is what it is," Shade retorted. "Hang on a sec…"

Shade lifted the tactical flashlight and turned it on. Much to the surprise of those with him, it lit up the entire street, practically all the way up to Lord Byron's front door. It wasn't as bright as broad daylight, but it provided an unexpected amount of visibility by bathing everything in its path in high-intensity light – including a couple fucking in a nearby car.

The couple weren't the only ones caught by surprise, as a deep baritone suddenly shouted, "What da fuck???!!!"

Looking ahead of them, in the direction of Byron's place, Shade saw a couple of thuggish niggas holding hands up to their eyes, trying to shield them from the flashlight's beam. He also noted that they were carrying what looked like assault rifles, which suggested they were some sort of guards or security detail.

"Turn that shit off!" the voice boomed.

Shade quickly dialed down the brightness and pointed the flashlight towards the ground.

"Sorry – my bad," he shouted towards the guys he'd seen, then slowly continued walking towards the mansion with the others beside him.

"Who da fuck is that?" one of the guards demanded.

Rather than answer directly, Shade said, "Got some girls here that Lord Byron told me to round up for the party."

"He tell you to blind a nigga, too?" the second guard muttered angrily.

"Like I said – my bad," Shade responded.

As he spoke, he kept the flashlight beam pointed down, and swept it from side to side. Hopefully, the light was helping the girls see where the road was bad (which was the reason he'd turned it on in the first place). In addition, the luminescence – coupled with where his voice was coming from – should have given an indication of where he was. Finally, there should have been enough light for anyone around to note that four of the five people in his unit were in high heels, thereby proving up his statement that he was indeed bringing girls to the party.

All in all, he was hopeful that those facts, when taken jointly, would keep the niggas he'd seen from getting itchy trigger fingers, which was a distinct possibility after the flashlight's beam had caught them off guard.

When his group got close, they slowed down and came to a halt, giving the two guards – who were standing near a lamppost – a chance to thoroughly look them over. One of them, a nigga with bloodshot eyes and no front teeth, lewdly eyed the girls while his partner looked Shade up and down.

"So you the muhfucka tryin' to blind niggas," the man stated.

"I didn't know you were there," Shade explained.

The man appeared to mull on this for a moment, then said, "Get the fuck outta here." As he spoke, he tilted his head towards the mansion.

"And don't do dat shit no mo'," the guard added.

Shade gave him a curt nod, and – after attaching the flashlight to one of his belt loops with a metal clasp – headed towards the mansion with the girls.

THUG LIFE: EMANCIPATED

Chapter 26

They had heard the music as they approached, and when Shade's group got inside it was clear that the party was in full swing. There were people everywhere – even in the foyer when they entered – and almost every one of them was holding either a drink or something they were smoking. (As a matter of fact there was a strong scent of weed in the air, which caused Shade to frown. He was here on business, so he didn't need anything that would affect his judgment – not even a contact high.)

Not really sure of which way to go, Shade took the lead and began walking towards an area where most of the partying seemed to be taking place. The girls followed, and a minute or so later, they found themselves in what Shade recalled as being the great room.

"Wow..." droned Dumplin', and Shade could understand her sentiment.

The room was at least two thousand square feet in size – bigger than most homes in the hood – with a twelve-foot ceiling. As Byron had mentioned, there was hardwood flooring and also a gorgeous two sided fireplace. In addition, there was a built-in bar at one of the far walls, while a DJ, turntables and all, was set up at the other end. But the most spectacular feature of all was a window wall that stretched from one side of the room to the other, giving a panoramic view of a luxury patio and pool outside.

There were even more people here than in the foyer – mostly niggas, but a handful of ladies (including a couple of White chicks). It was then that Shade also noticed something else that caught his eye: there were already strippers in the room.

Just taking a cursory head count, he thought there were about four of them, scattered haphazardly throughout the place, plying their trade. Unlike those with him, however, the woman already working the room appeared to be professionals, and each already had an intimate circle of people around them.

Shade frowned. Byron hadn't said anything about there being other entertainment present. But at the end of the day, it probably didn't matter. The girls with him were getting decent scratch just to show up, so why give a fuck?

"Should we get started?" Dumplin' asked, plainly noting the strippers already in the room.

"Not until we get paid," Yoni answered, then looked at Shade.

Understanding what was expected of him, Shade simply said, "Hang tight for a sec." At that juncture, he had already spied who he was looking for: Lord Byron.

Frankly speaking, still dressed as he'd been earlier – with royal mantle and scepter – Byron hadn't been hard to pick out. It was merely the sheer number of people in the room that had kept Shade from seeing him earlier at the bar. Now that he had his quarry picked out, Shade headed straight for him, gently but firmly pushing his way through the crowd.

At some point, however, Byron saw him coming. He then immediately broke off the conversation he was having with a voluptuous chick in a bikini top and began walking towards Shade, meeting him halfway. Unlike Shade, however, he didn't have to push his way through; people generally stepped out of his way if they saw him coming.

"Shade," Byron said, grinning as he gave him some dap. "Glad you made it. I take it you brought my girls?"

Shade hooked a thumb over his shoulder. "I take it you got the cash?"

Byron reached into a pocket, took out a roll of bills, and handed it over. Shade immediately stuck it in a pocket.

"You not gone count it?" Byron asked.

124

"I trust you," Shade replied. "And if the shit ain't correct, I know where to find you."

Laughing, Byron threw an arm around Shade. "Man, you funny as fuck. Come on, let's get you a drank." He then began guiding Shade towards the bar.

"Maybe later," Shade said, breaking away. "I need to go tell the girls it's okay to go to work."

"A'ight," Byron muttered with a nod. "I get that – business first."

"Any particular place you want 'em?"

"Naw," Byron declared, shaking his head. "Any place they wanna do they thang is fine. But you should tell 'em, the basement and the guest house out by the pool are for, uh, *private* interactions."

"I'll pass that on," Shade promised, then turned and walked away. A minute or so later, after making his way through the crowd once more, he was back with the girls.

"Everything good?" Taranda asked.

"Yeah," Shade confirmed. "I can give y'all the rest of your money now or–"

"Just hold it," Yoni told him. "You can divvy it up when we done."

The others simply nodded in agreement with her. Shade then told them what Lord Byron had said about the basement and guest house, deliberately avoiding looking at Yoni as he spoke.

When he was done there was silence for a moment, then Donna said, "A'ight, let's get to work, bitches."

Seconds later, they were all moving through the crowd, each looking for a spot to start doing their thing. He watched them for a moment as they scattered, hoping that the weird vibe he'd gotten earlier (and was still getting, to be honest) wasn't anything serious.

It was then that he heard a familiar masculine voice say his name.

"Shade – fancy meetin' you here."

Chapter 27

Shade turned towards the speaker.

"Mr. Jamison," he said, extending a hand. "Nice to see you, sir."

"You, too," Jamison said, shaking his hand. "By the way, thanks for comin' by this morning. My wife said you did a good job."

"No problem, sir," Shade said, looking away as he felt his cheeks turning red.

Mr. Jamison merely laughed and clapped him on the shoulder, finding his discomfort humorous. He then looked down at what Shade was holding and raised an eyebrow in curiosity.

"It's not mine," Shade blurted out, indicating the purse. "I'm just holdin' it for a friend."

"Gotcha," Jamison said with a nod. "She run off to the bathroom?"

Shade shook his head. "No, she's part of the entertainment. That's her over there."

He tilted his head towards a corner of the room where Dumplin', having removed her coat, was starting to sway in time to the music while a couple of niggas nearby started closing in around her. There was an elegant, floor-to-ceiling column near her, and she swung around it once, plainly using it as a stripper pole (although it was actually a little too large to properly serve that purpose).

"So she with you?" Jamison asked.

"Yeah," Shade confirmed with a nod. "Byron asked me to bring by a couple of girls I knew that might be interested in earnin' a few bucks. The others are 'round here somewhere."

"Well, that's interestin'," Jamison said. "I thought you were here 'cause you was friends with Byron or sommin'. I didn't realize we were in the same line of work."

"Huh?" Shade muttered, and then understanding dawned on him. "Wait a minute – you here with strippers, too?"

"Yeah, that's one of mine over there." Jamison pointed to one of the strippers Shade had noted earlier – a pretty White chick with monstrous tits. "Usually we the only ones Byron brang in for his parties, but I guess he decided to spice thangs up."

Shade nodded, noting that what he was hearing kind of aligned with what Byron had told him earlier, but it still left an odd tingling in his gut.

"So those girls work for you?" he asked after a few moments.

"Naw," Jamison declared. "Callin' 'em '*my*' girls is just for easy reference. To be honest, I'm just the muscle, here to keep shit from gettin' outta control. I'm assumin' that's why you here, too, right?"

Shade shrugged. "I guess."

"Okay, well show me whachu got."

Shade gave him a nonplussed look. "Huh?"

"Whachu brang in case you gotta put one of these niggas in they place?"

Shade unclipped the tactical flashlight from his belt and held it up.

Mr. Jamison took it from him and then examined it for a few seconds, looking it all over and then tapping it on his open palm a few times.

"This is pretty good," he finally said, still giving the flashlight a once-over. "Heavy duty, military grade. Depending on how dark it is, the light from this is bright enough to blind and disorient a muhfucka for a few seconds.

And it's solid enough to crack a nigga's skull if need be. But if the cops pull you over and find it on you, it's just a fuckin' flashlight, not a lethal weapon."

"What about you?" Shade asked.

"A coupla pairs of brass knuckles," Jamison told him. "Also an expandable police baton – that shit will fuck up a nigga's day – and finally, a rinky-dink twenty-two caliber, but I only brang it out as a last resort."

"Wow," Shade intoned. "Now I feel like I brought a knife to a gunfight."

Jamison laughed. "Naw, you fine. Shit rarely gets outta hand, and Byron usually runs a tight ship in terms of keepin' niggas from gettin' too crazy. But if you lookin' for a coupla tips…"

"Sure," Shade said as Jamison trailed off. "Whatever you got."

"Cool," Jamison said. "Now the first thang to know is this…"

****

Apparently moonlighting as a bouncer and hired muscle had given Jamison both breadth and depth of knowledge on the subject at hand. To say he had a lot of insight would be an understatement.

Of course, some of it was info that Shade was already aware of, such as when Jamison told him, "Don't drink, smoke, or snort anythang. You on the clock, so the last thang you need is sommin' that's gone inhibit you in any way."

The vast majority of the information, however, was incredibly helpful, like when Jamison advised, "Never stand in the same spot for more than a few minutes. If you stand still for too long, you start gettin' complacent, so always be movin'. Plus, you should make sure you set eyes on yo girls every twenty minutes or so – even if you have to bust in on 'em fuckin' somebody. If too much time go by and you ain't seen 'em, they might be outside gettin' they throat cut."

All in all, Jamison gave him some great tips, although it wasn't clear how much of the info Shade would use beyond that night. When they were done talking, Jamison followed his own advice and began working his way through the crowd, apparently trying to keep tabs on his girls. Shade followed his lead and began walking around the party as well, trying to keep an eye on his quartet of females.

He spotted two of them right away. Dumplin' was still in the corner where he'd noticed her earlier, while Taranda had staked out a spot in the middle of the floor. He didn't see Yoni or Donna, but that wasn't surprising. Despite the size of the room, there really wasn't enough space for a bunch of exotic dancers to showcase their skills, so presumably the other two had moved on to other rooms. In fact, he only saw one other stripper in the great room at the moment, so he assumed that Jamison's other girls had also drifted to other parts of the mansion.

Surprisingly, Shade found himself saddled with an urge to go find Yoni. Based on what he'd glimpsed of her personality that afternoon, he simply couldn't believe that she'd spread her legs for cash. She just didn't seem the type, and on some level he was still convinced that she really didn't know what she was getting into with this party.

At the same time, though, she had hit the nail on the head earlier when she said he didn't know her. They'd basically had one conversation – albeit a lengthy one – so what the fuck did he really know about this girl? Maybe she was just a flat-out hoe with a vivacious personality. Or maybe he wasn't as good at reading people as he thought. Or maybe…

He pushed the thought away. Yoni had made it clear that she could handle herself, so he didn't need to stick close like some guardian angel. She wasn't some damsel in distress who needed a white knight to save her. That being the case, he didn't need to give her special consideration. He'd treat her no differently than the other girls.

As if to prove that point to himself, he stopped walking. Turning his attention back to Taranda and Dumplin', he decided he'd stay in the great room and keep an eye on them for a few minutes.

And if Yoni gets her throat cut in the meantime, maybe that'll teach her to listen, he said to himself (although he immediately recognized the thought as being petty and juvenile).

Looking towards Taranda, he saw that she was not only dancing but – using a chair as a prop – was starting to draw an enthusiastic crowd. Her top was off and her tits looked great, as always. Even from across the room, Shade could see that her nipples were hard. Truth be told, her nipples always seemed to be hard, and he momentarily wondered if there was some kind of trick to it.

Probably, he thought as he forced himself to avert his eyes and looked towards Dumplin'.

She was still in the same spot as before, and – like Taranda – Dumplin' had already bared her chest. Nudity made her size more apparent, but Dumplin', confident as ever, strutted about like she was a svelte runway model. It also didn't hurt that she actually had a decent set of boobs.

Her tits were large (which was common with overweight girls), and in truth, Shade had half-expected them to be sagging below her waist like sacks of overripe fruit. Much to his surprise, they were more shapely than he would have imagined. It would have been a stretch to call them perky and they weren't in the same league as Taranda's, but they were firm enough to catch the eye.

Given Dumplin's weight, the comely appearance of her tits was presumably the result of youth and good genes.

Over time, gravity and age would probably start pulling them down and bring them more in line with Shade's initial expectations. At the moment, however, given the niggas who were starting to gather round her waving singles, it clearly wasn't a problem. Basically, some men like big women, and quite a few don't give a shit about size when it comes to nudity – a bare tit's a bare tit.

"Want a hit of dis?" asked someone next to him, interrupting Shade's reverie.

He turned in the direction of the voice and saw a thin nigga with a scraggly goatee, maybe eighteen years old. Shade recognized him as one of Lord Byron's flunkies, but couldn't put a name to him. He also saw that the dude was holding out a joint towards him.

"Want a hit?" the guy asked again.

"Naw, but thanks," Shade replied.

"You sure? This shit's prime."

"Thanks, but I'm good."

The guy simply shrugged, then took a puff, tilting his head and blowing the smoke up at an angle.

"Damn, this party's off the fuckin' hook!" the nigga commented.

"It's nice," Shade noted.

"Yeah, but this is how we roll in Byron's crew. Lots of cash, lots of bitches, and the best high. That's how it is when you know how to move weight."

Shade grunted noncommittally in response, turning his attention back to Taranda and Dumplin', who both had niggas hooting and hollering around them now, and tossing bills at them.

"Anyway," the nigga next to him continued, "if you ever lookin' to make some cash, we can always use a good man. And if you know anybody with a connect – who can hook us up with some product – that's even better, cause we–"

"Sorry," Shade blurted out, cutting the nigga off. "I see somebody I gotta talk to."

With that, he began walking off, happy to get away from the nigga's incessant chatter. However, mindful of Jamison's advice, he didn't simply move to another part of the room but decided to locate the rest of his group.

Eventually he found Donna near the kitchen, dancing in what appeared to be the breakfast area. She had the policeman's hat on and was also sporting a pair of mirrored sunglasses. All in all, she pulled off the sexy police act like a pro.

Shade himself ended up near a large island counter in the kitchen, watching her. However, it turned out to be a high-traffic area, mostly because the island was covered with bottles of liquor, and people were constantly coming by to mix themselves a drink.

One of them – a heavyset nigga wearing a wife beater t-shirt – actually mixed two drinks.

"Hey man, you gotta try this," he said, extending one of the glasses to Shade.

"No, thanks," Shade told him.

"You sure?" the guy asked. "It's my own special mix. Everybody loves it. In fact, it's prolly the only reason Lord Byron keep me on the payroll."

Shade merely nodded at this rather than verbally comment.

"Speaking of Byron," the fat man continued, "that nigga's rollin' in cash these days. I mean, look at this place tonight, with the all the liquor and the music and the hoes…musta cost a muhfuckin' fortune. And even though he throw a kick-ass party, he always business-minded –lookin' for whatever he can put his money into and make mo' paper."

The man paused, seemingly waiting for Shade to comment. Shade just kept looking at Donna, hoping the fat muhfucka would move on. Instead, the man took a sip from one of the drinks he'd made.

"Mmmm," he droned, making a yummy sound. "Damn, that shit is good. You really gotta try it."

As he spoke, again extended a drink towards Shade, who simply said, "Naw, I'm straight."

"Come on, man – just a sip," the nigga pleaded, practically shoving the drink into Shade's free hand.

Shade glared at the man, wondering where the fuck the nigga went to school since he didn't seem to understand English. In fact, he was actually on the verge of saying something to that effect but caught himself. Instead, he simply stepped to the kitchen sink which was nearby and dumped the contents of the glass into it before setting the glass on the counter.

The fat guy just stared him in surprise for a moment, then muttered. "Damn man, you didn't have to waste it. That's alcohol abuse…"

THUG LIFE: EMANCIPATED

Chapter 28

Shade left the kitchen almost immediately after dumping the drink that had been forced into his hand. Having laid eyes on three of the girls he'd brought with him, he then went in search of Yoni.

It took him a little time to find her. He actually made two circuits of the ground floor – during which time he saw his other three charges – before he realized that she must be somewhere else.

There was always a chance that she was in the basement or the pool house, engaging in a private interaction (as Lord Byron had put it). But again, Yoni just didn't strike Shade as that type.

Or maybe you just don't want her to be that type, he said to himself.

There was more truth in that statement than he wanted to admit, but he was still convinced that his initial impression of her was right. That being the case, he decided to shun the areas lord Byron had designated for turning tricks and instead look for Yoni in a place he hadn't tried yet: upstairs. And that's where he found her.

Like the ground floor, the upstairs was spacious and well-designed. However, there didn't seem to be as many people around, and after a few moments Shade figured out why: seemingly everyone on that floor was crowding into one particular room.

From what Shade could tell, it was about five hundred square feet in size and appeared to be a game room. There was a sixty-inch flat screen mounted on one wall, right above an entertainment center that appeared to house a couple of game consoles. He also noted a poker table nearby and a nice wet bar that was fully stocked. But the most dominant feature, in Shades' opinion, was what looked like an oversized pool table that sat in the middle of the room. It was roughly twelve-by-six feet in size, and he actually recognized it as a snooker table. And dancing on top of it was Yoni.

THUG LIFE: EMANCIPATED

Chapter 29

Shade had to give her credit. Using the snooker table as a makeshift stage was genius. It lifted her up to a height that would attract attention, and its dimensions gave her ample room to dance. But to be honest, calling what Yoni was doing "dancing" was like saying a fish could stay underwater for a little while.

Above the waist, her body barely seemed to be moving. Later, Shade would recall that her arms actually were in motion at the time – slowly and rhythmically going up and down (as well as side to side), presumably matching the cadence and tempo of whatever music was playing. However, he barely noticed them at the moment. What drew his attention was what Yoni had going on below the waistline.

From the waist down, her body – specifically, her hips and ass – seemed to be moving at a hundred miles per hour. They stayed in constant motion, rapidly going back-and-forth and side-to-side in hypnotic fashion, while periodically engaging in quick gyrations with spellbinding intensity. Even when she dropped down on her haunches, her hips and ass never stopped moving, and the skirt she wore accentuated her movements perfectly.

Just watching her, Shade occasionally thought he saw something akin to hip rolls and pelvic thrusts (among other things), but her movements were so swift that he honestly had trouble categorizing what he was seeing. All he knew was that her dancing was mesmerizing. More to the point, the contrast between the glacial motion of her upper body and the rapid-fire oscillation of her hips and ass was provocative as fuck. Simply put, Shade had never seen anything like it. And judging from the reactions of others in the room, neither had anyone else.

Basically, the place was full of niggas, and they had pretty much surrounded the snooker table that Yoni was dancing on. Most of them had cash in their hands that they were throwing onto the "stage," while filling the room with shouts, catcalls, and wolf whistles. In fact, they were so loud that it was almost impossible to hear anything.

That said, Shade barely noticed them at first. He was so caught up in Yoni's dancing that he was nearly oblivious to anything going on around him. In fact, he might have watched her all night had not someone drawn his attention away.

"Damn!" uttered a voice next to him.

Having parked himself near the door, Shade glanced to the side and saw that Jamison had entered the room and was standing beside him. As to what had solicited his outburst, it was apparently the fact that, at the moment, Yoni's ass seemed to be vibrating like there was a jackhammer inside her, moving damn near faster than a hummingbird's wings.

"I'm gay," Jamison continued, "and even *I'm* thinkin' 'bout tappin' *that*."

Shade chuckled, noting that it was a sentiment almost everyone in the room was probably feeling. In fact, one of the niggas at the edge of the snooker table suddenly shouted something at Yoni that was presumably along those lines. It was too loud in the room for Shade to make out what he'd said (and being near the door he was too far away), but Yoni – not missing a beat – immediately shot a comment back at the muhfucka. Presumably it was somewhat emasculating, because the nigga who'd shouted at her suddenly turned red while everyone else in the vicinity suddenly howled in laughter.

Truth be told, Yoni must have been a comedienne in another life, because during the time Shade had watched her dance, she had made several comments – sometimes to hecklers, sometimes to the crowd in general – that always elicited roars of laughter, cheers, and the like. He, of course, had never been close enough to hear what was said, but recognized that Yoni was a pro at working the crowd. It was just one more thing to admire about her.

THUG LIFE: EMANCIPATED

Chapter 30

Jamison's appearance in the game room broke the spell that Yoni's dancing had put on Shade. Realizing he'd been in one place too long, he reluctantly left and went in search of the other three women he'd shown up with.

He spent the rest of the evening in continuous circulation, following Jamison's advice not to let too much time go by without setting eyes on Yoni and the others. Fortunately, he really didn't have to do as much searching as he initially thought. In short, he generally only had to keep an eye out for three of the girls, because Dumplin', regularly needing a place to dump her cash, sought him out all evening so she could put her earnings in her purse.

That said, he did occasionally lose track of the women. In those instances, he assumed that they were engaged in business transactions in the basement or pool house, and therefore gave them a little extra time to make a reappearance – despite Jamison's earlier admonition.

Even Yoni vanished once or twice, and Shade found himself dwelling more often than he should on who she might be with. However, that question was answered in at least one instance when he saw her coming from the direction of Lord Byron's bedroom. Of course, that made sense; with respect to the party, Byron was the nigga with the fattest bankroll, and Yoni was the baddest bitch in attendance. Thus, it was pretty much a given that they'd meet up at some point. Moreover, it was further proof that Shade really didn't know her at all.

Outside of that, the only other thing that caused him any degree on consternation was when Donna disappeared for an extended period. Or rather, what amounted to an extended period for *her* - about twenty minutes.

Usually, Shade was able to put eyes on Donna every ten minutes or so – including a couple of times when he saw her headed down to (or coming from) the basement. Ergo, since she was never gone for long, whatever business she was engaging in was normally conducted swiftly. That's why not seeing her for twenty minutes put him slightly on edge and triggered the decision to go find her. Bearing in mind that the basement appeared to be her preferred venue, he figured he'd check there first.

The main entrance to the basement was right off the kitchen. There was a light switch by the door leading down to it, but – knowing what was going to be happening down there during the party – someone had wisely decided to remove the bulb. Thus, going down the basement steps required exercising a certain degree of caution.

That said, Shade noted that it wasn't completely dark as he went down the basement stairs. Someone (presumably Lord Byron) had set up soft blue mood lighting throughout the place. In all honesty, it barely provided any illumination at all, but was better than nothing. Still, Shade stood at the bottom of the steps for a moment, letting his eyes adjust as much as possible to the dark.

After about a minute, he could make out more of his surroundings and immediately noted two things. First of all, the basement was expansive – not quite as large as the great room, but close enough. And, although he couldn't see a lot of specific details, he got the impression that the place was decked out like a swank man-cave.

The other thing Shade noted was that there were people everywhere. He couldn't see them clearly because of the lack of light, but he could distinguish human forms – lots of them. From what he could make out, there several sitting areas in the basement populated with what he assumed were sofas, loveseats and the like, and almost every piece of furniture had people on it. Most of them were in prone positions, or as close to prone as they could get on things like Barcaloungers and ottomans.

As for what all these people were doing, he didn't even need eyes for that. Although the basement appeared to have its own sound system and there was music playing, it wasn't loud enough to drown out the cacophony of moans and groans Shade heard all around him, as well as the rhythmic sound of bodies slapping together.

Shade frowned, feeling that something was off, and a second later he figured out what it was. Assuming that most of the people in the basement were paired up male-to-female, the number of women down here exceeded the number of prostitutes that were seemingly at the party. Of course, there were probably some streetwalkers in attendance who kept their profession on the down-low, but that still wouldn't account for the numbers he was seeing. Clearly then, some of those in the basement were there for something other than business reasons.

Probably the excitement of having sex in a semi-public place, he thought, then began moving through the basement, looking for Donna.

It was a bit of an odd search. Most of those present didn't seem to care about folks traipsing back and forth through the room. Given what the place was being used for, it was understood and accepted that it would be a high-traffic area. What pissed folks the fuck off, though, was a nigga who seemed to be a voyeur, doing nothing but drifting through the place, watching people fuck.

Of course, that's not what Shade was doing at all; he was looking for Donna. Unfortunately, his task required him to give each female that he saw a once-over, which probably gave the impression he was just a perv. More to the point, Shade could sense the ire of those around him (evidenced by low grumbles) as they pegged him as some type of Peeping Tom.

Staying focused on the task at hand, Shade did his best to ignore them. After a few minutes, however, he was pretty much ready to give up, convinced that Donna must be elsewhere. Thus, he was heading back to the stairs when he saw a bit of light reflect off metal on some nigga's wrist.

The muhfucka in question was down on the floor, on his knees. His hands were behind him, and his face was buried between the legs of some chick sitting spread eagle in a recliner. It was then that Shade noticed that the nigga's hands weren't just behind him – they were cuffed. Turning his attention to the woman in the chair, he suddenly realized that it was Donna. Her back was arched and she was moaning in ecstasy, as the nigga on his knees continued eating her pussy like his muhfuckin' life depended on it.

Shade chuckled to himself, now understanding why this one was taking Donna longer than usual.

If I could get a bitch to pay to go down on me, *I wouldn't be in any rush either*, he said to himself.

Still, it made him shudder a little on the inside to see the way the nigga on the floor was eating Donna out. He didn't seem to care that her pussy had probably played hostess to a score of dicks that evening. Or maybe that was a turn-on for him. Different strokes for different folks…

At that moment, Donna apparently become aware of Shade's presence, as her head suddenly seemed to swivel in his direction. From what he could tell, she appeared to smile at him (and he also got the impression that she winked) before going back to enjoying herself.

Noting that she was okay (actually better than okay), Shade hurried and got the fuck out the basement, doing his damnedest not to touch anything on the way out.

THUG LIFE: EMANCIPATED

Chapter 31

Fortunately, locating Donna was the closest Shade came to having trouble at the party. For once, despite the bulk of them being drunk and high, niggas were generally on their best behavior. That said, it wasn't a completely hassle-free evening.

Basically, in addition to the two he'd met in the great room and the kitchen, Shade occasionally found himself next to niggas from Byron's crew as he made his rounds through the party. On each occasion, they tried talking to him, but after dealing with that fool who'd shoved the drink into his hand, he essentially just tuned them out. Instead, he stayed focused on his quartet of females and ultimately those niggas just left him alone.

From what he could tell, the girls were making out pretty well, dollar-wise. Whenever he saw them dancing, they typically had niggas around them tossing bills (even if a lot of them *were* singles). He didn't know what they were pulling in with respect to turning tricks, but assumed things were good on that front as well. Thus, it came as a bit of a surprise when they ended up leaving the party after only a few hours.

In essence, the decision to depart started with Taranda, who approached Shade saying that she needed to get home to check on her siblings. At that juncture, the two of them sought out the other girls, ostensibly to let them know that Shade was taking Taranda home and would be back. However, in each instance, the other three indicated that they were ready to leave as well. In the end, Shade told them to meet him by the door while he went to tell Lord Byron that they were heading out.

He was only mildly worried that he would get pushback from Byron, who might feel that he'd paid for an entire evening of entertainment. But when Shade found him, Byron was cool about the whole thing.

"S'all good," he said when Shade told him that he was taking the girls home. "Thanks for comin' through for a nigga."

Shade simply nodded, then turned and walked away. A few minutes later, he and the girls were out the door and headed to his car.

THUG LIFE: EMANCIPATED

Chapter 32

En route to his car, Shade gave the girls their cell phones back, as well as the rest of their payment from Lord Byron (minus his cut). He also gave Dumplin' her purse back. In all honesty, going around with it all evening hadn't been as awkward as he'd imagined. He was used to carrying his tool bag everywhere, so only having one hand free was something he was used to. As for having a woman's accessory, only a couple of people tried to give him any shit about it, and they'd accepted his explanation when he told them he was holding it for one of the strippers.

Once they were on the road, there was virtually no conversation – mostly because Shade's passengers were all counting their money. Thus for a minute or so, the only thing being heard was the rustle of paper.

"Damn!" Dumplin' suddenly exclaimed. "How you get all that?"

Shade risked a glance towards the back seat, where – for some reason – Dumplin' had chosen to sit for the ride home, giving up the front seat to Yoni. Dumplin's comment seemed to be directed at Donna, who was seated next to her and holding a fat wad of cash.

"How you thank I got it?" Donna shot back. "I earned it, same as you."

"But I didn't get nearly that much," Dumplin' whined.

"Age over beauty, bitches," Donna said, giggling as she fanned herself with a sheaf of bills. "That's experience at work."

No one immediately said anything, but Shade was almost certain that Yoni's pile – which couldn't really be seen by the three in the back seat – was easily more than Donna's.

"So what I'm doin' wrong?" Dumplin asked, plainly concerned.

146

Donna just looked at her for a moment, then let out an exasperated sigh. "Look, baby girl – how long you take to turn a trick tonight?"

Dumplin' shrugged. "I don't know…fifteen or twenty minutes, I guess."

"See, that's yo problem right there," Donna explained. "A party like tonight, you gotta treat that shit like a volume business. Don't be tryin' to show them niggas a good time. Yo job is to make 'em cum fast and make 'em cum hard. That's it. And you shouldn't be takin' mo' than five minutes to do that shit."

"Five minutes?" Dumplin' repeated incredulously.

"Yeah – five fuckin' minutes," Donna declared. "Don't be lettin' them muhfuckas set some tempo they can maintain. You work they shit like a fuckin' speed demon – try to make them niggas cum before they dick out they pants good."

Dumplin' seemed to meditate on this for a moment. "But donchu need to make it last? Won't they be mad if it's over too fast and they didn't get they money's worth?"

"Well, let me thank," Donna said, scratching her temple in faux concentration. "When's the last time a nigga got mad at me for makin' him cum? Oh, that's right – fuckin' *never*."

Dumplin' nodded at this, but still didn't appear convinced. Looking towards Shade, she asked, "Is that true?"

"Oh yeah – I never get mad get mad at a girl for makin' me cum," he declared, nodding. "Now bitches, on the other hand? They get furious about that shit." He then switched to a whiny feminine voice, saying, "Nigga, who da fuck you thank you are, makin' me cum? I ain't ask you to make me cum. I didn't *wanna* cum…"

His passengers all erupted into laughter – even Yoni. And something about seeing her smile made Shade smile in

147

return, even though he really didn't want to. Or rather, it wasn't so much that he didn't want to; he was just wary now of getting too wrapped up in this girl.

"Here," Donna said, interrupting his thoughts as she extended her hand towards Shade. In it she held a small wad of cash, which Shade took.

"What's this?" he asked.

"Just a tip," Donna replied.

"You don't have to do that," he told her. "I already got a piece of what Lord Byron paid."

He didn't know if any of them had done the math, but his twenty percent, in total, actually came to the same amount that his passengers had received from Byron.

And I didn't have to strip or suck anybody's dick to get it, he thought.

"I saw you making the rounds tonight," Donna noted. "Constantly checkin' on us and makin' sure we was okay. That's the kind of shit a bitch appreciate, so you earned that."

"Okay, uh…thanks," Shade murmured, not sure how to respond.

It was a nice gesture on Donna's part, but not anything he was expecting in the least. However, he got an even bigger surprise when, moments later, the other three also gave him a nice tip.

"Wow," Shade muttered as he shoved the cash into a cargo pocket. "I feel rich – like I need to go celebrate."

"Well, I don't need to celebrate," Dumplin's said, "but I could stand to get sommin' to eat."

"Me, too," added Donna, while Yoni simply nodded.

"That's fine," Shade assured them, "but I need to get Taranda home first, so–"

"Actually," Taranda interjected, "if we stop someplace, I can pick up sommin' for my brother and sister to eat."

"A'ight then," Shade said. "Let's go get sommin' to eat."

****

They ended up going to a late-night diner. The place was a grease pit, but it was on the way and the food was cheap.

Bearing in mind that the girls had all given him a nice tip, Shade offered to pay – including buying something for Taranda to take back for her siblings. It was an offer that his companions eagerly took him up on.

Inside, the diner only had a handful of patrons, and Shade's group quickly found their way over to an empty booth. When the waitress came over a few minutes later, Shade ordered something from the breakfast menu (which was served all day) and the others followed suite. Thankfully, service was rather quick, and within ten minutes they had their food.

For the next fifteen minutes, they talked as they ate, although the conversation mostly consisted of the females exchanging humorous anecdotes about their experiences at Byron's party: some of the crazy shit niggas had said, how much money muhfuckas had flashed, etcetera. Shade spent the majority of that time simply listening, although he noted that Yoni didn't really add much to the conversation other than an occasional witticism that made everybody laugh.

All in all, it was an enjoyable meal. Moreover, the conversation continued after the waitress came and took their plates away, with the discussion moving generally to current gossip in the hood, like who was fucking who, who got busted for something stupid, and so on. Needless to say, that topic encompassed enough subject matter to keep them talking and laughing all night. Even Shade got more involved in the conversation, making a couple of droll comments about hood life that had the girls in stitches.

They were having such a good time that they might have stayed there talking indefinitely, despite Taranda's earlier statement that she needed to get home. However, as often happens, their good time soon came to a somewhat abrupt and unexpected end, courtesy of some other patrons in the diner.

THUG LIFE: EMANCIPATED

Chapter 33

Shade's group had been in the diner for maybe forty-five minutes when a trio of niggas came in. They were all a couple of years older than Shade, but he recognized them right away: two braindead muhfuckas called Deeter and Monk, and their leader – a wannabe gangster named Mario who tended to act like the world owed him a living.

Shade frowned. Mario was trouble – not because he was some kind of *bad*ass, but because he was a complete *dumb*ass. Almost any word more with more than two syllables would confound him, and anything he didn't understand he took as an insult. That meant it was easy to get on his bad side.

Surprisingly, however, Mario actually *knew* that he was dumb, but he decided that the fix for that particular problem was not to become smarter, but to surround himself with muhfuckas who were even dumber than him (like his present companions). Ergo, when Mario was around, you typically had to deal with multiple morons instead of just one. That, coupled with Mario's mental picture of himself as a gangster and the fact that he was quick to anger, generally formed a recipe for disaster.

At the moment, Mario and his boys were simply being loud and obnoxious – laughing boisterously at some private joke while shouting at the waitress to "get yo fine ass over here" as they flopped down at a table. A couple of other customers frowned in disapproval but didn't say anything. Perhaps – like Shade – they knew that if this was the worst that Mario did while at the diner, it would be a blessing.

On their part, Shade's group continued talking, but in more subdued tones. Or at least it felt subdued in comparison to the clamor coming from Mario's table, which was only a few feet away. However, it wasn't long before the inevitable happened: one of the women at Shade's table – Taranda –

laughed too loud at something humorous that had been said. Needless to say, it drew Mario's attention.

"What's so funny over there?" Mario asked in a somber tone.

There was silence for a moment, then Shade simply replied, "Private joke."

"Well tell *me*," Mario stated. "I wanna laugh, too."

"Like I said, it's a private joke," Shade told him. "I don't thank you'd get it."

Mario's eyes narrowed. "You mean I ain't smart enough to get it."

Shade let out an exasperated sigh. "That ain't what I said."

"Then send one of dem bitches over here to tell me," Mario insisted. "She can whisper it right *here*." As he spoke, he dropped a hand between his legs and grabbed his crotch, causing Deeter and Monk to laugh.

"Come on, man – don't be crude," Shade admonished. "This a public place."

"Then let me take one of dem hoes out back," Mario replied, which got another snicker from his boys. "I mean, they hoes, ain't they?"

Shade didn't immediately respond. Although the women with him still had their jackets on, they were all open, revealing their outfits underneath. More to the point, anyone seeing those wouldn't be out of line for thinking all the females at their booth turned tricks. (Plus, it was possible that Mario was a customer of one – or more – of them.)

"They not hoes," Shade said after a moment. "And even if they was, they off the clock. It's been a long day and everybody's tired."

As he finished speaking, Shade – who was sitting near the outside of the booth – stood up. Following his lead, Yoni and the others stood and slid out of the booth as well.

"Aww, come on," Mario pleaded. "Y'all ain't gotta go. I was just playin'."

"It ain't you," Shade lied. "It's us. Everybody's just worn out."

With that, Shade began walking towards the exit, with the women following in his wake.

"Hold up," Mario said, coming to his feet and stepping in front of Shade. Then, leaning in, he said, "Lemme just talk to you for a minute, huh? See if we can work sommin' out."

Shade fought the urge to tell Mario to fuck off. It would have felt good, but also would have motivated that dumb nigga to do something stupid. Plainly speaking, it was easier to just listen to what the muhfucka had to say than to possibly piss him off and have to deal with the aftermath.

Mind made up, Shade reached into his pocket and pulled out his keys. Tossing them to Yoni, he said, "I'll meet y'all at the car in a few." He then turned back to Mario, who gestured towards his table, indicating that Shade should take a seat.

The table in question was a standard, square-shaped unit. Mario had been seated on one side, with his two friends sitting diagonal to him, with one on each side. Shade moved towards the only empty spot and sat down as Mario – directly across from him – sat down as well.

There was cutlery at his end of the table – a fork, spoon, and steak knife – which Shade pushed to the side. He then leaned back and crossed his arms, simply staring at Mario.

"Look, dawg," Mario began. "Me and my boys just lookin' to have a lil' fun. It's Saturday night, we got some cash, and don't mind spendin' somma it on women."

"So just drive down the street," Shade advised. "Damn near every corner 'round here got hookers this time a'night."

It was a slight exaggeration, but hopefully got his point across.

Mario, however, just shook his head. "Now why we gone do dat when you got fine-ass bitches right here?"

"Oh, so this kind of a bird-in-the-hand thang," Shade noted.

Mario frowned in confusion. "Huh?"

"A bird in the hand," Shade repeated. Noting that he still got a nonplussed look from Mario (and his friends), Shade completed the adage. "A bird in the hand's worth two in the bush."

Mario appeared to concentrate for a moment, like he almost understood, then seemed to throw in the towel, angrily muttering, "Da fuck you talkin' 'bout?"

"Nuthin'," Shade replied, shaking his head in exasperation. "Just thankin' out loud, I guess."

Mario gave him a skeptical look, then said, "Anyway, we was talkin' about us spendin' time wicho hoes. We here; they here. What's da problem?"

"'Like I already said," Shade answered, "the girls with me is off the clock."

"Then have dem bitches clock in again."

"They tired," Shade explained. "They been workin' a big party all night."

"What party?" Mario asked, showing more than casual interest.

"Lord Byron had a big bash tonight," Shade informed him.

"Really?" asked Deeter, speaking for the first time. "How was it?"

"Shit was off the chain," Shade replied truthfully. "Lord Byron invited damn near everybody in da hood."

"Then how come we ain't know nuthin' 'bout it?" Mario inquired.

"Fuck if I know," Shade uttered. "Maybe yo invite got lost in the mail."

Someone at a nearby table snickered. It wasn't clear whether it was related to Shade's last comment or something else, but it was incredibly poor timing. In essence, it gave Mario the impression that Shade was making fun of him.

Mario pursed his lips in anger, simply staring at Shade for a few seconds.

"Maybe we don't need yo hoes, after all," he finally said. "Since they all tired from the party that *we* didn't get invited to, maybe we'll have our own party. At *yo* place."

"Oh yeah," mouthed Monk, grinning. "Now ya talkin'."

"Yeah, I bet yo sistas ain't tired," Mario continued. "That older one, Nissa, look like she could go all night. At that young one – what they call her?"

"Cherry," Deeter volunteered.

"Yeah, Cherry," Mario said, licking his lips. "When we done with her, they gone have to change *that* name."

At that, Mario and his boys all burst out laughing, high-fiving each other like they'd just heard a witty repartee.

"I'm going to the bathroom," Shade announced without preamble, then came to his feet. He then began walking in the direction of the men's room, which required him to go past Mario, who was still chuckling with his boys about Nissa and Cherry. However, just as he drew even the nigga, Shade quickly spun towards him, slipping a hand under Mario's chin and pulling his head back, while at the same time placing a steak knife at the fool's throat.

Mario and his idiotic friends immediately went silent. They had been so busy guffawing that they hadn't even noticed Shade take the knife from his set of cutlery when he stood up. But they damn sure noticed it now.

Mario gulped and then slowly lifted his hands, palms out – a gesture that was intended to tell his friends not to do anything stupid while simultaneously keeping his hands where Shade could see them.

"Do not mistake me for somebody who gives a fuck about consequences," Shade hissed, leaning close to Mario's ear. "I'll stab you in the neck in the middle of this fuckin' restaurant, and post a video of that shit online, unnastand?"

Mario nodded – or rather, nodded as best he could with his head pulled back and throat exposed.

"Good," Shade said. "Now listen, 'cause I'm only gone say this shit once. You can say whatever the fuck you want about *me*. I don't give a shit. In fact, I'm one of the few muhfuckas on the planet who'll let niggas get away with talkin' shit 'bout my *momma*. Again, I don't give a fuck. But if you *ever* mention my sistas again, I'm gonna do shit to you that's so fucked up, they gone need a new branch of science to describe it."

With that he tossed the knife onto the table, at the same time roughly shoving Mario on the side of the head. He then walked out of the restaurant, feeling Mario's eyes on his back like daggers the entire time.

THUG LIFE: EMANCIPATED

Chapter 34

Shade was mostly silent as he drove the women home. He was angry at himself for letting his temper get the better of him back at the diner. He usually had more control than that, but after Mario mentioned his sisters – especially that comment about Cherry – he had seen nothing but red.

The only good news was that, even though he'd threatened Mario in a public place, he didn't think anyone had really noticed. From the way his body had been positioned, the other patrons in the restaurant probably thought he was simply whispering something to Mario, and the waitress hadn't been around at the time. Ergo, the only witnesses to what transpired were Deeter and Monk, and as far as Shade was concerned they didn't count.

Still, it had been a stupid, knee-jerk response on his part. Mario was a vindictive fuck, so he was sure to want payback in some way, manner, or form. In short, Shade could expect him to retaliate sometime soon.

Oh, well, he thought. *I'll cross that bridge when I come to it.*

For the most part, the women in the car chatted amongst themselves as he drove. Other than asking him what Mario had said (to which Shade had given a vague response), they didn't express much interest in what had transpired after they left the diner. Only Yoni, who was again in the front passenger seat, seemed to note Shade's mood.

He essentially dropped them off in the same order that he had picked them up. That meant Yoni and Donna were the last ones in the car. When he got to their neighborhood, Donna surprised him by leaning forward and giving him a quick peck on the cheek as he put the car in 'Park.'

"Thanks, Shade," she said. "You really hooked a bitch up tonight." Then she slipped out the car, closed the door, and began walking towards her building.

Shade expected Yoni to follow suit (*sans* the kiss), but she surprised him.

"Why don't you come up for a minute," she suggested. "There's sommin' I wanna show you."

Chapter 35

It turned out that what she had to show him was their kindergarten yearbook.

"I dug it out after you left earlier," she explained.

"I'm surprised you still got it," Shade admitted as he flipped through the pages. "Mine got lost a million years ago."

"Well, I'm kind of a packrat," she told him with a smile.

At present, they were sitting next to each other on the couch in Yoni's living room. She had taken off her jacket but still had on her outfit, and was looking on as Shade went through the yearbook. They had reminisced earlier, but there was something significant about being able to put faces to the names they'd previously discussed. Moreover, seeing those old pics brought even more memories to mind, and before long Shade and Yoni were laughing and joking heartily, much as they had that afternoon.

"Who'd have thunk it?" Yoni uttered as she pointed at her kindergarten picture. "That this sweet lil' girl would grow up to be the baddest bitch on the planet."

"Oh, is that Taranda?" Shade joked.

Giggling, Yoni gave him a playful punch on the arm. "Nigga, you funny. Like you mo' interested in Taranda than me."

"Maybe I am," he offered.

"Then why you slinkin' 'round the party all night, lookin' at me?"

"In case you forgot, I made regular rounds through the party checkin' of all of y'all."

"So it was just professional?" Yoni inquired skeptically. "You weren't interested in seein' my tits or anythang like that?"

"Nope," Shade assured her.

"Not even a lil' bit?"

"Honestly, I barely even noticed you had tits," Shade declared with a snicker.

Yoni laughed as well, then said, "A'ight – I'll take that bet."

"Huh?"

Instead of responding directly, Yoni grabbed her cell phone, which was sitting on a nearby end table. She spent a few seconds tapping on it, bringing up what Shade noticed was a music app. A few seconds later, the phone began playing a song he recognized as a current R&B hit. Yoni placed the phone back on the end table and then stood up.

There was a coffee table in front of the couch. Yoni placed a foot on the end of it and then extended her leg, pushing it out of the way. She then took a position a few away from Shade but directly in his line of sight.

"Now," she began, "since you claim you ain't notice my girls tonight, let's if you can ignore 'em now."

"Whachu mean?" Shade asked.

"What I mean is that we gone see how long you can keep yo eyes on my *face*."

With that, she began dancing. It wasn't the rapid-fire ass-and-hips thing she was doing earlier, but something more in line with the music, which was slow and sensual. Likewise, Yoni's moves – consisting of waist rollicks, hip whines, body rolls, and more – were steamy and arousing. It wasn't quite as hypnotic as her dancing at Lord Byron's party, but it was erotic enough to draw the eye – at least under normal circumstances. In this instance, however, Shade squarely met the challenge of keeping his eyes on Yoni's face, noting her dance moves with his peripheral vision.

Truth be told, it didn't require much effort on Shade's part. Yes, Yoni was fine as fuck, but you could come across plenty of fine-ass girls practicing their dance moves in hallways at school, on their front porches, and at backyard barbecues. So as far as Shade was concerned, although what Yoni was doing was enticing, it was in no way exceptional.

But then she took her top off.

Again, he wasn't looking directly at what her hands were doing, but he never got the impression that they went anywhere near her top. However, the next thing he knew, her chest was bare.

Or rather, somewhat bare, as her nipples were covered by a pair of red titty tassels. To his credit, Shade somehow managed to continue looking Yoni in the eye, but it took a monstrous effort not to glance down at her bosom. Even with just his peripheral vision, he could tell her tits were spectacular.

On her part, Yoni then adopted something of a more traditional stripper's routine. She kicked off her heels in a sultry fashion, then spun her top around an index finger before tossing it at Shade's feet. She followed this up with a shoulder shimmy that not only caused her breasts to bounce but made the titty tassels twirl like fan blades.

Miraculously, Shade continued to stay focused on her face, but at that point Yoni dealt the *coup de gras* to his concentration: she pulled off one of the titty tassels. At that moment, his eyes immediately cut to her exposed tit.

"Gotcha, muhfucka!" Yoni crowed triumphantly, laughing.

Shade shook his head in disagreement. "Actually, I was distracted by a bug or sommin' that flew out from between yo legs."

"Bullshit!" Yoni declared as she came over and sat back down next to him, smirking. "My shit is clean as a whistle."

"If you say so."

161

"Oh?" she droned. "You wanna conduct an inspection?"

Shade laughed. "I'll take yo word for it."

She snickered at that as well, then said, "Anyway, you get an 'A' for effort. You held out longer than I thought you would."

"Best two out of three?" he suggested, grinning as he picked her top up from the floor and handed it to her.

"Nigga, please," Yoni chided, smiling. "You was barely able to maintain eye contact with that shitty striptease I just did. If I really start dancin' and showcasin' my moves, you won't be able to keep yo damn eyes in yo head."

Shade chortled a little at that, then grew slightly pensive. "Speaking of dancing, what was that you was doin' at Byron's party?"

"Oh, you liked that, huh?" she teased, giving him a wink. "That was *Ori Tahiti*."

"What" he muttered, frowning.

"*Ori Tahiti*," she repeated. "Traditional dancing from Tahiti."

"Where'd you learn that?"

"My grandmother was Polynesian. She taught me."

"Seriously?" Shade asked. "Your grandmomma taught you to shake yo hips and ass like that?"

Yoni giggled wildly at that, her laughter seeming to suggest she found his question both humorous and impertinent. Her mirth was infectious, and Shade found himself chuckling along with her, at the same time trying not to be completely blatant about the fact that his eyes were constantly drawn to her bosom.

In essence, after Shade had returned her top to her, Yoni had placed it in her lap but appeared to be in no rush to put it back on. In fact, she hadn't even bothered to reattach the titty tassel she'd taken off. The end result was that she was presenting Shade with quite a bit of eye candy at the moment.

"Yes, my grandmomma seriously taught me to shake my ass," she finally managed to say between snickers. "What's so hard to believe 'bout that?"

"Didn't she know that was gone be like catnip to niggas in da hood?" Shade asked.

"Damn straight she knew. How you thank she snagged my granddaddy?"

Shade grinned at that. "So that dancin' shit is just a snare – an elaborate fuckin' man-trap to hook a nigga."

"Now you gettin' it," Yoni teased. "But it can't just be *any* nigga. It's gotta be the *right* nigga."

"Well, from what I saw tonight, you gone have the pick of the litter. No wonder you made the most money at the party."

Shade had meant it as a kind of half-joke, half-compliment. However, his words had a chilling effect, as they immediately highlighted the fact that Yoni had picked up a lot of paper at the party, and were also suggestive of how she had earned it.

There followed a few moments of awkward silence, following which Yoni lowered her eyes and simply said, "Just so you know, I didn't do anythang with anybody tonight."

Shade shrugged. "Not my business if you did."

"I mean, I did some lap dances, but nuthin' more than that."

"Again, not my business."

Yoni's eye narrowed. "So you tellin' me it wouldn't bother you one bit if it turned out that I fucked fifty niggas up in that party tonight?"

"Naw," Shade assured her. "Like you said, if you wanna let a nigga stick a dick in every hole, that's yo right."

"So you don't believe me," she stated.

"Actually, I do," Shade countered. "After seein' yo tiny lil' tits, I don't think you were able to close the deal with anybody."

"Fuck you, nigga!" Yoni shrieked, laughing.

And just like that, the tension was gone. Shade's little joke had effectively lightened the mood, brought them back to where they'd been just a few minutes earlier.

"My girls are fuckin' glorious," she continued with a smirk, cupping her breasts (which were nowhere near tiny). "I cudda had any muhfucka I wanted up in there tonight."

"Maybe you cudda had ninety-nine percent of 'em," he said smugly. "But not *all*."

"And just who's this one percent that ain't interested in what I got to offer?"

"I guess that's me."

"Oh, really?" Yoni intoned. "You wanna challenge me again this soon?"

Without waiting for a response, Yoni suddenly shifted position, swinging a leg over and straddling him. She then placed her arms around his neck, and at the same time started grinding on him, her hips moving back and forth in a sensuous fashion

"I know – you ain't interested," she whispered in a husky voice as she stared into his eyes. "You got no interest in this tight-ass pussy between my legs. You don't care 'bout the way it's strokin' yo pole right now, beggin' for a deep dickin'. You could give a fuck 'bout how easy it would be to just pull my panties to the side, whip yo shit out, and ram it all the way up in me. Naw, you don't care 'bout that – don't care 'bout that at all. Ain't even thought about it."

Shade drew in a deep breath. Yoni's words were starting to put all kinds of ideas in his head, but of course, that was the point. And the grinding she was doing in his lap was having the intended effect: his shit was getting hard enough to dent steel. When she had first climbed into his lap, Shade – taken somewhat by surprise – had placed his hands on the couch cushions on either side of him. Now however, with everything Yoni was doing, he was having a tough time keeping them there.

On her part, Yoni kept up the pressure, saying, "And you definitely not thankin' 'bout the fact that I'm gettin' wet enough to drown yo ass. 'Bout the way my pussy done prolly soaked the front of yo pants and how you'd love to just slide yo' big-ass dick up in there. Uh-uh. That shit ain't even crossed yo mind. And I know you ain't even considered the notion of flippin' me over onto my hands and knees and fuckin' me doggy style – maybe smackin' me on the ass while you tear it up from the back, or reachin' up and squeezin' my tits while you pound that shit."

"And speaking of tits," she droned, suddenly sitting up a little straighter so that her bosom was thrust out, "I know this flat-ass pancake I call a chest don't appeal to you, and these tiny lil' pimples I consider tits ain't nuthin' to get excited about. Hell, I doubt you even noticed them bitches before now, and even if you did, ain't shit about 'em that would make a nigga's dick get hard."

As she spoke, Shade felt something firm but yielding press against his chin. Instinctively, he knew it was her nipple, the one that was still exposed after she removed the titty tassel. Having it (and the rest of her tit) pressed teasingly against his him was practically torture, and at that juncture, he knew this was a game he couldn't win. Ergo, in preparation for telling Yoni she'd won this round, he licked his lips.

And that's when it happened.

Whether it was chance, an accident, or intentional on Yoni's part, Shade wasn't sure. However, the fact of the matter was that as Shade licked his lips, Yoni's exposed nipple gently brushed his mouth…touched his tongue. And that was all it took.

Whatever poise and self-control Shade had maintained up until that moment evaporated like a fucking raindrop in the desert. Without realizing what he was doing, he reached up and placed one hand behind Yoni's head.

"Plus," Yoni was saying, "you don't–"

Her words were cut off as Shade pushed her head forward, forcing her lips onto his. He kissed her then – deeply, longingly, and hungrily. More to the point, she kissed him back with the same fervor, although there was a brief moment when Shade felt her lips broaden into a wide grin – something he recognized in the back of his mind as her declaring victory with respect to this latest challenge.

Shade, of course, didn't care. If this was what losing felt like, he'd take it every time.

The hand he had used to initiate their kiss now loving stroked Yoni's face, while the other hand found the offending the nipple – the one that had shattered his resolve – and punished it severely, tweaking and rubbing it hard enough to make Yoni groan in pleasure before moving on to fondle her tits.

Her kisses were intoxicating, an exhilarating drug that aroused both his body and mind. Shade wasn't sure exactly how it happened, but the next thing he knew they were stretched out on the couch, with Yoni under him. He continued kissing her, taking delight in the softness of her lips, the scent of her skin, the feel of her body as he caressed her. He was so enraptured that it was probably a full thirty seconds before he noticed that something was off.

He was in the process of kissing her when the realization hit him. However, it only took him a moment to identify what was wrong: Yoni wasn't responding to anything he was doing. She wasn't moaning in pleasure, returning his kisses, or letting her hands roam over his body as he was doing to her. She was simply lying there.

His eyes had been closed while he kissed her, but he opened them now and found Yoni giving him a deliberate stare. It was a look that made him incredibly self-conscious, and left him feeling like he'd misread the entire situation.

"You done?" Yoni asked casually, as though inquiring if he'd gotten enough to eat.

"Uh, yeah," he replied sheepishly as he slid off her and took a seat on the couch near her feet.

"Good," she declared as she sat up. "Because I think it's time for you to go."

Shade merely stared at her for a moment, as if he couldn't quite comprehend what she'd said. Obviously he'd fucked up somewhere, but he had no idea what he'd done. Regardless, he wasn't the type of guy who couldn't take "No" from a female. That being the case, he rose to his feet.

Struggling for something to say, he muttered, "Thanks for, um, showing me the yearbook."

He then began trudging towards the door, still trying to figure out where he'd made a misstep. Just as he reached for the doorknob, Yoni suddenly slid in front of him. Shade had been so lost in thought that he hadn't even realized that she'd gotten up from the couch.

Still topless, she placed her back to the door, thereby preventing him from opening it.

"There's an old saying," she mused saucily. "You have to *cum* before you can *go*."

She then caressed his face with her forefinger, winked, and then went bounding down the apartment hallway, giggling.

Shade merely watched her for a moment, his brain trying to divine meaning from what she'd just said. Then, just as Yoni stepped into a room at the end of the hallway, her words suddenly rang clear. A second later, he was dashing down the hallway after her, a bright smile on his face. He was going so fast that when he checked his speed at the door Yoni had entered, he actually slid for a moment on a runner rug that was on the hallway floor. Plainly speaking, he was barely able to keep his balance and avoid landing on his ass.

Quickly recovering from his near-fall, Shade reached for the doorknob, then paused. Yoni had essentially been a cocktease at every opportunity: when he asked for her number, when he kissed her on the couch, etcetera. That being the case, there was a good chance that she had locked the door and was just waiting to taunt him when he tried to open it.

Fuck it, he finally said to himself. The possibility of what lay beyond that door was worth getting ridiculed for. Mind made up, he grabbed the doorknob and attempted to turn it.

The door was unlocked.

THUG LIFE: EMANCIPATED

Chapter 36

Shade found himself in a bedroom – presumably Yoni's, based on what a quick scan of the place revealed: perfume on a nearby dresser, a makeup mirror on a nightstand, and so on. Yoni herself was already under the covers of what appeared to be a full-sized bed. She smiled as Shade closed the door behind him, then waggled her eyebrows flirtatiously.

Shade didn't need any more of an invitation than that. He rapidly stripped his clothes off (making Yoni laugh when he almost tripped getting out of his pants) and then scrambled over to the bed. Preparing to join Yoni under the covers, he lifted the bedding, which appeared to consist of light gray sheets and a matching comforter, with a large blue blanket on top. Unexpectedly heavy, the bedding slipped from his fingers almost immediately.

Confused, Shade stared at the bed linen for a second. It had been surprisingly dense, having far more weight than he had anticipated. Reaching out once more, he got a firm grip on the bedding and tried lifting it again. Not only was he more successful on his second attempt, he also identified the problem.

"Da fuck's up with this blanket?" he demanded, indicating the blue blanket that was on top of the comforter.

Yoni gave him a curious look. "Whachu mean?"

"It weighs like a hundred pounds."

"Mo' like thirty," Yoni corrected, laughing. "It's a weighted blanket. It's s'posed to help you sleep better by makin' you feel mo' snug and shit."

"And you sleep better under this damn thing?"

Yoni gave him a frank stare. "Actually, I sleep better after I've had a dick inside me." She then raised an eyebrow salaciously.

"Fuck sleep," Shade said, forgetting about the blanket as he climbed into bed with her. "Yo ass about to go into a coma."

****

After getting into bed, Shade ducked under the covers and made a beeline for Yoni's pussy. Once there, he started eating her out immediately.

She tasted exquisite. If Mrs. Jamison was strawberries, then Yoni was ambrosia – a deliciously divine esculent reserved for deities.

Shade devoured her with relish. Somewhere in the back of his mind, however, he realized that he probably came off as less than romantic. In essence, he had completely sidestepped foreplay – hadn't given Yoni so much as a kiss or a nipple-squeeze after getting into bed. Instead, he had simply gone straight for the goods.

On Yoni's part, if she was disappointed at not being showered with kisses or caresses before Shade buried his face in her snatch, it didn't show. In fact, if her moans and gasps were any indication, the notion of foreplay wasn't even a fucking afterthought.

Unlike Mrs. Jamison, Yoni didn't verbally dictate what she wanted or announce how much she enjoyed it. Still, she made her wishes – and satisfaction - known by her reactions: the moans she let out when his mouth was on her pussy lips. The way her back arched when he slipped his tongue inside her. The brazen manner in which she grabbed his head and held it in place with a grip of steel when he vigorously licked her clit. All that and more told Shade everything he needed to know about what Yoni liked and how to get her off.

From Yoni's perspective, the cunnilingus was mind-bending. It wasn't simply that Shade seemed to enjoy it; he was actually good – no, fucking *fantastic* – at it. It was as though the nigga had gotten lessons in eating pussy, because he was a certified pro at that shit. Thus, when she came, it was hard and fast – an overwhelming feeling of unbridled ecstasy that engulfed her with the speed and intensity of a flash flood, washing away every other sensation.

"Hmmm! Hmmm! Hmmm!" she muttered in a sort of whimpering purr. It wasn't an exceptionally loud sound, but there was a fervor and passion to it that was undeniable.

At the same time, as the orgasm sent waves of pleasure rippling through her body, her hips began moving up and down in a jerky, almost spasmodic, fashion. It had the effect of pushing her pussy further into Shade's face, then pulling it away before repeating the motion. It caught Shade slightly by surprise at first, but not enough to truly interfere with the efforts of his mouth and tongue.

After about ten seconds, the hip motion ceased and her entire body seemed to relax as Yoni let out a long, lingering sigh. Afterwards, she simply lay there for a few seconds, breathing deeply, while Shade – sensing that she had climaxed – moved his mouth over to the inner part of her thigh, which he gently kissed. Then, with her hands on both sides of his head, Yoni gently tugged, indicating that he should move up.

Shade did as he was bid, kissing his way up her body as he inched forward. Moments later, he was in position, with his dick at her pussy. Balancing himself on one hand in order to keep the bulk of his weight off her, he nuzzled her neck while reaching down between his legs with his free hand.

Grabbing his dick, he began running it around her pussy lips. She was sopping wet, and he had to fight the natural urge to just go balls deep in her right then and there. Instead, he only put the head in, joggling it up and down in a tantalizing fashion.

Yoni, however, was apparently in no mood to be teased. Without warning, she wrapped her legs around his and then made a sudden thrusting motion with her hips, an action that made her pussy shoot forward and completely envelope his dick. At that same moment, she put her arms around him, locking her hands together behind his back. And then she went to town.

Much like when she had danced at the party, her hips seemed to take on a life of their own, swiftly and repetitively lunging back and forth, taking in the length of Shade's cock over and over again with unchecked ferocity. In the meantime, her arms and legs seemed to tighten, getting a death grip on his body while Yoni, in essence, fucked him from the bottom position.

Shade had, of course, been caught off-guard by the hip thrust that had resulted in his dick basically being gobbled up by Yoni's pussy. It had culminated with him being balls deep in her – as he had imagined just moments earlier – except that Yoni had initiated the action. That said, sliding inside her had felt so amazing that he had almost gasped. But it was nothing compared to what followed, when her pussy began vigorously and methodically gliding back and forth along his dick, creating a mind-altering sensation that defied description.

Needless to say, Shade had fucked in the missionary position before. More to the point, all of those girls had been active participants – they had lifted their hips, gotten into the rhythm, and so on. That said, Yoni was in a class by herself. Her body had a suppleness and flexibility that was damn near unnatural, so that the movements of her hips and pelvis – and more specifically, her pussy – were unlike anything he had ever experienced. Add to that the fact that she was wrapped around him like a boa constrictor and was starting to buck like a fucking bronco, and it was safe to say that, sexually, Shade felt like he was on the verge of a new frontier. However, it would

172

be a short-lived adventure if he didn't get things under control. Basically, if he couldn't get his partner to slow the fuck down – literally – he was going to shoot his load in record time.

With his face still nuzzling Yoni's neck, Shade reached down with both hands and gripped her ass. It was a bit like trying to grab a jackhammer that was already going at full throttle, but he managed it. He then physically began trying to slow the manic cadence of her hips and pelvis.

Initially, she wasn't responsive; she seemed solely intent on extracting a fierce, deep dicking from him. After a few seconds, though, she appeared to catch on and deliberately slowed the pace of her exertions, while also loosening the death-grip her arms and legs had on him. It was only at that point that Shade mentally relaxed a little. Yoni was still working her pussy in an incredible fashion, but at least now it was at a manageable rhythm, which he was able to match.

That said, it wasn't long before the fucking started feeling way too good – a fact that Shade later attributed to the uncanny movement of Yoni's all-too-limber pussy. The way she worked that shit was damn near mystical, and in almost no time at all their tempo increased dramatically and he found himself right back where he'd been just a short time earlier: practically on the cusp of cumming.

Likewise, Yoni was also at the brink. As far as she was concerned, the sex was off the fucking hook – even after Shade forcefully changed their momentum. Every stroke was ecstasy; every bump of their crotch and groin was bliss. And when they started speeding up again, with Shade thrusting harder and faster, it was damn near euphoria.

Yoni came as she had before – hard and fast, with the same whimpering sound and spasmodic hip thrusts that had accompanied her earlier orgasm. Shade came with her, audibly groaning in elation as he released his load before practically collapsing on top of her.

He simply lay there for a moment, breathing heavily and gathering his strength. Then, just as he rose up and prepared to roll off her, an unexpected sensation caused him to draw in a sharp breath and shudder all over.

Yoni's pussy – moving in conjunction with the convulsive motion of her hips – had once again gobbled up his dick. Now it was sliding up and down the length of his rod once more, as if attempting to draw out every last drop of cum before releasing him.

Somewhere in the back of his mind, Shade recognized that the spastic hip motion was an involuntary reaction on Yoni's part. It was her tell – a surefire indication that she had cum. Some women screamed when they climaxed, some clawed your back… Yoni, apparently, just continued fucking your brains out.

As if in proof of this, conscious thought didn't even exist for Shade at the moment, having been completely overridden by tactile sensation. In short, having just orgasmed, every nerve ending in his dick was still tingling – damn near on fire! – which made what Yoni was doing feel so fucking exquisite that he couldn't even think. Thus, he simply stayed there, rhapsodically groaning, until Yoni's pelvic thrusts ended – at which point he collapsed on top of her again.

THUG LIFE: EMANCIPATED

Chapter 37

Shade awoke to the sound of a door closing. His eyes snapped open, and for a moment he didn't know where he was; then he saw Yoni – still naked – walking towards the bed and everything came back to him: after her pussy had finally finished draining his dick, he had rolled off her. Apparently he had then fallen asleep, but didn't think he'd been out for more than a few minutes.

As Yoni got into bed, he could hear water running somewhere in the apartment. He recognized the sound as that of a toilet tank refilling, and assumed that Yoni had just come from the bathroom. Now in bed, she cozied up next to him, laying her head on his shoulder as he put an arm around her. Neither of them immediately spoke, instead, they both just stared up at the ceiling, lost in their individual thoughts.

"Well, that was definitely worth the wait," Yoni said after a few moments. "I was startin' to thank yo ass was gay."

Shade's head jerked in her direction. "Huh?"

"Nigga, I been tryin' to get yo attention for weeks," she explained. "Didn't you notice all the tight-ass shit I was wearin' to school every day?"

Shade shrugged. "Bitches wear tight-ass shit all the time. How am I s'posed to know you doin' it for my benefit?"

"Most niggas see a chick in some shit that look good on her, they don't care whose benefit it's for – they gone step to dat bitch."

"Well, maybe I wasn't interested."

Yoni gave him a disheartened look. "And I thought we were past all that."

"Okay, fine," he grumbled. "I was interested, but you done had a million pussy hounds sniffin' 'round since the minute you moved back. I got enough shit goin' on without havin' to compete with a bunch of knuckleheads over a girl, no matter how pretty she is."

"So," she purred, "you think I'm pretty." Shade rolled his eyes in faux annoyance, causing her to giggle. "Still, it's disappointin' that a lil' competition scared you off."

"I ain't scared of competition," he countered. "But most bitches in the hood don't go for a nigga like me." He paused for a moment, and then continued. "I'm not some dopeboy tryin' to come up in the game. I ain't got aspirations of makin' it as a pro baller. I'm not spendin' all my cash tryin' to make some rap demo tape." Shade looked her in the eye, and then went on. "I'm a brutha who makes straight-A's in school. I'm takin' community college courses to try to get ahead. I work odd jobs as a handyman to earn cash."

"Damn, nigga – you sound like a complete square," Yoni noted. "Except you left out the part where you pimp out women."

Shade gave her a sidewise look. "I ain't no pimp. I just help some girls out from time to time."

"Fine. We'll leave 'Pimpin'' off yo résumé. You obviously got other shit goin' on, though, but I guess you want everybody thankin' you a square, for some reason. But that's okay – some girls like squares." As she finished speaking, she took the arm he hand around her and brought his hand up to her lips, then kissed it.

"Some girls *do*," Shade agreed. "At least for a hot minute. But shit changes when yo best friend's man is taking her to a Kanye concert, and I'm askin' you to go see *Shakespeare in the Park* for free."

Yoni snickered at that. "Well, maybe you just ain't met the right girl yet." Shade merely shrugged. "Anyway, as far as competition goes, I guess you got braggin' rights: the first one to tap that new-chick ass."

"Ha!" Shade blurted out. "Who da fuck would I brag to? I don't really hang out with anybody."

"So you one of those lone wolf muhfuckas."

"I guess. I mean, there are people I'm friendly with and know well enough to ask for a favor if I need it, but nobody I go out and party with, or get together with to try to watch the game on Sunday."

"Well, I'll watch the game wichu," Yoni declared with a smile.

"Cool. Just let me know when you wanna come over," Shade stated. "Or is that just another tease?"

"Tease?" she repeated quizzically.

"Yeah. You been teasin' me since I bumped into you in the hallway. When you offered me lunch, when you got me to ask for yo number, when we was on the couch just now and you told me to leave…all damn day.

Yoni seemed to consider for a moment. "Yeah, I guess I have been teasin' you a lil'."

"A lil'?" Shade uttered skeptically.

"Okay, maybe more than a lil'. But just so you know, I only tease guys I like."

She gave him a wink then that made him smile. A moment later, however, he frowned and then squirmed a little.

Noticing how he was fidgeting, Yoni asked, "What is it?"

"Sommin's pokin' me. I didn't really notice it at first, but I feel it now."

As he spoke, he reached behind him with his free hand, towards his lower back. A moment later, he drew it back and then held up the offending item: Yoni's other titty tassel.

"Damn," she muttered, taking the tassel from him and then rolling onto her side, facing him. "I forgot all about this fuckin' thang. I ain't even notice when it came off."

"Me neither," Shade added, rolling onto his side as well and facing her. "But I thank the other one's still in yo livin' room."

"Oh?" Yoni droned, sounding skeptical. "I ain't thank you noticed."

Shade looked at her in surprise. "Da fuck make you thank I wouldn't notice sommin' like that?"

"Because I'm next to you on the couch, bare tit exposed, and you just sittin' there like a muhfuckin' statue. I said to myself, 'This nigga *must* be gay,' but I figured I'd give you one last shot."

"We just left a party where you got paid to strip," Shade argued. "So I assumed you wasn't modest 'bout shit like that – that takin' off yo top was like other folks takin' off gloves."

"Lemme give you a piece of advice, and you should prolly write this shit down," Yoni told him. "If you alone with a bitch and she show you her titties, she thankin' that either you gone grab them muhfuckas, or you gay."

"I'm not sure that's true," Shade countered. "'Cause this bitch showed me her titties in the Champagne Room one time, so I grabbed 'em. But then she slapped me and started screamin' 'bout me touchin' her. Next thang I know, this huge fuckin' bouncer came rushin' in and did a suplex on my ass. And then–"

"Stop!" ordered Yoni, who at that point was freely laughing at Shade's anecdote. "Just stop."

She continued giggling for a moment and Shade just watched her, smiling. He liked seeing her laugh.

"Anyway," Yoni said after a moment, "you actually the first one to see my girls in all they glory tonight."

"Huh?" Shade muttered in confusion.

"The titty tassels," Yoni explained. "I never took 'em off at Lord Byron's party."

Shade gave her a dubious look. "So you didn't fuck anybody tonight and really didn't strip."

"I took my top off, but with the tassels on nobody saw my nipples or anythang."

"So how you make so much money tonight?"

"By charmin' the audience." Noting that Shade responded to this with a befuddled expression, Yoni continued. "At its core, strippin' ain't about gettin' naked. It's about entertainment."

Shade shook his head in confusion. "You lost me."

Yoni seemed to contemplate for a moment. "You ever heard of Gypsy Rose Lee?"

"I don't think so."

"She was an old school burlesque star. Back in the nineteen-forties and fifties, she was the most famous stripper in the world. She made around ten grand a week. That's like, a hundred kay today."

"Damn," Shade muttered. "That's drug lord money."

"Yeah, but the thang is, she rarely ever stripped all the way down. Matter of fact, she would take thirty, forty-five minutes just to take a fuckin' glove off."

"And that was worth ten thousand a week?"

"Yeah, because Gypsy knew the secret of how to keep muhfuckas captivated. As she put it, it's not how *much* you take off – it's *how* you take it off. In other words…"

She trailed off, but Shade picked up on what she'd left unsaid. "She was entertainin'."

"Exactly."

"And that's what you did tonight," Shade surmised, remembering how Yoni's comments had kept the niggas at the party in stitches. "How long you been using that act?"

She gave him a petulant look. "How you know tonight wasn't my first time?"

"'Cause you obviously been on the pole b'foe. I mean, you knew 'bout the garter and rubber band for ya money."

Yoni was quiet for a moment, then said. "When we moved away, things were good for a long time. Well, good if you don't count my momma takin' off because my daddy couldn't keep his dick in his pants."

"Shit," Shade mumbled. "Sorry."

Yoni simply shrugged in a *that's-life* kind of way, then went on. "Anyway, a few years back, my daddy lost his job. Shit got tight, and I thought I could help out with our cash flow problem."

"By strippin'," Shade concluded. "How old were you."

"Fourteen."

Shade stared at her, incredulity stamped on his face. "And somebody hired you at the age?"

"Fake ID, muhfuhcka," Yoni explained.

"But don't you need a permit or some shit like that?"

"In some states you do, but they only had an age requirement where I was. And the niggas runnin' strip clubs don't give a fuck 'bout yo actual age, long as you look old enough when you on stage."

"And I'm guessin' that in no time at all you became the number one attraction."

"I wish," Yoni stated. "I ain't know shit about bein' on the pole – plus I was nervous – so my strip routine was shit. Niggas watched me on stage, but nobody was gettin' excited about the shit I was doin' – stumblin' around in five-inch heels and then takin' my top off. I could barely get niggas to pay for a lap dance."

"What was your stage name?"

"Thumbelina. I thought it sounded cute, and it was different than "Bambi,' 'Star,' 'Jade,' and all the other stale, unoriginal names that strippers always use."

"Thumbelina," Shade repeated. "I like it."

"Well, those other hoes actually called me *Stumble*-lina because of the way I was always flounderin' 'round on stage."

"So what happened? I mean, you obviously got better."

"What happened was that after about a week, the owner told me that I was fuckin' terrible at strippin'. He said he'd give me one more night, but he'd have to let me go if I couldn't give him a reason to keep me on. He was anglin' for some pussy, but no way was I fuckin' his old ass – he was like, fifty!"

"So what did you do?"

"I just decided that if I was gettin' fired, it wasn't gonna be because I couldn't perform some shitty striptease to some other muhfucka's satisfaction. If I was goin' out, it was gonna be doin' sommin' I loved."

"*Ori Tahiti*," Shade concluded.

"Yeah," Yoni confirmed with a nod. "So I told the DJ what I needed him to play, kicked those ugly-ass pumps off, then went out there and did my thang."

"Let me guess: those niggas loved it."

"That's puttin' it mildly," Yoni told him. "Niggas went fuckin' bananas – screamin', shoutin', and throwin' mo' money on the stage in ten minutes than I had made in a fuckin' week."

She paused for a moment, then went on. "You wanna know what was really funny, though? I got so into the music, that I never even took my top off. I didn't even strip, and still had those muhfuckas makin' it rain."

"And that's when you had yo 'A-ha,' moment," Shade assumed.

Yoni nodded. "I realized it wasn' just about strippin'. If it was just 'bout being naked, niggas wudda been throwin' money on stage every time I showed my tits. But I hadn't even taken shit off and cash was flowin' like a river. I knew then

181

that strippin' was secondary. The primary thing niggas wanted was to be entertained."

"And Gypsy Rose Yoni was born."

"Sommin' like that," she stated, grinning. "After that, my routine was strictly *Ori Tahiti*. A week later, I was making mo' money than any other bitch up in there."

"And you never had to strip?"

Yoni shook her head. "Naw. Sometimes, just to mix things up, I'd wear some titty tassels and take my top off, but niggas didn't seem to care either way – not even when they paid for a lap dance, and I charged an arm and a leg for that."

"What did the other strippers thank?"

"Bitches be hatin'," Yoni declared a little angrily. "They got mad that I was suddenly the number-one attraction, so one of 'em broke into my locker, stole my student ID, and showed it to the owner. After that, with the proof shoved in his face that I was underage, he had to let me go."

"That's fucked up. Right when you started makin' money, too."

Yoni nodded in agreement. "I admit I was pissed, but it didn't take me long to get hired at another club – 'cept this time, I knew what to do. I started off with my Tahiti dancin' and pretty much had niggas throwin' they whole paycheck at me by the end of the first night. But it didn't last long."

"What happened?"

"Same shit as the first club: jealous bitches. One of 'em found out my real age, told the manager, and he gave my ass the boot."

"How long did you work at *that* one?" Shade asked.

"About a week. After they let me go, I got on at a third club, but that only lasted about a day before somebody ratted me out again. After that, the word was pretty much out and I was basically blacklisted. And that was essentially the end of my strip club career."

"So no mo' easy money," Shade deduced.

"Not exactly," Yoni stated. "I started gettin' hired to do private parties – shit like Lord Byron's shindig."

"And they didn't care about yo age?"

"Assumin' they knew, these were private parties – not strip clubs – so it wasn't like cops were gone be raidin' those muhfuckas and chargin' the owner for havin' minors on the premises. Even if that did happen, the people throwin' the party would just say, 'I don't know that hoe. She musta just showed up with somebody. How's it my fault if the bitch just start takin' off her clothes?'"

She spoke that last part in a faux masculine voice that made Shade chuckle.

"Anyway," Yoni went on, "workin' those parties let me perfect my routine."

"So you figured out what worked and what didn't it terms of keepin' niggas entertained."

Yoni nodded. "I also heard just about every vulgar fuckin' comment you can imagine, and came up with comebacks for all that shit."

"I think I saw some of that tonight," Shade noted, reflecting on how Yoni had kept a room full of niggas at Byron's party completely beguiled with retorts and witticisms. But that suddenly brought up another point that he initially thought to avoid, but then decided to address head on.

"That reminds me of sommin' else," he continued. "At one point tonight I saw you comin' from Byron's bedroom."

Yoni lowered her eyes. "Okay, I have a confession to make. I lied earlier: I did fuck one guy tonight."

Struggling to keep his face passive, Shade simply stated in a monotone voice, "Like I said before, it's none of my business."

Yoni looked at him with a doe-like expression. "But it was only the one, I promise."

"Again, not my business."

"You don't wanna know who it was?"

Shade shrugged. "I'm assumin' Lord Byron, but – Oww!"

He yelped slightly as Yoni punched him – not really powerful enough to be painful, but hard enough to get his attention.

"Listen very carefully," she instructed. "I fucked *one* guy tonight." As she finished speaking, she looked him up and down.

"Yeah, I heard you the first–" he began, then his eyebrows shot up as he said, "Oooohhh…"

"Took you long enough," Yoni announced in mock anger as Shade suddenly smiled at her. "I got everybody in the hood tellin' me how smart you are, but damn if I see it."

"In case you didn't know, 'smart' is a low fuckin' bar around here," Shade said, still grinning. "Anyway, if you didn't bang Byron, what were you doin' in his bedroom?"

"Oh, he tried to get a taste – asked me what my price was."

Intrigued, Shade asked, "What did you say?"

"I told him I didn't know, but I'll know it when I hear it."

"I take it you didn't hear it from him."

"Nope, so he ended up settlin' for a lap dance, but that shit cost him a pretty penny."

"I saw yo stack, so I'm sure he's not the only one."

Yoni smiled. "What can I say? I know how to entertain."

"Well, considerin' how much money you made tonight, I'm startin' to wish I'd learned to shake *my* ass like that," Shade quipped, causing her to giggle. "But I'm sho' yo grandmomma would want you usin' what she taught you to get *out* the hood, not entertain niggas *in* it."

"I wouldn't bet on that," Yoni advised. "My grandmomma loved the hood."

Shade just stared at her for a moment, then blurted out, "You fuckin' kiddin', right?"

"No," Yoni insisted, shaking her head. "You have to unnastand – my grandmomma was from a poor island. She grew up with ten bruthas and sistas in a fuckin' two-room mud hut with no A-C or indoor plummin'. Compared to that, livin' conditions in the ghetto are like fuckin' paradise."

"I guess so," Shade concurred.

"Anyway, my granddaddy was in the military when they met. When he got out and brought her home with him, she thought she'd been rescued by Prince Charmin', even though he'd just brought her to the hood."

"So, did she teach yo momma how to dance like that, too?"

Yoni's eyes narrowed. "How you know it ain't my *daddy's* momma that I'm talkin' 'bout?"

"'Cause I remember yo momma, and she was a redbone. You daddy, on the other hand, had a complexion like burnt toast."

"Fuck you," Yoni muttered, snickering. "My daddy ain't that dark."

"Speakin' of which," Shade said, "do I need to leave?"

Yoni frowned. "Huh?"

"Yo daddy," Shade explained. "I don't thank it's a good idea for him to catch us like this."

"Oh, so now that you done hit that shit, you ready to run out on a bitch. Is that it?"

Recognizing that she was joking, Shade said, "Yo shit was whack. I just wanna get outta here and find a bitch who can really put it on me tonight."

"Keep talkin' shit," Yoni warned him. "Next time, I'm gone make yo ass beg for it."

Shade raised an eyebrow. "So there's gonna be a next time?"

"Don't get cocky, nigga," Yoni told him. "Anyway, as to my daddy, you don't have to worry 'bout him. I don't expect him home tonight."

"You sure? 'Cause I ain't lookin' to get shot. I already had that experience, and it ain't worth repeatin'."

As he finished speaking, Yoni appeared to notice his scars for the first time. Gingerly, she reached out and touched one that seemed to stretch across his abs.

"It happened a long time ago," he volunteered before she could ask.

"How old were you?"

"Six."

Yoni got the impression that there was more to the story, but sensed that Shade didn't want to talk about it at the moment. Withdrawing her hand, she returned to the subject at hand, telling him, "Anyway, like I was sayin', my daddy's out for the night."

"Okay, but don't you have a brutha?"

Rather than respond, Yoni just stared at him for a moment with a stunned expression on her face. Unsure of what had happened, Shade went on. "I think his name was Ben or Brian or–"

"Bo," Yoni interjected. "His name's Bo."

Shade nodded. "Yeah, Bo. I wouldn't want him catchin' us either."

"He's not here," Yoni informed him. "He didn't make the move with us. He knocked up some girl back home – our *old* home – and decided to stay and help take care of the baby. He's eighteen and grown now, so it's his decision, so only me and my daddy moved back here."

"Okay," Shade droned. "For a second there when I mentioned him, you looked like you didn't know what I was talkin' about."

"You just caught me off guard," Yoni admitted, then was silent for a few seconds. "See, I had another brother. He died."

"I'm sorry," Shade said in consolation. "I don't remember him."

"He had a different momma – some hoe my daddy used to fuck around with – but he was about our age."

"Were you close?"

"Yeah, believe it or not. After my momma took off, he used to come spend summers with us."

"What happened to him?"

"He got caught up in some drug shit. To be honest, though, he had no business bein' in the game. He didn't have a gangsta personality or a hustla mentality. He ended up owin' some bad muhfuckas a lot of money, and it looks like they took that shit outta his hide."

"Do the cops know who did it?"

She shook her head. "Naw, but those muhfuckas seem braindead half the time – don't have a clue what the fuck's goin' on. Plus, if they thank drugs involved, how hard you thank they really lookin'? And if they can't tie it to drugs, they just say, 'Wrong place, wrong time,' like that settles everythang."

Shade didn't say anything, but felt her words reflected his own experience with the police.

"But you wanna know what was really fucked up 'bout my brother gettin' killed?" Yoni continued. "He did it to help *us* – to get money for us 'cause my daddy was outta work. So now my daddy feel responsible 'bout what happened to him and spends all his time drinkin'. That's how I know he won't be home. And if he does show up, he'll be blind drunk and won't remember anythang he saw or heard."

As she finished speaking, something dawned on Shade: Yoni's situation with her dad was much like the one that he and his sisters had with Gin. She had a parent in name only; she was basically alone and fending for herself – doing whatever it took to survive.

Suddenly feeling protective of her, Shade reached out and put an arm around Yoni, then drew her in close. Snuggling in next to him, she put her arm around him, returning the embrace.

THUG LIFE: EMANCIPATED

Chapter 38

Shade woke up the next morning to someone incessantly ringing the doorbell. He groaned in irritation, as the visitor had interrupted a dream he was having of Yoni. As he rolled out of bed and wiped the sleep from his eyes, he spent a moment reflecting on the previous night.

Despite Yoni's assurance that it was okay, he hadn't stayed over. Although tempted, he didn't like the idea of leaving Nissa and Cherry by themselves. (Plus, they kind of had an unwritten rule about staying over in situations like that – basically, don't do it.) Thus, after snuggling for a while, Shade had reluctantly gotten dressed and gone home. Yoni had seen him to the door, but – as if trying to entice him to stay – hadn't bothered to put on a stitch of clothing. Moreover, as he left, she had brazenly stepped into the hallway in all her glory and told him, "You better fuckin' call me."

A smile came to his lips as he remembered the way she looked standing there naked. Fortunately, there had been no one in the hallway at the time, but Shade doubted that would have been a hindrance to Yoni.

However, before he could give any more thought to the subject, their visitor decided to alternate between ringing the bell and pounding on the door. Glancing at his watch, he saw that it was still early – after sunrise, but still early. *Too* fucking early to be honest, and on a Sunday morning at that.

Somebody better be dying, Shade thought as he popped a stick of gum in his mouth. And then it occurred to him that his thought might be prescient – maybe even prophetic. *Shit. Gin…*

Swiftly throwing on a pair of sweats and a t-shirt, he headed to the door, passing his sisters in the hallway. Like him, they had apparently been awakened by whoever was at the door. He could see the concern in their eyes, but basically just gestured that they should stay back and stay quiet – which is what they were going to do anyway.

Rather than go directly to the door, Shade went to the living room window that faced the front of the house. Peeking out through a crack in the blinds, he saw a cop outside. He was in plain clothes, but had a demeanor that Shade would have identified as law enforcement, even if he hadn't been wearing a badge on a chain around his neck.

Shade took a deep breath. After Gin's numerous overdoses over the years – as well as run-ins with the law and physical altercations with other junkies – he had long-expected someone to come knocking on their door at an ungodly hour to say that their mother was dead. Maybe it had finally happened. Then he frowned as something began nagging at him.

Basically, the cop outside had seemed familiar for some reason. Peeking out again, Shade looked the guy over again and then it clicked: it was the cop he'd glimpsed in the unmarked police car the previous day. The one that had given him a bad fucking vibe. He had only seen him for a second or two, but Shade was pretty sure it was the same guy. (He also noted what looked like the same cop car parked at the curb in front of their house.)

Shade spent a moment concentrating as the cop continued pounding on the door and ringing the bell. Sensing movement, he looked towards the hallway and saw Nissa starting to walk towards him, with Cherry behind her.

Shade motioned then back, then mouthed "Five-O" at Nissa.

His sister simply nodded, then led Cherry back to the hallway. Shade took a moment to collect his thoughts, then stepped to the door and unlocked it. At the sound of the lock being thrown the officer ceased ringing the bell and knocking, and a moment later Shade opened the door.

THUG LIFE: EMANCIPATED

Chapter 39

The officer seemed to size him up for a moment as Shade stepped outside and closed the door behind him. Shade knew what he was doing: assessing the likelihood that Shade had a weapon on him, among other things.

"Joshua Green?" the cop asked after a few seconds. He phrased it as a question, but it was pretty clear he already knew who he was talking to.

"Yes, sir," Shade answered in his most articulate tone. "How can I help you, officer?"

"It's 'Detective,' actually," the cop replied. "Detective Gummerson, but most folks call me 'Gummy.' I was hopin' to ask you some questions about a case I'm workin' on."

"Of course. Happy to do whatever I can to help law enforcement."

That statement earned him a dubious look from Gummy, but rather than comment on it, the detective simply said, "Any chance we can talk inside?"

"Unfortunately, my sisters are asleep and I wouldn't want to wake them up." It was a blatant prevarication on Shade's part, given the pounding the door had received (as well as the way the doorbell had been abused), but the detective seemed to take it in stride.

"Fair enough," Gummy noted. "Anyway, you may have heard sommin' about some bodies being found in an abandoned buildin' a few weeks back. You know anything about that?"

"Not to be flip, sir, but bodies in abandoned buildings aren't that unusual in this part of town. Could you be more specific?"

"Three bodies found in a condemned high-rise. Two bangers named Glen Simon and Chris Little, and a kid named William Waddell – went by Sneak."

"Yes, sir," Shade said with a nod. "I know what you're talking about now."

"Do you know anything about it?"

"About the bodies?" Shade inquired, giving the detective a look of surprise. "No, sir."

"Did you know any of the deceased?"

"Not really."

"So what does that mean – 'not really'?"

"I knew Glen Simon by reputation," Shade explained, "but only because his brother is Zerk Simon. If you don't know that name–"

"I know who Zerk is," Gummy interjected. "Local drug dealer."

Shade gave a short nod, then continued. "Anyway, I don't think I knew the other gang member you mentioned – something Little."

"*Chris* Little," Gummy clarified. "What about the last one – Sneak. Did you know him?"

"Only in passing."

"So you and he weren't buddies…didn't hang out or anything?"

Shade shook his head. "No, sir. I didn't even know his name was William."

"Well, that's funny, because a couple of witnesses say they saw you two talkin' maybe a day or so before he got killed."

That was a flat-out lie, but Gummy wasn't really concerned about that. Hell, cops lied to suspects all the time, trying to get them to own up to shit. In this instance, he was simply trying to see how Shade would react.

"It's possible that he asked me for a quote about repairing something," Shade said after appearing to concentrate for a few moments.

"It's possible, or it actually happened?"

"I don't have a specific recollection of it, but people ask me things like that all the time."

"So you're sayin' that you never talked to him around the time he died."

"No, sir - not that I recall," Shade assured him. "Sorry I couldn't be of more help."

"No problem. I appreciate your time," Gummy said. Then, as Shade prepared to go back inside, he uttered, "Oh, wait. There is one other thing."

"Yes, sir?" Shade replied.

"You mentioned repairin' stuff a minute ago. What did you mean by that?"

"I do odd jobs for cash, mostly repair work."

"On what types of things? We talkin' cars, boats, what?"

"Some of that, but mostly household items – appliances and things of that nature."

"Hmmm," Gummy droned. "So if you fix appliances, you must know sommin' about electricity and wirin'."

"Yes, sir."

"So you do any electrical work?'

"Yes sir, but I'm not licensed."

"What about plumbin'?"

"Yes, sir. But again, I'm not licensed."

"Still, that's impressive. How'd you learn all that?"

"My grandfather taught me. Before he passed."

"Sorry to hear that," Gummy declared. "Anyway, even if you're not licensed, I assume you got all the tools you need for the jobs you do."

"Yes, sir."

"So for electrical work, I'm guessin' you got things like insulated tools, wire strippers, and a volt meter."

"Multimeter," Shade offered.

Gummy frowned. "I'm sorry – what was that?"

"I use a multimeter instead of a voltmeter. It's a more versatile tool. But yes, sir – I have all of that and more for electrical work."

"And what about plumbin'? I s'pose you've got things like a torque wrench, faucet key, pipe cutters, and so on."

"Yes, sir. All of that is standard plumbing paraphernalia."

"So you have them?"

"Yes, sir."

"Great," Gummy noted. "Any chance I could take a look at them?"

"Uh, sure," Shade replied. "Any particular reason why?"

"Well, it turns out that the forensics team found tool marks on some equipment in that buildin' where we found the bodies, and also on some items near the deceased."

"Tool marks?" Shade repeated quizzically.

"Yeah," Gummy confirmed, taking a folded piece paper out of his back pocket. As he opened it up, he began reading. "Let's see…'Analysis confirms marks consistent with the following tools used in plumbing: torque wrench, pipe cutters, pipe wrench…' blah, blah, blah."

As he finished, the detective held the paper up for Shade to see. Scanning it quickly, Shade noted that it looked like some kind of report, and it did indeed contain a list of plumbing equipment (some of which the detective had just rattled off) with a circle drawn around them.

After a few seconds, Gummy drew back the hand holding the report. As he began to fold and put the piece of paper away he said, "Just to be clear, I'm not accusin' you of anything. It's just that witnesses have said you carry around a tool bag and that you also do plumbin' work. Basically, I wouldn't be doin' my job if I didn't check it out. You understand that, right?"

"Yes, sir," Shade stated.

"Good. So if I can just see those, I'll be on my way."

"They're in the garage," Shade told him, pointing towards that part of the house. "I'll go let it up and you can take a look at them."

As he finished speaking, Shade turned to go back in the house, but the cop's voice brought him up short.

"Honestly," Gummy said, causing Shade to turn back towards him, "it's probably easier if I just go through the house with you."

Shade shook his head. "Like I said before, I prefer not to disturb my sisters."

Then, without waiting for further commentary or acknowledgement from the cop, he went back inside and locked the door.

Chapter 40

Once inside, Shade headed to his room, which – despite what he'd told the cop – was actually where his tool bag was. As he suspected, his sisters were near the living room window when he came in; clearly they'd been peeking out and eavesdropping, which obviated the need to tell them what was going on.

Once he retrieved the tool bag, Shade went towards the kitchen. As he passed through the living room, he motioned for his sisters to stay where they were. Their kitchen connected to a small utility room, which in turn had a door leading to the garage, and that's where Shade found himself a few seconds later. After going into the garage, he closed the door behind him.

Aside from light around the perimeter of the external garage door, the place was dark. Shade reached for a light switch on a nearby wall and flicked it on, causing a single bulb in the center of the ceiling to bathe the area in light. Now able to see, he took a quick look around.

As usual, the garage was full of sundry items – so many that it was impossible to park the car inside. In addition to a workbench that was against one wall, there were several stepladders, some saw horses, and other tools Shade used in his work. Paint cans of various sizes were also scattered around, as were a couple of old metal toolboxes. There were even some planks of lumber and a small pallet of bricks.

That said, a good number of the garage's holdings were concealed beneath several broad expanses of tarp and drop cloth. Among the equipment thus covered were an assortment of power tools and a generator that Shade used when they occasionally lost power in the winter. The hope, of course, was that with the bulk of the items in the garage covered, there was little to catch the eye of a potential thief should such a person be in the vicinity when the garage was up. Presumably it worked, because they hadn't been burgled in a while, but that might also have stemmed from the fact that the last guy who tried it ended up having a bad fucking day.

Smiling as he remembered what had happened to the would-be burglar, Shade set his tool bag on the workbench. He then headed to the external garage door, which was a common model comprised of sectional panels. Unfortunately, they did not have a garage door opener, so he had to unlock it and lift it by hand.

It was only the work of a few seconds to roll the door up overhead. At that moment, Shade noticed that Detective Gummerson – whom he'd expected to be standing front and center in the driveway – was actually standing off to the side, near the edge of the garage. With one hand resting on his sidearm, the cop eyed Shade studiously for a moment.

Obviously, the man was no fool. For all he knew, Shade could have been holding a shotgun when the garage door went up and used it to saw him in half. Ergo, he had picked a strategic position from which he could see the garage go up, but without making himself an easy target if things went sideways. Now noting that everything was kosher, the detective stepped forward.

"I'll get the tools," Shade announced casually before turning and walking towards the workbench. However, he'd only taken a step or two before he heard something unusual – an odd sound like the call of a bird, but one that he'd never heard before. It had come from just outside the garage and was bizarre enough to make him to glance over his shoulder in curiosity.

Behind him, he saw nothing out of the ordinary. In fact, the cop was just standing there watching Shade like he hadn't heard a thing. That seemed surprising, but not worth making an issue out of, so Shade continued walking to the workbench. Grabbing his tool bag, he marched back to the detective.

"Here you go," Shade said, holding out the tool bag.

As the cop extended a hand to take it, Shade caught movement with his peripheral vision near the edge of the garage – not where the detective had previously been standing, but the opposite side. Immediately looking in that direction, he saw another plainclothes cop – also identifiable by the badge around his neck – walking towards him.

Shade turned his attention back to Gummerson, giving him an inquisitive look.

"My partner," Gummerson explained, inclining his head towards the new arrival. "Detective Blanchard."

At that moment, several things clicked into place in Shade's mind. First of all, he immediately understood that the new detective, Blanchard, hadn't just shown up out of nowhere. The man had been at the rear of the house, presumably there to make sure no one tried to slip out the back. And the weird bird call? That had been Gummerson, giving the all-clear signal and telling his partner to join him.

Those thoughts and more were flitting through Shade's brain when he suddenly realized that Blanchard had spoken to him and was extending a hand his direction.

Assuming that the man had introduced himself, Shade reached out and shook his hand, saying, "Nice to meet you."

While Shade and Blanchard were introducing themselves, Gummy, had spent a moment looking over the tool bag. It was a bit heavier than he'd anticipated, constructed out of some kind of tough canvas material, and was roughly rectangular in shape. It had no zipper running down the middle as one might expect, but instead had zippers running lengthwise on both sides.

Setting the tool bag on the ground, Gummy dropped down to his haunches. Next, he took a few seconds to unzip each side of the bag and take a look inside. Seemingly satisfied that it did indeed contain tools, he zipped it back up before rising to his feet.

"So," Gummy droned, hefting the tool bag. "These are all your tools?"

"Well, not *all* of them," Shade countered before gesturing to the rest of the garage behind him. "As you can see, I actually own a fair amount of equipment, but pretty much everything I use on a daily basis is in the bag."

"That should be good enough," Gummy attested. "We'll get 'em back to you as soon as possible."

"Excuse me?" Shade muttered, not hiding his surprise. "You're taking them?"

"Yeah," Gummy affirmed with a nod. "The forensic guys need to check 'em out. It shouldn't take long, though – no more than a couple of days."

"But I've got jobs lined up, including today," Shade insisted. "I need them for my work."

"We can understand that," Blanchard chimed in. "How 'bout this? We'll put a rush on it – have Forensics do their thing within forty-eight hours. That way, it'll cost you no more than two days."

That didn't seem to satisfy Shade, who asked, "But don't you need a warrant in order to just take private property like that?"

There was silence for a moment, then Gummy confirmed, "You're absolutely right. Technically, we *do* need a warrant. But look, all we're tryin' to do is eliminate you as a suspect. If you make us go get a warrant, it's gonna look suspicious – like you got sommin' to hide."

Brow furrowed, Shade plainly contemplated this for a moment, then seemed to come to a decision. "Alright, that makes sense."

"Great," Gummy uttered. "So we'll get these checked out and get them right back to you."

With that, he turned to go, only to stop a moment later when Shade asked. "Do you want the receipts as well?"

The detectives shared a glance, and a moment later they both turned back towards Shade.

"Receipts?" Blanchard repeated, openly curious.

'Yes, sir," Shade stated with a nod. "All of those are brand new tools. Even the bag is new. I only got them a few weeks ago, so I still have receipts for everything."

"Everything?" Gummy echoed skeptically.

"Yes, sir," Shade declared. He then turned and began walking towards the workbench, indicating that the detectives should follow him, which they did.

When he reached the workbench, Shade opened a drawer on it and – moving slowly so as to not agitate his visitors – reached in and pulled out a mid-sized manila envelope. It was unsealed, so Shade opened it and took out the contents: a stack of receipts bound together with a paper clip, which he then held out towards the detectives.

Gummy, still holding the tool bag, frowned slightly as he stepped forward and took the proffered receipts with his free hand. He glanced at the one on top for a moment, then placed the tool bag on top of the workbench. Taking the paper clip off the receipts, he spent a few seconds flipping through them. He followed this up by unzipping one side of the toll bag, revealing a myriad of hand tools all sitting in various slots and pockets.

Pulling out what appeared to be a socket wrench, Gummy examined it for a moment, then began scanning the receipts. After maybe ten seconds, he seemed to find what he was looking for – proof of purchase for said socket wrench. Somewhat irritably, he put the socket wrench back and took out a pair of vise grips. As before, he looked through the receipts and, after a quick search, found those listed as well.

Gummy selected a few more tools, but each time was able to locate a receipt for the item in hand. (In fact, on two occasions, the tools still had price tags on them.) It wasn't definitive proof by any means, but Gummy couldn't deny the obvious conclusion: as Shade had indicated, all of the tools were new. More to the point, the dates on the receipts indicated that they were purchased *after* the estimated time of death of the trio found in the condemned building. In short, these tools weren't going to match the tools marks that Forensics had found.

Plainly frustrated, Gummy tossed the receipts onto the workbench and stepped away.

"So," Shade mused, "is it safe it assume that you aren't going to need my tools after all?"

"No, we won't need them," Gummy confirmed somewhat sharply. "Based on the purchase date, they couldn't have been used durin' the time frame that we're interested in."

"Then that's good news, right?" Shade suggested. "I'm eliminated as a suspect, *and* I avoid losing my tools for a couple of days."

"Yeah," Blanchard muttered flatly. "I'm glad it worked out for you."

Shade smiled. "So am I."

"Hmmm," Gummy droned. "That kind of begs the question, though: what happened to your *old* tools?"

"Oh," Shade muttered. "They were stolen."

Gummy and Blanchard looked at each other for a moment, then Blanchard asked, "So when did this happen?"

Shade appeared to reflect for a few seconds. "Maybe a day or two before I bought the new tools."

"I don't suppose you reported the theft?" Gummy inquired.

"Absolutely," Shade stressed. "I have a police report and everything. In fact, when I looked out this morning and saw your badge, I thought that's why you were here. But when I opened the door, I realized that you weren't the detective assigned to the case."

There was a slightly awkward silence after Shade's last statement. The detectives didn't seem to care for his response, although he had told the truth about filing a police report with respect to his old tools.

"Anyway," Shade continued, "I should get back inside to check on my sisters, so if there's nothing else…"

As he trailed off, the two detectives shared a look, then Gummy turned to him, saying, "No I believe that's all we need for now. Thanks for your help."

"No problem," Shade asserted, but he was talking to the cops' backs, as they had already turned and begun walking towards the garage entrance. Shade followed, intending to let the garage door back down after the two men left.

"Just to be clear," Gummy said over his shoulder to Shade, "we'll contact you if we have more–"

He suddenly stopped mid-sentence, eyes going wide as he seemed to take note of something off to the side. Curious, Shade followed the detective's gaze and then saw what had grabbed the cop's attention: over by the wall, sticking out from under part of a drop cloth that was covering some equipment, was a pair of bare feet.

Chapter 41

Shade couldn't see who they belonged to, but the feet themselves were scrawny and dirty, with cruddy yellow toenails that actually looked diseased. They were also heavily callused, like the person had never worn shoes in their life.

Shade noted all of this in just a second, but before he could turn back to the detective he felt cold, hard metal pressed to his temple.

"Don't fuckin' move!" Gummy hissed, holding his service weapon on Shade.

On his part, Shade did as ordered and stayed stock-still; he didn't even speak. The detective with the gun stepped to his rear, moving his gun to the back of Shade's head. Meanwhile, the other cop – Blanchard – moved swiftly towards the spot where the feet were located. Gingerly, he lifted the drop cloth, then seemed to draw in a breath.

"We got a body here," he said. "Female."

Shade suddenly felt the gun press harder as the detective holding it ordered, "Hands behind your back – now!"

As before, Shade silently complied with the command he was given, placing his hands behind him. A moment later, Blanchard stepped over and cuffed him while Gummy kept the gun at his head. After the cuffs were on, he felt the pressure from the gun ease up as Gummy holstered his weapon.

"I'll call it in," Blanchard remarked, pulling a cell phone from his pocket.

Gripping Shade's shoulders, Gummy spun him around.

"You got a weapon on you?" Gummy asked as he began frisking Shade.

"No, sir," Shade replied.

"Needles? Syringe? Any shit like that?"

"No, sir."

"Good. Now I'm gonna take a wild guess here and bet that you got no fuckin' clue who that is over there," Gummy chided, tilting his head to where Shade could still see the feet sticking out.

"Most likely my mother," Shade offered.

"Most likely?" Gummy echoed dubiously as he finished the pat-down. "You keepin' that many bodies in here, that you don't even know who they are?"

"No, sir. I don't keep any."

"Really?" Gummy growled. "Care to explain what *she's* doing out here, then?"

Shade shrugged. "Probably sleeping one off."

His statement seemed to catch Gummy by surprise; the cop just stared at him for a moment, frowning, then glanced at his partner. Blanchard, who had his cellphone up to his ear, had obviously been paying at least partial attention to the conversation, because he stopped speaking mid-sentence.

There was a wordless exchange between the two detectives, then Blanchard, speaking into the phone, said, "Standby on that mortuary transport. I'll call you back in a minute."

Ending the call, Blanchard put away his phone and then stepped back towards where he'd seen the body. Gummy took a few steps forward as well, grabbing Shade by the elbow and dragging him along.

From his vantage point, Shade still could only see feet sticking out. Blanchard, looking down, bent over and reached towards the body. He pulled his hand back a second later, holding up an angular, emaciated arm by the wrist.

"No rigor mortis," Blanchard noted out loud. "Track marks on the arm."

Still bent over, he then spent a few moments appearing to fumble with the wrist that he held. Watching him, Shade understood that he was trying to find a pulse. Suddenly, Blanchard turned towards Shade and Gummy, his eyes wide in surprise.

"Holy shit!" he exclaimed. "She's alive!"

Turning his attention back to the person whose arm he held, Blanchard softly said, "Miss? Miss? Are you okay?"

As he spoke, he gently pulled on the arm he held, thereby coaxing the person on the floor to rise into a sitting position. As Shade had suspected, it was Gin.

She looked a complete mess, starting with the fact that her hair was a wild bush at the moment. As Blanchard had observed, she had a medley of track marks on both arms, a number of which were inflamed and scabby. Her lips were dry, cracked, and peeling, while her eyes had black circles around them and were completely sunk in her head, giving her a rawboned and wasted – almost skeletal – appearance. All in all, she looked much like the corpse Blanchard had initially mistaken her for. (Add to that the fact that Gin often slept with her eyes half-open, and it was easy to see why someone would have assumed she was dead.)

"Your mother?" Gummy inquired casually.

"Yeah," Shade intoned.

Blanchard snapped his fingers in front of Gin's face, asking, "Miss, do you know where you are? Can you tell me your name?"

Although she seemed to be awake to some extent, Gin was obviously still out of it. She was thoroughly unfazed by Blanchard's questions and attempts to get her attention. Rather than respond, she simply looked around slowly like she was in some sort of stupor – until she set eyes on Shade. All of a sudden, she came out of whatever fugue state she'd been in. She spent a moment looking him up and down, then let out a snort of disgust.

Noting this, Blanchard gestured towards Shade and asked, "Ma'am, do you know this young man?"

"Yeah, I know 'im," Gin answered. "I gave birth to that sorry nigga." Turning her attention to Shade, she cackled, "Ha-ha! I see the law finally caught up to yo shifty ass. It's about time."

Shade's brow furrowed and he stiffened slightly at her words, but didn't say anything.

Gin eyed the two detectives for a moment, then muttered conspiratorially, "Hey, it's okay with me if y'all wanna shoot his black ass. I'll back you up – say he had a gun."

"Uh, that won't be necessary, ma'am," Gummy stated.

"Then what the fuck good are ya?" Gin angrily demanded.

Ignoring Gin's comment, Blanchard asked, "Are you okay ma'am? Do we need a doctor or–"

"I'm fuckin' fine," Gin grumbled. "But if you ain't gone shoot his ass just leave me the fuck alone."

With that, she marched angrily from the garage, still barefoot.

"I love you," Shade shouted at her retreating form. Gin responded by sticking her arm out behind her with the middle finger raised.

Seemingly undeterred, Shade asked, "Will you be home for dinner?"

Spinning around, Gin bellowed, "Fuck you!" at her son, then resumed walking away.

"That's the drugs talking," Shade stated, giving the detectives a forlorn look. "Any chance you can take these cuffs off now?"

THUG LIFE: EMANCIPATED

Chapter 42

"Okay, that was a new one on me," Blanchard declared as he and Gummy got back in their car. "I mean, I've seen some shitty parenting before, but I don't think anybody ever asked me to take out their kid."

"People say all kinds of shit when they're angry," Gummy responded, "and she's obviously pissed at *him*. But at the end of the day, almost every parent I know – especially mothers – will take a bullet for their kid. Even junkies."

Blanchard simply nodded at that. Obviously, neither detective had taken Gin seriously. Still, there was no doubt that she had made an impression.

"Anyway," Gummy continued, "she only said what she did to try to get her son riled up."

"I don't think it worked."

"No, he seems too cool for sommin' like that to faze him. Did you notice how he was all 'Yes,sir' and 'No,sir' the entire time – even when we had him cuffed?"

"When we took the bracelets off, too," Blanchard added.

"Yeah," Gummy murmured in agreement.

Most assholes would have been screaming about how they were going to sue the whole fucking police department if they had been in Shade's shoes. However, after the detectives took the cuffs off and apologized for the misunderstanding, Shade had essentially said it was water under the bridge.

"Well, we know one thing now," Blanchard said. "He doesn't rattle easily."

"Maybe, but I noticed sommin' else back there in the garage," Gummy stated. "His momma said sommin' about the law finally catchin' up to his 'shifty ass.' He kind of froze for a second then, like he was worried she would say more, but she didn't."

"Definitely sounds like he's into sommin'," Blanchard concluded. "But whatever he's doin', he's obviously smart enough to stay off the radar."

"And sharp enough to cover his tracks," Gummy added. "You think it's a coincidence that all his tools were 'stolen' around the time those fools ended up dead in that condemned buildin'?"

"It *is* a bit of a coinky-dink."

"It's more than that. Even if we found his old tools and the marks match up to what Forensics found, he's got a ready-made alibi now. He can just say the tools were stolen, so anybody could have used them in that buildin'."

"So he's got a leg up on us now," Blanchard noted. "You still like him for this triple-homicide?"

"I like him now more than ever," Gummy said. "And he obviously thinks he's smarter than us. That little act with the receipts was just too cute. He was ready for us on that one."

"So how you wanna play it?"

"I think we need to keep eyes on this kid," Gummy said.

"Surveillance?" Blanchard muttered in surprise. "On a Sunday, with no notice, and with the department already stretched thin."

"Well it can't be *us*. He knows us – knows this car."

Blanchard sat silently for a moment, then acquiesced. "Alright, we can try, but I'll be shocked if we can get anybody."

THUG LIFE: EMANCIPATED

Chapter 43

After the detectives left, Shade went inside and washed up properly – brushed his teeth, washed his face, etcetera – but then spent much of the morning brooding. A visit from the cops was rarely beneficial, although – aside from when they cuffed him – those two had been fairly congenial. But Shade wasn't fooled; they obviously considered him a "person of interest" with respect to their case. Ergo, aside from an occasionally random thought about Yoni, he spent the bulk of his time reflecting on their visit.

The only other thing Shade devoted any significant thought to during that time was Gin. In short, he wasn't sure how the fuck she had gotten into the garage. However, Gin had been sneaking in and out of that house since she was a teen. For all he knew, she might have been adept at picking the garage door lock. But the most likely explanation was also the simplest: Cherry had probably let her in.

Basically, no matter how shitty Gin was as a mother, his youngest sister always tried to be a good daughter. Thus, if Gin had knocked on the door, Cherry would probably have let her in. (And, showing strong presence of mind for once, Gin might have gone to the garage to avoid potential confrontation. Or to shoot up.)

Nevertheless, despite his suspicions, he hadn't confronted Cherry about it. She was a good kid, and she still had faith that, deep down inside of Gin, there was a decent mother struggling to get out. In Shade's opinion, she'd figure out the truth over time on her own, in much the same way that kids eventually discover the truth about Santa Claus. Therefore, although he had told his sisters what had happened in the garage, he hadn't made an issue out of Gin's presence there.

Thankfully, as the morning wore on, Shade was eventually able to put thoughts of Gin, cops, and other distracting shit out of his mind. Truth be told, he had enough to deal with and couldn't afford to lose focus.

At that point – around late morning – he grabbed his tool bag and prepared to head out.

Finding Nissa in the kitchen, he said, "I got some errands to run and a couple of jobs. I'll be back in a few hours."

"Try not to get arrested," she joked, referencing his experience with the cops earlier.

"Not funny," Shade declared.

THUG LIFE: EMANCIPATED

Chapter 44

The next few hours actually flew by from Shade's perspective. As always, keeping busy made the time go faster for him. Thus, it was late afternoon before he knew it, at which point he found himself working his last job of the day: repairing a beat-up, decades-old washing machine for a single mother of five in the projects.

The washer was actually a job he had postponed from the day before, when Lord Byron's crew had scooped him up. Because he'd been the one to reschedule, he only charged half his quoted price when he was done. It was that kind of thing, in addition to being competent, that kept a steady supply of repair work coming his way.

After collecting his money, Shade left and began walking back to his car. For whatever reason, this part of the hood was one of those areas where there was never any place to park; every spot on the street was always taken. Shade suspected it was because there were way more adults living over here than what was actually allowed in government housing. Regardless, the end result was that he had parked several blocks away.

Fortunately, that wasn't a problem. The place where he'd parked was actually centrally located with respect to a couple of things he'd had to do earlier. (The only exception was a job located on a road full of potholes, so Shade hadn't wanted to drive there in his own car, but the guy hiring him had agreed to pick him up and bring him back.) In any event, because he'd known there would be a logjam of cars, he hadn't attempted to find a spot in this area. Basically, after finishing his earlier errands and other tasks, he had simply walked to that last job.

Heading back to the car, Shade kept a watchful eye out. He wasn't really expecting trouble and didn't see a lot of people on the street, but it was still the hood. Anything could happen – especially since he had a penchant for cutting through backstreets and alleys.

Thankfully, he was known by reputation to a certain extent, so people generally didn't fuck with him. Still, every now and then, some nigga would get bold and try some shit – like attempt to take his tool bag, intimidate him into giving up whatever cash he'd just made, and so on. It was a move they typically came to regret.

All of this flitted through Shade's mind as he walked, along with occasional thoughts of Yoni. (Truth be told, Yoni had been randomly popping up in his mind all afternoon.) At present, he was cutting through an alley – using it as a shortcut to his car. The alleyway itself was sandwiched between the back of two sections of row houses, about half of which were boarded up.

Looking at them, Shade noted that this was actually some of the oldest subsidized housing in the hood. Aside from the design and construction, he could tell by the fact that they all had basements, signified by steps next to the back door that led down to the substructure.

There was a time when families living in these houses would rent out the basements as apartments. But as soon as the government found out about it, they made those kind of basement rentals a housing violation – something that could get you kicked out of your home. Then they took the extra step of removing basements altogether from this type of government housing construction. It seemed extreme, but they couldn't have them poor folks making extra money now, could they? (At least, that's what Shade thought as he strolled along.)

Upon exiting the alley, he found himself about a block away from his car. At that point, he noted that there was a car parked behind his. There was nothing unusual about that in

212

and of itself, but something about the other vehicle – a gray sedan – made him wary. Nevertheless, he continued walking towards his car, trying to figure out why the other automobile was giving him a bad vibe. A moment later, the truth dawned on him.

At the same time, the driver's door on the sedan opened and Mario stepped out.

THUG LIFE: EMANCIPATED

Chapter 45

Shade stopped in his tracks, now realizing why seeing the sedan had rubbed him the wrong way. It was Mario's car, although he hadn't recognized the vehicle until just before Mario himself stepped out of it. But he wasn't alone; the same two dipshits who had been with him the night before – Deeter and Monk – were now climbing out of the front passenger side and back seat, respectively.

There was a confrontational tone to Mario's body language, but it wasn't hard to figure out why. The nigga was presumably still pissed about Shade putting a knife to his throat the night before.

He probably drove around the hood all day looking for me, Shade thought, *then lucked up on my car.*

If that was the case, Mario had shown more patience than Shade had thought him capable of, because he'd probably been waiting for hours. Needless to say, that would have just pissed him off even more.

Despite all that, however, Shade's first inclination was to keep heading towards his car. Whatever issues he and Mario had, his preference at the moment was to deal with them head-on and get them resolved – one way or the other. But at that point, two things changed his mind.

The first was the look on Mario's face, which telegraphed the fact that a peaceful resolution was out of the question. The second was an item that Mario held loosely in one hand: a gun.

Shade took all of this in within just a few seconds, then immediately did an about face. Moments later, he was headed back down the alley he had just exited. He wasn't running, but he was definitely moving at a fast clip.

Behind him, he thought he heard Mario say, "Get 'im," and then the sound of feet pounding on pavement reached his ears.

Shade's thoughts were racing. The alleyway actually ran perpendicular to the street that his car was parked on. Thus, when he ducked back down the alley, he was no longer in the line of sight of Mario and the others. Still, that only gave him a few seconds to come up with some kind of plan.

Unfortunately, his present circumstances didn't give him a lot of options. The row houses were actually connected to each other, so a nigga couldn't dash in between them and make a getaway like he could if they were single family homes. He could kick in the door of one of the homes that was occupied and dash inside (there wasn't time to be polite and knock), but that was just an invitation to get shot, which was the very thing he was trying to avoid. That just left...

Basement! Shade said to himself, and a moment later he was headed down the basement steps of the closest boarded-up home. As he went down the steps, he saw Mario and his buddies run into the alley. He wasn't sure if they'd seen him, but he was going on the assumption that they had.

Like the rest of the place, the basement door was boarded up, but with just a single piece of rectangular plywood. Shade yanked a pair of gloves from his tool bag and quickly put them on. Next, he placed his hands on both sides of the door and then quickly ran his fingers down the side of the plywood, the gloves preventing him from getting any splinters. A few seconds later, he found what he was looking for: a spot where the plywood wasn't quite flush with the wall. Wedging his fingers into the gap, Shade yanked as hard as he could and wrenched the wood off.

Coming free, the plywood made way more noise that he cared for. It probably didn't pinpoint his exact location, but certainly provided a better indication of where he was.

However, Shade put those thoughts out of his mind as he noted that the wood had been covering an actual door. More to the point, it appeared to be locked – secured by a keyed knob and what looked like a firm deadbolt.

Feeling pressed for time, Shade lifted a leg and planted a solid kick on the door right next to the lock. The deadbolt, as he had suspected, was of sturdy construction, but the door frame was shit wood. It splintered easily and the door flew open. Shade dashed inside, kicking the door closed behind him. Like the plywood, his antics with the door had made too much noise. But even if he'd been silent, one look at the wood and the door would be all anyone needed to figure out where he was.

The basement was pitch black. Unzipping his tool bag, Shade reached in and – after feeling around for a second – took out the tactical flashlight. Turning the beam on low, he quickly scanned his surroundings.

Like most basements, this one had a fair amount of clutter: old, moth-eaten furniture, boxes of various sizes, and more. Ignoring the hodgepodge of shit around him, Shade spent a few moments trying to figure out the best means of egress.

He was fairly certain that there would be a set of stairs leading up to the first floor of the house (and hopefully a way out), and going that route would put some space between him and his pursuers. But the basement was bound to have a front door that he could use to make an exit, and utilizing it would probably be quicker. However, he apparently wasted too much time trying to decide which was the better option, because seconds later he heard footfalls on the exterior steps leading down to the basement. They had found him.

Shade frowned as he turned the flashlight off. He didn't relish the idea of trying to slip by these assholes once they were down in the basement with him, and it was probably too late to pursue other options. However, he did have one more card up his sleeve, and he got ready to play it as the trio chasing him entered the basement.

They didn't say anything at first, but simply stepped forward slowly, with Mario in the middle. With light from the open door coming in behind them, Shade had no trouble making them out. The reverse, however, was not true; Shade knew that the dark interior of the basement would make it difficult (if not impossible) for them to see him. More importantly, they didn't have a flashlight and their eyes hadn't adjusted to the dark yet, so they were plainly being cautious. But having the gun seemingly made Mario bold, because he suddenly started talking shit.

"Come on out, nigga," Mario grumbled. "We know you ass down here. It's time to face the music muhfucka, 'cause – Ahhh!!!"

Mario screeched in pain, and his friends did likewise, as Shade – having turned the flashlight up to full luminosity – suddenly shined the light in their faces. As Mr. Jamison had said, it clearly left them blind, as all three were now vigorously rubbing their eyes.

Seeing his chance, Shade dashed forward, flashlight in hand. He came at them from the left, but he must have made some noise because Deeter – who was closest on that side – seemed to become aware of his approach.

Eyes still closed, Deeter reached wildly for him. Shade easily avoided his grasp by ducking low, then kneecapped him with the flashlight. Deeter howled in pain as the injured leg buckled. As he went down to the ground, Shade whacked him in the back of the head. Deeter pitched forward onto the floor and didn't move.

Apparently the sound of his friend being attacked, suddenly made Mario conscious of just how vulnerable he was. Without sight, he was basically a sitting duck. That being the case he raised the gun and fired in the direction of the commotion he'd heard, the weapon's report booming like a cannon in the enclosed space. But Shade was no longer there, having already retreated once again to the dim recesses of the basement.

At this point, Mario had the gun up in front of him, letting it oscillate from side to side as he listened for some telltale sign of Shade's position. On his part, Shade took the opportunity to once again shine the light brightly in the faces of Mario and Monk. Unsurprisingly, both of them still had their eyes closed. That said, they did flinch under the flashlight's glare, indicating that – even with their eyes shut – they could still sense the light to some degree.

At that juncture, Mario fired again, clearly aiming for what he thought was the source of the light. As before, his shot didn't even come close, but again the sound of gunfire was deafening. In fact, it seemed to hurt Mario's ears, because he grimaced and put a finger up to his ear, then began wiggling it, as if trying to clear something out of his ear canal. Monk, on the other hand, had dropped down to his haunches at the sound of gunfire, shoving a forefinger into each of his ears to block out the sound.

Following the second shot, Shade's own ears were ringing. Thus, he realized that Mario – being in closer proximity to the weapon – almost certainly had to be having a tough time hearing. Later, Shade would surmise that that was an accurate assessment because Mario suddenly seemed to go into panic mode, firing randomly in all directions. The obvious conclusion was that, despite being a dumbass, Mario had swiftly recognized that being both blind *and* deaf made him even more susceptible to attack. However, he was so indiscriminate in his gunplay that he actually shot Monk, who screamed in agony as a bullet struck him in the side.

THUG LIFE: EMANCIPATED

Mario either didn't know he'd shot his friend or didn't care. He continued firing until he was all out, and even then he continued pulling the trigger, seemingly not cognizant of the fact that he was out of ammo. At that point, Shade charged at him and walloped him viciously on the jaw. Mario's head jerked to the side from the force of the blow, then he dropped to the ground, unconscious.

Chapter 46

"So tell us again what happened," Gummy said, popping a stick of gum into his mouth.

"What, from the top?" asked Mia Watkins, the person Gummy was speaking to.

"Sure," Blanchard told her. "That way we we'll be sure to get everything."

The three of them were currently in an alley that ran between two sets of dilapidated, old-as-fuck row houses. About half of them were boarded up, but in Gummy's opinion every last one of them should have been condemned. Surprisingly though, those that weren't boarded appeared to have tenants, many of which were now standing outside chatting amongst themselves. However, a half-dozen uniformed officers stood nearby and kept the crowd from pressing in too close.

The alleyway itself was somewhat narrow and could best be construed as a one-lane thoroughfare. At the moment, there was an ambulance parked in it. Gummy and Blanchard, worried that they might get blocked in, had chosen to park on the street that ran perpendicular to the alley and had then walked over to meet with Watkins and her partner, who at present was nowhere in sight.

Watkins herself was flipping through a small memo pad that had a lot of handwritten notes on it. She was a tall woman – about five-ten – in her mid-thirties, with a well-toned figure and long lustrous hair. However, she was the type of woman that people would describe as handsome rather than pretty, although from what Gummy had heard it didn't affect her love life.

"Okay," Watkins began, looking at her notes. "At eight-seventeen, received a call from Detective Blanchard, requesting assistance–"

"Hold on," Gummy interjected. "We don't need the official play-by-play. Just give us the straight dope."

"Fine by me," Watkins declared, tucking the memo pad into a pocket of the sweatshirt she wore. "Alright, got a call this morning asking if I could help out surveilling a person of interest. Sure, it's my day off, but this is for my fellow boys in blue, so what the fuck. Plus I can use the overtime. So I roll out of bed, call my partner, and tell him to be ready in ten. Then I turn to the couple I had a threesome with the night before, tell 'em I can't do breakfast, and they gotta get the fuck out."

At this point, she gave Blanchard a wink, which caused Gummy to cast a sideways glance at him.

"I go pick up my partner, and we start surveillance of the subject's home," Watkins continued. "We sit there for a couple of hours until someone matching the subject's description comes out. According to our information he's the only male in the home, so we assume that's our guy. He gets in a car parked in the driveway and leaves. We follow."

"When was this?" Gummy asked.

"Late morning – maybe close to noon," Watkins replied. "Ultimately, we end up in this neighborhood, with the subject parking on a street that intersects with this alley. He gets out carrying a tool bag and starts walking down the street. My partner gets out and follows him on foot. He goes around a corner and I lose sight of him, but my partner still his eyes on him – says the subject reaches the next intersection where there's a black truck parked. Subject says something to the driver, then gets in and they leave."

"So where'd they go?" Blanchard inquired.

Shrugging, Watkins gave him a confused look. "How the fuck should I know?"

Now it was Gummy and Blanchard who looked confused, with the former saying, "You didn't follow him?"

"My partner was behind him on *foot*. Nobody expected this guy to jump into another car."

"Well, why weren't you followin' behind your partner in your vehicle?" Gummy inquired.

"Maybe you haven't done this shit in a while," Watkins chided, "but when people look over their shoulder and see a car creeping behind then at two miles an hour, they get suspicious as a motherfucker."

"We get it, Mia," Blanchard remarked. "You didn't wanna get made. But did your partner at least get a license?"

Watkins shook her head. "Nope. Too far away."

"Shit," Gummy muttered.

"What about the driver?" queried Blanchard.

Watkins shook her head. "My partner says the subject obscured his view. He did get the make and model of the vehicle, though."

"A lot of fuckin' good that'll do," Gummy blurted out. "This city must have a million black trucks of every stripe. And you losin' the subject means that we don't know if this was somebody who just gave him a lift for a few blocks, or if they went a hundred miles off to make a drug deal."

Watkins gave him a hard stare. "You wanna keep bitchin' 'bout the shit job my partner and I did as a *favor* for you, or you wanna hear the rest of the story?"

Gummy looked like he had something to say, but Blanchard interjected, saying, "Go on, Mia. What happened next?"

Watkins continued glaring at Gummy for a moment, then let out a deep breath. "Since we lost the subject, we simply decided to sit on his car. So we parked down the street and kept it in view. Nothing happened for a few hours – just normal people and traffic patterns – until one particular car came through. As it passed by the subject's car, it slowed down. Then it continued down the street, made an illegal u-turn, then came back. Again, it slowed down when going past the subject's vehicle before continuing on. It then made another illegal u-turn, came back, and parked behind the subject's car."

"Did you get the license of *that* one?" Gummy asked sarcastically.

"Yeah," Watkins said. "But if you're worried we fucked it up, you can always check it out yourself since the car's still parked over there."

"So what happened next?" asked Blanchard.

"Maybe another hour passed with no action," Watkins stated, "then the subject appeared, exiting from this alley onto the street where his car was parked. At that time, doors on the second car opened and three black males, mid- to late teens in age, got out."

"So they were waiting on our guy," Gummy surmised.

"Apparently," Watkins agreed. "And from our position, it looked like one of them had a gun. I'm assuming the subject noticed the same thing, because he immediately turned around and came back down the alley here. At that point, we lost visual on him, but the trio who had been waiting went after him. That's when my partner and I exited our vehicle and went after *them*."

"Okay, go on," Blanchard coaxed.

"We entered the alley with weapons drawn," Watkins continued. "We didn't see our subject, but saw the three black males going down the steps to *that* basement." As she finished speaking, she tilted her heads towards a nearby basement entrance. "A few seconds later, we heard gunfire."

"What, like a shootout?" Gummy inquired.

Watkins shook her head. "Single shot, but it sounded like it came from the basement, so we halted our approach to call it in. While we were doing that, we heard the report of more gunfire."

"So *that* was the shootout," Blanchard guessed.

"Don't think so," Watkins countered. "I'm sure we'll find out when the CSI team goes through the place, but to me it sounded like a single small-caliber being fired repeatedly."

"And it was coming from the basement?" Gummy asked.

"No doubt," Watkins assured them with a nod. "Anyway, when the gunfire ended, we crept forward and shouted down into the basement, identifying ourselves as law enforcement. We then told them to toss out their weapons and come out with their hands up. Usually that elicits a response – either motherfuckers firing back, or scrambling for a way out – but we got nothing. We gave it about half a minute, then yelled again for them to toss their weapons and come out. Again, no response. At that point, my partner and I pulled out our flashlights and went inside."

That was bold," Blanchard noted. "Nobody would have blamed you if you waited for backup." His comment was, of course, a reference to the fact that backup would have automatically been sent to their location after they reported that shots had been fired.

"Well, we could hear someone moaning inside," Watkins told them. "And we figured it wouldn't go over well on the six o'clock news if it was reported that someone died because a couple of armed cops were too chickenshit to do their jobs."

Gummy nodded in agreement at this. "So what did you find?"

"The trio of males we'd followed were all down," Watkins answered. "Two of them were unconscious; the third was conscious but looked like he might be going into shock. He'd been shoot – a through-and-through in the side. Then, while my partner checked and secured the premises, I stayed with three males, although I called back in to state that we'd need medical transport for three."

Neither Gummy nor Blanchard commented on this, but both understood what Watkins was talking about. In addition to backup, the original report of shots being fired would have caused an ambulance to be sent as well. Normally, at least two would show up, but since she had a trio of people in need of medical attention, Watkins had wisely stressed the need for three ambulances, since each could typically only transport one person.

"After that," Watkins continued, "I called you two and gave an overview of what had happened and suggested you get your asses over here. By that time, we had backup on the scene and my partner had come back and stated 'All clear' regarding the premises."

"So what's the status of the three you found?" Gummy asked.

"According to the EMTs, our gunshot guy will make it," Watkins informed them. "Of the other two, one has a shattered patella and a concussion, the other has a broken jaw. Also, that last would appear to be our shooter – he was still holding a gun when we found him, although it was empty."

"So our subject took those three down?" Blanchard asked.

Watkins shrugged. "Couldn't say. We didn't see him enter, never saw him leave."

"So you can't even place him on the premises," Gummy concluded.

"Nope," Watkins confirmed. "Also, after backup arrived, I hustled back to where the subject had parked, but his car was gone. Then I came back here, and a short time later you two showed up."

"And that's everything that happened?" said Blanchard.

"Pretty much," Watkins stated. "But you can double-check with my partner and see if I missed anything."

"Where's he?" Gummy asked.

"Inside," Watkins stated, tilting her head towards the basement. "The last set of EMTs wouldn't go in unless they had an officer with them. Apparently they got surprised by a shooter before at a site that was supposed to be clear, and they've been gun-shy ever since – no pun intended."

Gummy seemed to concentrate for a moment. "You said your partner checked the premises. Did he notice any way that the subject might had gotten out, assuming he was down there in the first place?"

"The only thing he mentioned was that the basement's front window had been smashed in," Watkins told them.

"So our subject could have done that when fleeing the scene," Gummy suggested.

"Unlikely," Watkins offered. "As I said, the window was smashed *in*. In other words, all the glass was *inside*, which you wouldn't expect if someone was breaking *out*. Also, the window wasn't actually boarded up – there was just a sheet of plywood resting against it. At least that's how I remember my partner describing it, but I can call him out here if you like."

"We can catch your partner later," Gummy told her. "I don't suppose any of the three you found in there said anything about what happened."

"Yeah," Watkins said. "The gun-shot-wound said *nobody* shot him."

"Figures," Blanchard muttered. "What about the other two?"

"The one who got kneecapped is talking," stated Watkins, "but outside of screaming about his leg he's not making much sense. Then again, he's got a concussion. As to the last, he's not saying much of anything with a broken jaw, but they should be bringing him out in a minute."

"What's taking 'em so long?" Gummy asked.

"They may have trouble getting him stabilized," Blanchard offered. "A broken jaw can cause all kinds of problems. There might be some kind of spinal injury, trouble breathin', bleedin'… All kinds of bad shit."

Gummy let out a frustrated groan. Keeping eyes on that Shade kid had seemed worthwhile, but hadn't really paid any dividends. To be honest, Watkins and her partner had done a decent job, but they hadn't seen Shade do anything that was actionable from a law enforcement standpoint.

But maybe someone *did*, he thought, as he scanned the crowd that was still nearby. Turning to Watkins, he asked, "Did you guys canvas the neighborhood yet? See if anybody saw anything?"

"No," Watkins stressed. "There hasn't been time for shit like that. Also, not my case, so not my job. Besides, you already know what the response will be: nobody saw a damn thing."

"Could you do it anyway?" Blanchard asked. "As a favor?"

"Oh, so a *second* favor on my day off?" Watkins intoned acerbically. "Sure, since you guys were so appreciative of our surveillance efforts."

With that, she turned to the crowd that was gathered. Holding up her badge, she then bellowed in a surprisingly loud voice, "Hey, I'm Officer Watkins. Anybody see what happened here?"

There was a general chorus of 'No's' from the folks gathered, along with almost synchronized head-shaking. In addition, about a third of the crowd suddenly started to meander off, like they suddenly remembered important business elsewhere.

Turning back to Blanchard and Gummy, Watkins simply shrugged while making a tsking sound and then muttered, "Sorry."

Blanchard merely stared at her for a moment, then sighed. "Fine, we'll get a couple uniforms to go door-to-door."

"Best idea I've heard all day," Watkins said with a smile.

THUG LIFE: EMANCIPATED

Chapter 47

After finishing their conversation with Watkins, Gummy and Blanchard had a quick conversation with her partner, who basically told the same story. At that point, they walked back to their car in silence, each of them seemingly lost in his own thoughts.

Once inside the car, however, Gummy turned to his partner and asked, "You fuckin' her?"

"Huh?" Blanchard muttered in confusion.

"Watkins," Gummy explained. "Are you hittin' that?"

"Geez, Gummy!" Blanchard exclaimed, shocked. "You need help."

"Hey, you two are the ones sending signals. She's giving you sly winks. You're all, 'Mia this' and 'Mia that,' but with anyone else – man or woman – you typically just call 'em by their last name. So now you act all surprised that someone would think you two–"

"She's my cousin," Watkins interjected.

Gummy looked at him in surprise. "Who, Watkins?"

"Yeah."

Gummy let that roll around in his head for a moment. "Then why was she winkin' at you when she was talkin' about threesomes and shit?"

"She's the baby of the family – at least in *my* generation – so she says shit like that for shock value, and as a reminder that she's an adult. For all I know, it's true, though. But hey, she's grown, so she can do what the fuck she wants."

"But still...your cousin? I'm yo fuckin' partner, and you didn't tell me?"

"She didn't want anyone to know – said she didn't want to be treated differently after she transferred here just because her cousin was a detective on the force. So the only person I told was the captain, and he agreed to keep it under his hat."

"Well, for future reference, I can keep a secret. And only an asshole keeps sommin' like that a secret from his partner."

"Anyway," Blanchard droned, ignoring Gummy's comment. "Our guy?"

"It's my guess he fucked up that trio in the basement. But he took it easy on them compared to the victims in *our* case – at least he left *these* shitheads alive."

"But if he was down there, maybe CSI can find some prints to tie him to the scene."

"He's too smart to leave prints. Or if he did, he'd have some way to explain them."

"Well, regardless of that, we learned one thing today."

"What?"

"Lamp was wrong: somebody's got it in for this kid."

"Guess we can talk to these knuckleheads he stomped on today. If we can find out why they were after him, we may get a clue as to what he's into."

"Good luck with that. You'll get as much out of them as Watkins got with the spectators back there."

"Hmmm," Gummy mused. "Maybe they'll talk if we find a way to lean on them."

"You got something in mind?"

"Maybe. You remember the Carson case a few years back?"

"Yeah," Blanchard replied, nodding in reflection. "Some high schoolers with too much time on their hands during summer decide they're gonna break into their old elementary school, which has been shut down. One of the kids who's in on it, Carson, arrives late. The door to the school is propped open, so he goes in. The others are already inside, raising hell – spraypaintin' walls, throwing chairs through windows, smashing mirrors in the bathrooms… But Carson isn't involved in any of that - doesn't touch anything, doesn't deface any property, doesn't tear anything up. Still, when the cops show up, he gets arrested along with the others."

"They charged the Carson kid under a conspiracy theory," Gummy added. "Basically, he conspired and agreed with the others to break into the school. Once you're part of the conspiracy, you're guilty of anything your co-conspirators do as part of the crime."

"Yeah," Blanchard stated in agreement. "It's a variation of the felony murder rule."

"Exactly," uttered Gummy, who had been thinking the same thing.

Basically, the felony murder rule was a legal doctrine which stated that if someone – in fact, *anyone* – died during the commission of a felony, all persons involved in the crime could be charged with murder. So if two guys rob a bank and a teller has a heart attack during the robbery and dies, both robbers are guilty of felony murder. If one of the robbers is shot and killed by cops during the getaway, the survivor is guilty of felony murder. Moreover, anyone else involved in the criminal enterprise – a getaway driver, a lookout, and so on – could also be charged with felony murder.

Basically, it didn't matter who died or what the cause of death was; if it happened during the commission of a felony, it was felony murder. More to the point, all of the criminals involved would be considered equally guilty in that regard.

Similarly, with the case they were discussing, anyone involved in the criminal enterprise could be charged.

With that in mind, Gummy continued, stating, "So, even though the Carson kid didn't do anything inside the school, he was charged just like the rest of his buddies. Under conspiracy law, everything they did in there – the vandalism and so on – was a foreseeable result of the break-in, and as part of the conspiracy he was just as guilty."

"I remember," Blanchard told him. "The media had a fucking field day with that – said an innocent kid was being railroaded."

Gummy shrugged. "The DA was trying to show she was tough on crime. After all, it was an election year. Just like now."

Blanchard merely stared at his partner for a few seconds before speaking. "So you're thinkin' we go at those three hard – get the DA's office to charge them with everything under the sun."

"It doesn't have to be a *lot* of charges. They just have to be serious as fuck."

"Like in the Carson case. The charges were so severe because the school was a government building, and they up the ante for government-owned facilities."

"Right, and in this instance our three culprits also took a gun inside. That by itself is a first-degree felony, let alone shooting the place up."

"There's an exception for government-owned *housing*," Blanchard reminded him. "You're not prohibited from bringing a firearm into a residence just because the government owns it."

"That's only if it's *your* residence," Gummy shot back. "If you're the legitimate occupant of government housing, sure you can have a gun. That's Second Amendment, right-to-bear-arms shit. But if it ain't yo house, you're fucked."

"True," Blanchard noted with a nod.

"I just wish it was a federal buildin' they'd gone into," Gummy continued, "because federal charges are the harshest on the books. But all the subsidized housing around here is owned by the County Housing Authority."

232

"Damn, Gummy. You almost sound like you *want* these charges to stick."

"No," Gummy intoned, shaking his head. "I just want them serious enough to make these dipshits cooperate – make 'em think broken jaws and busted kneecaps are the least of their problems. The DA can whittle them down and charge these clowns with a lesser offense later, if that's what she wants to do."

"Alright, I'll reach out to the DA's office about our three shitheads," Blanchard stated.

"And I'll contact Gills," Gummy said, "and tell him to get his ass over here, and that he'd better have something solid for us on this Shade kid."

THUG LIFE: EMANCIPATED

Chapter 48

Shade drove home in a piss-poor mood, angry at himself for what had happened. He'd known that Mario was a vengeful nigga, so he should have been expecting something like the ambush that muhfucka had tried to pull. But despite allegedly having an eye out for crap like that, he had damn near walked straight into a trap.

Fortunately, he'd been able to get out of that shit. After taking care of Mario and his boys, he had raced to the front of the basement. The door had been locked (and presumably boarded up on the outside), but luck was on his side: there was a window next to the door that someone had smashed in at some point – presumably to gain entry to the basement. There was a piece of plywood on the outside of the window in question, but it was simply leaning against the frame rather than being nailed in place. It was clearly there just to give the impression that the place was still boarded up. That being the case, Shade had shoved it aside and then quickly gone through the window, taking care not to cut himself or get his clothes caught on any of the jagged pieces of glass remaining. He had then put the plywood back in place in front of the window.

Thankfully, the basement's front door and the adjacent window were, like the back entrance, below street level. Ergo, someone would have had to be standing on the basement steps to notice him slip out. At that point his only issue had been getting up the basement steps without being seen. However, Lady Luck had smiled on him again in that - if memory served him correctly – the houses of either side of the one he'd emerged from were both boarded up. Even better, a quick peep up the steps revealed the same to be true of the house across the street.

Taking a deep breath, Shade had raced up the basement steps, but then immediately slowed once he reached the top in order not to draw attention. There had been a couple of people out on the street at that point, but none were close by or seemed to have noticed his sudden appearance.

Thankful to have made it up the steps unseen, Shade had then begun walking as swiftly as he could towards his car without giving the impression that he was in a rush. Eventually people did notice him, but at that juncture he didn't care. He was always out doing odd jobs throughout the hood, so being spotted in and of itself was no big deal. All that mattered was that he hadn't been seen coming from the basement.

To the extent that anyone nearby might have taken an interest in him, their curiosity clearly waned a few seconds later when another item caught the attention of everyone within earshot: the sound of sirens approaching. It was something Shade had been expecting after Mario's antics in the basement. With that much gunfire, somebody was bound to call the cops, so the whine of sirens hadn't caught Shade by surprise. In essence, it had served as his cue to get to his car (and get gone) as soon as possible, which was what he did.

Reflecting on everything that had happened as he drove, the only silver lining Shade could see was that he probably wouldn't have to worry about Mario for a while. Shade didn't know how badly he'd hurt him, but the injury wasn't what was likely to put Mario out of commission; it was the gun.

With Mario being a dumbass-supreme, he wouldn't have sense enough to use a *clean* gun for any shady business. Thus, the weapon he had fired in the basement had probably been used for all kinds of shit: stick-ups, carjackings, armed robbery… Hell, it wouldn't even surprise Shade if there were bodies on that gun. Long story short, that heater was likely to tie Mario to all kinds of bad shit.

The end result, then, was that Shade didn't think he'd have to worry about Mario for a long time. Moreover, without Mario out of the picture, his shit-for-brains compadres, Deeter and Monk, were unlikely to be a problem, although they'd probably have their own legal woes to deal with.

All in all, by the time Shade arrived home, his mood had lightened considerably. In fact, as he parked the car in the driveway and walked to the door with his tool bag, he damn near felt like whistling.

Once inside, he heard his sisters in the kitchen. Given the time, he assumed they were preparing dinner and began heading in that direction. However, he'd gone no more than a few steps when something made him stop short – a third voice. There was someone in the kitchen with Nissa and Cherry.

Slightly worried, Shade set down his tool bag, and at that moment Nissa came out into the living room.

"Thought I heard you come in," his sister said. Then, stepping close, she said in a low voice, "Just so you know, we have company."

Goose, Shade thought, letting out a frustrated groan. Speaking in a soft tone, he said, "Nissa, I really don't feel like dealing with anybody today."

Nissa simply stared at him for a moment, then nodded in acquiescence. "That's fine. I should have texted you that she was here."

"She?" Shade repeated, sounding perplexed.

At that moment, their guest walked out of the kitchen, and Shade found himself staring in surprise.

It was Yoni.

Leaning close, Nissa whispered, "Want me to send her home?"

THUG LIFE: EMANCIPATED

Chapter 49

The sight of Yoni, wearing a black jumpsuit, brought an involuntary smile to Shade's face, which she returned.

Ignoring his sister's comment, he asked, "What are you doing here?"

"Well, hello to you, too," Yoni replied snarkily as she walked towards him.

"I'm sorry," Shade apologized with a slight snicker as Nissa went back to the kitchen. "It's nice to see you. I just wasn't expecting you."

"Nice to see as well," Yoni told him. "And in case you forgot, you invited me over to watch the game."

"Huh?" Shade muttered. "I'm not sure that's exactly right. Plus, football season's over."

"Well I can leave if you want."

"No," he insisted, almost too eagerly, but in a way that made her smile. "I mean, it's okay. I'm glad you're here."

"You better be," Yoni warned, before leaning in to give him a kiss. She then grabbed his hand and led him into the kitchen.

Once there, he noticed that the place was a hub of activity. There were mixing bowls and baking pans out, as well as various baking staples like flour, sugar, and so on.

"What's goin' on here?" Shade asked as Yoni released his hand.

"Did you forget?" Nissa asked. "Cherry got a hundred on her Spanish test. We told her she'd get a treat for anythang over a ninety."

"That's right," Cherry chimed in, "so we're havin' cake and ice cream. Right now we're bakin' the cake."

"Actually, she couldn't make up her mind about the kind of cake she wanted," Nissa said, "so we're makin' *two*."

"And Yoni's helpin'," Cherry beamed.

"Yes, I am," Yoni confirmed, grinning, "so I better get back to it."

With that, she went to a mixing bowl on the counter and, apparently picking up where she'd left off, began measuring a cup of sugar. At the same time, Cherry was busy flouring a pan while Nissa was blending ingredients in a bowl using an old hand-held mixer that had belonged to their grandmother, who had died about a decade earlier.

"Anyway," Nissa droned. "I was just about to tell Yoni that I've been wanting to meet her for a while now."

"Oh?" muttered Yoni, her interest piqued. "Why's that?"

"I just wanted to see the girl who threw him out," Nissa said, tilting her head towards her brother.

"Huh?" Shade stated, perplexed. "Whachu talkin' 'bout?"

"You remember a few weeks back," Nissa prodded. "You came home with almost no clothes on because some girl threw you out—"

At this point Nissa had turned to Yoni, preparing to give her a knowing wink. Instead, she stopped mid-sentence as the look on Yoni's face made it clear that this was all news to her.

"Oh shit," Nissa mumbled. "It wasn't you."

Cherry suddenly started giggling as Yoni, shaking her head, declared, "Nope."

Nissa looked at her brother, who was giving her a fixed *da-fuck-you-doin'?* stare.

"Sorry," Nissa apologized. "I think I'm all confused on dates and stuff. It was actually more like a coupla *months* ago, not a coupla weeks, and—"

"Stop," Shade ordered, making Cherry laugh all the more. "Just stop. Don't compound the situation with a bunch of lies."

Horrified that she might have fucked things up between Yoni and her brother, Nissa just stood there for a moment. Then she glanced at Yoni, but was surprised to find her grinning.

"It's okay," Yoni told her. "Yo brutha hadn't said so much as 'Boo' to me b'foe yesterday. What he was doin' weeks ago ain't got nuthin' to do with me."

"Really?" Nissa chirped, sounding incredibly relieved.

"Yeah," Yoni assured her. "But I still wouldn't mind hearing the rest of the story."

"Oh, there's not much more to it," Yoni stated. "Shade came creepin' into the house in the middle of the night half-naked. Seem like he'd been with some girl and did sommin' to tick her off, so she tossed his ass out without even lettin' him get his clothes. When you came by today, I assumed it was you."

"No – not me," Yoni declared, shaking her head before turning to Shade and demanding, "So who was she?"

"There was no 'she,'" Shade replied. "Even though I told her what happened, my sista just prefers to twist facts around to fit her on distorted worldview."

"Then what's the real story?" Yoni asked.

"The truth," Shade stressed, "is that I had just finished a job and was on my way to the car when some hobo threw up all over me, from shirt to shoes."

Nissa and Yoni started laughing while Cherry, wincing, simply muttered. "Ew."

"Exactly," intoned Shade. "I smelled like a dead dog, stuffed inside a burning tire, that had been tossed into a dumpster full of elephant shit. I knew I'd never get the stink or the stain off my clothes, so I just stripped and tossed them into a trashcan. And that's the whole story."

Nissa gave him a skeptical look. "And what happened to your tool bag?"

"Huh?" Shade blurted out. "I told you b'foe - somebody stole it. I was strugglin' to get my friggin' clothes off without gettin' vomit on me, so I set it down. When I looked around for it a minute later, it was gone."

"See, that's how I know he lyin'," Nissa declared. "He don't ever take his eye off that tool bag when he out. The only time he ain't a hundred percent focused on it is when some chick catch his eye, 'cause when he like a girl he get so distracted that he forget his own name."

"Oh, really?" Yoni intoned as she smiled at Shade. "So there *was* some girl."

"No, there wasn't," he maintained. "You're as bad as Nissa."

Yoni then looked at Nissa. "And did he really show up half-naked?"

"He was wearing some raggedy-ass pants that he prolly stole off somebody clothesline," Nissa answered. "But that was about it."

"Actually, I still had on underwear," Shade countered. "And I didn't steal those pants – I bought 'em off a bag lady for five bucks."

"Sure you did," Nissa said, her disbelief evident.

"Whatever," Shade stated dismissively. "I just finished my last job so I'm gonna go take a shower. You two can just stay here and keep makin' up stories about me."

"Me, too," chirped Cherry, who had mostly been giggling while the others were talking.

"Say what?" asked Shade, giving her a curious look.

"I wanna make up stories, too," she explained.

Rather than respond, Shade merely looked at Nissa with a *See-what-you-did?* expression, at which she – and Yoni – burst into laughter.

Shaking his head in faux disgust, Shade left the kitchen, grabbed his tool bag, and headed to his room.

THUG LIFE: EMANCIPATED

Chapter 50

As usual, Shade tossed his tool bag on the floor of his room, then grabbed some clothes – specifically, underwear, a t-shirt and a pair of sweats – then headed to the bathroom. Out in the hallway, he could hear his sisters and Yoni laughing in the kitchen. He couldn't make out what they were saying, but they seemed to be having a good time.

Thinking about Yoni as he went into the bathroom and locked the door, Shade couldn't help smiling a bit. Her showing up had been unexpected, but a welcome surprise. If nothing else, it took his mind off his earlier run-in with Mario and his boys. After that visit from the detectives this morning, the last thing he needed was any other heat flowing in his direction.

With that thought, it suddenly occurred to him that the cops would probably be asking Mario, Deeter and Monk a lot of questions about what happened in that basement. However, he felt that trio were unlikely to link him to any of the afternoon's events, so Shade wasn't too worried. Typically, no matter how much you hated a muhfucka, you didn't rat him out. That was *Hood 101*. Like most rules, though, there were exceptions, but that was generally the code of the streets and even a bunch of fuckups like Mario and his buddies understood that.

At that moment, Shade turned on the water in the shower. As it began to run and heat up, he started getting out of his clothes. A minute later, he was in the shower, lathering up and starting to scrub himself clean.

Under normal circumstances, he would have taken his time. The hot water cascading over him was always relaxing, and the day had been more tense than usual. However, Yoni's presence acted as a spur, and as a result he finished showering faster than usual.

Turning off the water, he quickly stepped out of the shower and began drying himself. But he had barely started before someone rapped sharply on the door.

At that juncture, having lived together their entire lives, group dynamics had allowed Shade and his sisters to develop uncanny insight and perception with respect to each other. Each of them was well-acquainted with the quirks and mannerisms of the other two. Thus, they could tell who was in the hallway by their footfalls, who was in the kitchen by how loudly they closed a cabinet, and so on. In this instance, Shade knew by the knock that it was Nissa outside.

His gut reaction was to tell her that he'd be out in a minute. Then – thinking it might be an emergency (like if Cherry needed to use the toilet) – he wrapped the towel around his waist and stepped to the door. Making sure to stay behind it, he cracked the door open. As expected, Nissa was standing there.

"Hey," she said before he could ask what she wanted. "I'm gonna take Cherry out to pick up the ice cream she wants. It's okay to leave Yoni in the living room 'til you come out?"

She spoke her question in a whisper, and Shade responded with a nod. "Yeah, that's cool. I'll be out in a minute."

"Also, we put the cakes in the oven, so listen for the timer so you can take 'em out."

Shade frowned. "Won'chall be back by then?"

"We'll prolly be gone at least an hour," his sister replied, then cut her eyes towards the living room (where Yoni presumably was). She then gave him a sly smile before walking away.

Shaking his head in disdain, Shade shut the door and finished drying off. Then, while he was in the process of getting dressed, he heard the front door open and close, indicating that his sisters had left. Quickly putting on deodorant, Shade made a last-second inspection of himself in the bathroom mirror. Deciding that he look presentable, he was about to walk out when he noticed his toothbrush in its holder by the bathroom sink.

Better safe than sorry, he said to himself.

With that thought, he grabbed the toothbrush, put toothpaste on it, and then rapidly brushed his teeth for about thirty seconds. Once done, he washed his face, gave himself a final once-over, then hurried to the bathroom door. He opened it and was about to step out, then stopped in his tracks.

Directly across from the bathroom, leaning against the wall, was Yoni. And she wasn't wearing a stitch of clothing.

"It's about fuckin' time," she remarked testily. "And I mean that literally."

THUG LIFE: EMANCIPATED

Chapter 51

Yoni stepped forward and kissed him hungrily, at the same time reaching down into his sweats and giving his dick a solid squeeze before cupping his balls. Shade wasn't sure how it happened, but he suddenly found himself with his back to the wall across from the bathroom. At that moment, Yoni broke off the kiss and then unexpectedly dropped to her knees. As part of the same motion, she gripped his sweats and underwear as she went down, pulling them down to his ankles. And then she took his dick in her mouth.

Shade drew in a sharp breath as Yoni began working his rod with her mouth, lips and hands. It felt fucking sensational, and in no time at all his shit was as hard as galvanized steel. Gently, he placed a hand at the base of her neck – not for control, but because feeling the oscillating motion of her head as she sucked him off was a complete turn-on.

Pulling his cock out of her mouth for a moment, Yoni lithely ran her tongue all around the head like it was the world's most delicious lollipop. Then she pursed her lips and blew gently on it, creating a cool, tingling sensation that had Shade flicking his toes. Then, before the feeling faded, she deep-throated him.

The sudden warmth of her mouth was such a startling, delightful contrast to the briskness he'd felt a moment earlier that Shade audibly groaned. Glancing down, he watched her for a moment, noting that the way her head bobbed as she sucked his dick was erotic as a muhfucka. And then their eyes met.

She had obviously been watching him, getting off on his reaction to her oral skills. But when they made eye contact, something electric passed between them – a potent and irresistible power that immediately forged a connection, a bond that Shade instinctively knew would be difficult to sever.

Somehow, Shade managed to break eye contact after a few seconds. However, the feeling of a cogent connection and affinity for Yoni lingered. In fact it left him almost maddened with desire. He wanted – no, *needed* – to fuck this girl. Immediately.

Using both hands, he began to pull her to her feet. Although she seemed reluctant to stop sucking his dick, she acquiesced. Shade then immediately bent down, wrapping his arms around Yoni just below her ass cheeks, and lifted her up. Her bosom was now level with his face, and he began sucking one of her titties. Moaning in delight, Yoni wrapped her arms around his head as Shade – gingerly stepping out of the sweats and underwear around his ankles – carried her to his room. A moment later, he laid her gently on the bed, maneuvering himself so that he was on top on her.

Yoni, however, wasn't having it. She shifted her weight and rolled slightly, subtly indicating to Shade that she wanted to get on top, and he went with it. A moment later he was looking up at her as, smiling, she reached down and guided his dick into her pussy. And then, Shade's world flipped completely on its axis.

Apparently, he had learned nothing from their previous night together. Somehow, he had it in his brain that the fucking would start slow and build in tempo (which is what he'd have done if he'd been on top). But it seemed that Yoni had different plans.

The second he was inside her, she began her fanatical hip motion – a horizontal *Ori Tahiti* – making her pussy fly up and down the length of his dick at what felt like supersonic speed. It caught Shade completely by surprise and damn near took his breath away, subjecting him to a sensation that was so physically overwhelming that for a second he couldn't even think.

The sex had felt incredible the night before, when she was beneath him and thrusting wildly. But now that she was on top, unfettered by his weight and unrestricted by sheets or blankets, she really had free range of motion. The result was a feeling of blissful pleasure that was so intense that Shade thought he saw lights and colors. (The experience was so psychedelic, in fact, that later he briefly wondered if Yoni had somehow drugged him.)

With Yoni relentlessly riding his dick, Shade inherently understood that he was in trouble. The way she was working her pussy, there was no way he'd be able to hold back.

In desperation, he reached for her hips, hoping to physically slow her down like he'd done the night before. At the same time, he breathlessly pleaded, "Yoni...you gotta...slow–"

"Shhh," Yoni ordered in a breathy whisper, putting a finger to his lips but barely slowing her momentum. "It's alright. This is how I like it."

"But..." he implored, trying to grab her hips with his hands "I can't...hold it... I'll–"

"It's okay," she said as she grabbed his hands, interlocking their fingers. She then leaned forward, pushing his hands onto the bed on either side of his head.

Her face was over his at that point, and she spent a moment looking deep into his eyes.

"It's okay," she assured him again. "You have my permission to cum. As soon as you want."

With that, she released his hands, raised up so that her hands were on his chest, and began fucking him harder and faster than before, moaning loudly the entire time.

Of course, in addition to being incredibly arousing (especially her permission-to-cum statement), Yoni's words were also liberating to Shade – a sexual Emancipation Proclamation. Therefore, he essentially threw in the towel in terms of trying to establish a sustainable rhythm. Truth be told, however, it had only been a half-hearted attempt anyway. In all honesty, he really hadn't want Yoni to slow the fuck down or anything like that. The way her pussy was gliding up and down his dick was like an out-of-body experience – the erotic equivalent of receiving enlightenment from Buddha. No way did he want anything interfering with that.

In the end, he came in record time, but with an earth-shattering, mind-blowing intensity that left him so drained he didn't think he could speak. Later, he would understand that, in part, it had felt so amazing because he hadn't most of his time trying to keep from cumming. Instead of trying to control his body's natural reaction to being ball's deep in tight-ass pussy, he had let go. As a result, he got to experience the most spectacular sex he'd ever had (although that was due in large part to the rapid-fire antics of Yoni's hips and pussy).

On her part, Yoni came as well, once again making the whimpering noise – but notably louder – as she collapsed on top on Shade, out of breath. As before, her hips engaged in their spasmodic, post-orgasmic thrusting routine, causing her pussy to continue feasting on Shade's dick for a little longer. Shade – who had put his arms around her and given her a gentle, loving squeeze – seemed to shudder and groan loudly in response.

Needless to say, Yoni had thoroughly enjoyed the ride Shade had given her. Although she could cum when the sex was at a slower pace, going at it fast and hard always culminated in a far more intense and satisfying orgasm for her. Thus, given her druthers, she favored a short, rigorous fuck over nice-and-slow lovemaking. As for what the guy wanted, it was like Donna had said after the party: Yoni hadn't met the nigga yet who complained that she made him cum too fast.

As her hip thrusts came to a halt, she glanced up at Shade. His groans and shuddering had stopped, but his eyes were still closed and he was breathing hard. She smiled to herself.

Never had a bitch put it him like that *b'foe*, Yoni thought, not without undue pride. She wasn't one to brag, but she knew that her fuck technique was second to none.

Then, with a great degree of reluctance, she finally lifted her hips and slid off his dick, then just lay on top of him while he held her close.

THUG LIFE: EMANCIPATED

Chapter 52

They only stayed in a bed a minute or so after fucking. At that point, Yoni insisted that they had to get up.

"I think I'm on yo sistas' good side," Yoni said, "but it won't last if they come back and find us all naked and shit, and the cakes burnt up."

Thus, she hurried out of bed and went to get her things – specifically, her purse and the jumpsuit she'd been wearing earlier – before scurrying to the bathroom. While she was in there, Shade quickly got dressed. However, it didn't occur to him until a few minutes later that Yoni might be in need of a towel or something in order to freshen up.

With that in mind, he knocked on the bathroom door. It was opened a second later by Yoni, who was in the middle of brushing her teeth.

Shade just stared at her for a moment, finding himself speechless. Of course, he had kissed Yoni – more than once, in fact, and with quite a bit of tongue action. Still, he found it disturbing that she would think it was okay to use his toothbrush. Hell, husbands and wives didn't even do that. Ergo, Yoni taking the liberty of doing it was simply fucked up. Even worse, there was no way she could have known whose toothbrush was whose, so she might have been using Nissa's or Cherry's. (And from the way she was holding it, Shade himself couldn't tell who it belonged to.)

All of this flitted through his mind in just a second or two after Yoni opened the door. Still brushing, she raised her eyebrows in a *What-is-it?* fashion.

That broke the spell Shade was under, and as he came back to himself he muttered, "I just, uh, just wanted to, um, let you know where the linen closet was in case you needed a towel or sommin'." As he spoke, he pointed towards a narrow door on the bathroom wall.

Yoni held up a forefinger to indicate that she needed a second, then walked to the bathroom sink. After turning on the water, she spat out the toothpaste. Next, cupping her hand under the faucet, she brought some water up to her mouth and rinsed, then spat it out.

"I found it," she said, holding up a washcloth that has been resting on the counter. Using it to quickly wipe around her mouth she added, "I was hopin' you wouldn't mind, but I'm guessin' it was okay."

"Sure," he intoned, stepping in to the bathroom.

He spent a moment reflecting on how to address the toothbrush situation. He liked Yoni – he really did – but she needed to understand that, regardless of how magical her pussy was, certain shit was off-limits. (And using his toothbrush was high on that list.) Of course, given everything that had happened since his sisters had left, it was likely to be a touchy subject.

Miraculously, the situation resolved itself when, a moment later, Yoni rinsed off the toothbrush she'd used, dried it with the washcloth, and then folded it before placing it into a small plastic case on the bathroom counter. She then put case in her purse.

Of course! he thought in relief. *It's part of a travel pack.*

Basically, Yoni had come prepared; she had brought her own toothbrush. Once he realized this, Shade starting laughing.

"What?" Yoni inquired. "Did I leave toothpaste around my mouth?"

As she spoke, she looked at herself in the bathroom mirror, turning her head from side to side to see what Shade was laughing.

"No," Shade told her, as he stepped close. "There's nothing on you."

Then he pulled her close and kissed her.

THUG LIFE: EMANCIPATED

Nissa and Cherry took a bit longer than an hour to get back, but – bearing in mind the look Nissa had given Shade before they left – it was probably by design. Regardless, by the time they returned, Shade and Yoni had the cakes out of the oven and had put icing on them.

In addition to ice cream, Nissa had also stopped by a chicken spot and picked up some bird for dinner. It was something of an indulgence for them since Nissa normally cooked. More to the point, they were watching every penny these days, so they normally didn't grab a lot of takeout. However, Shade had picked up a nice piece of change by virtue of Lord Byron's party, and going out for ice cream had meant that Nissa didn't really have time to prepare anything. In short, it was one of those occasions where it seemed okay to splurge a little.

Without wasting time, the four of them dug in. In addition to the chicken itself, there was also rice, corn, rolls, and mashed potatoes. Everything was delicious, and Shade actually had to make an effort to leave room for dessert, which, of course, was cake and ice cream.

After dinner, despite Nissa and Shade insisting she was a guest, Yoni helped clear the table and clean the kitchen. Then, while Cherry went into the living room to watch television, the other three sat around the kitchen table talking. In truth, however, the conversation mostly consisted of Yoni and Nissa engaging in girl-talk, with the latter occasionally telling a humorous anecdote about her brother. At that point, Shade would usually interject, ostensibly to either defend himself or explain something that Nissa claimed he'd said or done.

All in all, Shade enjoyed the conversation, essentially because it was lighthearted and fun. It made him realize that, all too often, he and Nissa (and occasionally Cherry) spent too much of their time discussing weighty shit. He made a mental note to try to inject a little more jocularity into their day-to-day lives.

After a while, Shade heard the shower in the bathroom turn on. Maybe ten minutes later, Cherry came back into the kitchen dressed in pajamas.

"I just wanted to say goodnight," she announced. "I'm about to go to bed."

She then gave everyone a quick hug – including Yoni. Then she left, with Nissa going with her to tuck her in.

"I'm impressed," Yoni declared to Shade. "With ninety-nine-point-nine percent of the kids in the hood, you gotta drag they ass to the tub for a bath, then force 'em to go to bed at gunpoint. But yo sister just did it all without being told."

Shade simply nodded. "Yeah, she's a sweet kid – always has been. Maybe *too* sweet."

"Anyway," Yoni droned, coming to her feet, "I'm gone take that as my cue."

"You're leavin'?" Shade asked, rising as well.

Yoni nodded as she slung her purse over her shoulder. "Yeah. When people start goin' to bed, that's a hint. Plus, this was just s'posed to be a short visit anyway."

"That brings up a question," said Shade. "How'd you know where I live?"

"You had a birthday party here when we were in kindergarten," she answered. "You invited the whole class."

"And you remembered where our house was from that?"

"Of course," Yoni stated matter-of-factly. "I got, like, a photographic memory."

"Bullshit," Shade said, chortling.

"Okay, I might have asked someone for directions," she conceded with a snicker. "But I remembered the general area."

Shade was about to make a smart-ass response when Nissa came back into the kitchen with her cell phone to her ear.

"A'ight," Nissa said into the phone. "Sounds fine." She then hung up.

"Everything good?" her brother asked.

"Yeah," Nissa confirmed with a nod.

"Okay, cool," Shade continued "Anyway, Yoni's gettin' ready to go."

"Oh?" droned Nissa, looking at their guest.

"Yeah, I need to be headin' back," Yoni confirmed.

"Wait a minute," Shade muttered with a frown. "How'd you get over here?"

Basically, he had just recalled that there wasn't a car in their driveway when he got home, and he hadn't seen one parked on the street in front of their house.

"I walked," Yoni declared in answer to his question.

"Well, you ain't walkin' back," Shade stated. "I'm givin' you a ride."

"Fine by me," Yoni told him before turning to Nissa. "It was great to meet-chu."

"You, too," Nissa replied, giving Yoni a hug. "Come back any time."

"We'll have to see about that," Yoni told her. "Your brother may not want me comin' back by."

"Fuck him," Nissa said. "We'll hang out and do girl shit – he ain't gotta be around."

The two of them started laughing at that, while Shade rolled his eyes in faux annoyance.

"You got everythang?" he asked Yoni.

She nodded, saying, "I think so."

"Great," Shade muttered. "We outta here."

With that, he started marching her from the kitchen. A few seconds later, they were at the door. Shade opened it for Yoni and then turned to his sister, what was seeing them out. He was intending to tell her that he'd be right back, but never got the chance.

"After you drop her off," Nissa began, "can you find somewhere to be for 'bout an hour?"

"Huh?" Shade uttered, perplexed.

"That was Goose on the phone," Nissa explained.

"Goose?" Shade repeated, trying not to sound annoyed. Then, noting a look of curiosity on Yoni's face, he added, "My sister's boyfriend."

As Yoni nodded in understanding, Nissa went on, asking, "So, can you find sommin' to get into for at least, like, forty-five minutes?"

"Forty-five minutes?" Shade echoed. "With Goose, I'll be shocked if you need forty-five seconds."

Somewhere in the back of his mind, Shade realized that – given his recent performance with Yoni – he was being somewhat hypocritical, but he didn't give a shit about that at the moment.

In response, Nissa just laughed. "That was the old Goose, back when we first started dating. I got his ass trained now. He's a sixty-minute man."

"Ha!" Shade barked. "I'll believe it when I see it." Then, realizing his poor choice of words, he added, "That's just an expression. I don't need to see *shit*."

Nissa giggled. "Just make sure you gone an hour – maybe an hour-and-a-half."

"No problem," Shade assured her. "I'll go to the library and see if they got this book I been waitin' on: 'Aimless Muhfuckas and the Women Who Love Them.'"

His sister merely laughed at that and then shut the door.

Turning to Yoni, he said, "Come on," and then began guiding her towards the car.

"You know what?" Yoni countered unexpectedly. "Why don't we walk?"

"Walk?" Shade uttered, almost like it was a foreign concept.

"Sure. It'll give us time to talk."

Shade seemed to consider for a moment then shrugged, "Cool with me."

THUG LIFE: EMANCIPATED

Chapter 53

It was already dark as they began the walk to Yoni's tenement. There was light from street lamps, but Shade was wishing he'd brought the tactical flashlight.

"So," Yoni intoned. "You and your sister always talk to each other like that?"

Shade frowned, trying to figure out what she was talking about – then it hit him. "You mean the sex stuff."

"Yeah," Yoni confirmed with a nod. "I mean, I know my brother Bo is out there fuckin' – he knocked some bitch up, remember? – and he knows I ain't no virgin, but I couldn't imagine havin' a direct conversation with him about some guy I'm about to bone."

"I guess it *is* a lil' weird," Shade admitted.

"Maybe just a lil'," Yoni added sarcastically.

"Well, b'foe you start thinkin' we grew up in some freaky household, let me just tell you that it wasn't like that. I mean, Nissa and I were always close, but we weren't talkin' 'bout stuff like sex as kids, watchin' a bunch of porn on cable, or playin' doctor, or any shit like that."

"I get it – you were just regular kids."

"Exactly. But then… shit went sideways."

Yoni was silent for a moment, then asked, "So what happened?"

"Life happened," Shade declared. "Fuckin' life in the hood." There was silence for a few seconds, and Shade realized that his answer had been somewhat vague. Taking a deep breath, he then added, "Our granddaddy was shot and killed."

"I heard about that," Yoni told him. "I'm sorry."

"It's okay," Shade stressed. "It was a while ago. But you have to understand, up until that point, Nissa had been a *good* girl."

256

"You mean a virgin."

"I guess," Shade replied with a shrug. "But our granddaddy gettin' killed really got to her. After he died, certain things just hit home for her, like about how fleetin' life is and how tomorrow ain't promised to you. How you can go at any time – 'specially in the hood. All that stuff just got in her head."

"And she started wonderin' what she was savin' herself for," Yoni concluded.

"Yeah," Shade confirmed, nodding as he looked at Yoni with new eyes.

She obviously had some insight into the situation he was describing, and she verified it a moment later, saying, "Lots of girls go through shit like that in the ghetto. I dealt with sommin' similar when my grandmomma died."

Shade merely took that in stride, then went on. "Anyway, at some point she ended up hooking up with some nigga called Tony. I forget his last name, but everybody called him Tony Macaroni because it seemed like that's all he ate. But he had no business bein' with Nissa, 'cause she was only thirteen at the time and this muhfucka was seventeen – damn near grown."

Yoni snorted in derision. "Like niggas in the hood care about that."

"True, but that alone is enough for you to know that the nigga ain't no good. Ain't no decent muhfucka that age gone be chasin' some girl barely outta elementary."

That was a slight exaggeration, but not by much in Shade's estimation.

"So Tony actin' like he all in love and shit," Shade continued. "Callin' Nissa all the time, tellin' her how pretty she is, how much he wanna be with her, takin' her to the movies…"

"Basically, the same bullshit niggas always spout when then wanna get in a bitch panties," Yoni summed up.

"Pretty much," Shade remarked. "So you can prolly guess the rest: she slept with him, and he dogged her – acted like she didn't exist. No mo' phone calls, no mo' dates, no mo' nuthin."

"Typical nigga," Yoni noted flatly. "How'd Nissa take it?"

"It fucked with her head – had her in tears all the time. I mean, she knew niggas in the hood did shit like that, but she didn't expect it to happen to her. She had been a virgin and thought they were in love, but all that muhfucka wanted was a taste."

"And after he got it he was gone," Yoni said. There was an emotion in her tone that seemed to suggest that she wasn't just making a comment, but speaking from experience.

"It was good riddance as far as I was concerned," Shade attested. "As to Nissa, in most situations like that, I guess girls will turn to their sistas, momma, grandmomma, or girlfriends... Some female who's maybe been there and can give 'em advice. But Nissa didn't have any of that. Our grandmomma died back when I was in elementary, our mom's a junkie, and Cherry was too young for that kinda talk. We're really not close to any other family, and Nissa didn't have many friends back then – all the girls tended to think she was a stuck-up prude because she hadn't so much as kissed a guy up to that point. So basically, at that juncture, I was the only one left. And if she didn't have *me*, she didn't have *anybody*."

"So you became a sympathetic ear," Yoni noted, then teased, "That's so sweet."

"It was fuckin' uncomfortable, is what is was," Shade countered, "'cause she told me everythang. Not blow by blow, thankfully, but way more than I thought she'd share."

"Well, the main thing is that you were there for her."

"I guess," Shade conceded. "But that wasn't the last guy she told me about, and over time I s'pose I became comfortable with it."

"And now you're at the point where she can ask you to leave so she can bang some nigga."

"That moron Goose," Shade muttered, almost in disgust. "She could do a lot better. I'm just glad she makes that nigga wear a condom."

"Well, that's good," Yoni commented. "At least you know she bein' careful."

And with that statement, something suddenly occurred to Shade – an issue he should have conferred with Yoni about much sooner.

"Um, that actually brings up an interestin' topic," he began. "I probably should have asked this before, but, uh, are you–"

"Nigga, are you for real?" Yoni interjected, coming to a halt under a street lamp. "You gone wait until after you squirt yo jizz all up in me – twice, mind you – and *then* ask if I'm usin' birth control?"

Shade gave her a sheepish look. "I guess I kinda got carried away before, so I, um, didn't thank to ask."

"Well, the answer is no, nigga – I ain't on shit," Yoni declared. "No IUD, no vaginal ring, no diaphragm, no nuthin'."

"Nuthin'?" Shade echoed, looking shocked.

"On top of that, I'm ovulating."

"What?" Shade blurted out.

"And I also have overactive ovaries that produce more than one egg at a time," Yoni stressed. "As a result, the doctor says I'll probably always have multiple births – at least twins every time some fool knocks me up."

Shade didn't immediately say anything. In essence, he was still trying to process everything Yoni had just said. It was all too fucking overwhelming, and he couldn't get his head around all the implications. Still stunned, he looked at Yoni – and saw her with a hand to her mouth, struggling to stifle her laughter. And then he caught on.

"You fuckin' bitch," Shade muttered, grinning as Yoni suddenly laughed out loud.

Stepping close, Shade grabbed her wrist and pulled her to him. Grinning broadly, Yoni gave him a quick peck on the lips.

"I'm on the pill, asshole," she told him. "But maybe that'll teach you to ask a few more questions next time yo dick's leadin' you around."

"But all my 'next times' are gonna be with you," Shade said contritely, looking at Yoni with puppy-dog eyes. "At least, I hope so."

Yoni appeared to blush for a moment, then demanded, "Nigga, stop tryin' to sweet-talk me."

"Can't help it," Shade retorted. "You just so sweet."

"Whatever," Yoni said, although Shade noted she was still smiling. Now holding hands, they resumed walking to Yoni's place.

"So," she continued, "after your sista told you how the guy fucked her over, what did you do?"

"Initially, I ain't do shit," Shade replied. "Because honestly, what did he do? He didn't slap her. He didn't throw her out of his place naked. He didn't kick her out his car on the other side of town. What he did was fucked up, but it was romance shit."

Yoni raised an eyebrow skeptically. "Romance?"

"You know what I mean. This was related to the relationship, and it's the type of stuff that happens, not just in the hood but everywhere. Niggas get what they want from a chick and then act like she's a fuckin' plague of locusts. But it's not the kind of thang you normally get in a nigga's ass about, and even Nissa realized that. In fact, she *asked* me not to do anythang – said the key here was not for me to go after guys because they dogged her; she simply needed to become a better judge of character."

Yoni appeared to reflect momentarily. "You said that *initially* you didn't do shit about the guy."

Shade didn't immediately respond. But after a few seconds, he stated, "I was gonna leave it alone like Nissa asked me to, but that muhfucka Tony took shit too far. He had some video of a chick givin' a blowjob on his phone, and he started tellin' everybody it was Nissa suckin' him off. The bitch didn't even look like Nissa, but you know how it is. Shit like that will spread like wildfire, even when it's an obvious-ass lie. So I went to Tony and told him to chill with that shit."

"Did he?"

"No, he just laughed, and I left. Guess he figured that was the end of it."

"I'm guessin' it wasn't," Yoni suggested. "So what happened?"

"Oh, he had an accident," Shade answered.

"An accident?" Yoni echoed with a frown.

"Actually, he had a couple of 'em," Shade clarified. "First, he had a test tube explode in his hand during chemistry class. He was s'posed to be demonstratin' some minor chemical reaction – making bubbles or some shit like that – but seems like he used the wrong ingredients."

"And it blew up?" Yoni asked, sounding incredulous.

"More like shattered. Tony got cut and had to get stitches, but that was about it. He claimed somebody must have switched the chemicals around or sommin', but from what I heard the teacher considered Tony a dumbass and assumed he either fucked up the experiment or deliberately used the wrong chemicals cause he thought it would be funny. And to be honest, he was the type of nigga who'd do sommin' like that as a joke, so most everybody assumed that's what happened."

"Then a few days later," Shade went on, "he's driving this piece-of-shit car he owns, and the engine catches fire."

Yoni gave him an inquisitive look. "Was he hurt?"

"Not really. He slammed on the brakes, threw the car into park and jumped out. The fire blew some kind of exhaust into the car before he stopped so he had some smoke inhalation, but nothing serious."

"Do they know what caused the fire?"

Shade shook his head. "Naw. The fire department showed up and put it out, but from what I heard they never figured out exactly what happened. They just assumed it was shitty maintenance on Tony's part. Anyway, a day or two after that, he broke both legs."

"Da fuck?" Yoni muttered in surprise. "How the hell he do that?"

"He lived on the third floor of a tenement with an overprotective grandmother," Shade explained. "She didn't want him goin' out at night, so she had a deadbolt installed that required a key to unlock it and get out, and she always kept the key on her."

"So basically," Yoni surmised, "when Tony came home at night, she locked him in."

"Yeah, but Tony found a workaround. The buildin' had an old drainpipe that ran right next to his bedroom window, so when he wanted to get out at night, he'd open his window and shimmy down that pipe. Then, when he came home, he'd shimmy back up it again."

"Okay, that's fuckin' crazy."

Shade shrugged. "Depends on how bad you wanna get out. Anyway, this particular night, Tony decides he's goin' out, so he opens his window and gets on the pipe. But apparently it's old and rusted – been there for years – and it breaks away from the buildin'. Tony lets go and falls three stories."

"And breaks both legs," Yoni concluded.

"Yep. After that, he found religion, a twelve-step program, or some shit like that because he called my sista and apologized, then started tellin' folks he was jokin' when he said that was her in the video."

Yoni said something then, but Shade didn't take note of it. Instead, his attention had been drawn to an SUV that had just passed them, going in the opposite direction. More importantly, it had slowed down significantly as it drew abreast of them. Although the windows were tinted, Shade had gotten the distinct impression that whoever was inside was eyeing him and Yoni.

"Are you even listenin' to me?" Yoni suddenly asked.

"Huh?" muttered Shade as the SUV sped up again..

"I was asking what Nissa said when Tony called."

"Oh, uh… She told 'im she'd accept his apology if he promised to never fuckin' speak to her again."

"Damn straight," Yoni said with feminine pride.

Shade, however, wasn't really paying attention to her. His focus was still on the SUV, which had done a u-turn and was now headed back towards them.

Not good, Shade thought. The u-turn didn't necessarily mean that the vehicle's occupants were interested in him and Yoni; they could have just been looking for an address. Still, it was suspicious as fuck.

He spent a quick moment trying to recall who – like Mario – he might have pissed off enough lately to make them want to come after him. A couple of people immediately came to mind, but it suddenly occurred to him that he might not be the person the SUV's passengers were interested in. It could be some nut fixated on Yoni.

He then briefly considered taking some kind of evasive action – maybe grabbing Yoni by the hand and sprinting between some nearby houses. But it seemed like that would be an overreaction when he didn't know who or what they were running from. And again, he didn't even know if the folks in the SUV were even focused on him and Yoni. It was just instinct telling him that was the case.

However, his instincts were proven correct when the SUV pulled to a stop next to them a moment later. Still holding Yoni's hand, Shade stepped protectively in front of her as the front passenger window rolled down, then a male voice said, "Zerk wants to talk to you."

Chapter 54

Shade recognized the person who'd spoken. It was a nigga called Spinner, who was the lieutenant of drug dealer Zerk Simon. More importantly, it was clear that his statement had been directed at Shade.

"Why don't you hop in?" Spinner said, although it wasn't really phrased as a question.

At that point, the rear passenger door opened and a big, brawny muhfucka stepped out. Through the open door, Shade could also see another nigga in the back seat.

"I need to walk my girl home first," Shade replied after a moment.

"We can drop her off," Spinner assured him.

"You already got two niggas in the back seat," Shade noted. "It'll be too tight back there. Plus, I promised her we'd walk."

"Well, I'm bettin' yo girl would rather ride than keep hoofin' it back to her crib. Come on, get in."

"That's okay. We'll finish our walk."

Spinner gave him a hard look. "I wasn't really askin'."

"I know," Shade told him. "But I'm still walkin' her home."

Suddenly the big nigga by the rear door stepped forward, and Shade realized that he held a gun loosely in his hand.

"Muhfucka, you don't hear so good," the big guy said. "Get in the fuckin' car."

Shade shook his head. "Not happenin'."

Without warning, the big guy raised his gun, pointing it directly at Shade's forehead. Shade didn't flinch; he just tugged on Yoni's hand to make sure she stayed safely behind him

"Nigga, you thank I'm playin' wichu?" the brawny nigga demanded. "I'll end you *and* this bitch right here, right now.

"Yo, yo, yo, Beemer!" Spinner exclaimed. "Chill with that shit. This s'posed to be friendly."

The big nigga – Beemer – didn't look friendly at all, but he slowly lowered his gun and took a step back, glowering at Shade the entire time. Spinner gave him a disapproving look, then turned his attention back to Shade.

"Hey, gone walk ya girl home," Spinner told him. "We'll scoop you up after."

Rather than verbally respond, Shade simply gave him a terse nod.

"Where you live at, by the way?" Spinner asked Yoni.

"The Quad," she replied, looking a little shell-shocked. At the same time, she raised her hand and pointed at a cluster of four tenement buildings that appeared to be a couple of blocks away.

"A'ight," Spinner uttered with a nod as Beemer got back inside. "See you over there."

He then rolled up the window as the SUV drove off. When it reached the next intersection, it turned and then was lost to sight. At that moment, Yoni seemed to collapse inward on herself.

"Oh, shit!" she exclaimed, placing a hand over heart and breathing hard. "Oh shit."

"Just breathe," Shade suggested. "In and out. Slow. You're okay."

"No, I'm *not* fuckin' okay," she countered. "We almost got shot."

"But we didn't, and those fuckfaces are gone now."

"Shit," she uttered again. "I've never been so scared in my life – and I'm not the one who had a gun in my face."

She then looked at Shade, and for the first time seemed to notice that he was utterly calm – had been throughout that entire encounter.

"Weren't you scared?" She finally asked.

"Ha!" Shade barked. "I ain't been scared of nuthin' since I died."

Chapter 55

"It happened when I got shot," Shade explained as they resumed walking. "I actually coded out on the operating table. I was clinically dead for six minutes."

"How'd it happen?" asked Yoni. "You gettin' shot, I mean."

"My shithead gangsta daddy showed up one day high as a muhfuckin' kite. He got into with my moms, and I guess she said sommin' he didn't like 'cause he pulled out a gun. Nigga was so stoned that he didn't even realize my momma was holdin' Cherry, who was just a baby at the time. So, right b'foe he pulled the trigger, I stepped in front of 'em"

"Damn…" Yoni muttered sympathetically. "Tell me again how old you were?"

"Six," he said, looking nostalgic for a moment. "Anyway, the doctors managed to bring me back, but since then, nuthin' scares me."

"For real?"

"Yeah," Shade confirmed with a nod. "I can't explain it, but it's like when I came back, some shit got left behind. Or maybe it's just a natural side effect. I mean, after you dead, what the fuck else is there to be scared of?"

"Nuthin', I guess," Yoni concurred. "So what happened to yo daddy?"

"They locked his ass up."

"For how long?"

"Hopefully 'til the muhfuckin' sun goes out – and then some."

"So he's still inside?"

"Far as I know."

Yoni gave him a quizzical look. "Do you ever talk to him?"

"Indirectly."

268

"How's that?" inquired Yoni, frowning.

"Through the Parole Board," Shade answered. "Every year when his parole hearin' comes up, I send the Board a nice picture of me lyin' all gutshot in the hospital, with tubes and wires runnin' out of every orifice. I also include a nice letter, explainin' how my lifelong dream is to be able to eat solids again, and to go to the bathroom without pissin' blood."

"What?" muttered Yoni. "Nigga, ain't nuthin' wrong wichu."

"Yeah, but the Parole Board don't know that."

Yoni eyed him skeptically. "You bullshittin'. You ain't wrote no Parole Board."

"Maybe, maybe not," Shade said with a smirk. "The main thing is that he stay behind bars."

Yoni seemed to dwell on that for a moment. Then, changing the subject, she asked, "So who's this Zerk guy?"

"Just your friendly, neighborhood sociopath," Shade responded.

"Well, every hood needs at least *one*," Yoni said with a grin. "Keeps thangs interestin'."

Shade chuckled at that, then continued. "He's a local drug dealer, about the same level as Lord Byron. But I wasn't kiddin' 'bout what I said b'foe. He's a certified, grade-A psycho. He'll be laughin' with you one minute, then tryin' to shove a tire iron down yo throat the next. You never know what'll set 'im off."

"So what he want wichu?"

"Prolly wants me to read 'im a bedtime story," Shade answered sarcastically. "Fuck if I know."

"Sounds like you should be careful."

"That's the damn understatement of the year," Shade declared.

****

THUG LIFE: EMANCIPATED

For the remainder of the walk, they simply made small talk until they reached the street where Yoni lived. Her tenement was actually one of a four identical buildings constructed around a central courtyard. As expected, the SUV with Spinner and the rest of Zerk's goons was parked out front in plain view. Ignoring them, Shade began escorting Yoni to the door of the closest building.

"Uh," Yoni droned as they approached the entrance, "you know this ain't my buildin', right?"

"I know," he told her. "But I prefer that those fuckin' gorillas workin' for Zerk not know where you live."

"Oh, shit," Yoni mumbled. "I hadn't even thought about that." Then she frowned. "You thank they might come after me or sommin'?"

He shook his head. "No, but right now I just feel like the less info those muhfuckas have, the better – 'specially since I don't know what the hell Zerk wants."

"Sounds good to me," Yoni said as they reached the front door. Coming to a halt, she turned to Shade, stepped in close, then put her arms around his neck.

"Since you told those niggas you was walkin' yo girl home, I figure we need to make it look good." she said. "But don't take this as meanin' I like you."

"It never crossed my mind," Shade told her with a grin, then kissed her.

It wasn't a long or lingering kiss, but it was deep and passionate. When their lips parted a few seconds later, they stayed close, foreheads touching.

"Hey, momma," said a masculine voice that seemed to come from behind Yoni. "You brought enough for everybody?"

"Fuck off!" Yoni yelled over her shoulder, without even turning around to see who the speaker was. Glancing behind her, Shade saw that it was a thin, middle-aged man leaning against the side of the building smoking a cigarette.

"Damn, baby," the man whined. "Nigga can't even joke wichu."

Still not turning around, Yoni flicked a middle finger up the air, causing Shade to chuckle.

"Aw, hell," the man said. "I don't have to take this shit."

With that, he dropped his cigarette butt on the ground, stomped it out, then went into the building.

"Damn," muttered Shade. "Hard to believe you were scared back there with Zerk's crew."

"Nigga's like that I know how to handle," she said, nodding of the direction of the man who gone inside. "I know what they want and how to put 'em in they place. Niggas with guns is a different story."

"No argument there," Shade told her. "Anyway, I better get going before those fools start gettin' antsy. Just go inside like you live here, wait about a minute, then head to yo buildin'."

"Got it," Yoni told him. "Call me later?"

"Definitely," he promised.

They kissed once more, and then Yoni went inside while Shade walked down to the SUV and got inside.

THUG LIFE: EMANCIPATED

Chapter 56

As was fast becoming the norm for them, Gummy and Blanchard were once again parked in their car in a deserted alley in the hood.

"Where da fuck is Gills?" grumbled Gummy. "He was s'posed to be here thirty minutes ago."

"You know how he is," Blanchard responded. "Thinks bein' tardy is a damn badge of prestige."

"Well, he better have sommin' on this Shade kid."

"Yeah," Blanchard agreed. "It's too bad those three knuckleheads at the hospital didn't wanna cooperate."

Gummy frowned. None of those dipshits who had gotten fucked up in that basement had really been willing to talk – despite having a bunch of serious charges being levelled at them. Even when the detectives stressed that Shade was who they were really interested in, they didn't make much headway. The most they got was a hint from the one who'd been kneecapped – Deeter – who said that Shade might have taken issue regarding a joke they'd made about his sister. But – like his shithead compadres – Deeter hadn't been willing to put Shade in the basement when the gunplay occurred.

Noting his partner's expression, Blanchard asked, "You thank we should have kept a tail on 'im?"

Gummy shook his head. "No, that didn't work out too well earlier today, and I don't wanna burn a bunch of favors havin' 'im followed 'til we have more to go on."

"Well, hopefully we'll get sommin' solid soon. Here comes Gills."

A moment later, their confidential informant slid into the back seat with a cordial, "Evenin' gents."

"Da fuck you been?" groused Gummy.

"We been sittin' here half an hour waitin' on yo ass," Blanchard added, "so you better have sommin' for us."

272

"That depends," Gills remarked with a grin. "Wha'chall got for *me*?"

The two detectives shared a glance, then Blanchard grabbed an envelope that was sitting on the seat between them. He held it up over his shoulder, towards the back seat. A second later, Gills took it.

"Now that's what I'm talkin' 'bout," Gills muttered as he peeked inside the envelope. Satisfied, he folded the envelope and tucked it into his pocket.

"Alright," Gummy said. "You arrived fashionably late, you got paid in full, now tell us what the fuck you know about Shade."

"Sure," Gills replied. "His real name's–"

"Stop," Blanchard ordered. "We cops, okay? And we good at our jobs. That mean we already know the fuckin' basics like name and address. Yo ass is here to tell us shit we *don't* already know."

"Okay," Gills droned. "Then I guess you already know that he basically goes around the neighborhood fixin' shit up."

"Yeah, he's the hood handyman," Gummy commented. "We got all that. We need to know what he's into, and who he's got beef with, like these three dipshits he had a run-in with this weekend."

"Somebody had a run-in with Shade?" Gills uttered in surprise. "Shit, they lucky they not in the hospital."

Gummy and Blanchard suddenly looked at each other. Then, in an almost synchronized motion, they both turned towards the back seat.

Feeling a little nervous all of a sudden, Gills looked from one of the detectives to the other, then muttered, "What?"

"They *are* in the hospital," Gummy said.

"Huh?" Gills responded, looking confused.

"You just said those guys who had a run-in with Shade were lucky not to be in the hospital," Gummy noted. "Well, that's exactly where they are."

Gills seemed to consider this for a second, then remarked with a shrug, "Can't say I'm surprised."

"And why is that?" inquired Blanchard.

Gills looked pensive for a moment, then stated, "Look, there's two things you gotta know 'bout Shade. First is that people generally don't fuck with him or his family. Those that do, tend to have accidents."

Gummy's brow creased. "Whachu mean, 'accidents'?"

"*Accidents*, muhfucka," Gills chided. "The get into car wrecks, slip down the stairs, fall through open manholes..."

"Seriously?" asked Blanchard.

"As a fuckin' heart attack," Gills answered.

"Bullshit," Gummy declared.

"A'ight, lemme tell you a lil' story," Gills said. "Shade got this lil' sista go by the name of Cherry. Now, she 'bout nine, ten years old and just a sweet girl from what I hear. Anyway, a lil' while back this crew of four or five niggas started harrassin' her every day when she on her way home from school. They sayin' how they gotta have them some Cherry, how Cherry need to popped and all kinds of shit like that."

"Now they like sixteen or seventeen," Gills continued. "Idle niggas who don't do shit but cut school and ain't got no business talkin' to a lil' girl that way."

"So what happened to 'em?" Gummy inquired.

Gills seemed to consider for a moment. "You know how it is when it come to hangin' out in the hood. Just about everybody and they friends have a favorite handout spot. It might be somebody's backyard, or a deserted warehouse, or abandoned train car. Whatever. There's usually someplace y'all go that nobody else know about or go to, so it's like it's ya own space."

"I know whachu mean," Gummy told him. "When I was a kid, my friends and I used to play in this abandoned used car lot. It was overgrown with weeds and people used to just dump shit there, but it was our spot. It's where we played kickball, baseball, everything. We even climbed into some of the old cars that were left and pretended to drive."

"Sound like a cool spot," Gills said. "And in the same way, these muhfuckas who messed with Shade's sista had a place they liked to kick back. It was over on the Gold Coast – where the rich niggas used to live. They found this old mansion that had been deserted for like forty years."

"And that's where they hung out?" Blanchard surmised.

"Not exactly," Gills replied, shaking his head. "The mansion had a huge back yard – a couple of acres with lots of trees and shit, and in one of 'em was this treehouse. *That* was their spot."

"A treehouse?" Gummy repeated dubiously.

"They ain't got shit like that in the hood," Gills explained, "so these muhfuckas felt like they hand found sommin' extra-special. They used to take girls there, go up in that bitch to smoke weed, plan shit, whatever. Anyway, one day, all them niggas was up in the treehouse with it fell out."

"Wait a minute," Gummy said, frowning. "One of them fell out the treehouse?"

"Uh-uh," Gills replied, shaking his head. "The *treehouse* fell out. It fell out the *tree*. Just fuckin' collapsed or some shit."

"Hold on – I think I remember seein' that on the news," Blanchard stated.

"Yeah, they had ambulances and news crews all over there," Gills told them. "Nobody died, but those niggas got fucked up pretty good."

"And Shade did that?" Gummy asked.

"That's the rumor," Gills said, "but the police investigated and said there was no foul play. Anyway, that's the kind of shit that happens to people who fuck with Shade or his family. They have accidents."

"Hmmm," Gummy droned. "You said there were two things we needed to know about Shade. What's the second?"

"Again, it's just rumor," Gills stressed, "but word on the street is that if you have enough cash, Shade can make anyone you want have an 'accident' – includin' a fatal one, if the price is right."

"Bullshit," Gummy declared. "You tellin' me this kid's a hitman?"

"I'm with my partner on that one," chimed in Blanchard, "and callin' bullshit, too."

"Well, which part you thank a kid in the hood can't do?" Gills asked. "Kill somebody, or do it for money?"

The two detectives exchanged a glance, but neither immediately said anything.

After a few seconds, Gummy said, "I'm assumin' you got a source for this bullshit you shovelin'. Are they reliable?"

"I got no particular source," Gills answered. "This is all shit I learned over time just keepin' my ear to the ground."

"I don't suppose the ground also gave up who might have hired Shade," Gummy prodded. "Assumin' any of this assassin shit is true."

"I knew you were gonna ask that," Gills said. As he spoke, he pulled a folded piece of paper from a pocket and held it out.

Gummy took the piece of paper and, with his partner looking over his shoulder, opened it up. There was a list of names written on it – presumably the people who had hired Shade to kill someone.

"So which of these good people is most likely to cooperate with the police?" asked Blanchard after a few seconds.

"Probably none," Gills answered. "But why you need to talk to 'em? Just do what they do on those cop shows."

"Which is what?" asked Gummy, plainly curious.

"Follow the money," Gills said in a matter-of-fact tone. Then, sensing that the meeting was over, he slid to the door and opened it, preparing to exit. However, he'd barely put a foot out before Gummy called his name.

"One more thing, Gills," Gummy said. "You said you learned this shit about Shade over time."

Gills shrugged. "Yeah, so?"

"That means you already knew it yesterday when you met with us. Why da fuck didn't you just tell us then?"

"Well, for one thing, you muhfuckas practically threw my black ass out the car," Gills said. "And for another, if I had told you yesterday, I wudna got paid again."

Then, laughing and waggling the envelope they'd given him, he stepped out of the car.

THUG LIFE: EMANCIPATED

Chapter 57

The ride with Zerk's crew gave Shade an odd sense of déjà vu. It was eerily reminiscent of his jaunt the day before with Lord Byron's gang. Then, like now, he had found himself sandwiched into a vehicle with four thuggish muhfuckas. However, his meeting with Lord Byron felt like it had happened a lifetime ago because of everything that had occurred in the interim: the party, his chat with the cops, the run-in with Mario… And now this.

Ultimately, they ended up at an ancient, beat-up warehouse that had been converted into an auto body shop. At least that's what the faded sign outside said. Shade and the others got out of the SUV, and he found himself following Spinner to the warehouse entrance, which was seemingly guarded by a couple of niggas outside wearing jogging suits. One of them gave Spinner a what's-up nod, which Spinner returned before opening the door.

Inside, the place actually looked a bit like an auto shop – at least to the extent that there were a couple of cars inside. However, none of the half-dozen or so niggas Shade saw in there appeared to be working. They were just standing around talking, shooting the shit (although they appeared to look a little more alert when they saw Spinner).

Shade's escort led him to a door situated on the back wall. Still accompanied by the others he'd ridden with, Shade followed Spinner inside and found himself in a narrow hallway. After a few twists and turns, the corridor terminated at a doorway with stairs leading to a basement. Still following Spinner, Shade went down the steps.

Needless to say, Shade wasn't wild about the way things were shaping up. Him alone in a basement with four possibly adverse muhfuckas (five, if Zerk was down there as well), was less than an ideal scenario. Even worse was the fact that he obviously wasn't here for any type of handyman shit; he had mentioned to Spinner in the SUV that he didn't have his tools with him, only to be told that he wouldn't need them.

All of this flitted through Shade's mind as he reached the bottom of the stairs and took a look around. There wasn't a lot of light, but the basement was expansive and appeared to be divided into a couple of rooms. It probably would have made a great man-cave, but was currently devoid of furniture except for an antiquated couch that had seen better days.

"Come on," Spinner said to Shade. He then told the others, "The rest of you muhfuckas stay here."

With that, Spinner began heading towards a nearby hallway, with Shade on his heels. The passageway, which had initially been dark, was suddenly illuminated when Spinner flicked a light switch on the wall. A few seconds later they stopped in front of a door on the right side of the hallway. Spinner knocked once, loudly, then opened the door.

At first, Shade only saw one person in the room: a big nigga – maybe six feet tall and heavily muscled. He had his back to them, but Shade didn't have any trouble recognizing him: Zerk.

At the sound of the door opening, Zerk glanced over his shoulder.

"Shade," Spinner said in answer to Zerk's unasked question, at the same time tilting his head in Shade's direction.

At that, Zerk turned around to face them, and that's when Shade realized something: Zerk wasn't in the room alone.

He had initially been blocked from view by Zerk's body, but there was a man in the room as well, sitting in a chair. Or rather, *tied* to a chair – at least that was Shade's impression based on the way the man's arms seemed to be pinned behind him.

Shade didn't think it was anyone he knew, but it was hard to tell because the nigga's face had been beaten to a pulp. His eyes were swollen shut, his lips were split, and he had a wicked gash on one cheek. Blood was dribbling from the man's mouth and his shirt was so stained with it that Shade would have sworn that he'd been stabbed in the chest.

However, he wasn't the only one covered in blood, because at the moment, Zerk looked like the very essence of his nickname. He had blood spatter (not his own, of course) all over his face, chest and especially his hands, each of which was adorned with a pair of brass knuckles. But the most telling feature, the one aspect of his that really made him look as crazy as he actually was, was the fact that he had a lazy eye.

Zerk merely stared at Shade for a moment, apparently sizing him up. Shade met his gaze, but found it difficult to stay focused when, after a few moments, Zerk's right eye started drifting to the side, like it had better things to do. That, in conjunction with the fact that he was covered in blood, made Zerk look brutal and unhinged (which was pretty much an accurate description).

"I'ma need a minute here," Zerk finally said. "Take 'im to my office."

At that moment, the guy in the chair – who appeared to be semi-conscious – mumbled something that sounded like, "Please...please..."

Spinning back towards his victim, Zerk bellowed, "Shut the fuck up!" At the same time, he swung a vicious blow at the guy's jaw.

There was a weird cracking sound, like someone simultaneously snapping several pencils in two as the head of the guy in the chair snapped to the side. At the same time, something akin to a couple of white buttons seemed to fly across the room and strike the wall. One of them ricocheted and came tumbling across the floor towards the doorway. It came to rest just a few inches from Shade's foot, giving him a good look at. And of course, it wasn't a button.

It was a bloody tooth.

THUG LIFE: EMANCIPATED

Chapter 58

Zerk's "office" turned out to be a men's room off the hallway on the first floor. In Shade's opinion, the place had obviously seen better days, as one of the bathroom stall doors was missing and at least one of the urinals was missing a handle to flush with. It also stank of urine, which meant that the niggas hanging out around here probably pissed on the floor half the time, and nobody was cleaning this bitch up on anything close to a regular basis. He also doubted that any of these muhfuckas washed they hands.

Aside from the smell and possible hygiene issues, Shade didn't like the psychological aspects associated with meeting in a bathroom. For one thing, it suggested that he was no better that the piss and shit that got disposed of in here. In addition, simply being in a bathroom created a subconscious desire to use the facilities, and the last thing Shade needed was to have his back to these muhfuckas and his dick in his hand if shit went sideways.

That said, he seriously doubted that psychology was the reason they were meeting here. That nigga Zerk's thinking didn't run that deep. Much like Mario, Zerk wasn't particularly bright and he knew it. However, he did have good instincts. Also, unlike Mario, Zerk shored up his shortcomings in the area of brains by putting smart muhfuckas on his payroll, like Spinner.

But it was a double-edged sword; while Zerk knew he needed niggas around who were brighter than him, he didn't trust them. In essence, he knew that, sooner or later, smart muhfuckas always end up at the same crossroads in their thinking: *If I'm the brains of this fuckin' crew, then how come I'm an employee and not the boss?* Zerk generally took action when things reached that point, and as a result, the job of being his lieutenant was not a position with long-term prospects.

Bearing that in mind, Shade felt a little sorry for Spinner, who – by all accounts – really wasn't that bad of a guy. For a drug dealer, that is.

After that, Shade had no more time for introspection as Zerk unexpectedly kicked the door open and came in.

"–nd clean up that mess in the basement," Zerk growled over his shoulder as he entered and headed to one of the bathroom sinks. Taking off the brass knuckles, he dropped them into the sink and began washing his hands.

Looking at Shade via the bathroom mirror, he grumbled, "Muhfuckas be tryin' to test me, know what I'm sayin'? Nigga take shit that he *know* belong to me and then act like he don't know what I'm talkin' 'bout when I ask for it. I try to be a nice guy, tell 'im that if he just give the shit back, we cool. There'll be a penalty he gotta pay for puttin' his hand in the fuckin' cookie jar, but we'll be straight after that. But naw – nigga wanna play dumb. Then I got to drag yo ass to the basement and make an example outta you – use you to send a message."

Zerk paused for a moment to cup his hands under the faucet, then used the water to wash his face.

"Anyway," he droned as he snatched a couple of paper towels from a dispenser on the wall, "I'm sorry you had to see that."

"Don't worry about it," Shade told him, although he was certain that Zerk had *absolutely* wanted him to see that shit in the basement. He wanted Shade to know that he wasn't a nigga to be trifled with. And as he watched Zerk wash up, Shade also had a better understanding of why they were meeting in the bathroom. "Anyway, Spinner said you wanted to see me?"

"Yeah," Zerk confirmed with a nod as he dried his face and hands with the paper towels. "We got a problem."

He didn't move, but Shade's body suddenly tensed and his eyes darted back and forth between the other two. Thankfully, neither made any type of aggressive move, which suggested that they were just there to talk – for the moment.

"I'm listenin'," Shade said.

Zerk, who had begun stripping out of his bloody clothes, simply nodded at Spinner.

"I'm not gonna fuck around," Spinner began. "It's ya moms."

Shade gave a perplexed look. "What about her?"

"She's into us for a lot of money."

"What?" uttered Shade in surprise.

"She owes us," noted Zerk, who had now stripped to the waist and tossed the bloody clothes into a nearby trashcan. With the gore and bloody clothes off, he genuinely look less crazed – but only slightly.

"Okay, I'll bite," said Shade. "She owes you for what?"

"For product that she got from us," Zerk replied as he kicked off his shoes and started unbuttoning his pants. "We gave her the shit, but she never came back and paid like she was supposed to."

"Ha!" barked Shade. "You expect me to believe you sold my momma crack on credit?"

Spinner snickered slightly at that. Zerk, who had just finished unbuttoning his pants, let them drop to his ankles as he glared at his lieutenant.

"Da fuck you laughin' at?!" he screamed at Spinner.

"Nuthin', Zerk," replied Spinner, sobering immediately. Turning to Shade, he said, "We didn't *sell* to Gin. We *fronted* her."

"Da fuck you talkin' 'bout?" demanded Shade. "Nobody fronts a junkie."

"*We* do," declared Zerk, who had now shed not only his pants but also his underwear, and now stood there wearing nothing but his socks.

Somewhat stunned at having an almost completely nude sociopath just a few feet from him, Shade gave Spinner a *What-the-fuck-is-this?* look. Spinner's response was a vague gesture accompanied by a *What-do-you-want-me-to-say?* expression.

Oblivious to any discomfort that his nudity was causing, Zerk went on, stating, "I guess you could say we're…innovators."

As he finished speaking, Zerk looked at his lieutenant, who nodded in approval at his choice of words.

"Basically," Spinner said, "ya moms came to us to buy, but got to talkin' like she could move some product. Since she a user, we figured she definitely knew people she could sell to, so we took a chance. We fronted the product, and she was supposed to come back at the end of the day and pay ten percent of the cost. Then it was supposed to be another ten percent the next day, and the next…every day until she paid in full."

"Okay," Shade intoned, ignoring Zerk's nudity. "What's that gotta do with *me*?"

"She never came back with the cash," Spinner replied.

"Well, I'm guessin' you know how to handle shit like that," Shade retorted. "So feel free to make an example outta her ass. Go beat the stuffin' outta her, cut off her thumbs, slice her throat, or whatever the fuck you need to do to send a message."

"And you cool with that?" asked Spinner, sounding surprised.

"Yeah," Shade insisted. "She made this bed, she can damn sho' lie in it."

"Well, she actually offered us another option at the time we made the deal," added Spinner.

"Which was what?" Shade inquired.

"She said *you'd* be good for it if she couldn't pay," Zerk answered while reaching down to scratch his exposed balls.

Shade snorted derisively. "Well, that's a fuckin' joke."

"Nigga, do I look like I'm laughin'?" demanded Zerk, at the same time giving his dick a tug. That being the case, it actually looked to Shade like the muhfucka was about to jerk off, but he kept that thought to himself.

"I'm just tryin' to figure out what the fuck I'm doin' here," Shade said after a few seconds.

"We just told you," Spinner attested. "Gin put you on the hook for the shit she took, so *you* liable."

Shade spent a moment looking back and forth between the other two, his incredulity evident.

"Hold on," Shade muttered, shaking his head in disbelief. "You tellin' me a nigga can obligate some other muhfucka just by *sayin'* that's who'll pay? 'Cause in that case, I'ma say the President is good for any shit *I* owe, so y'all can pull up to the White House and tell *his* ass to pay up."

Rather than respond directly, Spinner let out a sigh. "This is on *you*. If you don't handle the debt, it falls to yo sistas."

Shade merely stared at him for a moment, then muttered, "What?"

"Yo sistas," Zerk chimed in. "If you won't take care of it, then they can pay the debt…or work it off."

Shade fought to keep his face impassive, but inside he was seething.

"So how much she into you for?" Shade inquired.

"Twenty large," Spinner told him.

Shade's eyes went wide. "You fuckin' kiddin', right?"

"Say that shit again!" boomed Zerk, punching the mirror over the sink and causing it to break. "You got one mo' time to talk like this a fuckin' joke and see what happen!"

"Hey, Zerk – it's cool," stated Spinner, playing peacemaker. "I'm sure Shade didn't mean anythang by it."

He then looked expectedly at Shade, who concurred saying, "Naw, I didn't mean anythang."

That seemed to pacify Zerk, who had been glowering at Shade with fists balled and breathing heavily. Then suddenly he laughed.

"Shit man, I'm sorry," Zerk apologized. "This shit s'posed to be friendly and I'm all actin' like an asshole."

"Oh naw," Shade assured him. "I didn't think you were *actin'* like one." That earned him an alarmed look from Spinner, but before the comment could sink in with Zerk he asked, "So when exactly did this deal take place?"

"Today," Spinner replied. "We gave her the shit around noon, and she was s'posed to bring us the money around five."

"So she owes you ten percent of twenty thousand," Shade muttered, calculating. "That's two kay. So I assume that's what you want me to pay."

"That was the *original* deal," Spinner clarified, "but when she didn't show up with the cash she forfeited. Now the entire balance is due."

"Is that a jo–" Shade began, then caught himself. Zerk, still nude, had looked like he was about to launch himself at Shade. "If you askin' for twenty gees, I ain't got it."

"Well, maybe you got sommin' else you can trade for it," suggested Zerk. His right eye was still wandering, but there was an intensity about him now that was unsettling.

"I don't think I got anythang worth that kinda money," Shade declared after a few seconds.

"Don't be modest," urged Spinner. "You got skills we can use."

"Uh, sure," Shade concurred, nodding as he looked around. "I'd say there's at least twenty large worth of repairs I can do around here – startin' with the bathroom."

Spinner shook his head. "No, not *those* skills."

"Then what?" asked Shade.

Rather than reply, Spinner reached into a pocket and pulled out a folded piece of paper, which he extended to Shade.

Shade took the paper but – unsure if he wanted to be involved in whatever was going on – didn't look at it. "What's this?"

"Just a name," Spinner told him.

"And you want me to do what – spell-check it for you?" Shade asked.

"Now *that's* funny," said Zerk. "But it's the name of a nigga who needs to have a 'accident.'"

Suddenly, Shade found himself giving Zerk a cold, hard stare. Still not bothering to look at it, he held the piece of paper back out to Spinner, announcing, "Sorry, I don't do that."

"Sure, you don't," replied Spinner sarcastically. "It's just coincidence that anybody who fucks with you or yo family ends up in traction – or the morgue."

"That's called karma," Shade shot back. "You do bad shit, the universe does bad shit to you in return."

Spinner rubbed his chin in thought for a moment. "Does failin' to fulfill your obligations count as bad shit? 'Cause I could see the universe retaliatin' hard against a muhfucka for some shit like that."

As he finished speaking, he glanced at the piece of paper that Shade was trying to hand back to him, then back at

Shade's face. Letting out a grunt of resignation, Shade drew his hand back and put the slip of paper in his pocket.

"You not even gonna look to see who it is?" Spinner asked.

Shade shook his head. "Right now, I don't even wanna know."

He then spent a moment rubbing his temples. This entire meeting had already been bizarre, with the shit in the basement and Zerk becoming buck-ass naked. Now it had become completely surreal.

"It's gonna take time – at least two weeks," he finally told them.

"That shouldn't be a problem," Spinner noted with a nod.

"Hold on, muhfucka," Zerk grumbled at his right-hand man. "*You* don't make decisions 'round this bitch – *I* do."

Spinner spread his arms in a compliant gesture. "Whatever you say, Zerk,"

Satisfied, Zerk seem to contemplate for a moment, then said, "Two weeks shouldn't be a problem."

"Great," Shade muttered acerbically.

"Don't disappoint me on this," Zerk warned. "It won't go well for you – or ya sistas."

Shade's eyes momentarily narrowed in anger, then he let out a deep breath and said, "Anythang else?"

"Yeah," Zerk stated with a nod. "You met up with that muhfucka Byron yesterday. What was that about?"

"Not much," Shade disclosed. "He just wanted to know if I could supply some dancers for his party last night."

"And that was it?" Zerk asked suspiciously.

"Yeah," Shade confirmed. "I knew some girls who wanted to make some extra cash, so I brought 'em over."

"So you and he ain't all buddy-buddy or any shit like?" inquired Zerk.

Shade shook his head. "Naw."

"Good," Zerk told him. "'Cause that's *his* name you just got."

THUG LIFE: EMANCIPATED

Chapter 59

After that, the meeting – for lack of a better term – was over. Zerk essentially told Shade and Spinner to fuck off, and they immediately left.

"Hang tight for a sec," Spinner said after they exited the bathroom. "I need to check on sommin', then I'll have the guys to take you back."

With that, he had headed back down the hallway towards the basement. Shade, wanting to put some distance between himself and Zerk (who was still in the bathroom), began meandering towards the main area of the warehouse.

Once he got there, he saw that nothing much had changed – that is, no one was doing any body work – but there were only two niggas in the place now. Presumably the others had found something to do or been given an assignment. Seeing that Shade was by himself, the remaining duo eyed him suspiciously but didn't take any action. He didn't note any weapons, but he was sure they were packing, so he tried not to do anything to alarm them in case they had itchy trigger fingers.

Maybe a minute or so later, Spinner reappeared.

"This is for you," he said, holding out what looked like a small white jewelry box, maybe two-by-two inches in size.

"What is it?" Shade asked.

"Just a small token of our esteem – sommin' that will hopefully keep you motivated over the next two weeks."

Shade studied it for a moment, then was about to open it when Spinner blurted out, "No, no. no. Wait 'til you get home."

"Whatever," Shade muttered irritably as he put the box in one of the cargo pockets of his pants.

"A'ight, let's go," said Spinner.

"Okay, but before I leave, I wanted to ask–"

"Not here," Spinner interjected. "Outside."

With that, they began walking towards the exit. Once outside, Shade noted that the guards were still by the warehouse door. He also saw a couple of the niggas he'd ridden with hanging out around the SUV he'd arrived in. Spinner yelled at them to start the car. A moment later they were inside with the engine running

Spinner then waited until they were out of earshot of the guards, then came to a halt.

"Acoustics inside are fucked up," he explained. "Sometimes muhfuckas nowhere close to you can hear what you say, so usually it's best to just talk outside."

"Makes sense," Shade told him, nodding.

"Okay, so what's your question?"

"I just need you to tell me, what the fuck was that in there?"

Spinner chuckled. "You mean the medieval beat down, the bare-assedness, or the psychotic overreactions to minute shit?"

"All of the above."

"Shit man, that's just typical Zerk – on a *mild* day. You don't wanna see 'im when he's *really* worked up. But as for him standin' around with his dick hangin' out, there's actually a shower in the back of that bathroom. Him waiting for us to leave before he showered up was just Zerk's way of being polite."

"It wudda been polite enough if he'd just kept his damn clothes on."

"That don't work for Zerk. The nigga can't stand blood and hates havin' it on 'im. So he has to wash up asap every time he, uh, 'chats' with somebody in the basement like that."

"Well, Zerk don't like niggas in his crew bein' smarter than him. You might wanna watch out, b'foe *you* end up down there in the basement havin' one of those chats."

"Don't worry about me," Spinner said. "I can take care of myself."

"Yeah, that's what Zerk's last two lieutenants thought," Shade commented solemnly. "We gone go put some flowers on they grave later, if you wanna come."

Spinner just stared at him for a moment, then burst out laughing.

"Shit nigga," he chortled. "For a second there, I thought you were serious."

"Come on, man – that was an obvious fuckin' joke," Shade chided. "Nobody even know where those two fools are buried."

Chapter 60

Shade stormed angrily into the house after being dropped off by Zerk's thugs.

"'Bout time you brought yo ass back," he heard Nissa say from the kitchen. "I appreciate you stayin' gone, but that was way longer…"

She trailed off as, walking out of the kitchen, she saw her brother's face.

"You seen Gin?" he asked a little forcefully.

Nissa shook her head. "No. Haven't seen her all day."

"Shit," Shade grumbled.

"What happened?" his sister asked, plainly concerned.

Rather than answer, Shade swiftly headed to the garage. Gin had somehow found her way there that morning – presumably without anyone knowing it – so maybe she'd done so again. However, a quick inspection of the place turned out to be fruitless: no verbally-abusive, junkie mom.

Plainly disappointed, Shade went back inside, silently stalking past Nissa, who had followed him and stood at the garage door.

Now frustrated by her brother's silent treatment, Nissa trailed him back into the living room and demanded, "What da fuck is goin' on?"

Shade flopped down on the couch then gestured towards the loveseat that was diagonal to it.

"You gonna wanna sit down for this," he told her.

****

"Twenty large?" Nissa practically exclaimed when Shade finished describing his recent escapades and the pile of shit Gin had dumped on them.

"That's what they said," Shade remarked.

"But it don't make no sense. You don't give twenty kay worth of drugs to a fuckin' junkie to sell. They just gone use it."

"True, but this was never really about the drugs. This was 'bout Zerk gettin' me under his demented fuckin' thumb."

Nissa frowned. "Whachu mean?"

"Basically, he want me to work for 'im," Shade replied.

"Doin' what?"

Shade contemplated for a moment, then said, "He got an errand he want me to run."

"You don't need to be doin' nuthin' for that fuckin' psycho."

"If I don't, he gone come after you and Cherry."

"He can try, but being crazy don't shield yo ass from buckshot, and we still got granddaddy's shotgun."

Shade simply nodded at that. With most girls, that kind of talk would have just been braggadocio, but his sister was dead serious.

"Anyway," Shade droned, "let's hope it don't come to that. In the meantime, let's keep an eye out for Gin."

Nissa was pensive for a moment. "You thank they'll go after her, too?"

"I doubt it," Shade said. "They didn't seem that interested when I told 'em they could cut her throat as payback."

"What?!" his sister screeched. "Tell me you didn't."

"Look, Gin's the chink in our armor. We can't have muhfuckas thinkin' we care about her, 'cause they'll use that shit against us. Remember when Mrs. Annie Mae said Gin broke in her house and stole her TV? Said she wouldn't call the cops if we bought her a new one?"

"Yeah," Nissa snickered, recalling the incident with a neighbor down the street. "She swore up and down that she saw Gin run out her back doe' with it, but at the time it happened Gin was in the hospital gettin' her stomach pumped."

"That's the kind of shit I'm talkin' 'bout," Shade stressed. "So, far as the outside world is concerned, we don't give a fuck about Gin. But if it comes down to it – even though I don't want her junkie-ass around here – I won't let anythang happen to her. Cherry would never forgive me."

"You gone go out lookin' for her?"

"Fuck, naw. It's late and I'm tired."

"But if she got that many drugs…"

Nissa trailed off, but Shade knew what she was thinking.

"Look," he told her, "even a hardcore junkie like Gin ain't stupid enough to do that amount of drugs at once. She'd OD for sure – and this time they prolly wouldn't be able to save her ass. Plus, if Zerk was basically just usin' her to get to me, what he gave her is most likely trash – some weak-ass shit that will give her the lowest high she ever had."

His sister giggled at that. "Yeah, you prolly right."

"I am," he declared with conviction. "But like I said, I'm tired so I'm goin' to bed."

As he spoke, he came to his feet. Nissa stood as well.

"I got a few more things to do in the kitchen," she told him, "but I'm right behind you."

"A'ight," Shade muttered with a nod. "See ya in da mornin'."

He then quickly made his way to his room. In all honesty, he wanted to just collapse onto the bed and pass out. However, after being jammed into a car with four other niggas, watching some muhfucka getting his face pulverized in a basement, and then hanging out in a bathroom with a nude sociopath, a shower couldn't wait.

That being the case, he grabbed some underwear and pajamas, and then headed to the bathroom. Once there, he started getting undressed, then double-checked the pockets on his pants to make sure he hadn't forgotten anything. Ultimately, it was a good thing that he did, because he came across something he had completely forgotten about: the jewelry box Spinner had given him – purportedly as motivation.

His curiosity now piqued, Shade flipped the lid of the box up. Inside was a small jewelry bag made of dark purple cloth, with drawstrings at the top.

Taking the bag out, Shade noted that it was rather light. That said, the contents of the bag made a slight clinking sound, like poker chips being shuffled. Shade loosened the drawstrings at the top and took a peek inside. Then he found himself staring, not quite convinced of what he was seeing inside:

Four bloody teeth.

THUG LIFE: EMANCIPATED

Chapter 61

Shade didn't actually go to bed as planned following his shower. Remembering his promise to call Yoni, he had given her a ring instead of simply crawling under the sheets and going to sleep. He had only intended for the call to be perfunctory, and thus had planned to chat with her for only a minute or two. However, they ended up talking for more than an hour, with the conversation culminating in Shade agreeing to give Yoni a ride to school the next day, which was Monday.

That being the case, he woke up in a chipper mood the following morning. The only thing that mildly spoiled his disposition was the fact that he was still indebted to Zerk, so-to-speak. (That also brought to mind the little pouch of teeth, which Shade tucked into his tool bag with the intent to dispose of it later.) He then put all things Zerk out of his mind for the moment.

After seeing Cherry off, he told Nissa he was leaving. Although they went to the same school, she typically caught a ride with Goose. Shockingly, Goose always managed to get her there on time, so – in Shade's opinion – it was one of the few things the nigga was actually good for.

He and Yoni had previously discussed when he'd pick her up, so she was already downstairs waiting when he arrived. She quickly made her way to the car and got inside.

Having someone ride to school with him was a nice change of pace for Shade. He hadn't realized how much he enjoyed having another person to talk to. (Of course, it was possible that it was simply this *specific* person that made the experience more pleasurable, but he wasn't about to split hairs.) The conversation was mostly just general chitchat, although Yoni tried to get details from him about his meeting with Zerk. She had attempted the same thing the night before when they had talked on the phone, but then – as now – Shade deftly sidestepped the topic.

Once they arrived at school, they had their first – and only – class together. However, Shade found it hard to concentrate because Yoni kept making goo-goo eyes at him the entire time.

After first period, the day kind of dragged by for Shade. His schedule was atypical in that he only went to formal high school for half a day – from morning to lunch time. His afternoons were reserved for dual credit courses at community college. However, all of his college coursework was recorded and online, so he didn't actually have to attend class. As long as he completed all of his assignments and tests, he never even had to set foot on campus. The end result was that it left his afternoons free, which was essentially the reverse of what his schedule had been the previous semester, when his high school classes had been in the afternoons.

Ordinarily, Shade would have tried to have work of some sort lined up after class in order to earn some cash. On this particular day, however, there was nothing on his schedule. Ergo, when his high school classes ended, he found himself with time on his hands.

Truth be told, it felt good to have nothing to do. Now that he had a moment to reflect on it, it seemed that he was always on the move, constantly hurrying from one hustle to the next. It was nice to finally have a breather, although it left him with the task of figuring out what to do with himself.

He mentally debated having lunch with Yoni, but then decided against it. In addition to picking her up that morning, he had also agreed to give her a ride home after school. If they also had lunch together, he would feel like he was smothering her.

In the end, with nothing better to do, he went to the library to do some research and work on some of his college assignments. On a whim, he also looked up *Ori Tahiti* on the library's computers. What he came across was numerous videos of island girls shaking their wares much as Yoni had done. However, as alluring as the online images were, it became abundantly clear after just a few minutes that Yoni's dancing transcended the traditional form of *Ori Tahiti* by a mile. Simply put, she was in a class by herself.

At the end of the day, as promised, he gave Yoni a ride home. In fact, he met her as she was coming out of her last class. Evidently she viewed it as a pleasant surprise, because she gave him a peck on the lips and then took his hand as they walked out. It was a little bold of her since affection between students was technically against the rules. Then again, this was the hood, so bullshit edicts like that were rarely enforced. Truth be told, considering all the shit kids in that school probably got into on a regular basis, a little tongue action should have been the least of the administration's worries.

And so it was then, while Shade was on cloud nine, that he had the rug yanked out from under him. Basically, as he and Yoni were leaving the school hand-in-hand, he saw one of the cops who had visited him the day before – Gummerson.

At the time, the detective was standing outside talking to one of the assistant principals. He didn't immediately notice Shade, but then it was like some internal radar switched on and he started looking around at the students leaving the building. He scanned the faces for a few seconds, then somehow seemed to home in on Shade and Yoni. Gummerson's brow creased for a moment as he watched them, but beyond that there was no real reaction on his part. Still, Shade was grateful when they finally got to the car and got on the road.

On the ride back, Yoni spent a few minutes trying to engage Shade in conversation, but wasn't quite successful.

Seeing the cop had unsettled him, and it showed in the way he gave simple, one-word responses to her questions and comments.

Finally, Yoni just asked, "What's wrong?"

"Nuthin'," Shade answered, but his tone was unconvincing – even to him.

"Come on, sommin's botherin' you."

"No, it's not. Seriously, I'm okay."

Yoni gave him a hard look. "I don't believe you. Seem like you been antsy ever since I kissed you in the hallway." Then she frowned as a thought occurred to her. "Is that it – the kiss? You thank you gone get in trouble about it?"

"What?!" Shade blurted incredulously. "No – fuck that. Ain't nobody worried about some bullshit rules on public displays of affection."

"So what is it then?"

Shade glance at her for a moment. One look at her face and he knew that she wasn't going to let this go until he gave her *some*thing.

Letting out a deep sigh, Shade said, "I think I fucked up on a test."

"A test?" Yoni echoed. "That's why you all tense and shit?"

"I guess," Shade offered, shrugging. "I'm worried it'll fuck up my GPA. I'm tryin' to go to college."

"I'm sure it'll be fine, so just relax."

"Easier said than done," Shade remarked.

"Well, if you havin' trouble relaxin', baby, don't worry – I'ma help you."

Suddenly, Yoni undid her seatbelt and slid closer to Shade. Next, she reached over and began unzipping his pants.

"Whachu doin'?" Shade asked, and immediately realized it was a stupid fucking question. Fortunately, Yoni didn't view it as looking a gift horse in the mouth.

Yoni smiled salaciously. "I'm helpin' you relax, like I said."

As she spoke, she reached into his pants and fondled his dick for a few seconds, which was seemingly all the time it needed to become engorged. Pulling his rod out, she stroked it lovingly for a few moments. Then she bent over and took him in her mouth.

THUG LIFE: EMANCIPATED

Chapter 62

Yoni sucked his dick all the way back to her place. She did a masterful job of taking him to the brink, but not making him cum. Shade was so damn near in ecstasy that he could barely keep the car on the road. He was just thankful that the windows were heavily tinted.

She didn't stop until he brought the car to a halt and parked. At that point, she raised up, then grabbed her purse and book bag.

"Let's finish this shit," she said without preamble, then opened the passenger door and got out.

Shade didn't have to ask what she was suggesting they finish. In fact, he was so eager that he almost stepped out the car with his dick still hanging out. He quickly tucked his shit back in his pants, zipped his fly, then went scrambling after Yoni.

****

They were barely inside Yoni's apartment before they started practically tearing each other's clothes off. Once they were naked, Yoni attempted to guide him towards the bedroom, but Shade couldn't wait even the few seconds it would take to get there. He threw her ass on the couch and started eating her pussy.

As before, she was absolutely delectable. Unlike a lot of dishes, Yoni tasted as good as she looked, and Shade made sure she knew it. Ultimately, when she came, it was with the same earthshaking intensity as before. This time, however, Shade was ready for her follow-up hip thrusts, and continued eating vigorously when they began.

303

From Yoni's perspective, the oral had once again been stellar, and she lay on the couch with her eyes closed, still trying to catch her breath

If I'd known the nigga gave head like this, she thought, *I wudda spread my legs the first time he stepped up in this bitch.*

That was a little bit of an overstatement, but captured the essence of what she was feeling. At the moment, she felt like Shade's tongue should be bronzed – preserved forever for her enjoyment.

However, before any more thoughts of cunnilingus entered her mind, she felt Shade moving her leg in a way that indicated he wanted her to turn over. The couch wasn't as wide as a bed, so it took a bit of squirming to get in the right position as opposed to simply rolling over. That said, she had barely gotten onto her hands and knees before she felt Shade get into position behind her. Suddenly, she found herself almost trembling in anticipation as his dickhead grazed around her pussy almost teasingly. A second later, she gasped as he slid what felt like a steel beam inside her.

Wasting no time, Shade grabbed her hips and began rocking them back and forth, quickly establishing a rhythm as he began ramming his dick inside her, going balls deep with every thrust. To Yoni, it felt glorious – not quite as fantastic as when she was on top doing her thing – but glorious nonetheless, and she found herself moaning in delight as Shade started tearing that shit up from behind. And then he smacked her on the ass.

Yoni yelped – more in surprise than in pain, although it stung a little. Then he did it again, to the other cheek, eliciting more of a moan from her. When he did it a third time, there was no denying it: getting smacked on the ass while being pounded from behind was a complete turn-on for her. And from that point forward, every smack on the ass increased how good the fucking felt and elicited a deep moan of pleasure from her.

But Shade didn't stop there. At some point in between slapping her ass cheeks, he found time to lean forward and squeeze her tits, occasionally pinching her nipples so hard that she cried out. But they were cries of bliss, not pain. She was thoroughly enjoying what he was doing to her and was so caught up in the moment that she wasn't fully cognizant of everything that was happening, such as when she suddenly noticed that the side of her face was actually resting on the couch. Shade had apparently put a hand behind her head and pushed her face down – presumably to get a better angle as he pounded her ass, which was still raised. Then he pulled on her hair – gently, but forcefully enough to raise her back up.

Basically, Yoni recognized that she was being handled. Not in a base or degrading way, but definitely handled, as Shade was fully and absolutely in control. And she loved it.

She loved it so much, in fact, that when he yanked on her hair a second time, she came – intensely, unexpectedly, and whimpering loudly. Moments later, Shade let out his own loud groan, and then his thrusts came to a halt as he slumped down on top of her, and she smiled knowing that he'd cum as well.

Yoni slowly lowered herself to the couch, with Shade still on top of her, seemingly too weak to move. And in truth, she really didn't want him to – not at the moment, anyway. She simply wanted a little time to enjoy the moment, because not only had the sex been amazing, but – for perhaps the first time in her life (excluding the times when she was on top) – she felt like she had truly and honestly been *fucked*.

As for Shade, it wasn't quite the out-of-body experience he'd had when Yoni had fucked him in his room, but it was damn close. He had done things in the heat of the moment that had made sex this time more intimate – allowed him and Yoni to bond on a deeper level.

Hell, he thought. *If this is the end result of seeing a cop at school, I'll gladly look at those muhfuckas everyday.*

Little did he know that he was about to get his wish.

THUG LIFE: EMANCIPATED

Chapter 63

After their sex session, Yoni kicked him out.

"I got some shit I need to take care of," she told him, "including schoolwork, and it'll never get done if yo horny ass is hangin' around temptin' a bitch."

However, she promised to call him later, which she did. As before, they ended up talking for far longer than either of them anticipated, and once again Shade found himself promising her a ride to school the next day.

Thus, for all intents and purposes, Tuesday started out as almost a repeat of Monday: Shade picked Yoni up, drove her to school, and they went to first period together. (This time, however, Shade ignored the looks she gave him and actually paid attention in class.)

Afterwards, the rest of the morning crawled by like a snail on crutches. Thus, when lunchtime finally arrived and Shade found himself done for the day, it felt like he'd been paroled. However, he knew that it was just eagerness to see Yoni. Basically, instead of taking off for the rest of the day, he had decided to surprise her at lunch. (Yeah, there was still the possibility that it could be viewed as smothering, but he'd take that chance.)

The surprise, however, was on him; Yoni was nowhere to be found. It left him a little confused, as he was sure she'd told him when she got out for lunch. He tried texting her, but got no response.

Of course, there were a million reasons why she might not be at lunch or responding to texts. She could be meeting with a teacher or counselor. She might have been sent to the principal's office. It's possible that she got sick and went home, or had a family emergency.

In short, there were a lot of variables that could account for Yoni not being around. More to the point, trying

307

to run them down probably wasn't the best use of his time. With that in mind, he decided to head home – maybe take a nap before picking Yoni up from school, or put some more thought into this fucked up Zerk situation.

The notion of Zerk made him frown. Needless to say, Shade didn't like associating with that nigga on any level, so he needed to figure a way out of what he was being ordered to do.

All of this went through his brain as he walked back to where he'd parked. He was so preoccupied with the Zerk thing that he was almost at his car before he realized that someone was there – sitting on his hood, in fact.

It was one of the cops he'd talked to on Sunday – Gummerson. As Shade drew close he slid off the hood.

"Detective Gummerson," Shade said in greeting. "Nice to see you again.'

"Well, that would make you one of the few people on the planet happy to find a cop waitin' for 'em," Gummerson replied.

"Something I can help you with?" Shade asked.

The detective nodded. "Yeah, but not here. I was hopin' we could talk at the station."

Shade swiftly debated saying that he had class that afternoon. Technically, it was true; but again, he didn't have to be present physically. Plus, although he really didn't feel like having a conversation with the police, he didn't want to be viewed as uncooperative.

"Actually, I have classes at community college in a bit," he stated after a few seconds. "But I can catch up online later."

"Great," Gummerson declared. "I'm parked right across the street, so if you wanna jump in I can take us–"

"If it's okay," Shade interjected, "I'd rather drive myself."

The detective seemed to ponder for a moment, then shrugged. "Suit yourself. Just follow me."

THUG LIFE: EMANCIPATED

Chapter 64

Gummy had to admit to being surprised. Ninety percent of the time when people agreed to follow him to the station, they ended up trying to take off. It usually began with them falling one or two cars behind him, as if they had trouble keeping up. Then they'd suddenly veer off – making a turn at an intersection where he kept straight, or vice-versa. Those assholes acted like he was the only cop in town (or the only one with an unmarked police car). Next thing they know, the cop they never knew about – the one that was tailing them – is pulling them over, and at that point the option to follow is taken out of their hands.

That Shade guy didn't do any of that, though. He stayed pretty much on Gummy's ass the entirety of the drive; when they finally arrived at the police station, he parked at the visitors' lot next door and then hustled over to meet Gummy, who was waiting for him at the entrance. At that point, he followed Gummy inside.

"We're heading to the back," Gummy told him as they walked through the waiting area. "There are some rooms back there where we can talk."

Shade merely nodded at that and Gummy smiled to himself. They were actually headed to an interrogation room, but if you called it that, it tended to put people on their guard.

Unsurprisingly, as they passed by a couple of departments, like Booking, Gummy noticed that Shade waved to a couple of folks. Given where he lived, Shade could probably come through here every day of the week and see someone he recognized.

After a few minutes, they came to a halt in a small hallway.

"Wait here for sec," Gummy said. "I need to see what rooms are open."

With that, Gummy proceeded from the office into an open area where several uniformed officers were sitting at desks.

Gummy approached one of the officers sitting and said in a low voice, "Hey Benson, you busy?"

The officer – Benson – shook his head. "The usual paperwork bullshit, but I can take a break. Whachu need?"

"I'm takin' the kid over there" – Gummy cut his eyes towards Shade – "to one of the interrogation rooms."

"Kid?" muttered Benson. "Looks grown."

"Yeah, he looks twenty, but he's only sixteen. He's one of those that grew up fast, I guess."

Benson nodded. "I know whachu mean. My sister's kid is fifteen – got a beard like a fuckin' mountain man."

Gummy chuckled at that. "Anyway, I may have to step out for a few minutes while we talkin', so I just need somebody to stand in there while I'm gone."

"No problem, Gummy."

Gummy clapped him on the shoulder. "Thanks, Benson. I owe you."

However, Gummy didn't immediately move away. After a second Benson looked at him and said, "Sommin' else?"

Gummy gave a quick shake of his head while looking at Shade out of the corner of his eye. "No, I'm just waitin' on sommin'… And I think it just happened."

As people in his position are wont to do, Shade had started looking around. The hallway Gummy had left him in had a door on one side with a glass window. As Gummy watched, Shade had glanced in that direction and then froze momentarily.

Gummy gave himself a mental pat on the back. Shade's reaction meant that he had seen what Gummy wanted him to see through the glass window: the girl he had kissed at school the day before – Yoni – sitting inside talking to the cops.

At that point, Gummy hustled back towards Shade, saying, "Okay, I got a room we can use."

THUG LIFE: EMANCIPATED

Chapter 65

Gummy quickly led Shade to an area at the back of the station, only stopping long enough to grab an accordion folder full of papers from his desk. Eventually, they ended up in a small room that was maybe fifty square feet in size. It was populated by a single wooden table and a couple of chairs – one on each side.

"Why don't you have a seat," Gummy said, gesturing towards the chair on the table's far side. "You want anything to eat or drink? We got snacks, sodas—"'

"No, thanks," Shade interjected as he nudged the proffered chair away from the table with his foot, then sat down with his hands in his lap.

"You sure?" Gummy asked dubiously, taking a seat as well and placing the folder on the table.

"Yeah, I'm fine."

"Well, let me know if you change your mind."

"Will do."

"Anyway, thanks again for comin' in, Joshua. Or do you prefer 'Shade?'"'

Shade shrugged. "Either is fine."

"How'd you get that nickname anyway?"

"My grandfather."

"So, he just started calling you 'Shade' out the blue or sommin'?"

"I didn't get the nickname *from* him," Shade explained. "I got it *because* of him."

Gummy simply waited, assuming a more detailed explanation was coming. After a moment, Shade continued. "He worked as a handyman for the most part, but was also a shadetree mechanic. After a while, that became his nickname: Shadetree. After I came along, I was always with him wherever he went, so people started calling me 'Shadetree Junior.' That was a bit of a mouthful, so eventually it got shortened to 'Shady J,' then 'Shady,' and finally just 'Shade.'"

"Interesting," Gummy said with a nod. "Now your grandfather is also the one who taught you how to do repairs, right?"

"Yeah," Shade confirmed with a nod.

"Now, he was in the military, right?" Gummy asked as he pulled a manila file from the folder. "Is that where he learned to work on cars and stuff?"

"No. He had a short stint in the Motor Pool, but he spent most of his time as a cook."

Gummy simply nodded as he looked through some papers in the manila folder. "Yeah, I see that here in his military personnel file: Culinary Specialist."

"Well, I've never seen his official file, but that jibes with what he told me."

"Now it's interestin' that you put it that way, mentionin' his official file. Because that's just what this is" – Gummy held up the manila file – "his *official* file."

As he finished speaking, he simply stared at Shade, who initially didn't respond.

"I'm sorry, sir," Shade apologized after a few moments, "but if there's some significance to that, I'm not sure I get it."

"Fair enough – I should explain," Gummy said. "See, for the average grunt in the military, their *official* record is also their *actual* record. It tells exactly what their job title was and what they did. But for a select few, the official record doesn't actually tell the story."

"What do you mean?"

Gummy contemplated for a moment. "You ever see those commercials for military video games, where you're a soldier on a black ops mission and shit like that?"

"Yeah," Shade stated with a nod.

"Well, those are the kinds of guys whose *official* records are complete bullshit – because they did a bunch of crap that can't be put into their personnel file. Guys like your grandfather."

Shade frowned. "I'm not sure I follow."

"Maybe this will clear it up," Gummy stated as he pulled a letter-size envelope from the accordion folder. It was stamped "Secret" on both sides, and had a fold-down metal clasp on the back. Gummy lifted the ends of the clasp, opened the envelope, and took of a small sheaf of papers. Like the exterior of the envelope, each page was stamped "Secret" and was heavily redacted.

Turning the papers so Shade could read them, Gummy said, "It's hard to glean anything from this because of everything that's blacked out, but this is your grandfather's *real* military record."

Shade simply ran his eyes over the first page for a moment, then looked at Gummy. "Should you be showing me this?"

"Oh, it's fine," Gummy assured him. "It's all been declassified."

That, of course, was a flat-out lie. Gummy had spent an hour on the phone with some bureaucratic asshole trying to explain that the veteran in question was dead and the files were needed for a homicide investigation. But the administrative shithead he was dealing with had refused to budge, saying there was no way those files could be declassified for ordinary review. It was easier to get Gummy secret-level clearance (which, in fact, was exactly what they'd done).

Even that, however, had only entitled him to review the documents in redacted form. And truth be told, they were only supposed to be viewed in rooms that met a stringent set of security requirements in terms of locks, bolts, and access –

essentially a vault. But Gummy didn't give a fuck about shit like that; as far as he was concerned, a bunch of pissant rules didn't apply when you were trying to catch a murderer.

"Anyway," Gummy droned, leaning forward and tapping a spot on the page, "if you look right here, you'll see that – rather than culinary arts – your grandfather specialized in sommin' called 'Malefic Event Simulation.'"

"I'm sorry, sir," Shade said, shaking his head. "I don't know what that is."

"Neither did I," Gummy admitted. "I had to call a buddy in the military to get an answer on that one."

That was another lie. Gummy had actually called around to a bunch of offices at the Pentagon, getting passed around from department to department like a two-dollar hoe until somebody was able and willing to tell him what the fuck that job title meant.

"Anyway," Gummy went on, "it turns out that your grandfather specialized in killin' people and making it look like an accident."

"What?" Shade muttered in surprise.

"Let me state it another way: yo granddaddy was an assassin."

Shade shook his head in disbelief. "I never heard anything like that. But even if it's true, it happened while he was in the military, so I would assume anything he did was sanctioned."

"I'm not so sure about that," Gummy said as he took the papers from in front of Shade and put them back in the envelope.

Shade gave him an odd look. "You don't think this kind of thing would have been sanctioned?"

"Oh, I believe it was sanctioned while he was in the service. I just don't think he did all of it in the military."

"I'm not sure I understand," Shade said with a perplexed expression on his face.

"Then let me break it down for you," Gummy said. "I don't think your granddaddy stopped 'Malefic Event Simulation' when he got out the army. I think he came home and continued plying his trade, but at a higher pay grade."

"No," Shade insisted, shaking his head. "He wouldn't do that. He wasn't that kind of person."

"I think Terrance Steele would say different."

Shade blinked in surprise. "Excuse me?"

"Terrance Steele," Gummy repeated. "You know that name, right?"

"Yeah. He was a friend of my grandfather. He died, maybe, four years ago – carbon monoxide poisoning."

"It was an accident, right?"

"That's what the police concluded. Apparently, something went wrong with the gas stove at their place. He had a wife and grown son – Tyrone – who lived with them, but they were both out at the time. Lucky for them, I guess."

"Lucky in more ways than one, because when Terrance died, his family got an insurance payout of…" Gummy trailed off as he pulled the right document from the file folder. "…two hundred and fifty thousand dollars."

"I wouldn't know anything about that," Shade declared.

"Yeah, it got deposited directly into their bank account. But on the day they get the money, Terrance Steele's widow goes and withdraws ten thousand of it. And guess who goes and deposits ten grand later that day? Your grandfather."

That last part was a bit of an exaggeration. Shade's grandfather had actually deposited nine thousand and some change, but Gummy felt okay rounding up.

"That could be right," Shade said after a moment. "There were lots of people my grandfather did work for who couldn't afford to pay right away, but he always said that was no reason to let folks freeze to death in winter because the heat went out, or die of heatstroke in summer because the air conditioner stopped working."

"So you're sayin' the Steeles were into your granddaddy for ten grand, and it all related to repair work."

"I don't know remember the exact amount, but I do recall that they owed him."

"And I suppose that's why Tyrone Steele went around after that complainin' about how they had to pay yo granddaddy ten thousand out of the insurance proceeds."

"I remember Tyrone. To be honest, he was something of a loafer and always complaining about stuff: taxes, the price of groceries, the forty-hour work week… everything. So I'm not surprised he'd complain about paying my grandfather what he was owed. But Mrs. Steele, his mother, was a nice lady. I heard she settled up all her husband's debts, then took the rest of the money and moved away to some place nice. And of course, Tyrone went with her."

"Hmmm," Gummy intoned. "Let's move on." As he spoke, he pulled another file from the folder and began leafing through its contents. After a few seconds, he asked, "Do you know the name Alma Carter?"

"Yes, sir," Shade replied. "I remember Miss Alma. She was a sweet old lady who died about two years ago."

"You remember *how* she died?"

"Not exactly. Some kind of allergic reaction to something."

"Actually, it was an *adverse* reaction, and it was in relation to some medication she was taking."

Shade nodded. "That sounds about right. I recall that she was taking a bunch of pills."

"Well, it looks like one of those pills was the wrong medicine, and it killed her," Gummy stated, laying the open file on the table. "No, I'm wrong on that. It was the right *medication*; it was the wrong *formulation*."

Shade shrugged. "I'm not sure I understand the distinction."

"Basically, it was the right medicine, but the wrong dosage. In other words, that particular pill was too strong, and interacted badly with other shit she was takin' and killed her."

"So it was like an overdose."

"Sort of," Gummy agreed.

"Then the doctor who prescribed it is the one who killed her," Shade offered.

"That's one way to look at it, but the pill bottle had the correct dosage on the label."

"Then that seems to suggest that the pharmacy is responsible."

"So you'd think, but here's the thing: the pharmacy information on the label was completely illegible. So was the info about the doctor who prescribed it. You couldn't read any of that shit. The only thing you could make out was the dosage and the date the prescription was filled. Not a lot to go on, but the investigatin' officers were thorough. They reached out to every pharmacy in town, and guess what? Nobody had a record of that drug prescription being submitted or filled."

Gummy just stared at Shade, who – after a few moments – uttered, "Sounds like a real mystery."

"Well, you wanna know what *isn't* a mystery? The fact that her family got a nice six-figure life insurance payout after she died. They had to wait until the police classified her death as an accident and closed the case, but ultimately they got it. And after they have the cash in hand, guess what they do that exact same day?"

"I couldn't imagine, sir" Shade responded.

"Then I'll enlighten you," Gummy said. "They withdraw ten thousand dollars."

"Maybe it was for funeral expenses," Shade suggested.

"No," Gummy stressed, shaking his head. "There was a separate policy for that. Apparently Mrs. Carter was a big believer in insurance."

"Good for her."

"Even better for her two granddaughters, who got a massive payday – minus ten thousand, that is."

"Well, there's no way you can say *that* was for my grandfather," Shade insisted. "He was dead by then."

"Now that brings up an interestin' point," Gummy remarked. "See, you're right in that your granddaddy couldn't have killed Mrs. Carter. The timing doesn't work. That's why I believe it was *you*."

Shade blinked in surprise. "Excuse me?"

"You heard me," Gummy told him. "See, I don't think your grandfather stopped at teachin' you about auto mechanics, plumbin', and all that handyman crap. I think he taught you the exact same thing he did in the military: how to kill people and dress that shit up to look like an accident."

"No, sir," Shade shot back, vehemently shaking his head. "That's not true."

"So you're sayin' Mrs. Carter's granddaughters didn't give you anything after collectin' on her life insurance?"

"No, I recall that they gave me *something* – they owed me for some work at the time – but I don't remember exactly how much."

"Do you recall what you did with it?"

"Huh?" Shade muttered. "You mean the money? I don't know… Paid bills, maybe. Uh, bought–"

"It's fine," Gummy interjected. "See, we got forensic accountants who can hunt that down all that shit. Of course, it was easier with your granddaddy, but I guess it was because he was old school. He was fine with just takin' money to the bank and makin' a deposit. But you're trickier – you got that new-age, millennial, Gen Z mindset. The type who thinks he can hide his trail because he's smarter than the cops, right?"

"No, sir," Shade maintained. "That's not me at all."

"But you *are* smart, aren't you? I mean, I looked at your transcript, and you're kickin' ass not just in high school but in your college classes, too. You got a list of awards a mile long. 'Best Website,' 'Best Coding,' 'Best App Developer'… And that's just from your IT classes."

Shade shrugged his shoulders. "My grandparents stressed academics."

"I can understand that," Gummy said with a nod. "It takes brains to kill someone and make it look like an accident."

"Except that's not something I do," Shade retorted.

"Well," Gummy said, patting the accordion folder, "I got a stack of documents here that say different."

THUG LIFE: EMANCIPATED

Chapter 66

Gummy spent the next twenty minutes relentlessly grilling Shade. He brought out more files of people who allegedly died in accidents, accusing Shade (or his grandfather) of killing each one, only to be met with denial in each instance.

For the most part, Gummy didn't hold back. He yelled, cussed, pounded the table…even came around and got directly in Shade's face. All to no avail.

Gummy had to admit to being impressed. He had seen hardened criminals break under the same treatment; Shade, however, never seemed shaken. He showed enough emotion so that anyone watching wouldn't think he was a robot, but for the most part he gave Gummy the impression that he was unfazed.

Needless to say, Gummy had been a little surprised that Gills' information hadn't turned out to be total bullshit. It had seemed more than a little far-fetched, but Gills was one of the best snitches he'd ever recruited. Ergo, it had made sense to check out the info he'd provided.

Thus, Gummy had gone to a forensic accountant that the department used as a consultant and told him to look for any fiscal connection between the names on Gills' list and Shade's family. In essence, as Gills had put it, they needed to follow the money.

In addition to the names themselves, Gills had also given them a little extra help by jotting down the fact that Tyrone Steele had bitched about having to fork over part of the insurance money. That had led Gummy to taking a harder look at Shade's grandfather, including a check to see if he served in the military and getting his personnel file.

More to the point, Gummy had dealt with *faux* official service records before, so he could recognize the telltale signs. He immediately knew that the official file was bullshit and that

Shade's grandfather had a classified personnel file out there somewhere. Once he got his hands on that and found out about the "Malefic Event Simulation," everything fell into the place. He knew in his gut that everything that Gills had told him about Shade was true.

The problem was, he couldn't prove any of it.

Of course, that wouldn't keep a stubborn asshole like Gummy from trying, which is how he wound up trying to browbeat an admission – if not a confession – out of Shade.

It was shaping up to be a fruitless endeavor. Even when he switched gears – coming at Shade about the shootout in the abandoned basement – he didn't make any headway. When Gummy lied, saying he had witnesses who saw Shade enter and leave the place, the most he could get from his suspect was an admission that he was in the area. Not even the threat of trumped-up charges based on a conspiracy theory and damage to a government-owned building earned him any progress. Likewise, he didn't make any headway when he broached the subject of the bodies in that condemned building. Basically, the kid seemed to know that all the cops had were supposition and coincidence.

Gummy did leave the room twice during the interrogation at about ten minute intervals. This was calculated on his part; sometimes it paid to let a suspect stew in his own juices for a while and think about how much shit he was in. On those occasions, he had Benson go into the room to keep an eye on Shade.

Benson was an experienced cop and knew his role. In addition to making sure Shade didn't try to leave, he also offered him something to eat and drink. Shade politely declined each time, a fact which Benson whispered into Gummy's ear when he returned. It was news that Gummy didn't like. Most times after being put through the ringer, a suspect would be nervous and sweating – so much so that they'd jump at the offer of something to drink at the very least. The fact that Shade turned it down repeatedly suggested he knew what Gummy was after: a DNA sample.

After he returned the second time, Gummy once again shifted to a new angle, this time asking Shade about the treehouse incident Gills had mentioned. However, he'd barely gotten started before he heard a commotion outside. A moment later, the door flew open and a woman burst in.

She was short, maybe five feet tall, and a little on the stocky side. Dressed in a business suit, she appeared to be in her forties. Her hair was done up in an eye-catching beehive, and when combined with the three-inch heels she wore had the effect of making her seem taller than she was.

"Don't say another word!" the woman bellowed at Shade. "Come on – we're leaving."

Shade stood up, as did Gummy.

"Wait just a damn minute," the detective said. "Who the hell are you?"

"Bronwyn DuBose," the woman said as Shade came to stand next to her. "Legal counsel for Mr. Green."

Gummy had trouble hiding his surprise as his gaze shifted from the woman – Bronwyn – to Shade, and then back again. "You're his lawyer?"

"That's what legal counsel means," she snapped. "I was retained by Mr. Green to provide legal services a while back. Right now, I'm taking him out of here."

"We're in the middle of an interview," Gummy told her.

"Don't bullshit me," Bronwyn responded. "This isn't an interview; it's an interrogation. And I would think, *detective*, that you've got enough years on the force to know that you can't talk to a minor without a parent or adult representative present."

"That's if they've been arrested," Gummy explained. "Your client's not in custody. We were just talkin'."

Frowning, Bronwyn looked at Shade. "I thought I told you not to say anything."

Shade shrugged. "I didn't want it to look like I wasn't cooperating."

His lawyer let out a grunt of disgust and turned back to Gummy. "Look, I know how talking works with you assholes. You lean on a kid and coerce some kind of admission out of him, then arrest him and say he freely confessed. Well, I'm not going to let you railroad my client. We're getting the fuck out of here."

As she finished speaking, Shade leaned towards her ear and whispered something.

Narrowing her eyes at Gummy, she added, "And my client tells me that you're also interrogating another minor – Yolanda Archer?"

THUG LIFE: EMANCIPATED

Chapter 67

"You let him make a phone call?" Blanchard asked incredulously. "Seriously Gummy, you're slippin'."

"Fuck you," Gummy replied. "He didn't make a call when me or Benson was in the room. He must have done it in the car on the way here."

Blanchard simply nodded at the conclusion his partner had reached. At the moment they were standing outside the station, having walked out behind Shade, his lawyer, and Yoni. The lawyer had shared a few choice words with the detectives as they exited the building, with the upshot being, "Stay the fuck away from my client." Now they simply watched – out of earshot – as she had a quick discussion with the two teens in the visitors' lot.

"You get anything?" Blanchard asked.

"Just complete and utter denial of everything I accused him of. He also refused the offer of food or a drink…"

"So no DNA" Blanchard concluded.

"…and kept his hands in his lap and didn't touch anything," Gummy added.

"So no fingerprints either."

Gummy was silent for a moment, then asked, "How'd it go with the girl?"

"She was cooperative," Blanchard replied. Needless to say, he had been the cop chatting with Yoni while Gummy was raking Shade over the coals. "Of course, she didn't know jack shit about these accidents her boyfriend was involved in, but that's to be expected. I mean, she just moved back to the city. And, of course, him being our number-one suspect in that triple-homicide really threw her for a loop."

"I can imagine. So where's her head at on all that?"

"About where you'd expect, given the facts. In my opinion, she really wants to know the truth."

"If she's as close to our suspect as it looks, she might be in position to get it so let's stay on top of that."

"Done," Blanchard told him. However, noticing that his partner appeared to grow pensive, he followed up with, "What is it?"

"I was just thinkin' about sommin' that lawyer said – that she instructed Shade not to talk to us. Presumably she did that when he called her."

"Yeah, so?"

"Well, he talked to us anyway. I'm just curious as to why. He said it was because he wanted to appear cooperative, but I'm not buyin' it."

"You don't think that could be the reason? Criminals do that shit all the time, thinkin' it'll make you less likely to suspect them.'

"Except he didn't really cooperate," Gummy groused. "He didn't actually give us anything to work with. In fact, I did most of the talkin', layin' out…" Gummy trailed off as a thought suddenly occurred to him. Then, shaking his head in disgust, he muttered "Shit."

"What is it?" inquired Blanchard.

"He played us," Gummy said. "He fuckin' played us."

Blanchard looked at him with a nonplussed expression. "Whachu mean?"

"He wasn't there to cooperate and *give* us information – he was there to *get* it. And I obliged. I basically laid out for him everything that we thought he was involved in or suspected him of. That's why he was willin' to talk when his lawyer told him not to, why he pretended to cooperate when he knew all along she was on her way. He wanted to find out what we knew. Now he knows all the shit we'll likely come after him for."

"But he doesn't know *how* we'll come at him," Blanchard countered. "And remember, we've got at least one weapon in the arsenal that he doesn't know about."

"True," Gummy admitted with a nod. Shade had once again outsmarted them, but they had an ace-in-the-hole that was sure to give them the last laugh.

"There's only one other thing that bothers me," Gummy stated after a few seconds.

"What's that?" asked his partner.

Blanchard frowned for a moment, then said, "Why the fuck does a sixteen-year-old need a lawyer on retainer?"

THUG LIFE: EMANCIPATED

Chapter 68

Bronwyn Dubose may have been small in stature, but she was big on client rights. More to the point, she shared her thoughts on said rights with Shade and Yoni in the visitors' lot after they left the station. Although she took a roundabout method of conveying it, her general advice with respect to talking to the police was "Don't fucking do it." (At least, not without legal counsel present.)

After she left, Shade turned to Yoni, saying, "Come on. I'll give you a ride back–"

"Is it true what they said?" Yoni demanded, cutting him off.

"Huh?" Shade muttered. "Is *what* true?"

"They said you kill people – that you do it for money."

"Who, the cops?"

"Yeah," Yoni confirmed with a nod. "They also said you killed three people in a buildin' a few weeks back."

"And you believed them?" Shade asked incredulously.

"Fuck what I *believe*. Just tell me if it's *true*."

Shade glanced towards the police station, where those two detectives – Gummerson and Blanchard – were still outside, watching them.

"Come on," Shade said. "Let's get outta here."

"I'm not goin' anywhere with yo ass 'til you tell me the truth," Yoni stressed.

"Okay, I will," Shade promised. "But not here."

As he finished speaking, he glanced at the two detectives again. Yoni, following his gaze, noticed them as well. Shade then tilted his head towards his car and began walking in that direction.

Yoni appeared to debate for a moment, looking back at the detectives once more before turning again to Shade. Then, almost reluctantly, she followed him to his car.

THUG LIFE: EMANCIPATED

Chapter 69

They didn't really talk after driving away from the police station. Their entire conversation basically consisted of Shade asking Yoni if she wanted something to eat, and her declining because she'd had a candy bar at the police station. Shade had given her an odd glance then, but hadn't said anything further. He himself ended up eating a bag of chips that he'd put in the glove compartment a few days earlier to serve as a snack between jobs.

As to their destination, Shade ultimately took Yoni to a spot she'd never been before – a hilly, slightly wooded area about an hour out of town. It was obviously farther than she'd assumed they go to talk, but she hadn't felt the need to voice any concerns.

As they pulled into an unpaved lot at the base of a small slope, Yoni noticed a sign identifying the place as Grosvenor Pointe. The name didn't mean anything to her, but – as the place seemed semi-secluded – she figured it was some sort of lovers' lane.

They got out of the car, and Shade swiftly went to the trunk. Once there, he opened it and took out a blanket, which he draped over one arm. It was an item that he occasionally used to avoid lying on a bare floor when he had to work under a sink or counter.

"Come on," he said to Yoni, and then went trudging up the hill. A second later, Yoni followed him.

The incline of the hill wasn't too bad, so the walk didn't take an excessive amount of effort. More importantly, it only took a few minutes to reach the spot that Shade apparently had in mind: a grassy area of the hilltop overlooking a quaint suburban neighborhood.

Shade spread the blanket out on the ground and then sat down on it, crossing his legs. Yoni sat down next to him.

She was a city girl and didn't go much for the outdoors, but she had to admit that their current location offered a breathtaking view of the surrounding area. The only thing detracting from the scene was a nearby electrical transmission tower, but apparently they had to put those things somewhere.

"This is nice," Yoni remarked in sincerity after a few moments. "You come here a lot?"

"Not a lot," he confided. "Just occasionally when I need to think or just get away. But I unnastand it ain't for everybody. A lot of people can't adjust to the quiet. They're used to the sounds of the city – traffic constantly going by, horns honkin', sirens screamin'..."

"I know what you mean," Yoni told him. "But I kinda like it."

Shade simply nodded at that before once again gazing out at the scene before them. Yoni stayed silent. She could tell he was working his way up to something and didn't want to distract him. After a few minutes, he finally spoke.

"My granddaddy had this friend – Mr. Steele," Shade began. "A nice guy for the most part...worked hard, took care of his family, and so on."

"The cops mentioned his name," Yoni offered. "They said yo granddaddy killed 'im for money, and that you was prolly involved."

Shade shook his head in disdain. "Like I said, granddaddy was his *friend*." He then went silent for a moment, letting that sink in, then continued. "Anyway, Mr. Steele got sick – cancer, stage four."

"Damn..." Yoni muttered. "My aunt had cancer. It was stage two, but that was scary enough."

"Yeah. They obviously caught his shit late, so when Mr. Steele went into treatment, the odds were fuckin' grim. Practically no chance of survival. But what do you do – just throw in the fuckin' towel?"

It was clearly a rhetorical question, so Yoni just stayed quiet, listening.

"Anyway," Shade continued, "he's in treatment for like four months, and it ain't really doin' shit for 'im, and then this damn domino effect of bad shit suddenly starts happenin'."

"Whachu mean?" asked Yoni.

"Well, first his job tells him they're lettin' him go," Shade began, then frowned. "No, that's not exactly right. He'd been there almost thirty years, but because of his treatment he hadn't been to work in a coupla months. So they said they'd keep him on another four weeks – until he hit his thirty-year anniversary – and then they were gonna force mandatory retirement on him. Pension him off."

"A pension?" Yoni repeated. "That don't sound so bad."

"'Cept the job is how he got health insurance. Without it, ain't no money to pay the ever-growin' stack of fuckin' medical bills. And you ever priced private insurance, when you have to pay for that shit yo'self? It's a damn arm-and-a-leg."

Yoni gave him a curious look. "What about Obamacare? That shit's supposed to be affordable."

Shade snorted in derision. "Half the doctors don't take it. Apparently the reimbursement system is all fucked up, and doctors wanna be paid like everybody else."

"What about Medicaid?"

"Medicaid is based on income and assets. With Mr. Steele havin' a pension, he didn't qualify, even though it wasn't a shit-ton of money."

"That still leaves Medicare. I know everybody can get that, because my grandmomma had it."

"It kicks in when you turn sixty-five. Mr. Steele was only in his late fifties."

"Yeah, but if you disabled you can get it early, like my aunt did."

"Havin' cancer don't automatically make you disabled," Shade told her. "We had a teacher in middle school, Mrs. Cross, who had breast cancer. Never missed a day of work...had fuckin' surgery over like, Christmas break, and then did that radiation shit after school. Of course, her diagnosis was stage zero – a hundred percent survival rate – but still."

"And Mr. Steele?"

"I don't know what brainless fuck reviewed his paperwork, but they wouldn't declare him disabled. So there he was: no job, no insurance, no Medicare, no Medicaid, no disability."

"But he still had the pension, right?"

"His family was gonna need that to survive. He didn't want them wastin' the money on insurance, doctor bills, or any of that shit. As he put it, as long as he was alive, *he* was gonna be the cancer, eatin' at the people he loved. So he asked my granddaddy to help him."

"Help him how?"

"By removin' the cancer in his family."

Yoni mentally chewed on that for a moment, then the light bulb came on. "He asked yo' granddaddy to kill 'im?"

Shade sighed. "He didn't want to be a burden to his family. They were already livin' in the fuckin' ghetto, losin' his job and insurance wasn't gonna help, and – even if he hadn't been sick – the pension was gonna give them just enough to get by."

"But askin' yo friend to kill you? Why not just shoot yo'self, jump off a bridge, or some shit like that?"

"Well, there was one mo' piece to the puzzle. Mr. Steele had a life insurance policy through his job – two-hundred-and-fifty thousand. But life insurance don't pay if the person commits suicide, and – like the health insurance – it was goin' away when his job ended."

"So he wanted to die, needed it to happen soon, but couldn't commit suicide."

"Pretty much, which is why he wanted my granddaddy's help," Shade said. "See, "Mr. Steele knew that my granddaddy had been in the army, and somehow he found out what Granddaddy had been trained for: Malefic Event Simulation."

"The police told me about that. They said the military taught him how to kill people and make it look all accidental and shit. Is that what he did with Mr. Steele?"

Shade seemed to reflect for a moment. "The Steeles had an old gas stove that was always on the fritz. Nobody was fuckin' surprised when it filled the house with carbon monoxide one day, killin' Mr. Steele."

Yoni thought about that for a moment, then asked, "What about the money?"

"Huh?" muttered Shade.

"The cops said yo granddaddy got paid for killin' Mr. Steele."

Shade let out a deep sigh. "What Mr. Steele was askin' my granddaddy to do was fuckin' illegal. At best, it would be considered assisted suicide; at worst, somebody could claim it was murder. Regardless, it was definitely insurance fraud, conspiracy, and a laundry list of other shit."

The mention of conspiracy immediately brought to mind Shade's earlier interrogation, when that cop Gummerson brought it up while pressing Shade about what went down in that abandoned basement. Shade had played dumb, but he knew all about the doctrine of legal conspiracy. He had first learned about it from his grandfather, who had wanted Shade to know all the risks involved in helping Mr. Steele. Since then, Shade had done plenty of research on his own and was well-versed on the topic, especially after taking a Criminal Law course at community college.

"Anyway," Shade went on, "Mr. Steele said Granddaddy should be compensated for any risk, so he told his wife that if anythang happened to him, my granddaddy was owed ten thousand dollars."

"And when he died, his widow gave yo granddaddy the money."

"It's not like she was hurtin' for cash at that point. She got the rest of the insurance money, and she qualified to collect his pension."

Yoni appeared to contemplate for a moment, then asked, "So how many times did yo granddaddy do this?"

Shade gave her a sharp look. "This wasn't his *job*. He was a neighborhood handyman, fixin' shit like heat lamps and leaky faucets. But somehow, word got out that he had this particular skill set. So yeah, people would occasionally approach him, but he wasn't out there handing out business cards for this shit, tryin' to drum up business."

"But he did do it again – and got paid for it."

"If and when my granddaddy did this," Shade retorted heatedly, "it wasn't so he could go around with stacks in his pocket or make it rain at the strip club on Friday nights. It was to help people who didn't have options, like Mr. Steele or Miss Alma."

Yoni looked at him with a perplexed expression. "Who?"

From her reaction, Miss Alma wasn't someone the cops had mentioned to Yoni. Noting that he'd let the cat out of the bag, Shade let out a deep breath. "Miss Alma was another friend of the family – a sweet old lady raising two granddaughters by herself. She got diagnosed with early-onset Alzheimer's, right around the time her oldest granddaughter, Nikki, got a full ride to an Ivy League college."

"Wow," droned Yoni. "Fucked up timing."

"True dat. But the real problem for Miss Alma was that Nikki wanted to put college off in order to stay home and take care of her. Miss Alma had raised Nikki and her lil' sista, so Nikki felt like she'd be desertin' her if she went off to college then."

"I get that."

"Me, too, but Miss Alma hated the thought of it. As far as she was concerned, Nikki had a chance to get the fuck out the hood, and she didn't want her to waste it, because the same thang happened to her."

A curious expression settled on Yoni's face and she asked, "Whachu mean?"

"Miss Alma had a chance to get out the ghetto when she was young, but she stayed to take care of the grandmomma who raised *her*. In the end, she regretted it – not that she didn't love her grandmomma, but she lost her shot to get out. And she knew that of Nikki stayed, the same thang would happen to her. She'd end up with some shiftless nigga who wouldn't do nuthin' but give her babies that he himself didn't want, and she'd spend the rest of her life strugglin' to make ends meet. Even worse, Nikki's lil' sista tried to do everythang Nikki did. So if Nikki went to an Ivy League school, her lil' sista would try to go to one, too. But if Nikki stayed in the hood…"

He trailed off, but Yoni knew where he was going. "If Nikki stayed, then so would her sista."

"Right," Shade concurred. "But Nikki was fuckin' hardheaded and wouldn't listen to reason. Fuck college – she was gonna stay and take care of her grandmomma. So, Miss Alma only saw one solution."

"She needed to check out," Yoni concluded, "in order to save her grandkids."

"Yeah, but she also didn't like what Alzheimer's was doin' to her. She had always been pretty sharp, so it was killin' her to suddenly not remember simple shit, like what she had for breakfast. She didn't wanna reach the point where she'd forget her name every time the doorbell rang, or take a dump in the kitchen sink because she thought it was the toilet. But the thang that pushed her over the edge was the insurance."

That earned him a perplexed look from Yoni, so Shade started to explain. "Miss Alma had this life insurance policy she had bought, like, forty years ago. Back then, there was a fuckin' cottage industry that revolved around sellin' life insurance to people in the hood – at least in *this* city."

"I thought they didn't like sellin' life insurance to people in the hood,' Yoni commented. "They say we die too often. Most times you have to get it through yo job."

"This wasn't like normal insurance – it was a predatory fuckin' practice," Shade stated. "First of all, it wouldn't pay anythang if you died within the first two years of the policy."

"What?" Yoni blurted out. "You shittin' me, right?"

"No," Shade assured her, shaking his head. "They said that was their way of accountin' for the elevated level of violence in the hood. But even if you made it through the two years, they still knew that almost everybody in the hood goes through hard times sooner or later. You get laid off, yo car breaks down, and so on. When that happens and you need cash, the first thing you do is cut back on non-essentials – shit that ain't providin' an immediate benefit."

"Like life insurance."

"Bingo. The insurance companies were bankin' on it, and if you missed a single payment or the muhfuckin' check was so much as a day late, they cancelled the policy. No grace period, no catch-up provision, nuthin'. Yo ass was just shit outta luck if that happened."

"Is that what happened with Miss Alma? She missed a payment."

"No, she never missed a payment in forty years. But because of the Alzheimer's she *almost* missed a payment – completely forgot about it until the last minute, and then had to overnight the fuckin' check. But you know what was really funny? The damn insurance premium was only ten bucks. Overnightin' the check cost three times as much."

"The insurance payment was ten dollars? That don't seem like much."

"That's how they'd get you – the cheap premium," Shade noted. "If you can get a thousand niggas in the hood to buy that policy, that's ten grand a month – one-twenty large every year. And if you don't have to pay anythang within the first two years, you're up almost a quarter-mill before anybody can collect a dime. And if muhfuckas let the policy lapse or have it cancelled due to a missed payment, you don't give a fuck. You already pocketed they money."

"Anyway," Shade continued. "almost missin' the insurance payment freaked Miss Alma out. As far as she was concerned, that was her granddaughters' inheritance, and she wasn't about to let Alzheimer's fuck up four decades of tenacity on her part, or let her granddaughters continue the cycle of poverty."

Yoni's brow crinkled for a moment, then she asked, "So how'd she go out?"

"Because of the Alzheimer's and some other health problems, she was on a lot of meds. Somehow though, she got the wrong dosage for one of her pills."

"Somehow?" Toni repeatedly skeptically.

Shade continued without addressing her comment, saying, "The higher dosage caused a bad reaction with her other meds and she died."

338

"That doesn't sound like a fun way to go," Yoni surmised."

"Well, you'll be happy to know that the coroner said she died peacefully in her sleep."

"And her granddaughters?"

"Nikki was eighteen, so she got appointed guardian of her lil' sista – took her with her when she went off to college. The university had some family housing and helped them get settled in. Plus, they got the insurance payout and their grandmother had a funeral policy, so they're good on funds. My guess is we'll never see their asses around here again – which is exactly what Miss Alma wanted."

"And I assume your granddaddy got part of the insurance money again?"

"No," Shade told her, shaking his head. "He was dead by then."

Yoni simply stared for a moment, then softly uttered, "So they paid *you*. Because you're the one who did it."

"They didn't pay me for killin' her. All they knew was that they grandmomma told them she owed me money, so they needed to pay if anythang happened to her."

"Sounds just like the instructions Mr. Steele's family got."

"Except Nikki and her sista didn't bitch about it like Tyrone Steele," Shade observed. Then, noting a confused look on Yoni's face, he went on. "Anyway, as you done prolly figured out, my granddaddy taught me that particular skill set."

"What – killin' people and makin' it look like an accident to everybody?"

"It's not about makin' it look like an accident," Shade countered. "It's about meetin' people's expectations."

Yoni shook her head in confusion. "I don't follow."

"Think about it like this: nobody's surprised if a junkie dies of an overdose. It squares up with the type of thang they thank is prolly gonna happen if you addicted to drugs. Likewise, if some fool is always zippin' around on a motorcycle at a hundred miles an hour, nobody's shocked if he goes flying off the road and crashes into a transformer. In those cases, the end result squares up with the kind of shit people expect to happen, so there's no reason to thank it's anythang other than what it looks like: an accident."

Yoni spent a few seconds thinking about that, then asked, "Well, do you ever just do it for the money? I mean, if somebody just said, 'I hate my brother and want him dead – here's ten thou,' would you take job?"

"No!" Shade barked. "That's not what I do. I'm not some fuckin' assassin, no matter what the cops said."

Yoni eyed him dubiously. "So you ain't never caused any 'accidents' outside of situations like you told me about – where the victim wanted you to."

Shade shrugged. "There may have been one or two occasions when some lowlife muhfucka got what he deserved."

"Like the nigga who dogged yo sista – Tony?"

Shade frowned as he dredged up a particular memory. "I went to see 'im after he broke his legs – explained the concept of karma to his black ass...how if you do a bunch of repugnant shit, the universe does repugnant shit to *you*. And the universe will keep doin' it 'til the scales are balanced. He seemed to get the message."

I bet he did, Yoni thought. A moment later her brow furrowed as a new thought occurred to her. "Do yo sistas know about this...this stuff you do?"

"Only Nissa, but we don't talk about it – not directly anyway. We just describe it as 'errands.' So if I say I gotta go run some errands, she know what I'm talkin' about."

"Okay, but why beat around the bush like that?"

"Because I need her to have deniability. If shit hits the fan, I don't want her gettin' splattered. If there's a screw-up, she needs to be able to tell the cops, *truthfully*, that she had no fuckin' clue what was goin' on. That way they won't be able to come after her on some bullshit conspiracy theory."

Yoni let that sink in for a moment, then asked, "So when's the last time you planned one of these things – an accident."

Shade gave her a sober stare, as if wondering how much he could tell her. Then he seemed to mentally flip a coin.

"This past weekend," he admitted. "A guy I know, an honest worker, has been puttin' in crazy overtime on the job. But his supervisor don't wanna pay him for it, says the company will chew his ass off for payin' that much oh-tee, so the muhfucka's been writin' the time off. He said he'd take care of my friend another way, basically pay him extra under the table, but now he's refusin' to make good on it."

"So the supervisor's gonna have an accident?"

"No," Shade replied, chortling. "That won't help anybody. If you just gotta know, my friend's gonna have an 'accident' in a company vehicle and mess up his back."

"You're gonna intentionally fuck his back up?" Yoni asked incredulously.

"Ha-ha," Shade laughed. "You obviously don't know how this shit works, so let me explain: backs are tricky. If a nigga gets in a car accident and says it fucked his back up – that he's in muhfuckin' agony all the time – nobody knows if he's lyin', not even doctors. That's why the damn insurance companies send investigators out when niggas makes claims about they back bein' hurt. And if they catch yo ass turnin' cartwheels or helpin' somebody move a two-hundred-pound sofa-bed, they gone say you fakin' and not pay you shit."

"So your friend's gonna have an accident and just *claim* his back's fucked up? And then what, try to get an insurance payout?"

"Not exactly," Shade told her. "The outfit he works for is a douchebag operation that doesn't give a shit about the workers. All they care about is the bottom line – savin' money. So, despite OSHA regulations, they spend almost nothing on safety gear, properly maintainin' equipment, storin' hazardous materials, etcetera. They're the fuckin' definition of unsafe workin' conditions, and a nigga can get fucked up pretty bad there if he's not payin' attention to what he's doin'."

"Okay," Yoni droned, "so how exactly does that relate to your friend?"

"Whenever a worker there gets seriously hurt, it's supposed to trigger an OSHA investigation. Before that happens, the company lawyers typically swoop in like fuckin' vultures and try to get the muhfucka that was injured to accept a settlement. Usually, as part of the settlement, you have to sign a confidentiality agreement, which normally includes a statement that says the company wasn't responsible for you gettin' hurt. The main thing, though, is that – since it's confidential – you can't talk about it or the accident that led to the agreement. That essentially keeps you from cooperatin' with any OSHA investigation, and without the person who was injured the investigation is pretty much dead in the water."

"I think I get it," Yoni declared. "After your friend claims his back is hurt, he expects the company to settle up, and that'll make up for the overtime stolen from him."

"You got it," Shade stated, clapping her on the shoulder.

"So how much did they owe him in overtime?"

"Maybe a coupla thousand."

"And how much will they settle for?"

"Prolly mid five-figures."

"Damn," Yoni blurted out. "They should have just paid him the oh-tee."

"Well, five figures is a lot cheaper than the fine they'd get hit with if OSHA investigated and found all the occupational safety and health regs those muhfuckas are violatin'."

"And you'll get a piece of whatever your friend's settlement is."

"This type of shit ain't risk-free," Shade informed her.

As he spoke, he reflected on the fact that he'd spent time that past Friday, Saturday *and* Sunday setting up the particular "accident" in question. Bearing in mind the number of times he told Nissa he had errands to run, she probably knew something was up, even if she wasn't privy to the details. As to the accident itself, the area where it was slated to occur was populated by a bunch of fucked-up roads, making Slade thankful once again that on Sunday he'd been driven there and back by the guy he was helping out rather than risk messing up his own car.

Shade was so wrapped up in his thoughts, that it was a second before he realized that Yoni was speaking to him.

"Huh?" he muttered.

She let out an exasperated sigh. "I said, what about the three people in that buildin'. Was that you, too?"

"No," Shade insisted. "I ain't have nuthin' to do with that."

Yoni gave him a hard look. "You sure?"

"Yeah," he insisted. Those bodies ain't on me."

Yoni simply nodded at that, but the expression on her face suggested that she didn't quite believe him.

Chapter 70

They spent a few more minutes on the hill simply enjoying the view, but didn't really say much more. About the only other topic they discussed was how Yoni had come to be at the police station. (Basically, during the last period before lunch, a note had been sent to Yoni's class saying she needed to come to the Principal's office. When she arrived the two detectives, Gummerson and Blanchard, had been waiting for her.) Other than that, there wasn't much chatter, even during the ride back.

Despite the lack of conversation, Shade was in a better mood on the return drive. It had been a long time since he'd openly discussed with anyone the malefic skill set he'd learned from his grandfather, and how he put those talents to use. It had felt good to openly discuss it with someone, and he was particularly happy that the indicated someone was Yoni.

Of course, Nissa knew what he did, but it wasn't the same. (Plus – as he'd told Yoni – he tended to avoid giving his sister too many details.)

As to how Yoni was taking everything, it was hard to say. She appeared reflective and pensive as they drove back, but that wasn't surprising given everything she'd learned. Shade had answered all of her questions, and had been honest for the most part. The only time he had prevaricated was when she had asked about the three bodies in the abandoned building, but *nobody* other than Shade knew the full story of what had happened there, and he preferred to keep it that way.

When they finally arrived at her tenement, Shade asked to come up, but Yoni nixed the idea.

"I'm sorry," she told him as she got out of the car, "but I need more time to process all this shit. It's a lot to digest."

"Okay," Shade acknowledged regretfully. "Call you later?"

Yoni mumbled something in response that Shade didn't quite catch before turning and walking away. Shade watched her retreating form until she reached the entrance, then drove away.

He spent the drive home thinking about everything that had happened the past few days. Between Zerk, the cops, and everything else, his life had spun completely out of control.

He was still thinking about the shitstorm he now found himself in as he pulled into the driveway and parked. However, he'd barely gotten out of the car before he heard someone call his name.

"Shade, my man," called out a familiar voice.

He turned and saw what appeared to be a brand new SUV parked near the curb in front of his house. He had been so lost in thought that he hadn't noticed it before (or else it had just pulled up). It wasn't a vehicle he recognized as belonging to someone he knew, but he recognized the nigga who'd called to him through the rolled-down window of the backseat: Lord Byron.

"Come on," Lord Byron said to him. "Let's take a ride."

From the tone of his voice, it wasn't a request.

THUG LIFE: EMANCIPATED

Chapter 71

There were two niggas in the front seat, while Shade sat in the back with Lord Byron. After he had gotten into the SUV, Shade had expected Byron to tell him why the fuck he was there. Byron, however, didn't initially say anything. More to the point, it appeared that they were just driving around aimlessly, with no particular destination in mind. With nothing better to do, Shade simply stared out the window on his side, noting that it was already dark.

"I love this fuckin' town," Lord Byron suddenly stated out of the blue. "'Specially the hood. Some niggas hate it, spend they whole life tryin' to get out the ghetto, but not me. Wanna know why?"

"Sure," Shade sad flatly. "Tell me why."

"Because there's opportunity here," Byron declared. "A way to get ahead. A nigga with grit – with ambition – can make sommin' outta hisself." He then gave Shade a somber look before adding, "And right now, there's a massive opportunity in the streets."

Shade gave him a blank look. "I'm not sure whachu talkin' 'bout."

Byron drummed his fingers on his leg for a moment. "There's an outfit in town that was blowin' up – movin' weight and gettin' ready to take over the streets. It was run by a couple niggas called Kane and Jay-Cee."

"I heard of 'em," Shade remarked.

"Yeah, they were a coupla rungs higher on the food chain than me, but all of a sudden, those niggas jumped ship. They stopped sellin' powder and switched to weed, became part of an organization run by this muhfucka called Bush. I doubt you know that name, but he–"

"I heard of Bush," Shade interjected. "He's like, some kind of dope king."

"Ha!" Byron laughed. "Callin' Bush a king is like sayin' a T-Rex is a small lizard. It's a gross fuckin' understatement." He let Shade ruminate on that for a moment, the continued. "Anyway, with Kane and Jay-Cee crossin' trade lines, there's a void in the market. And that kinda hole is like the snatch of a horny housewife – somebody gone fill that bitch, don't matter who."

"But you wanna make sure it's you."

"That would be nice, but when shit like this happen, every muhfucka sellin' a dime bag on a corner thank it's *his* time. That destiny's opened a door for his ass. But they don't unnastand that you gotta prepare for moments like that. You gotta be ready. And that means having sommin' more than just a cocky attitude and hope. You gotta have *cash*."

"Cash?"

"Damn straight. See, to fill the void left by Kane and Jay-cee, you need product. The only way to get product is with money."

"I know how it work," Shade told him.

"Well maybe you should get in the game, then," Byron said, "'cause most of these niggas don't seem to have a clue. When the opportunity came along, most of those dumb fucks wasn't ready – didn't have a dime to spare."

"But you did," Shade surmised.

"Hell yeah. I been fuckin' frugal with my cash in anticipation of a chance like that."

"Yeah, that Gold Coast mansion you got just screams 'frugality.'"

"I got that at a tax sale, muhfucka, and it was relatively cheap," Byron countered. "But as I was sayin', most of these muhfuckas wasn't ready to move up to the next weight class."

"But I'm guessin' you were?"

"Fuck yeah," Byron insisted. "My team bought and moved product in, like, record time, then re-upped and sold that shit, then re-upped again. At that point it was just rinse-and-repeat. And with almost no other competition, we started making money hand over fist. That was part of the reason for the party the other night – celebratin' that success, 'cause at this point Lord Byron's house is in serious fuckin' order."

"Congrats," Shade told him. "Sounds like you in the catbird seat."

"No shit," Byron agreed. "In fact there's only one cloud in my personal sky at the moment."

"Which is what?"

"We been dominatin' for the most part, but there is one other crew that was givin' us a run for our money. They shitheads, but they money is as good as anybody else's as far as the connect is concerned. Still, I got the better team, so for a lil' while now we been pullin' ahead. *Way* ahead."

"Who's the other crew?" Shade asked, although he had a feeling he already knew the answer.

"Zerk Simon's gang," Byron said, confirming Shade's suspicions.

"Nice guy to be in competition with."

"Except competin' ain't his strong suit," Byron opined. "Like I said, they were vyin' with us for top status for a minute, then we started movin' into the lead. Seem like that drove Zerk wild, 'cause he went for a knockout punch not too long ago."

"In what sense?"

"Word on the street is, he got the connect to front him some keys maybe a month or so ago. How a psycho like Zerk managed that I don't know, but that's enough product to put him back on the map."

"And make it a two-horse race again," Shade concluded.

"So you'd think, but Zerk ain't been actin' like a nigga with a large inventory," Byron stated. "Take last night, for instance. I sent some of my boys to re-up, and after they leave the connect, some niggas on Zerk's payroll try to rip 'em off."

Shade frowned. "How'd Zerk even know about it?"

"He snatched up one of my people yesterday afternoon – a nigga named Moonie," Byron answered. "Basically tortured his ass, until he talked. From the way he got worked over, I'm bettin' he gave up info not just about the meet with the connect, but everythang he fuckin' knew: social security number, mother's maiden name…all that shit."

Recalling that he'd seen Zerk pounding some nigga just two days before, Shade simply noted, "With Zerk, I think that's par for the course."

"Don't I fuckin' know it," groaned Byron. "But I got tipped off about what he was tryin' to do, so now he short a coupla employees."

"Guess it pays to have contacts."

"That it does," Lord Byron agreed, "and I've got 'em all over: in the hood. Downtown. In the 'burbs. Everywhere."

"That must cost a pretty penny," Shade noted.

"It does, but it's worth it. It's how I stay on top of shit and know what's goin' on – like when niggas try to set up on me."

As he finished speaking, Byron gave Shade a hard stare. On his part, Shade simply said, "Sounds like it's money well spent."

"Oh, it is," Lord Byron attested. He then leaned towards Shade conspiratorially and asked, "You wanna know what else would be money well spent?"

"No, what?" Shade inquired.

"Zerk," Byron answered. "I'd pay good money to get rid of his ass."

As he finished speaking, Byron eyed Shade expectantly, as if waiting for him to say something in particular.

"Sounds like Zerk had a bad day already," Shade noted after a few moments

Byron frowned, as if Shade's comment was difficult to comprehend. Then he seemed to mentally shrug and said, "Shit, it's been way more than a *day*. See, for a few weeks now, some of Zerk's best customers been comin' to *me* for product. Weird, huh? He gets fronted a couple of keys, but his customers are comin' to *me*. Now why you thank that is?"

Shade initially took it to be a rhetorical question, but as Byron continued staring at him, it became clear that he was expecting an answer.

Shrugging, Shade said, "I don't know."

"I don't know either," Byron stated. "But here's sommin' I *do* know: I love the current situation – being able to sell product at will, havin' Zerk's customers blowin' up my cell, and so on. Life's fuckin' fantastic for the most part. So, as you can imagine, I don't want anythang interferin' with the muhfuckin' status quo. In fact, I will be royally pissed at anyone or anythang that does, and prolly take it out of somebody's hide – even if it's somebody I like. Ya feel me?"

Shade was silent for a moment, then simply replied, "Yeah, I feel you."

THUG LIFE: EMANCIPATED

Chapter 72

They let him out at home a few minutes later, with Lord Byron rolling down his window and giving Shade a final word about maintaining the status quo. Shade had merely nodded in acknowledgement, then waited until they drove off before heading to the garage. A moment later he had it unlocked. Raising the door, he quickly stepped inside and then lowered it again.

The conversation with Lord Byron had put a lot of things in perspective for him. In fact, quite a few pieces of the puzzle had suddenly fallen into place for Shade, which was why he was now in the garage. However, before he'd even taken a few steps inside, the garage door suddenly went up and three niggas stepped inside.

Shade recognized them. It was Beemer – the muhfucka who'd put a gun in his face a few nights back – and two other thugs from Zerk's crew that were called Bull and Caveman.

"Da fuck ya'll thank y'all doin'?" Shade asked as Bull pulled the garage door back down.

"That's the same fuckin' thang we 'bout to ask yo ass," replied Beemer. "Da fuck you doin' hangin' out with than nigga Byron, huh?"

"Oh, is he bad people?" Shade asked with faux anxiety. "Is hangin' out with him gone get me in trouble?"

"You could say that," Beemer answered, glowering. "Zerk said you s'posed to be handlin' his ass, but you and Byron look all buddy-buddy to me."

"Whatever," Shade muttered. "If you just here to deliver that message, consider it done. Now get da fuck out."

"There's a message alright, nigga, but that ain't it," Beemer stated. "We actually s'posed to ask you a question."

"Which is what?" inquired Shade.

Beemer gave him an intense look. "Where's the shit?"

Shade gave him a blank look. "Da fuck you talkin' 'bout?"

"I see – you wanna play dumb," Beemer grumbled. "Maybe dis'll jog yo fuckin' memory." As he finished, he raised his hand, pointing a gun at Shade's face. "Now I'ma ask again: where's the shit?"

"And I'ma tell you again," Shade retorted, "I don't know whachu talkin' 'bout."

Beemer flexed the fingers on the hand holding the gun, and the look on his face said he was itchin' to pull the trigger. Instead, he said, "Caveman, help this nigga with this fuckin' amnesia he got."

Smiling, Caveman began walking towards Shade. He was short – maybe five-six – but built like his nickname suggested, with a massive chest and arms like tree trunks. Shade had heard that the nigga could bench press, like, three hundred pounds, so he had no intention of grappling with that muhfucka. Instead, he shot his leg out as fast as a snake when Caveman got close, kicking him solidly in the shin.

Caveman howled in pain, grabbing the injured leg and hopping on the other.

Steel-toed shoes, muhfucka, Shade thought, watching Caveman continue to hop for a second. Then, comically, Caveman lost his balance, bumped into Beemer and they both went down in a heap.

Wasting no time, Shade scooped up a two-by-four about as long as his arm from where it was resting against a saw horse. He then brought it down sharply on the pile that was Caveman and Beemer, not caring who or what he hit in what he would later look back on as a kind of hood version of whack-a-mole.

Shade raised the piece of wood over his head again, but never go a chance to take another swing as he found

352

himself tackled around the midsection by Bull, whom he had almost forgotten about. The force of Bull's momentum sent him staggering backwards, until he checked up painfully against the worktable, dropping the two-by-four in the process. Still holding Shade around the waist, Bull began viciously punching him in the side.

There was a small, cup-shaped container of nails on the worktable, and it had fallen over when Shade had bumped up against the table. Shade reached for them, grabbed one in his fist, and then brought it down hard on Bull's right shoulder blade. His hand wasn't as efficient as a hammer, but Shade was able to drive the nail in hard enough to make Bull arch his back, screech in pain, and – most importantly – stop punishing Shade's sides and ribs.

Shade grabbed another nail and stabbed it in Bull's side. Again, it didn't go in far, but it was enough to make that nigga let go of Shade and back away. Furious, Shade bent down to pick up the two-by-four, intending to use it to go after that muhfucka, but suddenly found himself hoisted off the ground.

He immediately realized what had happened. While his attention was focused on Bull, Caveman had gotten up and now had him in a bear hug. In short, Shade had gotten tunnel vision, focusing on one antagonist at a time when there were multiple adversaries present. It was a classic blunder, and Shade had seemingly done it twice in the span of just a few seconds.

If Caveman found it awkward to lift someone half-a-foot taller than himself, it didn't show. More to the point, he was strong as a fucking gorilla, and Shade felt like he was having the life squeezed out of him. Caveman was holding him so tight that he couldn't breathe.

"Crush that nigga," he heard Beemer say. "Squish his ass like a muhfuckin' grape."

Shade wanted to make a smart-ass comment in response, but couldn't get enough air in his lungs. He suddenly realized that there was a good chance that Caveman actually *would* squeeze him to death – if all his ribs didn't snap first.

All of a sudden, Shade heard someone scream, "Let my baby go!"

A moment later, there was an odd sound, like someone trying to tenderize a piece of steak by slamming it on the sidewalk. At the same time, Shade thought heard Caveman let out a grunt of pain. His hold on Shade loosened slightly, allowing Shade to draw in a breath, and then he let go completely, at which point Shade collapsed to his hands and knees, wheezing.

After a few seconds, Shade felt like he was able to breathe again, but wasn't quite able to rise yet. Next to him, laid out on the floor was Caveman. He was obviously unconscious, and there was blood on one side of his face. In fact, the ear on that side of his head looked like it had been pulped.

Movement and shouting drew Shade's attention. Looking up, he found himself shocked by what he saw. Gin was standing between him and those other two niggas. In her right hand she held a brick that seemed to have blood on it, and she swung it back-and-forth in front of her, using it to keep Beemer and Bull at bay, all the while screaming at them to stay the fuck away from her son.

Shade blinked. Gin displaying any sort of maternal instinct was more than he'd ever thought was possible, but there she was, defending her child – *him*. He had always thought that, if required, she'd probably do something like that for Cherry, maybe even Nissa…but never *him*. Even though he was seeing it, he still couldn't quite believe it. Then the inevitable happen.

Whether because she was high, malnourished, or some other reason, Gin lost her balance while swinging the brick and stumbled slightly. Beemer took the opportunity to step in and pistol-whip her on the jaw. Gin dropped bonelessly to the ground, knocked out. Seeing that, Shade struggled angrily to his feet.

"Uh-uh, nigga," Beemer said, pointing his gun at Shade's head. "Playtime is over. We 'bout to end this shit."

"Muhfucka, you ain't about to end *nuthin'*," interjected a feminine voice from the door leading into the house.

Shade looked over and saw Nissa standing in the doorway holding a shotgun – one that had belonged to their grandfather. It was pointed at Beemer's head.

Beemer eyed Nissa for a moment. Obviously not viewing her as a real threat, he boldly asked, "Who da fuck you s'posed be?"

"I'm 'bout to be the muhfuckin' angel of death if you don't back the fuck off my brutha," Nissa fumed.

"Bitch," Beemer snapped, "I'll come over and shove that gun up yo snatch and pull the trigger."

"Nigga, there's two thangs you need to know when it come to me and this shotgun," Nissa said calmly. "One: it ain't my first time usin' it. Two: warning shots are for pussies."

There was an intensity about Nissa that made it clear that she wasn't joking. Beemer obviously picked up on it, because he lowered is gun.

"Now," Nissa continued, "you got ten seconds to get out that garage doe', or get yo insides splattered all over it – yo choice."

"Come on," Beemer muttered to no one in particular, then began backing towards the garage door.

"Hey," Nissa called out, then gestured towards caveman, who was still knocked out on the floor. "Pick up that piece of dogshit and take it wichu."

Beemer looked like he wanted to protest, but then thought better of it. Tucking his gun into the small of his back, he and Bull pulled Caveman groggily to his feet. Less than a minute later they were gone.

After they left, Shade walked over and locked the garage door – something he should have done the moment he entered, but he had been preoccupied at the time. Now he turned his thoughts back to what he'd come into the garage for.

With the garage now locked, Nissa seemed to relax a bit and lowered the shotgun.

"What da fuck did those animals want?" she asked Shade, who – after slipping a nearby glove onto his right hand – was busy taking the lid off a five-gallon paint bucket.

"I'm guessin' it's this," Shade answered as he pulled what looked like a black-leather overnight bag from the bucket with his gloved hand.

Nissa frowned. "What the hell is that?"

"A bag full of coke," her brother stated somberly.

THUG LIFE: EMANCIPATED

Chapter 73

"Okay, what da fuck is goin' on?" Nissa demanded.

At present, they were in the car, with Shade driving – heading to what he'd called a "safe spot." After mentioning the bag of coke, he hadn't given Nissa an opportunity to ask any questions. Instead, he had hustled her inside the house and told her she had two minutes to wake Cherry, pack whatever shit they'd need and be ready to go.

It had actually taken a little over three minutes, but was partially due to the fact that they took Gin with them. She was still unconscious, and currently in the backseat with a still-sleepy Cherry. She had a nasty-looking bruise forming where Beemer had hit her, but Shade had seen his mother with worse and was confident she'd be okay.

All things considered, though, they had actually made good time. His sisters now had a couple of bags full of clothing and essentials in the trunk, which also held Shade's tool bag. He hadn't worried about getting clothes or the like for himself; if necessary, he'd make do with a set of coveralls and some other pieces of attire that he generally kept in the trunk. Basically, aside from his tool bag, the only thing he really wanted was their stash, which he had quickly retrieved. However, once they were on the road and safely away from the house, Nissa had started pressing him for answers.

"Talk to me Shade," his sister said. "Da fuck you doing with a bag full of coke?"

To stress her point, she used a tissue to hold up the bag in question, which was near her feet on the front passenger side of the car.

"I found it," Shade stated.

"Bullshit," Nissa declared. "You don't just *find* a bag full of cocaine."

357

Shade let out a deep breath. "I came across in that condemned buildin' where Sneak died a few weeks back."

Nissa just frowned at him for a moment, then understanding seemed to dawn on her.

"Oh shit..." she muttered. "The bodies in that buildin'...that was *you*."

"No," Shade insisted, shaking his head. "I mean, I was *there*, but I didn't kill 'em. Not directly. Not *all* of 'em."

"Are you seriously tryin' to fuckin' equivocate on this shit?" Nissa almost barked. "Just tell me what da fuck happened."

Shade glanced in the rearview mirror to confirm that Cherry was asleep, which appeared to be the case.

"Well," he began, "the condensed version is that Sneak told me he needed help gettin' sommin' outta that buildin' that was worth a lotta cash..."

****

It only took about a minute for Shade to relay the salient details from his exploits in the condemned building, at which point his sister seemed to reflect for a second.

"So, let me see if I got this," Nissa remarked when he was done. "When the dust settles, Sneak's dead, and the two niggas chasin' y'all fell into a fuckin' bottomless pit."

"That pretty much sums it up," acknowledged Shade.

"So how does a damn bag of coke enter the picture?"

"I had flung a headlamp to the other side of the hole in the flo'. That's how I tricked one of those niggas – got 'im to fall into it. But I had to go get it."

"What, the headlamp?"

"Yeah. At some point, those bodies was gonna be found, and when they were the cops were gonna sweep that whole fuckin' buildin'. Sneak had been wearin' that headlamp, but it belonged to *me*. I wore it before, so it probably had my DNA on it. Couldn't let the cops get that. So I went to get it, and that's when I found the coke."

Nissa gave him a curious look. "Found it *where*?"

"The stairwell Sneak and I had come up when we was tryin' to get away. I'm assumin' one of the muhfuckas chasin' us was carryin' it, then it either fell or he dropped it so he could run faster. Either way, I knew it wasn't there on the way up, so when I noticed it comin' down I opened it up and saw bricks wrapped up in plastic."

"So why the fuck would you take it? You plannin' to start dealin' or some shit like that?"

"Fuck no," Shade insisted. "But soon as I saw what it was, I figured I might need it."

His sister frowned. "Need it for what?"

"Leverage," he responded. "I didn't know who they were at the time, but those two niggas who fell down that hole were obviously bangers. In case somebody in they clique came lookin' for payback later, the coke could be a bargainin' chip."

"Okay, I get that," Nissa told him, "but this is a lotta fuckin' blow. Somebody was bound to come lookin' for it, regardless of whether they wanted payback."

She hefted the bag for emphasis as she spoke, and suddenly her eyes narrowed as she noticed something on it.

"And what's this weird stain on here?" she continued. A moment later she went-bug-eyed and dropped the bag, saying, "Did one of those niggas nut on this?"

"What?" Shade said quizzically. "The bag?"

"Yeah," Nissa answered with a vigorous nod. "You got me holdin' some bag with muhfuckin' cum-stains on it?"

"Oh, so now you got a problem with cum? Goose'll be disappointed," Shade noted. Preparing to retort, Nissa drew in a deep breath, but before she could speak her brother went on, saying, "Calm down. It's not cum."

"Praise fuckin' be," Nissa muttered, spreading her arms and lifting her head up in faux supplication.

"It's blood," Shade continued.

Nissa's head snapped in his direction. "What?"

Shade let out a sigh. "I never finished tellin' you... When I went to get my headlamp, I had to go all the way down to the first level and then pass through the area where the hole was in order to find a stairwell on the other side that I could use to go back up. I had the tactical flashlight out 'cause it was brighter, and I saw where those two muhfuckas that chased us had fell. Matter of fact, I had to go by one of 'em – the one I later found out was Zerk's lil' brutha. Anyway, I wudda sworn that nigga was dead, that's how fucked up he looked, but when I went by he suddenly snatched at the bag."

"Shit..." Nissa muttered.

"He got a hand on it that was all bloody and tried to kinda claw it away from me – you can see where his nails sorta scratched the leather."

Lifting up the bag again, Nissa merely nodded at this.

"I just pulled away from him," Shade continued. "and he flopped back down. Then I hustled up the stairs, found the headlamp, and got the fuck out."

"Then you came home and hid the coke in our garage," Nissa concluded.

"Not exactly," Shade countered. "Like I said, I only took the coke for leverage. Even though I found the headlamp, there was still shit that could tie me to the buildin' and 'cause muhfuckas to head in my direction."

"Like what?"

"Tool marks, for one. And I got a bag full of tools."

"Oh, fuck," Nissa intoned.

"In a perfect world," Shade went on, "I wudda gone back and tried to buff the tool marks out, but I didn't have time for that shit. I needed to get outta there and I wasn't comin' back."

Nissa's expression showed that she agreed with her brother's logic, then her brow creased in thought. "But wait a minute...yo tools got stole."

That earned her a sideways glance from her Shade, and then the truth hit her.

"Shit," she spat out. "Yo tools was never stole. I shudda figured that – you never let that tool bag outta yo sight. So what the fuck happened?"

"As far as I knew, they were the only thang that could definitely link me to that buildin'," Shade replied. "So I took a ride over the bridge, stopped in the middle, and threw 'em in the river."

"Hold on – that's the night you came home naked," his sister recalled.

"Not naked," Shade corrected. "I was wearin' those pants you said look like they was stole off somebody clothesline."

"So what happened to *yo* clothes?"

"I didn't know what the fuck might have been on 'em that could be traced back to what happened in that buildin'. We're talkin' blood, drywall, mold...anythang. So I took everythang off but my draws, wrapped it in a plastic bag, then tossed 'em into a barrel fire that some drunk hobos had going under a bridge."

"And it didn't occur to you to toss the fuckin' bloody coke bag in there as well?"

"I told you: I wanted the coke for leverage."

"Nigga, I'm just talkin' 'bout the *bag* that shit was in," Nissa clarified.

"Oh, that wudda been great," Shade shot back. "Me running down the street half naked with a bunch of white bricks in my arms. Not suspicious at all."

"You had the car," his sister reminded him. "And you cudda bought a bag from somebody on the street, like those pants you wore home."

"I actually didn't buy those pants," he admitted. "I stole 'em off somebody clothesline."

Nissa looked at her brother, then burst into laughter so loud that she almost woke Cherry up. Shade snickered as well.

After taking a few moments to recover her composure, Nissa stated, "Here's what I don't unnastand: why those two thugs was up in that buildin' with a bunch of coke anyway."

"Based on what I heard," Shade told her, "I'm guessin' they had just got it in a drug deal. It's a lot of powder, so maybe they got excited about what that meant in terms of cash flow for their crew – Zerk's crew, that is – and couldn't wait to celebrate."

"So they head into the first place they see where they can have some privacy and decide to get it on?"

Shade shrugged. "Who da fuck knows? For all I know, that buildin' is where the deal went down. Then after it was over and the other party left, those two just decided to stick around and have a lil' fun."

"I guess that make sense," Nissa asserted. "But lookin' at this bag, this seem like a lotta weight for somebody like Zerk."

"At one point, you wudda been right about that," Shade conceded. "But there's shit goin' on now that you don't know about."

"Like what?"

"There's practically a fuckin' cocaine competition takin' place – muhfuckin' drug dealers tryin' to see if they good enough to get drafted into the pros."

Nissa looked at him in confusion. "You gone have to explain that."

"There's some muhfuckas who left the game, and they sudden absence created a void. Everybody on the street see it as they chance to move up, but most of those niggas ain't got the resources to advance to the next round. So we at the point where the contest has been whittled down to two contenders: Zerk and Lord Byron."

His sister seemed to contemplate for a moment. "How you know all this?"

"Byron laid it all out tonight – right b'foe those fuckin' gorillas showed up in our garage. But after talkin' to him, all the other pieces fell into place."

"Such as?"

"For starters, the reason he wanted me at that party. Remember when I said I had a weird vibe about goin'? It's because Byron didn't give a fuck about havin' new blood in there strippin'. He wanted to see what I knew. That's why, all night, his peeps was rollin' up on me, talkin' bought how much weight they move and how if I know someone with product they'd be interested. They were feelin' me out."

"Byron knew you had the coke," Nissa surmised.

"I don't think he *knew*. I think he just *suspected*."

"Well, why the fuck was he suspicious?"

"That fuckin' police report," Shade explained. "When those cops came to our house, one of 'em showed me a report that talked about findin' tool marks on pipes in the buildin'. It was date-stamped this past Saturday mornin'. That's the same day Byron had me come over to talk about bringin' some girls to his party. He knew about the police report."

"How would he know 'bout sommin' like that?"

"He told me he's got contacts all over – includin' 'Downtown,' meanin' the police."

"So some cop on his payroll slipped him the report. But unless it had yo name on it, how the fuck does that lead to you? There must be a dozen other niggas in the hood that can do pipework."

"Maybe, but half of 'em are junkies or alcoholics that are drunk or high b'foe noon everyday. So the list of reliable muhfuckas ain't that long. Then thank about how many of those left can find some keys of coke and somehow keep it to theyself instead of tryin' to sell that shit."

"Okay, it just became a short-ass list."

"Right, and from Byron's point of view I'm prolly at the top of it. Plus, he prolly know by now that the cops consider me a 'person of interest' regardin' the bodies in that abandoned buildin'."

"So what? I mean, how does Byron connect you bein' a suspect with the coke? How's he even know about the coke in the first place?"

"He's got contacts, remember? So he knows those two muhfuckas that fell were supposed to have picked up some bricks – which are now missin' – and he knows the cops think I'm involved in they deaths. At that point, it's just a matter of puttin' two-and-two together."

"So he thank you got the coke and wanchu to sell it to 'im?"

"Naw," Shade replied, shaking his head. "I mean, I don't think he'd *mind* me sellin' it to 'im, but he doesn't care that much 'bout gettin' the bricks for himself. All he gives a fuck about is that they don't go to Zerk, 'cause without that coke, Zerk's outta business."

"Seriously?" Nissa asked in surprise.

"Hell yeah. Somebody fronted him the coke, and if he ain't got it to sell then he can't pay 'em back. On top of that, he's out the runnin' in terms of this lil' coke contest, 'cause without product, he ain't in the game. He's like a nigga tryin' to shot hoop with no basketball. That leave the door wide open for Lord Byron."

"Well, Zerk's fuckin' bananas. He's not liable to take shit like that lyin' down."

"He's not," Shade assured her. "He tried to rip off Byron last night. And that errand he wants me to run?"

"Yeah?"

"He basically wants Byron to have an accident," Shade said. "And last but not least, he just came after *us*."

"So he knows you have his coke."

Shade shook his head. "I don't think so. If he was sure I had it, he'd have my ass tied up in some basement. Like Byron, I thank he just *suspects* I have it. In fact, Byron's prolly the reason he's suspicious?"

"How's that?"

"Zerk snatched up one of Byron's people – tortured him until he gave up some info Zerk could use to try to rip Byron off. But you can be damn sho' Zerk asked him 'bout the coke, too. See, up 'til now, Zerk's prolly been thankin' that Byron's the one killed his brutha and took his drugs."

"But now he suspects you," Nissa concluded.

Shade nodded. "Which is why those knuckleheads showed up at our house tonight."

"Well, can't you just give Zerk his drugs and walk away?"

"You forgettin' that his brutha's dead, and he might want some payback" Shade said. "Plus, Lord Byron's made it clear that he ain't gonna be happy if that blow finds its way back to Zerk, and he's gone take that out on somebody – namely, *me*."

"So let me see if I got this," Nissa said. "Zerk's prolly gone try to kill you if you don't hand over the coke, Lord Byron's comin' after you if you give it to him, and you got the cops breathin' down you neck about the bodies in that buildin'. Anythang I forget?"

"Yeah – Byron knows about the errand Zerk wants me to do."

"Holy shit!" Nissa exclaimed.

"But the thang is, he sorta made me a counteroffer."

Nissa gave him an inquisitive look. "Which was what?"

"Can't chu guess?" her brother shot back.

Her brow creased in thought for a moment, and then she simply said, "He wants Zerk to have an accident."

"In essence."

Nissa raised a hand and rubbed her temples. "This shit is way too complicated."

"Actually," Shade countered, "all this shit is finally makin' sense to me. After talkin' with Byron tonight, everythang came into focus. I just wished I'd figured it out sooner."

His sister's eyes narrowed. "So why didn't you?"

"Huh?" Shade droned, giving her a blank look.

"Shade, you the smartest nigga I know, and I ain't just sayin' that 'cause you my brutha. You can spot shit comin' a mile off and can practically see around corners. So why it take you so long to get yo arms around this shit?"

Shade didn't verbally respond. In fact, his only acknowledgement that he'd heard the question was a quick, uneasy glance in his sister's direction.

"It's her," Nissa muttered a moment later. "That bitch, Yoni."

"She's not a bitch," Shade said defensively.

"You know what I mean," Nissa told him. She then glanced quickly into the back seat to make sure Cherry was still dozing (as well as Gin), then practically hissed, "Didn't you already fuck her?"

Giving his sister an incredulous look, Shade blurted out, "What the hell does that have to do with anythang?"

"'Cause you always get like this when you chasin' a piece of tail. When you like some chick – I mean, *really* like her – you have this tendency to forget which way is up. Shit that should be easy for you to figure out suddenly become like fuckin' quantum physics, and you usually can't get your shit together again until you bang the chick in question."

"It's not like that with Yoni, it's–"

"Please don't tell me you in love," Nissa interjected. "'Cause I don't wanna hear that shit right now. All I wanna hear about is how you gonna take care of yo family – the peeps in this car – 'cause we the ones in danger, not yo girlfriend."

Rather than respond, Shade blinked as a new thought occurred to him.

"Shit," he muttered. "Yoni…"

Chapter 74

Shade went racing down the hallway towards Yoni's apartment, practically out of breath after having run up the stairs.

Basically, his sister's statement had made him realize that Yoni could be in danger; he wouldn't put it past a maniac like Zerk to try using her as leverage. Thus, he'd swiftly turned the car around and headed to her tenement. Once there, he'd told Nissa to get behind the wheel and gave her instructions about where they'd meet up later. Simply put, he didn't need his family hangin' around waitin' for him – not with everything that was going on. Then, as they drove off, he'd dashed into Yoni's building.

Fortunately, he hadn't run into anyone along the way to her apartment who appeared to be a threat. The closest thing he encountered in that regard was some drunk who came staggering down the corridor, continuously bumping from wall to wall like a human pinball. Shade slipped by him (noting that he smelled strongly of alcohol), and a moment later was pounding on Yoni's door. A few seconds later, he saw the peephole darken, and then Yoni opened the door.

"Look, Shade," she began. "I told you I needed–"

"We need to go," Shade interjected, pushing past her into the apartment and closing the door.

"Hold on, nigga," Yoni hissed angrily. "Who da fuck you thank you are bargin' into–"

"Yoni, we don't have time for this shit," Shade barked, cutting her off. "There's prolly some muhfuckas from Zerk's crew on they way here now, and they ain't comin' to talk."

"Huh?" Yoni muttered in confusion.

"What part didn't you unnastand?! Niggas with guns prolly on they way here! We can talk when we get outta here, but for now, you got two minutes to pack whatever the fuck you need."

Yoni still looked confused, but quickly dashed to her bedroom, sliding momentarily on the hallway rug like Shade had done a few nights earlier.

While she packed, Shade paced worriedly in the living room, looking at his watch every few seconds. He wanted to kick himself for not having come here immediately after leaving his house, for not realizing that Yoni might be in danger, too.

It felt like it was taking forever, but Yoni was actually back with an overnight bag within the designated two-minute time frame. However, rather than head to the door, she flopped down on the end of the couch.

"I need a sec to put my shoes on," she explained, at which point Shade noticed that she had a pair of tennis shoes in her hand. He also seemed to take note of the living room for the first time, and realized that it was kind of a mess.

There was a plate of fried chicken and mashed potatoes that looked like it had been knocked off the coffee table and onto the floor, along with a couple of napkins. On the coffee table itself a cup had been tipped over and spilled some juice or soda that someone had attempted to wipe up. There was also a pepper shaker laying on its side with the top off, and a small mound of black pepper that had seemingly spilled out.

"What da fuck happened here?" Shade asked, gesturing towards the mess.

"My drunk-ass daddy, that's what happened," Yoni answered as she continued putting her shoes on. "He came in smellin' like he just crawled out a whiskey barrel and sayin' he wanted sommin' to eat. I gave 'im some leftovers that he was eatin' out here on the couch, but he fell asleep in the middle of chewin', dropped the plate and knocked a bunch of shit over. I went and got a blanket to put on him" – she gestured to the arm of the couch, where Shade saw her weighted blanket – "but while I was in the kitchen gettin' some stuff to clean up this mess, he just left. That was about thirty seconds b'foe you barged in; I'm surprised you didn't pass 'im in the hallway."

"I think I did," Shade said, reflecting.

"Anyway," Yoni droned as she stood up. "I'm ready."

Shade grabbed her overnight bag and slung it over his shoulder before hustling Yoni to the door. He opened it, preparing to step out, then froze.

Right outside was Beemer, and he was holding a gun that was pointed directly at Shade's forehead.

THUG LIFE: EMANCIPATED

Chapter 75

Hands raised, Shade backed into the apartment without being told, keeping Yoni behind him. Beemer came in, followed by some other nigga that Shade didn't recognize, but who was also armed.

"Close that doe', Shep," Beemer said over his shoulder.

The other nigga – Shep – did as instructed. He was obviously the replacement for Bull and Caveman, who were probably feeling under the weather after what happened in Shade's garage.

"Guess you thought this shit was over, muhfucka," Beemer grumbled at Shade. "Nigga, we ain't even got started yet." Then, speaking over his shoulder again, he told Shep, "Go check out the back – make sure ain't nobody else here."

Inwardly, Shade smiled as Shep began walking down the hallway. After getting surprised by Nissa holding a shotgun earlier, Beemer was seemingly more vigilant this time.

"Now you two," Beemer growled at Shade and Yoni, "go sit y'all asses on that couch, and keep yo hands where I can see them bitches."

Yoni and Shade turned to go sit, and a second later Shade felt a searing pain at the back of his head, like he'd been clubbed with a nightstick. Dazed, he dropped down to all fours, with Yoni's bag slipping from his shoulder.

"Shade!" Yoni cried out, dropping down to help him.

"That's for tryin' to be all slick, nigga," Beemer informed him. "Makin' us waste our time at that other buildin' like this bitch lived over there. And *this*" – he stepped forward and kicked Shade in the ribs – "is for that shotgun that got pulled on me b'foe."

Shade shook his head, trying to clear his thoughts, at the same time trying to mentally push aside the pain he was now feeling in his side and head. Yoni started to drape one of his arms over her shoulder to help him up, but suddenly found Beemer's gun pointed at her.

"Bitch, get back," Beemer ordered.

Keeping her eyes on the gun, Yoni backed away from Shade, who had just put a hand on the coffee table for balance.

Beemer turned his attention back to Shade. "Now, muhfucka, we 'bout to—"

His words were cut off as the front door opened, drawing his attention, and the drunk Shade had seen earlier – Yoni's dad – staggered in.

The unexpected appearance of Yoni's dad gave Shade a small window of opportunity. Faster than seemed possible, he grabbed the overturned pepper shaker and flicked it at Beemer's face. As a result, Beemer – who was just turning back towards Shade – had a heap of finely ground black pepper fly into his mouth, nose, and eyes.

Letting out a grunt that sounded like a mixture of pain and irritation, Beemer instinctively closed his eyes. As he began rubbing them with the thumb and middle finger of his free hand, he opened his mouth and let out something like a strangled cough, then drew in a sharp breath and sneezed explosively. Almost immediately, he sneezed again. And again.

By that time, Shade was on his feet. Although still a little wobbly, he rushed Beemer, being careful to stay out of his line of fire in case that nigga intentionally or accidentally pulled the trigger. Of course, the gun was Shade's goal, and when he got close he grabbed Beemer's gunhand and pushed it to the side so that the barrel was pointed to the wall. Then, gripping Beemer's forearm with both hands, he brought it down sharply on a raised knee.

There was a cracking sound, and Beemer – who was still sneezing – somehow managed a yelp of pain between sternutations. His gunhand went limp, and Shade knocked the weapon from it.

At that juncture, Beemer clearly knew he was in trouble. Ergo, despite being afflicted by sneezes and unable to see, he fought back as best he could, trying to grapple with Shade using his free hand. But he didn't get a chance to do much before Yoni rushed forward brandishing the plate that the chicken and mashed potatoes had been on. She whacked Beemer on the side of the head with it, which apparently knocked him unconscious because he suddenly went down. Unfortunately, Shade – who had still been scuffling with him – went down as well.

Thankfully, Shade was able to twist as they fell to the floor, so that he ended up coming down on top of Beemer, who simply lay there and didn't move. Shockingly, Yoni's drunk-ass daddy had wandered through the mayhem and flopped down on the couch without seeming to notice anything.

An unexpected creak at the far end of the hallway drew Shade's attention, and he looked up to find Shep coming out of one of the bedrooms in the back.

"What da fuck?" Shep muttered as he looked at Shade and Beemer on the floor. Then, seeming to understand that his partner was down, Shep started to raise his gun.

By that time, Shade was already reaching out towards the hallway rug. Grabbing it, he yanked as hard as he could. Shep, who didn't seem to understand that he was standing on said rug, had his legs jerked out from under him. He landed hard, like he'd been bodied slammed, with the wind being knocked out of him and his head bouncing off the floor. Even worse, his gun went off, and Shep screamed as the bullet went into his thigh.

Shade rolled to the side, getting out of Shep's view and fetching up against the couch. Bumping it caused the weighted blanket, which had been resting on the sofa's arm, to tumble down on top of him.

It was still heavy as fuck. However, as he shoved it off, he was seized with a sudden inspiration. Standing up, he grabbed the weighted blanket. Holding it up overhead and spread out in front of him, he went racing down the hall.

It was foolhardy and impulsive, but he hoped that would be enough to catch Shep off guard. A second later, he wondered if he'd made a mistake as Shep fired two or three times in rapid succession, the sound booming in the narrow apartment hallway. The blanket jerked wildly as the bullets struck – like a heavyweight boxer was punching it on the other side – but surprisingly the ammo didn't fully penetrate. And then Shade went tumbling as he ran pell-mell into Shep, who was either still on the floor or just starting to rise.

Shep screamed again, the impact with Shade causing excruciating pain to his injured leg. Shade himself with down in a disorderly heap, releasing his hold on the blanket as he went to the floor and then banged his shoulder against a door frame. Quickly recovering, he saw that the blanket was now partially covering Shep, who was trying to squirm out from under it, moaning all the while. Most importantly, the hand holding the gun was under it.

Seeing an opportunity, Shade drew in a leg then extended it forcefully, kicking Shep right near the temple just as the muhfucka was pulling his gunhand free. Shep's head snapped to the side and he stopped moving, while the hand holding the gun flopped limply to the side.

Shade let out a deep breath, feeling tension leave his body as Yoni came down the hallway.

"That was stupid," Yoni commented. "You cudda got killed."

"I'm just lucky he didn't aim for my hands or feet," Shade countered as he began searching Shep's pockets.

"We cudda just left. You didn't have to go chargin' at his ass."

"I didn't know how bad he was hurt, and the nigga had a direct line of sight to the doe'," Shade explained. "Unless this muhfucka was completely out of it, we weren't makin' it to the hallway without one of us – or maybe both of us – gettin' capped."

"What about that other nigga's gun?" asked Yoni. "You cudda grabbed it."

"Same thing – I wudda had to step into this muhfucka's line of sight to get it. And at best that would have just earned us a standstill; at worst, a fuckin' shootout."

As Yoni contemplated what he'd said, Shade stood up holding Shep's keys and cell phone, both of which he then pocketed.

"A'ight," Shade intoned. "Let's check that other nigga and get the fuck outta here."

"Damn," Yoni muttered, looking at Shep. "He's bleedin' a *lot*."

Shade followed her gaze and realized she was right. He had avoided stepping in it and didn't seem to have any on him, but there was more blood present than he would have anticipated.

"Shit," he uttered as he realized what they were dealing with. "Musta hit the femoral."

Yoni's eyebrows went up in surprise. "The femoral artery?"

Shade nodded. "Yeah. You nick that, you'll bleed out in minutes. Or less."

"So he's dead?"

"If he ain't, he will be soon," Shade replied, noticing that Shep looked pale.

Yoni was on the verge of saying something else, when a voice shouted from the other end of the hallway.

"Don't move, muhfuckas!"

Shade and Yoni looked up to find Beemer, on his feet, cradling one hand and holding his gun in the other, with the barrel pointed towards them.

"Now, don't nuthin' stupid," Beemer said. "Put yo hands—"

He suddenly stopped speaking as movement appeared to draw his attention. It was Yoni's dad, still drunk but coming to his feet, singing.

Beemer appeared to react out of instinct, swinging the gun towards Yoni's dad and firing.

"No!" Yoni screeched, snatching Shep's gun and firing.

With the gun booming next to him, Shade couldn't tell how many times Yoni pulled the trigger, but two slugs took Beemer in the chest. He staggered back slightly, then slump down to the floor and didn't move.

Yoni immediately went dashing down the hallway, plainly trying to get to her dad, who could be heard saying, "I been shot... I been shot... I been shot..." over and over again like a broken record.

Shade, right behind her and knowing what she was likely to do, hissed, "Don't touch him!"

Whether because of what Shade said or shock at what she was seeing, Yoni froze in front of her dad, who was sitting on the couch. Shade looked at him, noting that he appeared to have taken a bullet in the upper right chest. Another seemed to have grazed his temple. Beyond that, however, he didn't appear to have caught any slugs.

Despite the close range, Beemer had done a poor job of hitting his target. However, that could have been the result of a lot of factors: shooting with his non-dominant hand, maybe not seeing clearly because pepper was still in his eyes, and so on.

Shade took a moment to scan everything, his mind racing. He then turned to Yoni.

"Okay, we only got a few minutes," he said to her as he took Shep's gun from her hand. "Does your daddy have a cell phone?"

"Yeah," Yoni said, with a nod, Shade's words having seemingly broken whatever spell she'd been under.

"Okay, find it – quickly – and don't get blood any blood on you."

Yoni went to her dad, who was still bitching in a sing-song way about being shot, and attempted to gingerly lay him on the couch. Her efforts made him groan in pain, but once he was down she started going through his pockets looking for his phone.

While she did that, Shade grabbed a napkin off the floor and began wiping off Shep's gun. By the time he was done, Yoni announced that she had found her dad's cell.

"Okay, just sit it on the coffee table for a sec," Shade ordered as he scrambled over to Beemer, who appeared to be dead. As he began going through Beemer's pockets, he told Yoni, "Real fast, without getting blood on you, kinda wipe your hands on your dad's hands and his shirt.

She moved to comply, but asked him, "Why?"

"Because you fired a gun," he answered. "You gonna have gunshot residue on you, and we need it to be on yo daddy."

"What's the purpose of that?" she asked.

"We need it to look like yo daddy shot these niggas," he told her as he stood up with Beemer's keys and cell. "If the cops test for gunshot residue and there's none on 'im, they gone know somebody else pulled the trigger."

"Wait a minute," Yoni muttered as Shade put Beemer's items in a pocket with Shep's. "You framin' my daddy for this shit?"

"I ain't *framin'* him," Shade explained as he walked to her, "but the cops are gonna be here soon and we need to be gone by then. This is too big a mess to clean up, but there needs to be some kind of plausible explanation. The best one is that these niggas followed yo drunk daddy home and tried to rob him, and he somehow took 'em out – wrestled the gun away from one of them after shootin' him in the leg, and then blasted the other one."

"Nobody gone believe that shit," Yoni declared.

"The evidence prolly won't square up exactly, but it'll be close enough," Shade told her. "Now, is yo daddy left- or right-handed?"

"He's ambi," she answered. Getting a confused look from Shade, she continued with, "Ambidextrous."

"Okay, great," Shade commented while putting Shep's gun in the right hand of Yoni's dad, making sure to put his finger on the trigger. "Now get his phone and use *his* finger to dial 9-1-1."

Yoni complied, and a second later, the phone was ringing. Within moments, it was answered by a 9-1-1 operator. Shade held a finger up to his lips to indicate silence, then pointed at Yoni's dad, who was still muttering about being shot. Yoni nodded in understanding and placed the phone near her dad's mouth. Apparently the 9-1-1 operator heard him, because she asked him for his location. At that juncture, Yoni hung up using her daddy's finger and tossed the cell phone onto the coffee table.

Shade spent a moment doing a quick mental check, trying to see if he had missed anything. To the best of his knowledge, he hadn't. As he had told Yoni, on the surface it would look like some would-be criminals had gotten the tables turned on them. From what he could tell, Yoni's dad was too drunk to be able to explain what happened, but that wasn't necessarily a bad thing in Shade's opinion, because the cops wouldn't have a story to try to tear apart. They'd only have the evidence to tell them what happened.

Satisfied, Shade grabbed the bag Yoni had packed and they got the hell out of there.

Chapter 76

Through divine providence, Shade and Yoni managed to make it out of her apartment without being seen. (Presumably anyone who heard the shots had hit the floor and stayed there until they were sure it was safe to get up.) Making it all the way outside without being seen would have been too much to ask, but thankfully, nobody appeared to connect them to the gunfire that had happened. Even better, no one attempted to speak to them.

In fact, the only conversation that occurred was when Shade whispered to Yoni that she'd need to text her father in a bit and tell him she was staying with a friend, which Yoni agreed to do. That would be enough to pacify the cops, who might otherwise think the worst after finding two dead bodies in Yoni's apartment and Yoni herself missing.

Shade still had the keys and cell phones of Shep and Beemer. The keys, of course, came in handy when they eventually left the building and hit the street. Thanks to a key fob that Beemer had been carrying – which turned out to belong to a four-door pickup truck they found parked outside – Shade and Yoni now had a ride. Thus, after Shade confirmed there was no GPS device, they were on their way. It was at that point that Shade brought her up to speed on everything that was going on.

****

"Wait a minute," Yoni muttered. "I just asked you about the bodies in that condemned buildin' and you told me you had nuthin' to do with it."

"I didn't wanna get you involved," Shade told her.

"I'm already fuckin' involved!" Yoni insisted, causing Shade to give her an odd look. "Did you forget the fuckin' cops yanked me out of school to talk to me about that shit?"

"They saw us together and just wanted to see what you knew. That don't make you involved."

"It damn sho' feel like involvement to *me*," Yoni stressed. "'Specially when niggas show up at *my* place with guns 'cause *you* got they cocaine. But the main thang is that you lied to me. You looked me right in my fuckin' face and lied to me."

"Like I said, I ain't wanchu involved."

"But if you lied to me about that, how do I know you ain't lie about anythang else? About *everythang* else?" she demanded. "How can I believe anythang that come out yo muhfuckin' mouth?"

Shade let out a groan of exasperation. "Look, I already told you why I said what I said. That's the simple truth. I don't know what else to say."

Rather than respond, Yoni merely crossed her arms and stared sulkily ahead, lips pursed in anger.

THUG LIFE: EMANCIPATED

Chapter 77

They met up with Nissa and the others in the parking lot of a grocery store in a middle-class neighborhood. Goose was also there, having been called by Nissa after she dropped Shade off, but that had been part of the plan. Of course, it had been Nissa's idea to recruit her boyfriend to help them, and Shade – not liking the idea of his sisters and mom being alone – had acquiesced. Thus, he was glad to see that the nigga was at least semi-reliable in that regard.

His family was actually in Goose's car when Shade and Yoni pulled up next to them. He had already called and told Nissa what they were driving, so they knew it was him as opposed to someone who might be after them. Shade quickly parked, then found himself being hugged tightly by sisters as he and Yoni stepped out.

"How's Gin?" he asked after they separated.

"In the back of Goose's car but still pretty much out of it," Nissa informed him, at which point Shade gave Goose a what's-up nod. "She came 'round once and asked about *you*, believe it or not, then kinda passed out again."

"You thank we need to take her to the doctor?" Cherry asked, plainly worried.

Shade glanced at Nissa, giving her a *Can't-risk-it* look that he knew she'd understand, but to Cherry he simply replied, "No, I'm sure she's alright. She'll be better when she wakes up."

Cherry nodded as he finished speaking, seemingly satisfied with her brother's assessment.

"So what's the plan?" Nissa asked.

"I need you, Cherry and Gin to lay low 'til I get this shit sorted out," Shade told her. "You remember where I told you to go?"

"Yeah," Nissa replied.

"Good," her brother stated. "I'ma need you to take Yoni wichu, 'cause—"

"Fuck that," interjected Yoni, who had been silent up to that point. "I'm not stickin' my head in the sand while muhfuckas are out huntin' for me."

Shade shook his head on disagreement. "Like I said b'foe, you not really involved in this. I'm the one they really want."

"And like I told *you*," Yoni countered, "I'm already involved in this shit, so my plan is to see it through."

Shade simply stared at her for a second, then sighed. "A'ight, but it's yo funeral."

He then turned his attention back to Nissa, who asked, "So whachu gone do?"

"I'm still workin' on it," he admitted.

"Well work the fuck faster," his sister practically ordered. "I hate havin' to sleep with one eye open."

Chapter 78

They spoke in the parking lot for a few more minutes, then split up, with Shade's family leaving with Goose in his car. He had given Nissa the bulk of their stash, so they'd be okay on funds for a while. (And Nissa, of course, didn't have to be told to keep Goose in the dark about the money, because even niggas in love – which Goose allegedly was – can get confused when cash enters the picture.)

On their part, Shade and Yoni headed back towards the hood, with the former in his car and the latter driving Beemer's truck. At Shade's direction, they headed to an area that was notorious for car thefts; once there, Yoni parked the truck under a bridge and left it running with the key in the ignition and the doors unlocked. Then, she hustled over to Shade's car and got in.

"Hang on for a second," Shade said as he took what looked like a cleaning rag from beneath his seat. A moment later, he stepped out the car and dashed over to Beemer's truck. Once there, he opened the door on the driver's side and leaned inside, seeming to poke around or something.

For a moment, Yoni wondered what the hell he was doing. They had moved her overnight bag to Shade's car before they left the parking lot, and he had double-checked the truck then to make sure they weren't forgetting anything. Unless he had OCD, he couldn't possibly be checking the pickup again. And suddenly, as she watched him, she understood: he was wiping the truck down.

It took Shade less than a minute to do both the driver and passenger side, as well as any other surface they might have touched. Still, it felt much longer, as he was constantly looking around to make sure nobody crept on him. In truth, this particular spot seemed fairly deserted, but he didn't doubt that someone would come by soon enough. Eventually satisfied with the job he'd done, he raced back to his car, got in, put the car in gear and hit the gas.

"That's one less thing to worry about," he noted as they drove away, tucking the rag back under the seat.

Honestly, he didn't think the car would get reported as stolen, but he didn't want to take a chance. That left him driving his own car, but he didn't think Zerk's goons were familiar enough with it to know it on sight. In other words, it was a calculated risk, but one that he was willing to take.

"So I take it *this* is what all this shit's about," Yoni said, interrupting his thoughts.

Looking towards her, Shade noted that she was holding up the bag that contained the coke. Obviously, Nissa had left it on the front passenger side of the car.

"Uh, yeah," Shade confirmed. "That's it."

Yoni placed the bag on her lap, then reached for the zipper, only to be brought up short when Shade spoke.

"Don't," he said firmly.

"I wasn't gone snort it," Yoni joked. "I just wanted to see it."

"Wait 'til we get where we're goin', then you can look."

Yoni frowned. "What's wrong with openin' it *now*?"

"'Cause I don't want anythang connectin' me to that bag or those drugs. No contact particles, no trace elements, nuthin'. So I don't want a string from the seat belt gettin' caught in the zipper. I don't want a piece of the upholstery fallin' from the roof into the bag while you got it open. No links from it to me. That's why I don't even touch that bag without gloves on."

"So wait," Yoni muttered worriedly. "Do I need to wipe it down?"

"No," Shade advised, shaking his head. "Prints don't adhere to leather very well."

"But you just said *you* use gloves when you touch it."

"Yeah, but I'm paranoid about shit like that."

Yoni's eyes narrowed. "Did your sisters touch it?"

"Nissa did."

"With her bare hand?"

Shade was silent for a few seconds, then sighed. "No, I made her use a tissue."

Yoni glared at him in fury. "Oh, so you won't let your sister touch it barehanded, but for me it's okay?"

"I didn't say that," Shade argued. "And now that I think about it, I really didn't *make* Nissa use a tissue. She kinda just knew to do it."

"Just pass me that fuckin' rag," Yoni demanded.

Shade reached down and retrieved the cleaning rag, which Yoni snatched from his hand when he held it out to her a moment later.

"Fuckin' asshole…" she mumbled in Shade's direction as she began wiping the handle of the bag.

Chapter 79

"Where are we?" Yoni asked as they got out of the car.

"An old manufacturin' plant," Shade answered. "There was a worldwide financial crisis like ten or fifteen years ago, and the company that owned this place went bankrupt."

As he spoke, Shade looked around. He had left the car's headlights on to provide illumination, allowing him to see various types of industrial equipment and facilities around them: cooling towers, warehouses, an extensive piping system, and so on. The place was huge, and there was a lot more that they couldn't see.

"It's kind of isolated," Yoni noted, reflecting on the fact that – by her estimation – the plant was located at least five miles from the nearest house.

"That was intentional," Shade said as he went to the trunk, opened it and took out his tool bag. "Who wants a fuckin' manufacturin' plant next door, belchin' chemicals and spewin' fumes all the damn time?"

"And it don't bother you that there's only one way in and out of this place?" asked Yoni, referring to the long, winding (and unlit) road they had taken to the plant.

"There's actually three ways in and out of here," Shade informed her, at the same time pulling the tactical flashlight from his tool bag and turning it on. "But the other two are fenced off. Plus, they were never maintained too good, so you'd fuck up your car drivin' over 'em. And on top of that, they all overgrown with trees and bushes now."

"So after all that talk, you just proved me right: only one way in and out."

"Just come on," Shade muttered as he walked towards the front of the car and turned the headlights off.

****

They ended up at a building that Shade referred to as a shipping warehouse. Once there, they circled the outside until Shade found what he was looking for: a rectangular object similar to a utility box that was embedded in the ground.

"What's that?" Yoni asked.

"Standby generator," Shade replied, slipping on a pair of gloves from his tool bag. "It's s'pose to supply backup power if the electricity ever goes out. They got a big one for the whole plant, but this buildin' also had its own."

"If they got generators, how come none of the fuckin' lights on 'round here?"

"Da fuck they need the lights on for?" Shade asked as he removed a side panel and began fiddling with the generator. "They ain't makin' shit. They in bankruptcy, which mean they ain't got enough money to pay they bills, and all the muhfuckas they owe are fightin' over what's left of the company. So all the generators are off right now – most of 'em been off for years."

Yoni paused to consider that for a second, then asked, "You thank this one will still work?"

"Generators can last thirty or forty years. They might need a lil' maintenance, but long as nobody don't go whackin' 'em with a sledgehammer or sommin', they'll last a muhfuckin' lifetime."

"But they run on gas, right?" Yoni noted. "Don't gas go bad after a while?"

"Regular gas and diesel will," Shade commented. "But this one runs on propane, and propane never goes bad. And we in luck, 'cause it looks like there's a lil' fuel left."

Yoni was about to make another comment when the generator suddenly came on. It didn't actually make a lot of noise, but in the gloom of night it seemed incredibly loud.

"A'ight," Shade said as he put the side panel back on. "Let's go check this place out."

With that, he began walking towards the entrance that led into the warehouse, and Yoni followed. As they drew close, Yoni noticed that there was some kind of metal sign posted on the door, but Shade yanked it off and tossed it aside before she got a good look at what it said. Shade then tried the door knob; to Yoni's surprised, it was unlocked, and a moment later they were inside.

"They just leave the door unlocked like that?" Yoni noted as Shade flicked on a nearby light switch.

"Why lock it?" Shade shot back. "Ain't shit in here to steal."

As he spoke, the lights flickered momentarily, and then came on, at which point Yoni saw that they were in an expansive warehouse. There was a bunch of inventory shelving that was bolted in place, some workbenches and desks, a myriad of wooden pallets haphazardly tossed around, and some kind conveyor system. There was also some heavy equipment that she couldn't identify located sporadically along the walls, but for the most part she got the impression that Shade was right: nothing she saw was readily stealable.

As if reading her mind, Shade said, "Pretty much all the shit that could be lifted either got moved or sold off ages ago. But if you thank you can make off with a ten-story cooling tower or a fifty-ton boiler, knock yourself out."

At that point, he reached over and turned the light switch off and suddenly the place was pitch black again.

"Why'd you do that?" Yoni asked as she turned his flashlight on.

"I just wanted to make sure the generator was workin' right," Shade explained. "But it's got a limited amount of fuel, and I don't wanna use it up turnin' on all the lights in this muhfucka. Now let's move."

With that, he began walking towards a door at the rear of the warehouse.

Falling into step beside him, Yoni inquired, "So what we doin' here?"

"I got an idea about how to deal with this situation. This a good place to fine-tune it."

"So, yo sistas and mom hidin' out at some factory, too?"

"Fuck naw. They at a motel just outside the city limits." As if to confirm this, he pulled out his cell phone and spent a moment thumbing through apps. "Yeah, they made it there."

"So you treatin' me different than yo sistas...again."

Shade shook his head. "No, I told you to go with 'em, but yo ass is hardheaded."

At that point, they reached the door they'd been walking towards. Shade opened it and went into the next room, followed by Yoni. As expected, it was dark, and he spent a moment scanning the place with his flashlight. They were in what might have been a storage area, but it was hard to tell since the room was completely devoid of furnishings.

Shade and Yoni kept moving, going through a door in the opposite wall into a hallway.

"This place looks a lot better than I wudda thought," Yoni said abruptly as they continued walking. "I mean, it could stand to be swept – there's dust and cobwebs all the fuck over – but, from what I can see, it's not as bad as I expected."

"Whachu mean?" Shade asked.

"Well, even if there's nuthin' to steal around here, I'm surprised this place ain't full of graffiti, or that a bunch of homeless people ain't livin' here."

"Like you said b'foe, it's pretty isolated. Homeless folks usually ain' got no car, so why they gonna hoof it all the way out here to a spot with nobody to panhandle from and no place to beg for food?"

"So what about teenagers, maybe comin' up here and writin' all on the walls and shit?"

"It happened a coupla times, then maybe six or seven years ago, a gang of fuck-ups from the 'burbs cut class and came up here one day. They broke into a room full of hazardous materials – dumb fucks didn't recognize a hazmat symbol – and ended up screwin' around with a vat of chemicals and blew themselves to kingdom come."

"You jokin', right?"

"Nope. I thank two of 'em died. The rest lived – they just fuckin' maimed and disfigured for the rest of they life. After that, nobody was chompin' at the bit to come up here and do anythang."

"Wait a minute," Yoni uttered in concern. "That sign you yanked off the door…that wasn't a fuckin' hazmat symbol, was it?"

"Naw. It just said sommin' 'bout who owned the place and trespassers bein' prosecuted.

"So why you yank it down?"

"Actually, it kinda just kinda came off when I touched it. I think the nail holdin' it in was rusted or sommin'."

Yoni frowned. That really didn't jibe with what she remembered seeing, but it *had* been dark out there.

"Anyway," Yoni intoned, "shouldn't they have had security if it was a bunch of explosive shit around here?"

"You keep forgettin' that the company was in bankruptcy – still is. The plant was pretty much shut down, and the creditors didn't want a lot of money wasted on guardin' a place that didn't have much to steal. They wanted they money, and anythang that got spent was money they'd never get. Plus, the dangerous shit was already locked up. They never expected anybody to be dumb enough to break into a room with a bunch of hazardous shit in it – that's like smearin' yo'self with barbecue sauce and then walkin' into a cage with a hungry lion."

"So that was it?" Yoni droned quizzically. "Most times when shit like that happen to kids from the suburbs, you never hear the end of it. It's fine if it's Pookie and Peaches from the hood, but if it's Janet and Mark from a damn master-planned community, then sommin's gotta be done."

"Oh, the media bitched about it, so the creditors agreed to hire a security company to keep thangs in check. But they only come around like the once a month – usually the last *day* of the month – so we won't see 'em 'round here for a couple of weeks."

"A coupla weeks!" Yoni blurted out, giving him an incredulous stare. "I'm not stayin' in this shithole a coupla weeks."

"I wasn't sayin' we would," Shade stressed. "I was just tryin' to say we didn't have to worry 'bout any rent-a-cops comin' 'round. Anyway, here we are."

He flicked on a light switch and spread his arms in an expansive gesture meant to encompass the room they had just entered. In truth, Yoni hadn't been paying attention to where they were going; she had just been following Shade. Now she took a look around.

The room they found themselves in had lockers lining the walls. In addition, there were rows of lockers spaced equidistant from each other in the middle of the room, with benches in between them. Bearing all that in mind, it wasn't hard to figure out where they were.

Turning to Shade, Yoni said, "They had a locker room here?"

"Bet," he replied. "Occasionally the workers had to deal with that hazardous shit we were talkin' about b'foe. This is where they'd change into the proper gear – they even had connectin' showers so they could get cleaned up after."

"So why *we* here? You wanna take a shower together or sommin'?"

"Not exactly," Shade answered, walking towards one of the sets of lockers in the middle of the room. He then began opening lockers one at a time, apparently checking them as he mumbled, "Where is it? Where is it?"

Yoni was about to ask him what the hell he was looking for when he suddenly yelled, "A-ha!"

Reaching into a locker he'd just opened, he pulled out something that looked to Yoni like a folding camping chair – the type that people bring to little league football games and use to sit on the sidelines. However, as Shade moved to a more spacious part of the room and opened it up, she realized that she was only half right. It wasn't a folding *chair*; it was a folding *cot*.

"Shit," Yoni muttered. "You really do expect us to stay here."

"It's prolly just for a night," he assured her as he went back to the lockers. A moment later, he pulled a second cot from a different locker.

"Okay, there's no fuckin' way you just happened to find some cots in here," Yoni stated.

Shade smiled as he carried the second cot near the spot where he'd opened the first. "Guess I'm just lucky."

"Bullshit," Yoni declared. "How you know so much about this place?"

As he began trying to open the second cot, Shade started to explain. "A few months b'foe he died, my granddaddy did a job here."

"What kind of job?"

"Not whachu thinkin'," Shade told her, as he struggled to unfold the second cot. "No malefic shit. It was handyman-type work."

"Oh, okay."

"The company ownin' this place didn't have money to pay the creditors, but it still had assets."

"I know whachu mean," Yoni said. "Land, equipment…shit like that."

"Exactly," Shade concurred, taking a seat on a nearby bench as he continued trying to open the cot. "Anyway, they agreed to give a bunch of equipment 'round here to a creditor to pay off some of what they owed, but they didn't wanna pay union rates to get the work done. So they hired a bunch of skilled, non-union labor, like my granddaddy. They basically had to disconnect a bunch of equipment and prepare it for shippin' – things like chemical vats, turbines, heat exchangers…"

He trailed off as, glancing at Yoni, he realized a lot of the shit he was saying was going over her head.

"But as to how I got involved," Shade continued, "it was summer, and while my sistas were off visitin' relatives I stayed to help my granddaddy with work."

Yoni looked at him with raised eyebrows. "I'm surprised they let a kid hang around here with all the shit they had goin' on."

"Technically, I wasn't supposed to be here, but the dude supervisin' the work was a man named Mr. Ostertag. He had been the plant manager here, so they brought him back to oversee everythang. Anyway, he was divorced, but he had his daughter, Sally, stayin' with 'im for the summer. She was about my age, so he let me hang around as a playmate for her."

"So, just you and Snowflake Sally hangin' out together. Betchu loved that."

"I never said she was White," Shade shot back, pushing the cot away in frustration and reaching for his tool bag.

"You didn't have to – how many 'Sallies' you know in the hood?"

"You stereotypin'," Shade told her as he pulled an aerosol can from the tool bag.

"Whatever," Yoni droned monotonously. "But I'm surprised this guy let his daughter hang out with some kid form the hood. I wudda thought there was some summer camp she could go to, or some neighbor's kid that could have played with her."

"He was divorced and had her for the summer," Shade stated as he began spraying the hinges of the cot. "That was his time with her. What da fuck sense would it make to ship her off to camp? As for playin' with neighbors, after those kids blew themselves up, wasn't nobody lettin' they kids come play around here. So that just left me."

"Well, knowin' how niggas feel about White chicks, I bet it was the best summer of yo damn life."

"It wasn't like that, but yeah – it was fun," Shade admitted as he put the aerosol can away. "Sally and I roamed all over this plant, so that's how I know this place so well."

"I bet the plant's not all you roamed over," Yoni teased. "And now I unnastand how you know about these cots. I'm guessin' you and Sally broke 'em all in."

"Again, it wasn't like that," Shade insisted. "And if you just have to know, the cots have been here since back when the plant was actually runnin'. A lot of times niggas would be workin' double shifts, so Mr. Ostertag had the cots brought in so they could squeeze in a nap on they break. He did the same thang when he was supervisin' the work my granddaddy and other people were doin'. They had shifts runnin' 'round the clock sometimes, so Mr. Ostertag brought the cots out and let folks use 'em."

As he finished speaking, Shade tried the cot again.

"Finally," he muttered as the cot opened up this time. Turning to Yoni, he went on saying, "Anyway, I thank I've got a plan for gettin' us outta this hole we in."

"So what's that?" Yoni inquired.

Before Shade could answer, the lights flickered, causing him and Yoni to look up.

"Like I thought," Shade remarked, "the fuel may not last long."

"So what's the plan?"

"I'll probably have to go around to the other generators, siphon propane out of those, and then use it to keep this one runnin'."

"No," Yoni said, shaking her head. "What's the plan for getting us outta this fuckin' mess."

"I'll tell you later," Shade stated. "You should prolly try to get some sleep."

"But I don't wanna sleep," Yoni insisted. "I'd rather tie you up."

Shade chuckled as he leaned forward and placed his hand on the cot, seeing how much weight it could bear.

"Wow," he said. "I didn't know you were that kink – Oof!"

He grunted in pain as, for the second time that night, he got walloped on the back of the head. And then he pitched forward, unconscious.

THUG LIFE: EMANCIPATED

Chapter 80

Shade came to with a groan, his head throbbing like a sumbitch. Wincing, he tried to reach up and touch the injured area, only to find that he couldn't move his hands. Blinking, he came to the sudden realization that he was seated in a chair. No – *tied* to a chair, arms as well as legs.

"So, yo ass is finally awake," said a familiar voice. "Good – I was worried for a minute that I hit you too hard."

For a second, he couldn't focus, and then his vision cleared and he saw who had spoken to him.

"Yoni," he muttered softly. "What the fuck is goin' on?"

"Is it that fuckin' complicated?" she asked. "I knocked yo black ass out and tied you up."

At that point, Shade noticed that she was holding an item he recognized: a rubber mallet from his tool bag. He immediately understood what had happened: while he'd been wrestling with the cot, she had pulled out the mallet without him noticing and clubbed his ass with it.

"By the way," she added, "thanks for bringin' the twine. I was worried I'd have to hunt all over for sommin' to tie yo ass up with, but you had what I needed in yo bag."

"But why?"

"'Cause I need to get the truth, and you the type of nigga who can't seem to stop lyin'."

At that point Shade noticed something that he hadn't before. Maybe he hadn't initially detected it because it wasn't in his line of sight, or maybe he had a concussion and wasn't able to focus as he should have. Regardless, something that he had overlooked suddenly made his situation much more serious: in addition to the mallet, Yoni was also holding a gun.

"Where'd you get that?" Shade asked, inclining his head towards the weapon.

"This?" Yoni asked, holding up the gun. "It came in a box of crackerjacks. Where da fuck you thank I got it, nigga?"

"I mean, why do you have it?"

"Well, originally it was 'cause I got a daddy who's drunk all the time and never home. That means I practically live by myself, and everybody knows it, so a bitch need some protection – and I ain't talkin' 'bout condoms. Right now, though, I need it to make sure yo monkey ass don't keep lyin' to me."

Shade shook his head in confusion. "Lyin' about what?"

"About my brutha and why you killed 'im," Yoni hissed angrily.

"Who, Bo?" Shade said. "I ain't done shit to Bo. I literally ain't seen his ass in, like, ten years – prolly wouldn't know 'im if I saw 'im."

"Not, Bo," she stated, shaking her head. "William. William Waddell."

"Who?" Shade asked in confusion. "I don't even know no fuckin' William Wa…"

He abruptly trailed off as the name triggered something, and Yoni saw the light of recognition suddenly form in his eyes.

"Shit," Shade muttered. "Sneak…"

Chapter 81

It all made sense now. Sneak was the brother Yoni had mentioned before – the one who got killed, presumably in some kind of drug deal.

Yoni gave him a hard stare. "So, did you do it? Did you kill my brutha?"

"No!" Shade bellowed. "Sneak was my friend."

"Bullshit. The cops say you told 'em you didn't even know 'im that well."

"They're fuckin' cops," Shade insisted. "Why would I tell them anythang? Plus, half the time they don't care 'bout who did it; they just want somebody they can prosecute."

"So I should believe what you're tellin' *me* instead of what you told the *cops*, is that it?"

"Yeah. I'm tellin' you the truth. Sneak was my friend. I wudna killed 'im – I *owed* 'im."

Yoni frowned. "Owed 'im for what?"

Shade sighed. "There was a group of knuckleheads started messin' with Cherry on her way home from school every day. First it was just fuckin' talk – you know how niggas are. Then one day, these muhfuckas try to pull her into this car they got. Sneak comes along and stops 'em. I don't know how, 'cause Sneak wasn't no big, intimidatin' nigga, but he makes 'em back the fuck off and walks Cherry home. *That's* what I owed him for."

"And you paid 'im back how – by leavin' 'im to die?"

Shade shook his head. "I already told you everythang that happened. Sneak was already dead – there wasn't shit I could do for 'im. But it was that muhfucka Glen – Zerk's lil' brutha – who shot 'im. If you talked to the cops, I'm pretty sho' they told you the same thang."

"They did," she admitted with a nod. "They said sommin' 'bout forensics and ballistics and a bunch of other shit all indicatin' that Glen shot Sneak."

"That's what I'm tellin' you: I didn't do it."

"I hear you," Yoni said. "But here's my dilemma: I'm gettin' all this from a nigga who's trained to kill muhfuckas and make it look like an accident."

"But I swear, I'm tellin' you the truth."

"Oh, so I can believe everythang you say from now on, huh? It's all gone be gospel, right?" She appeared to ponder for a moment then continued. "Okay, let's try that out, but we'll start with an easy question: could you have killed my brutha?"

"No, I never wudda done that," Shade insisted. "Like I said, he was my friend."

"I phrased that wrong," Yoni told him. "What I meant was, if you had killed him, could you have arranged it to look like it did in that buildin' – like Glen had done it?"

"But I would never do that," Shade stressed. "Like I told you, Sneak was my–"

He stopped speaking mid-sentence as Yoni stepped forward and put the gun to his forehead.

"I need you to answer *my* question, and not ya own," She informed him. "And if you thank I won't cap yo ass just 'cause I fucked you, you might wanna reassess. I had an ex b'foe we moved back here, thought this pussy was still his even after we broke up so he tried to take it one day. I blew his balls off. So, as you probably gathered from back at my apartment, this is one bitch with no compunction about pullin' the trigger, unnastand?"

Shade simply nodded, not daring to speak, because at the moment Yoni seemed a little bit crazy.

"Good," Yoni declared in response to his nod. "Now, listen to my question. I'm not askin' if you *wudda* killed Sneak.

I'm askin' if you *cudda* killed 'im. Could you have done it and made it look exactly the way the cops think it happened – like Glen capped 'im?"

Shade nodded. "Yeah, I cudda."

Yoni stared at him for a few seconds, then lowered the gun and said, "A'ight, now we gettin' somewhere. But b'foe we go any further, there's sommin' you need to know 'bout me."

"What's that?"

"Basically, there's three thangs I can't stand: anchovies on my pizza, a nigga who too good to go down on a bitch, and muhfuckin' liars. And that last is the one I hate the most. I absolutely fuckin' hate bein' lied to."

Shade stared at her for a moment and then asked, "Why you doin' this?"

"You really have to ask that?" Yoni blurted out incredulously. "Well, let me ask you, what would you do if it was Nissa or Cherry that got killed like that?"

Shade's brow furrowed, then he simply uttered, "Prolly the same thang."

"Now you get it. By the way, what ever happened to those niggas who messed with Cherry?"

Shade was silent for a moment, then stated flatly, "They had an accident."

"An accident," Yoni echoed. "Now, I'm not gone ask you if you did it, 'cause even if you did, it sound like those sumbitches deserved it. But the point is that Cherry is still walkin' 'round alive and healthy. She wasn't kidnapped, didn't get assaulted, ain't traumatized…none of that shit. My brutha's in the ground, rottin', gettin' ate by worms. If somebody was willin' to go after the niggas who hurt Cherry – who's still alive and unharmed, by the way – why are you surprised that I would want to get whoever killed my brutha?"

Shade just nodded as she finished speaking. "Like I said, I'd be doin' the same thang in yo position. Believe me, I get it."

"So you unnastand that I'm gonna do what I need to do to get the truth?"

"Yeah."

"And you okay with that?"

"I'd do the same thang if it was my sistas," Shade answered. "And for the record, everythang I've been tellin' you really is gospel, and I'll tell you whatever else you wanna know, 'cause you deserve the truth."

Yoni stared at him fixedly for a few seconds, then declared, "You know, I actually believe that. Or rather, I believe that *you* believe it. But the problem is that you lie so much and so often, that you even fool yo'self into believin' that yo bullshit is true."

Shade looked at her in confusion. "I'm not even sure whachu talkin' about."

"Well, let's think about it. You go 'round actin' like you some square doin' a straight job, but that's bullshit," Yoni declared. "You run women. You make muhfuckas have fatal accidents. And now you walkin' the streets with a bag full of blow. That mean that you really a pimp, a hitta, and a drug dealer. Yo ass is every fuckin' male ghetto stereotype all rolled into one."

"No," Shade objected, shaking his head. "That's not me."

"Really? Well, which part ain't true?"

"I ain't no pimp, or a drug dealer, or—"

"So much for only tellin' me the truth," Yoni interjected. "That didn't last long."

"Just 'cause we interpret thangs differently don't mean I'm not tellin' the truth."

Yoni seemed to reflect for a moment, then said, "Okay, I'll buy that. I'll agree that some shit is subject to interpretation. But here's a question where you can't waffle on the answer: where yo mom and sistas at?"

Shade blinked in confusion. "Huh?"

"Yo mom and sistas," Yoni repeated. "You claim you only gone tell me the truth from now on, so answer my question. Where da fuck are they?"

"They ain't got nuthin' to do with this," Shade blurted out.

"I didn't say they did," Yoni retorted. "But you said you'd tell me the truth about whatever I wanna know, so I'm askin' where Gin, Nissa and Cherry at."

Shade just stared at her, but didn't reply.

"You know what, I don't need you to answer," Yoni said after a few seconds. Dropping the mallet, she reached into a rear pocket and pulled something out. With a start, Shade realized it was his cell phone.

"Got this off you while you were nappin'," Yoni told him. "I also lifted the phones of those two fucks who died in my apartment. Now let's see…" She then began manipulating the applications on his phone. "Okay, got 'em – thank goodness for these fuckin' trackin' apps. And look at that. They just where you said they were: at a motel outside of town. Guess you didn't lie about that. Oh, but there's a text from Nissa. Let's see…looks like Gin woke up and took off. But the girls are still there."

"They not involved in this," Shade stated again as Yoni put his phone away. "Just leave 'em out of it."

"I like yo sistas," Yoni told him, "and I ain't tryin' to see 'em hurt. I just want who ever killed my brutha, and right now, I'm really thankin' it's you."

"So what's yo plan?" Shade asked. "Shoot me in the head and leave me here to rot?"

"That would be fair," Yoni surmised, "since it's pretty much what you did to Sneak. Problem is, I'd prolly still have Zerk on my ass about his drugs."

"That's right," Shade concurred. "He'll keep comin' after you if he thank you got his shit."

"Unless I offer him a trade," Yoni said with a smile.

"What kind of trade?" asked Shade.

"I give him his drugs back, and he leaves yo ass to me." As she spoke, she produced a cell that Shade recognized as belonging to the recently-deceased Beemer.

"Zerk's a fuckin' psycho," Shade advised. "He'll stab you just for lickin' yo lips. You can't trust 'im."

"But I can trust *you*, right?" Yoni asked.

"Yeah, I swear you can," Shade said.

"And you say you have a plan for gettin' us outta this pile of shit we in?"

"I do."

"Okay great," Yoni intoned. "What is it?"

Shade's brow crinkled in concern. He didn't have a lot of cards to play at the moment, but the plan Yoni was asking about was one of them, and he wasn't quite ready to tip his hand.

"Come on," Yoni urged. "You say I can trust *you*, but sounds like you don't trust *me*. I still believe you killed Sneak, but I'm lookin' for a reason to believe you – to trust you. So tell me, what's the plan?"

Shade still didn't say anything. At the moment, Yoni was like a cop dead set on finding someone to pin a particular crime on, even if they were innocent. She was so focused on finding someone to blame for Sneak's death that she wasn't seeing straight.

"Last chance," Yoni said, holding Beemer's phone as if she was preparing to call someone. When Shade still didn't answer she simply shrugged, saying, "Okay, suit yo'self. We'll see if Zerk wants to do some horsetradin'."

She then began looking for Zerk's number in Beemer's contacts.

THUG LIFE: EMANCIPATED

Chapter 82

Zerk Simon was in his bedroom, deep in some pussy, but his mind was a million miles away. The girl under him was writhing like crazy and screaming her head off as Zerk pounded that shit.

"Oh yeah!" she shouted. "Fuck me, nigga! Fuck me! Tear that pussy up!"

"Bitch, will you shut da fuck up?!" Zerk bellowed. "I can't hear myself thank!"

The girl, some hoodrat Spinner had picked up for him a few hours earlier, immediately went dead silent.

"And stop all that fuckin' squirmin'!" he added. "It's distractin' the hell outta me!"

As commanded, the girl immediately stopped moving. Zerk continued thrusting like a maniac, oblivious to the fact that all the work he was putting in between her legs suddenly wasn't eliciting any type of response whatsoever.

He was obviously in a foul mood, but that wasn't an unusual state of mind for Zerk. Things just had a tendency to piss him off, and under the heading of "things" was a lot of shit: people, plants, doorbells, the weather... Basically, almost anything could set him off at any time.

At present, however, he had a reason for his unpleasant disposition, and it wasn't just the fact that it was late and he hadn't slept. In essence, just a few weeks earlier, his star had seriously been on the rise. He'd had a shot at moving up in the drug game, and had been making serious headway – and then everything had fucking collapsed. He had worked a deal that would give him a lot of product at once, and sent his brother to make the pickup. Then his brother had gotten killed and the product – several keys of coke – had vanished.

It was a situation that put Zerk in a serious fucking bind – not just because he had no product to put on the streets, but because he had gotten the connect to front him most of the blow. He still owed for that shit, and the connect had started bitching about getting paid.

After it happened, Zerk had been pretty sure he knew who had ripped him off: that pretentious muhfucka Lord Byron. They had been battling each other since the moment it became clear that there was room to move up. But then Byron had started pulling ahead – selling more, re-upping faster, making more money. That was what had prompted Zerk make the deal for the coke in the first place. Competing with Lord Byron had forced his hand, so as far as Zerk was concerned, the mess he found himself in with the connect was all Byron's fault.

At that point – like a camera flash unexpectedly going off in his eyes and distracting him – he randomly seemed to recognize that something was off about the sex he was currently having.

"Why da fuck you just layin' there like a corpse, all quiet and shit?" he demanded unexpectedly, looking at the girl as he continued fucking her. "My dick ain't big enough for you? I ain't hittin' the spot right? Is that it?"

"Oh no, baby," the girl blurted out. "It's just that, uh, you kinda stunned me with the way you hittin' it – left me speechless."

"Well act like you enjoyin' this shit," Zerk commanded.

"Hell yeah, I'm enjoyin' it!" the girl assured him as she began moving her hips again. "Yo dick is da bomb! You hittin' the spot now! Just keep on–"

"Not so fuckin' loud," Zerk groused. "I'm still tryin' to thank."

"Just keep doin whachu doin," the girl urged in a normal tone. "Just keep on fuckin'–"

"Still too damn loud," Zerk told her.

"Just keep fuckin' me," she said in something akin to a whisper. "Keep swangin' that dick like you doin'…"

She kept talking but Zerk tuned her out, his mind going back to how Lord Byron was the cause of his problems. That being the case, Zerk had felt justified in trying to get Shade to take Byron out, and also in snatching up a nigga in Byron's crew called Moonie. The latter had resulted in him getting two vital pieces of intel. The first was about about a buy, and Zerk had tried to use the info to rip Byron off. That shit had gone sideways and cost him some people.

The other info Zerk had gotten out of Moonie related to the missing coke. The nigga's mouth was fucked up by then, so his comment about Zerk's stolen product came out as, "Tink…Thate…gah ih…"

Zerk translated that as "Think Tate got it," mostly because he knew of a nigga on Byron's payroll named Tate. Therefore, he'd had a couple of muhfuckas following Tate since then, hoping to snatch his ass or that he'd lead them to the cocaine. But after what happened to Moonie, nobody on Byron's team was leaving themselves vulnerable enough to be grabbed.

In addition, Zerk also sent Beemer and a couple of niggas to talk to Shade, to tell him the timetable had been moved up on dealing with Lord Byron. That's when they called to say they'd just pulled up to Shade's house and saw him getting out of Byron's car in a way that was all-too-chummy.

At that point, shit suddenly became clear – in particular, what Moonie had been trying to say: "Think *Shade* got it."

Zerk had immediately told the niggas watching Shade to go get his shit. But those incompetent dickheads had somehow fucked it up – in fact, two of 'em got *themselves* fucked up and were out of commission for the night, if not longer.

Zerk had then sent Beemer to grab Shade's girl, hoping that would give him something to bargain with. Once again, the niggas on his team turned out to be incompetent. Both Beemer and a nigga he'd taken with him, Shep, had wound up with toe tags.

With so many of his crew either down or out, Zerk was going to have to hire niggas off the street. His funds were low, so he didn't know what the fuck he'd pay them with, but that was a problem for down the road. Or, if he could get his product back, it wouldn't be a problem at all.

Of course, the mere thought of the stolen coke was enough to get Zerk pissed. Right now, if he could get his hands on that nigga Shade, he'd love to use a pair of meat hooks to spread that muhfucka's butt-cheeks apart, and then shove a rabid squirrel up his asshole. But Shade and everybody connected to him – his sistas, his girl, his junkie momma – had all disappeared. None of them were around for Zerk to vent his anger on, and when he got worked up (like he was getting right then) he *definitely* needed to vent. The only person within reach was the bitch he was fucking.

Zerk looked down at her. She had her eyes closed, but was still speaking softly about how great his dick felt, how hard he was fucking her, blah, blah, blah…

Mentally, Zerk flipped a coin. A moment later, he slowly let a hand glide up her body, going past her stomach, taking a second to fondle her tits, then continuing on up to her neck. At that point, he put his hand around her throat…and then squeezed.

The girl's eyes popped open.

"Baby," she croaked. "Baby, I can't…"

She didn't say anything after that, having apparently exhausted her air supply. She then began trying to pull his hand away as Zerk squeezed harder. At the same time, he continued to fuck her – only now, he was starting to get into that shit. Suddenly, her pussy seemed tight as a muhfucka around his dick, and every stroke felt fucking amazing. Obviously, he should have started choking this bitch the minute he slipped his dick inside her.

In desperation, the girl began punching and clawing at him, trying to make him let go. Zerk pretty much ignored her antics; this wasn't the first time a bitch tried to get away while he was choking her ass.

Prolly won't be the last, he thought.

Suddenly, there was a knock at the door. Zerk heard someone talking – Spinner – but couldn't understand what he was saying.

"I can't hear you, nigga!" Zerk called out. "Just come on in."

Spinner opened the door, and then just stared at the scene for a second: Zerk fucking the girl Spinner had brought in earlier, while choking her out at the same time. And the girl, fighting for her life…

"What, nigga?" Zerk demanded, still thrusting and strangling simultaneously.

"Uh," Spinner droned, coming back to himself. "We, uh, we got a call."

"So handle it. Da fuck you botherin' *me* for?"

Trying not to look at the girl, Spinner said, "It's about the, um, *stuff*."

Suddenly, Zerk's head jerked in Spinner's direction, and he noticed for the first time that his lieutenant was holding a cell phone. Zerk abruptly pulled out of the hoodrat and released his grip on her neck; she immediately began coughing and gasping for air, while bringing a hand up gingerly to her throat.

"Get the fuck outta here," Zerk commanded almost angrily.

Although plainly still in distress, the girl didn't have to be told twice. Still coughing and with tears streaming down her face, she rolled out of bed, spent a few seconds grabbing her shit, and practically left a dust trail dashing from the room.

Spinner watched her retreating form for a minute then closed the door. Zerk, still naked, was now sitting on the edge of the bed.

Ignoring the nudity, Spinner said, "It's Shade's girl – Yoni's her name – callin' on Beemer's phone. She on mute, but she wants to make a deal."

"What kinda deal?" Zerk inquired, his curiosity evident.

"Haven't asked her yet. Didn't know if you wanted to talk to her personally."

"Naw, fuck that. You know I don't like talkin' on the phone to people I don't know."

Spinner simply nodded, as that was one thing Zerk was definitely paranoid about. Actually it was one of *numerous* things Zerk was paranoid about – like his belief that cell phones caused cancer. In fact, that was part of the reason why he often had Spinner hold his phone (as he was doing at the moment). About the only time Zerk carried his own phone was when Spinner wasn't around. But seeing as how his lieutenant was currently present, dealing with phone calls was a task Zerk was clearly delegating.

"Fine," Spinner said. "*I'll* talk to her."

He then tapped the cell phone and said, "A'ight, we listenin'…"

THUG LIFE: EMANCIPATED

Chapter 83

The girl Yoni had said she and Shade were holed up in a factory. She also gave pretty good directions, so it wasn't hard to find. In fact, Zerk had rounded up his crew and gotten over there in record time, driven by the thought of getting his coke back. However, once he got near the place, he started having second thoughts.

For one thing, the factory was in a secluded fucking location – nothing around for miles. That made it damn near perfect for setting somebody up. On top of that, there was a dark, unlit road leading up the place, and the entire facility was completely dark.

Correction: it was completely dark except for one building, but that was expected. Basically, when Spinner had asked Yoni during the call how to find them once they arrived, her reply had been, "Easy – it's the only fuckin' buildin' with lights on."

Still, bearing all the facts in mind, Zerk wasn't keen on walking into a trap. That being the case, he sent some of his boys up the road to the factory first. They made it there without incident – no ambush on the road or when they reached the main area of the factory. Sensing it was safe, Zerk followed, riding in the back seat of an SUV.

The building with lights on turned out to be some kind of warehouse – at least that's what it looked like from the outside. Zerk instructed the nigga driving him to park about a hundred feet away, then spent a minute thinking.

Once again, he didn't like the notion of walking into a trap. That said, everything had been cool thus far – it had all lined up just like that chick Yoni had told Spinner on the phone. Speaking of Spinner, Zerk was thinking that he could use that nigga now, but Spinner was off on a related errand.

Finally making up his mind, Zerk got out the SUV. His exit was the signal for everyone else to get out as well. He then spent a minute looking around at the folks with him. There had been two in the front seat of the SUV he'd been in, and another three in the other car. That made six of them altogether, but only two of the others were members of his regular crew; the others were some niggas Spinner had rounded up at the last minute.

Based on how quickly the new people had been recruited, Zerk suspected that Spinner had already been putting feelers out, maybe even signing niggas up behind his back. They did need soldiers to replace the people they'd lost – something Zerk had actually been thinking about earlier – but he didn't like the idea of Spinner making those decisions without him. In fact, just thinking about it was starting to piss him off, but it was clearly shit he'd have to handle later. For now, though, he needed someone to be a possible sacrificial lamb.

Looking around at those with him, he decided on a nigga called Downtown. He wasn't a regular member of Zerk's crew, but occasionally did some side work for them. He was a pretty-boy muhfucka that all the girls liked. For that reason alone, Zerk couldn't stand his ass.

"Downtown," Zerk said. "See if you can find a way into the back of this muhfucka, make sure it ain't a setup."

Downtown didn't look particularly pleased about the assignment, but knew better than to object. Therefore, he simply nodded and took off towards the back of the warehouse.

Zerk then settled in to wait, which wasn't his strong suit; he was not a very patient man. Thus, it seemed like an hour later (but was probably no more than a few minutes), before he finally thought he detected some type of action in the warehouse.

It came in the form of raised voices, but there was no way to discern what was being said. Unsure of what was about to happen, Zerk pulled out his gun and began creeping swiftly, but furtively, to the front of the warehouse; the others with him followed suit. However, when they were still about twenty feet away, the door of the warehouse opened and Downtown stepped out.

He spent a moment blinking, plainly trying to get his eyes to adjust to the dark.

"Zerk?" he called out.

"We here," Zerk answered, continuing to move forward until Downtown could clearly see him and the others. "Everything cool?"

"Yeah," Downtown answered. "But, uh, there's some muhfucka tied up in there and a girl."

"Nigga, I already know all that," Zerk grumbled.

"Yeah well, the girl gotta gun," Downtown explained. "And she say she ain't givin' it up."

Zerk just stared at him for a moment, and then burst out laughing.

This was basically a muhfuckin' drug deal. Niggas on all sides were always armed when it came to shit like this. It was fuckin' expected, and nobody would just hand their piece over because some sumbitch on the other side of the table asked for it.

"Come on," Zerk said, walking inside. The rest of his crew fell in step behind him.

The interior of the warehouse was well-lit. Zerk noticed some shelving and equipment around them, but the area of immediate focus for him was an open space near the center of the place. There he saw a couple of beat-up desks and a gorgeous redbone holding a gun in one hand and a black bag in the other. A few feet from her, tied to a chair, was that muhfucka Shade.

414

He had his head down, resting on his chest like he was exhausted. One of his cheeks was bruised, and the front of his shirt was covered with blood, like maybe he'd been cut or stabbed. Whatever had happened to him, the nigga deserved worse.

"'Bout fuckin' time," uttered the redbone – Yoni – as Zerk began walking towards them. "Let's do this."

With that, she stepped forward and tossed the bag she'd been carrying onto a nearby desk. Zerk glanced at it for a moment, then walked over and unzipped it before looking inside. Satisfied, he nodded towards the nigga who had chauffeured him there – a dude called Dunk – who stepped towards the bag while simultaneously pulling a small vial of liquid from a pocket of the jacket he wore.

Zerk gave Shade a once-over. "Hey, man. How you doin'?"

Shade looked up at him, then stated in a tired voice, "Never better."

Zerk laughed. Turning to Yoni, he said. "Ya boyfriend don't like so hot. Whachu been doin' to 'im?"

"Just getting' a lil' payback," Yoni replied. "I wudda done a lot fuckin' more, but you muhfuckas said you needed 'im alive."

"That's cause on the phone, you said you hadn't tested the coke. That basically mean you don't know what the fuck you holdin'. We need to make sure we got the right product and the right quantity, and if anythang's wrong or missin', we needed to be able to quiz his ass 'bout it. Or you."

"So, is all that shit right?" Yoni asked, ignoring the implied threat.

In response, Zerk looked back at Dunk, who held up the vial of liquid, which was now blue.

"We good," declared Dunk, who had apparently been testing the drugs in the bag.

Zerk smiled. "And all's good with the world," he declared to no one in particular. He then turned to Shade. "So tell me, what exactly happened in that buildin'? You saw my brutha and Chris makin' the buy for that coke and just decided to rip 'em off?"

"I ain't see nuthin'," Shade replied, "except yo brutha gettin' railed by his boyfriend, and lovin' it!"

Zerk let out a little chuckle. "You thank that bothers me? You thank I ain't know that my brutha was a homo – that he loved dick? I knew exactly what he was. I ain't give a shit, long as he did what I needed him to do. Hell, he could take it up the ass all day long and I wouldn't care. Matter of fact, I'm not even bothered that much by the fact that he died."

Noting a look of surprise on Shade's face, Zerk went on. "What – you thought I was gonna want revenge or some shit? Naw, see, I'm not like ya girl here" – he gestured towards Yoni – "tryin' to get payback and all that crap. That's just the biz we in – niggas get killed in this shit. You walk into a meet or a buy, ain't no fuckin' guarantee you gone walk out. Anythang can fuckin' happen, like…"

Without warning, Zerk raised his gun, pointed it at Downtown, and fired. The slug took him in the stomach and sent him staggering back a few steps.

"Da fuck, Zerk?!" Downtown howled, doubling over as his shirt started turning red with blood.

Ignoring him, Zerk turned to Shade with a crazier-than-usual expression on his face. He then began raising his gun, aiming in Shade's direction.

"Hold on!" Yoni shouted. "B'foe this shit get too crazy, let's talk about my money."

"Money?" Zerk echoed as he put the gun away.

"Yeah, my fuckin' money," Yoni stressed. "The deal we made was for you to getcha coke, and I get Shade's ass to do what I want with, plus a ten thou finder's fee for locatin' yo shit."

"I remember," Zerk informed her. "I was there when Spinner negotiated that shit wichu. But here's the thang: I ain't brang the money."

Yoni gave him a piercing stare. "Why da fuck not?"

"Because it turns out that brutha you all anxious to avenge – Sneak? Well, he was into us for a lotta cash. See, he asked us to stake him in the game, and we did. But that nigga wasn't built for this shit. I don't know if he couldn't do math or what, but he wound up way in the fuckin' hole."

Yoni shrugged. "So what that got to do with me and *my* money?"

"Well, you his sista, so his debt pass to you."

A look of incredulity settled on Yoni's face. "You must be fuckin' jokin'."

"Nope," Zerk assured her, shaking his head. "Ask ya boy Shade. He know all about how we operate in that arena."

"Fuck you," Shade said, causing Zerk to chuckle.

"We gone come back to you in a minute," Zerk told him before once again turning his attention to Yoni. "As I was sayin', Sneak's debt on you now. But bearin' in mind that we promised you a finder's fee, I'm willin' to call this shit even. Or, if you up for some mo' tradin', I'll give you the ten grand if you give Shade to me."

"Fuck that," Yoni stated. "His ass is mine. I owe it to my brutha."

"A'ight," Zerk said, "but that mean we square – no ten thou."

"Whatever," Yoni muttered. Then, distracted by a painful groaning, she looked towards Downtown, who had dropped to the ground. "Looks like yo bullet-test dummy might need a doctor."

"He'll be a'ight," Zerk noted casually. "But I need to talk to Shade for a minute."

"Kiss my ass," Shade muttered.

"Oh, I got some other thangs in mind for yo *ass*," Zerk told him, "but right now I just wanna have a friendly conversation."

Shade eyed him suspiciously. "About what?"

"Money – what else?" Zerk replied. "See, you stealin' my product really fucked thangs up for me, cash-wise. I might be able to get back on track now, but it don't change the fact that you caused me a lotta fuckin' grief."

"Let me guess," Shade said. "You wanna be compensated for the inconvenience."

"Bingo," Zerk declared, pointing a finger at Shade. "Now, I don't wanna get into a back-and-forth about all the shit you do or don't do for money. Let's just say that, based on the number of muhfuckas that done had 'accidents' in the hood, that you should have a sizeable bankroll by now. I want it."

Shade frowned. "Want what?"

"Yo bankroll. All of it," Zerk replied. "The way I figure it, you damn near cost me everythang I *have*, so I want everythang you *got*."

"And I done told you b'foe, I don't do this shit you thank I do," Shade retorted. "So I ain't got no bankroll to give you, muhfucka."

"See, I knew you was gone say some shit like that," Zerk noted. "That's why I got a lil' sommin' to incentivize yo ass."

"Like what – a lollipop?" Shade chided as Zerk pulled out his cell phone.

"Yeah," Zerk answered with a smirk. "It's Nissa-and-Cherry flavored.

Shade's mouth fell open and he blinked. "Wh-what?"

Rather than answer, Zerk put his phone on speaker as it started to ring. It was answered immediately.

"Hey, man," said a voice Shade recognized as Spinner. "Whachu need?"

"Just callin' to check in," Zerk responded. "You still got 'em?"

"Oh, yeah," Spinner attested. "Listen…"

There were sounds of something like scuffling, then a feminine voice screamed, "Get yo fuckin' hands off me!"

"NO!" Shade wailed. "No! No! No!"

"Yes, yes, yes, nigga," Zerk teased, smiling. "See, when yo redbone girlfriend called to make a deal, I was worried that you and her was settin' me up, so I asked for some insurance – sommin' to make sure I walked in and outta here of my own free will. She offered up yo sistas. Never hesitated."

"You bitch!" Shade bellowed, staring at Yoni with utter hate. "You fuckin' bitch! I'm gone kill you!"

Shade continued shouting obscenities at Yoni, and at the same time began rocking from side to side in the chair he was tied to, plainly trying to get free.

"Calm the fuck down," Zerk ordered. At the same time, he pointed his gun at Shade, who ceased yelling and became still. However, before anything else happened, the lights began to flicker.

"Da fuck's goin' on?" Zerk muttered, suddenly suspicious.

"It's the generator," Yoni replied, noting that – aside from Downtown (who was now whimpering) – all of Zerk's people had pulled out their weapons.

"Generator?" Zerk repeated.

"This buildin' is powered by a propane generator," Yoni explained. "But it's old as fuck and low on fuel."

"So what that mean?" Zerk asked.

"That the lights gone go out soon," Yoni said. "Then this place gone be dark as the rest of the factory."

"Then we need to step this up," Zerk decided. Turning again to Shade, who was still in his gun's line of fire, he said, "Now after that call, I'm sure you unnastand: I hold all the cards, and I'ma get my money one way or another. So you can tell me where yo stash is, and I let yo sistas go. Or you don't tell me, and I make them bitches work off what you owe."

Shade appeared to ruminate for a moment. "Even if there was a stash, how you know there's even enough in it to cover what you thank is owed?"

"'Cause you a smart nigga," Zerk commented. "You the type don't put all yo eggs in one basket, and always save for a rainy day. Well guess what, muhfucka? I *am* the rainy day. So you can tell me what I wanna know, or–"

Zerk abruptly stopped speaking as the lights began flickering again…and then unexpectedly went out.

It was suddenly pitch black in the warehouse. Almost immediately, there was the sound of scuffling, followed by shouting and something being knocked over. There was also the distinct patter of feet running as people seemed to dash around haphazardly, followed by a couple of muffled thuds as one or two people seemingly tripped and fell.

Presumably as a result of falling, someone's gun also went off. This precipitated a round of random gunfire that persisted for a few seconds before Zerk's shouting made everyone stop. Moments later, the lights flickered again before coming back on. All in all, they had been out maybe forty-five seconds.

Glancing around, Zerk noticed that everybody was on the floor, including Yoni, who had taken refuge between two desks. A moment later he revised his initial assessment: *almost* everyone was on the floor.

Shade was gone.

"Fuck!" Yoni exclaimed, coming to her feet. "He got away."

Zerk looked at Yoni. "You didn't tie him up good?"

"I thought I did," Yoni replied, "but I ain't no fuckin' boy scout.

Zerk gave her a disparaging look, then suddenly felt a moment of panic. The desk that the bag of blow had been on was knocked over. More to the point, he didn't immediately see his product.

"The coke!" he screamed, looking around anxiously. "Where da fuck is it?"

"Over there," Yoni said, pointing under some nearby machinery. "Looks like it fell when the desk got knocked over, and one of these brave-ass he-men you brought with you must have kicked it when they were scurryin' around in the dark."

Zerk scrambled over to the machinery in question, bent down, and retrieved the bag. Unzipping it, he glanced inside and seemed to breathe a sigh of relief.

"If you good," Yoni said, "we need to hurry so we can catch him. He can't have got too far."

"Who, Shade?" Zerk asked.

"Who the fuck else?" Yoni shot back irritably. "I don't thank he headed out the front, so I'm guessin' he went out the back" – she gestured towards a door at the rear of the warehouse – "the same way yo boy tried to sneak in."

As she finished speaking, Yoni glanced towards Downtown. He was still whimpering, and now lying in a growing pool of his own blood.

"So what you expect us to do?" inquired Zerk, drawing her attention. "Go wanderin' 'round a huge-ass factory that's mostly pitch-black? This the one buildin' with power, and accordin' to you, the lights 'bout to go off in *here*."

"That's why we need to hurry and go after his ass," Yoni explained.

"Uh-uh," Zerk declared, shaking his head. "You can go chasin' 'im if you want to, I ain't gotta go after that nigga. I got his sistas. He gone come to *me*." With that, he announced generally to his crew. "Come on. Let's get the fuck outta here."

Having nothing more to say, Zerk and his boys began heading to the exit, with two of them helping Downtown get to his feet and walk out. A few seconds later, Yoni found herself alone in the warehouse.

THUG LIFE: EMANCIPATED

Chapter 84

Drugs in hand, Zerk headed to the SUV with an extra pep in his step. Once he reached it, he quickly got into the back seat, placing the black bag almost lovingly beside him.

"Let's go," he urged as Dunk got behind the wheel and another muhfucka slid into the front passenger seat. Glancing out, he saw Downtown being put into the back seat of the other car by the two niggas helping him. Zerk reflected for a moment, then rolled down his window and shouted, "Get that nigga to a doctor after we leave."

The two helping Downtown both nodded in acknowledgement, and Zerk mentally gave himself a pat on the back.

You a good boss, he thought. *Providin' medical benefits and everythang.*

He then chuckled mentally as Dunk started driving. Taking a moment to glance out the rear window, he noticed the headlights of the other car behind them. It occurred to him then that maybe he should have let them go first so they could get Downtown some help as soon as possible.

Nah, Zerk said to himself. *I wasn't aimin' for nuthin' vital. He'll be a'ight. Most likely…*

Now that they were in motion, he felt a certain amount of relief wash over him. Up until that moment, it hadn't seemed quite real – hadn't felt like he had actually gotten his shit back. But reality was setting in now, and in his head he began making plans, seeing how shit was going to unfold. Now that he had some product he could start making money again, begin once more moving up the ladder, get straight with the connect, and so on. He still had Lord Byron to contend with, but he'd deal with that in due time.

Zerk smiled, thinking how amazing it was that shit had suddenly come together for him, and how fast it had happened. Upon reflection, he realized that he probably would have been completely fucked if that chick Yoni hadn't called. And now that she came to mind, it suddenly occurred to him that maybe they shouldn't have left her stranded back at that warehouse. From what he could tell, they were only about halfway down the road that led to the factory; they could always go back and scoop her up. She might even be grateful enough to...

Zerk frowned and let the thought trail off as something new suddenly occurred to him.

Where the fuck was her car? he thought, realizing that he hadn't seen another vehicle up at the factory.

However, he didn't have time to dwell on it as Dunk unexpectedly slammed on the brakes, and the entire road suddenly lit up.

"What da fuck?!" Zerk yelled as he pitched forward, straining against his seatbelt. "Dunk, you—"

He abruptly stopped speaking as he realized why Dunk had come to a screeching halt. Parked across the road and blocking their way were a couple of police cruisers. On the far side of the cruisers were at least four uniformed officers, all of whom had their weapons out and pointed at Zerk's SUV. The police sirens weren't on, but as he watched their blue-and-red lights started flashing.

In fact, he suddenly saw lights flashing from both his left and right – a clear indication that additional police cars were parked off-road on either side of him. Turning to look behind him, he saw what he expected: blue-and-red flashing from vehicles behind the car that Downtown was in.

As if he needed to be told, someone with a bullhorn suddenly said, "This is the police. You're surrounded..."

THUG LIFE: EMANCIPATED

Chapter 85

Zerk sat at a table in a police interrogation room, with his lawyer Hugo Goldstein next to him. It had been about ninety minutes since the cops had arrested him. Of course, he had immediately asked to call his lawyer and, surprisingly, they had let him. They didn't have to do that before they completed the booking process, but this time they had. And, although it was pretty late (or pretty early, depending on your point of view) Goldstein had rolled out of bed, gotten dressed, and rushed to the station.

The two of them had been in the interrogation room since Goldstein's arrival, conferencing for about the last thirty minutes. Zerk understood that cops weren't allowed to listen to conversations between lawyer and client, but it still made him nervous to discuss shit openly in the middle of a police station.

That said, Zerk felt somewhat secure at the moment. Goldstein was one of the best criminal defense attorneys in the city. He was also one of the most expensive, but he was worth it. He had gotten some serious fucking charges against Zerk dropped more than once, and hopefully would manage it again now. Zerk had no doubt that it would ultimately cost him an arm and a leg, but at the moment he didn't care.

A knock on the door interrupted Zerk's thoughts. A moment later, the door opened and a cop came in – some muhfucka in plainclothes.

Goldstein nodded at the cop, greeting him, with a flat, "Gummy."

"Goldstein," said the cop in return.

At that point, Zerk sat up straight, because he noticed two things: the cop was wearing latex gloves, and he was carrying the black bag containing Zerk's blow.

"You mind if we record this?" the cop asked, pointing up to a corner of the ceiling where a camera was located.

"Oh, I insist," replied Goldstein, smiling.

Zerk didn't notice the cop do anything, but suddenly a green LED light came to life on the camera.

The cop took a seat on the opposite side of the table from Zerk and Goldstein, putting the black bag on the seat of an empty chair next to him.

Turning to Zerk, he said, "I'm Detective Gummerson. I was one of the officers present when you were arrested a little while ago. Don't know if you recall, but I'm also the lead investigator on your brother's case. We spoke once before."

"I remember," Zerk said. Truthfully, however, he only vaguely remembered Gummerson. In essence, he didn't like cops and was reluctant to help them in any way – even one purportedly investigating his brother's death.

"Don't say anything," Goldstein ordered. Turning to Gummy, he then asked. "So what exactly are the charges against my client?"

Gummy seemed to consider for a moment. "Honestly, it's hard to know where to begin."

"Well, I understand there are some charges regarding property," Goldstein said. "Why don't we start there?"

"Okay," Gummy agreed. "Let's see… There's trespassing, breaking and entering, destruction of property–"

"So the owner filed a complaint?" Goldstein interjected.

Gummy frowned. "Excuse me?"

"That factory where you arrested my client is private property," Goldstein explained. "And, as I'm sure you already know, when it comes to private property, the owner has to make a complaint. So if you see a guy carrying a TV out of a house, you can't just assume he's a thief. The owner might be loaning it to him, he might be helping the owner move, or he

426

might have just bought it. It's only when the owner complains about it that it becomes a crime. So I'm asking you if the owner made a complaint."

Gummy drummed his fingers on the table for a moment. "I don't know if we have the formal paperwork for that yet."

"Well, let me save you the trouble," Goldstein told him. "The factory where you arrested my client is part of a conglomerate that went bankrupt ages ago. The creditors have been fighting over the company's assets for a good fifteen years, and will probably be fighting for a hundred more. That being the case, nobody knows who that factory belongs to, and by the time the bankruptcy court makes a decision on ownership, my client will be a grandfather. So good luck getting the owner to file a complaint, and without that all your property crimes are out the window."

Gummy just stared at him for a moment, then noted, "There's still nuisance."

Goldstein raised an eyebrow in curiosity. "Excuse me?"

"Nuisance," Gummy said. "A passing cop heard shots coming from the factory. Even if you're not shooting at anyone or anything, gunfire can be a nuisance and nuisance is still a crime. Your client was being a nuisance."

"Nuisance to who?" Goldstein demanded. "The essence of 'nuisance' as a crime is that you're disturbing somebody. You've got a loud party going at three in the morning on a weekday, or you got a dog that barks at all hours of the night, or you're playing ding dong ditch… It generally has to be something like that – an activity causing a disturbance – to be a nuisance. That factory is miles from the nearest home. No way was anybody bothered by anything my client allegedly did there. Moreover, did anyone actually *see* my client firing guns there?"

Gummy's jaw clenched for a second, then he simply said, "No."

"So it sounds like we're done with nuisance," Goldstein concluded. "What else you got?"

"I got *this*," Gummy told him, placing the black bag on the table. "A bag full of powder wrapped in plastic. Now, I'm sure you know the typical list of drug offenses, starting with possession, possession with intent to distribute–"

"I don't need the legal lesson," Goldstein interrupted to tell him. "But my understanding is that the bag was found stuffed under the front seat of the car my client was in – a car that he doesn't own, by the way. In fact, he was in the back seat and clearly a passenger. But the main thing is that whatever's in that bag can't be used to convict my client of a crime."

"How do you figure?" asked Gummy skeptically.

"We've already established that my client was on private property and that you had no cause to pull him over, let alone search the vehicle or arrest him – unless you had a warrant."

Goldstein looked at Gummy expectantly. After a few seconds, Gummy sighed and admitted, "No, we didn't have a warrant."

"Well, no warrant means any evidence obtained during that search or arrest is tainted. It's the fruit of a poisonous tree."

"Huh?" muttered Zerk. "Whachu say 'bout poison?"

Goldstein turned to his client. "The law looks at an arrest like a tree, and all of the evidence obtained when you're arrested is viewed as the fruit of that tree. It all stems from the arrest. But if the arrest itself is wrongful – if the police have no cause or right to take you into custody – then that tree is considered tainted and poisonous. In addition, any evidence from that arrest, like a bag found stuffed under a seat, is tainted as well and can't be used against you. It's the fruit of a poisonous tree."

Turning back to Gummy, Goldstein continued. "So it doesn't matter what's in that bag. It could be eight human heads and it still wouldn't matter. Because it's the fruit of a poisonous tree, you can't use it against my client."

Gummy was silent for a few seconds, then commented, "There were guns, too."

"Sure," Goldstein noted with a nod. "But it's the same story as the bag: some weapons were found under the seat of a vehicle in which my client has no ownership interest and that he was riding in merely as a passenger. On top of that, it's more evidence that resulted from an illicit search and illegal arrest – the fruit of a poisonous tree."

"Except we have a guy who was shot," Gummy retorted.

"Oh? Did he say my client shot him?" asked Goldstein.

Gummy stared at him in frustration but didn't answer.

"That's what I thought," Goldstein remarked. "Anyway, it doesn't sound like you have a case in this instance. So, unless you've got something else, my client and I are leaving."

With that, Goldstein stood up, smiling smugly. Zerk came to his feet as well, and they began walking towards the door.

As they came around the table, Gummy looked at Zerk and asked, "You want your bag?"

Rather than respond directly, Zerk looked at Goldstein.

"Might as well," Goldstein said. "They can't use anything in it against you."

Having been given the okay, Zerk reached for the bag and unzipped it. After peeking inside, he zipped it back up with a smile.

"Thanks for carrying this for me," he told Gummy as he lifted the bag from the table. "You'd make a great fuckin' bellhop."

He then resumed walking towards the door with his lawyer, but had only taken a step or two before the detective's voice brought him up short.

"Oh, wait," Gummy intoned. "There is one more thing."

Goldstein eyed him warily for a moment and then asked, "What's that?"

"I completely forgot to mention it," Gummy replied, "but that factory's been condemned."

"Good thang, too," said Zerk. "Fuckin' place looked dangerous."

"No," Gummy said, shaking his head. "Not *that* kind of condemned. There's a different type of condemnation – I'm sure your lawyer can tell you about it."

Zerk looked at Goldstein, who was frowning now, but said, "He's talking about *legal* condemnation. It refers to the government's ability to take private property – usually for a public use like a highway, school, or things along those lines."

"Exactly," Gummy concurred. "And it looks like that factory got condemned about a year or two back. That means it's government property now – not privately owned – and every building on the premises is a government facility. Also, as a representative of said government, I can lawfully arrest your client for trespassing, among other things."

Goldstein looked stunned. "But, uh, if it's government property, it has to, uh, be clearly identified as such."

"There are signs posted all around that factory stating that it's government property. Of course, somebody ripped one off the front door of the building we think your client was in, but there are still enough around to constitute adequate notice."

"But even if he was allegedly on the premises, you still don't have a witness putting my client inside any government building or facility."

"I think the evidence will do that," Gummy told him. "For instance, I got a nice pool of blood in a warehouse there, and a guy who's been shot. What do you think the odds are that those two will match up?"

"Assuming it does, a gunshot victim inside a government facility doesn't come anywhere near proving my client was in there," Goldstein argued.

"I don't have to prove he was actually in there," Gummy said. "Conspiracy law says that he's guilty of anything his co-conspirators do as part of the conspiracy."

"Conspiracy?" Goldstein muttered, like he'd never heard the word before.

"Yeah," Gummy intoned. "So if he's part of a group that decided to unlawfully enter government property, then he's part of a conspiracy and can be charged with anything the others in the group do. So if one of them goes into a government facility and shoots the place up or caps somebody – which seems to be the case here – they're all guilty of those crimes. And believe me, the preliminary evidence is showing a lot of shit we can charge them with: trespassing on federal facilities, destroying federal property, possessing a firearm in a federal facility… The list is damn near endless."

Goldstein just stood silently, his brow wrinkled as he weighed everything he was hearing.

"Also," Gummy continued, "a valid arrest uproots your fruit-of-a-poisonous-tree argument. So the guns are valid evidence, along with the bag that your client just claimed ownership of *on camera*. Speaking of which…"

As he trailed off, Gummy gestured towards the bag Zerk was holding, and then asked, "May I?"

Zerk looked at Goldstein – who nodded – then handed the bag to Gummy.

"See, I'm still investigating your brother's death," Gummy told Zerk. "It was actually part of a triple-homicide – three bodies in a condemned building." He glanced at Zerk and added, "It's the kind of condemned you were thinking about before."

Zerk felt the detective was taking a subtle jab at him, but kept his mouth shut.

"Anyway," the detective went on, "one of the victims – your brother, in fact – had particulates under his nails, some of which turned out to be leather. And if you take a look *here*" – he pointed to the side of the bag where some of the leather had been lightly scored – "you'll see some faint scratch marks. Now, we'll have to wait for Forensics to do their thing, but I'm betting it's going to match up."

"What are you trying to say?" Goldstein demanded. "That my client killed his own brother?"

"That's a damn lie!" Zerk shouted angrily. "I ain't killed my brutha!"

"Quiet," Goldstein uttered in irritation. Turning his attention back to Gummy, he went on. "If that's your theory – that my client killed his sibling - what's the motive?"

"Maybe it's because his brother was gay," Gummy offered. "He's a hardcore thug, and having a fairy for a brother hurts his reputation."

Goldstein shook his head in derision. "If you think you can sell that to a jury, knock yourself out. I seriously doubt they'll find sexual preference to be motive for murder."

"I've seen siblings kill each other for less," Gummy retorted. "I had a case last year where some fool stabbed his brother in the head for cheating at cards. So yeah, I think I can sell it."

"Not with the evidence you've got," Goldstein argued. "Some bits of leather that may match up? It's pretty lightweight."

"Well, here's something that falls in the heavyweight category," Gummy retorted. He then pointed to an area of discoloration on the bag. "See this blotch here? Preliminary analysis indicates that it's blood. My money says that when we get the full report back, it's going to belong to one of my triple-homicide victims – most likely his brother."

"So what if it does?" Goldstein mused. "My client's brother could have cut himself at home months ago and bled on that bag."

"As a matter of fact, that's what happened," Zerk chimed in. "He cut hisself at the house – bled all over the place and–"

"Shut up!" Goldstein roared at his client. "Don't speak unless I tell you to."

"It's a little late for that," Gummy announced. Turning to Zerk, he asked. "So when did this bleeding episode happen?"

Zerk looked at his lawyer, but kept his mouth shut.

"So you're going to take your attorney's advice and stay silent?" Gummy asked, to which he received no reply. "That's fine, we got it on camera that your brother bled a lot at home. That's enough to get us a warrant to go analyze the scene and see if it's true. Of course, if we don't find anything, we'll know you're lying."

Zerk suddenly looked as though he wanted to speak, but one look from his attorney changed his mind.

"Also," Gummy continued, "if you're thinking of saying something later about having cleaned up the blood and that's why we may not find anything, let me warn you: blood stays around a long damn time."

Gummy paused for a moment to let that sink in, then went on.

"Ever hear of Lizzie Borden?" he asked Zerk, but only got a confused look in response. "She was this chick who lived in the eighteen hundreds – got accused of a couple of vicious murders. Basically, they said she hacked up her father and stepmother with an axe. It was pretty brutal, but get this: the house where the murders took place is still standing. It's a fucking bed-and-breakfast now, can you believe that shit? But it's true."

"Anyway," Gummy continued, "a couple of years ago, some scientists went in there to do some forensic work. Do you know that, more than a hundred years later, they were still able to detect the blood from the murders? That's how good the science is on that shit now. So believe me when I say that if you're lying about your brother bleeding all over the place, we're going to find out."

"Okay, that's enough of you trying to intimidate my client," Goldstein said. "Get your warrant – if you can – and test for what you want, but I still say your murder case has a lot of holes in it."

"Maybe, but here's one that's pretty airtight."

As he spoke, he unzipped the bag and reached into it. He seemed to fiddle around for a moment, then pulled out a small pouch made of dark purple cloth with drawstrings at the top.

"This was kind of buried at the bottom of the bag," Gummy noted as he loosened the drawstrings and then poured the contents of the pouch into his gloved hand. Both Goldstein and Zerk leaned in close to get a good look.

"What are those?" Goldstein finally asked after a few seconds.

"Teeth," Gummy told him. "And we believe they're going to match a toothless body the Harbor Patrol recently pulled from the river."

"She set me up," Zerk hissed softly. "That bitch set me up."

"What was that?" Gummy asked him as he put the teeth back into the purple pouch.

"Nothing," Goldstein answered on behalf of his client. "He didn't say anything at all."

"Anyway," Gummy droned, putting the purple pouch back into the bag, "we've got a laundry list of stuff we can charge your client with – practically everything except drug charges."

"So wait," Goldstein uttered, frowning. "You're not planning to charge him for the drugs?"

"What drugs?" inquired Gummy.

"The drugs you claimed were in the bag," Goldstein replied, gesturing towards the black bag.

"I never said there were drugs," Gummy corrected. "I said there was *powder* in it wrapped in plastic, and that's what it seems to be. We'll have to wait for the full analysis, but the lab thinks it's baby powder. But it's definitely not coke or any other narcotic. They tested for those and it all came back negative."

"Aahh!" Zerk screeched like he was in pain, ignoring his lawyer's admonition to be quiet. "That fuckin' bitch! She set me up *and* played me!"

Chapter 86

Two days after Zerk Simon's arrest, Shade showed up at Lord Byron's mansion shortly before noon with a newspaper tucked under one arm. He was let in by some nigga wearing a shoulder holster and then shown to the breakfast area, where Byron was sitting at a table eating a sandwich and chips. With him was someone Shade recognized: Zerk's former right-hand man, Spinner.

"Shade, my nigga," Byron greeted him between bites. "Sit the fuck down."

Shade took a seat, at which point Byron looked him up and down, apparently noting that Shade was dressed in somewhat formal attire: a navy blue blazer, white button-down shirt, slacks and loafers.

"Damn, look atchu!" Byron blurted out. "Dressed all fancy and shit. You got sommin' goin' on?"

"Yeah, my bar mitzvah's later today," Shade replied drolly.

"Anyway," Byron chuckled, "you already know Spinner."

"Yeah," Shade acknowledged before looking at Spinner and saying, "Wassup?"

"'S'all good," Spinner replied.

Shade tossed the newspaper he was carrying onto the table. "Page B-sixteen. Local news. Zerk Simon copped a plea to manslaughter regardin' a body fished out the river. Official sentencin' is next week, but minimum is twenty years and this his third strike."

"I heard about it," Byron told him. "I like it, but that ain't what we agreed to."

"The agreement was that I'd get rid of his ass," Shade countered, "and I did."

"I wanted 'im *gone*."

"You bitchin' 'bout form over substance," Shade declared. "For all practical purposes, the nigga *is* gone. Now where's my fuckin' money?"

Byron just stared at him for a second, then chuckled. "Like I said b'foe, I like the way you just say what's on yo mind." As he spoke, he reached towards the floor and then lifted up a large paper bag, the top portion of which had been folded over so you couldn't see inside. However, rather than hand the bag to Shade, he placed it on the table in front of himself.

"The money's yours," Byron informed Shade. "But first, tell me how it went down."

Shade frowned. "Ain't shit to tell. Plus, you already know most of it."

"Tell me anyway," Byron insisted.

Shade let out a sigh of irritation. "That muhfucka Zerk somehow got the crazy idea that I had his coke, so he came after me, my family, and my girl. We all went to ground, but I knew we couldn't stay that way forever, and that nigga Zerk would never stop lookin'. Sommin' had to be done."

"And that's when you reached out," Byron concluded.

"Not right away. I mean, I knew you were willin' to pay to get rid of that nigga and I needed him gone anyway, so it made sense to kill two birds with one stone. Plus, you had resources. You knew that Zerk was settin' up on you, and got a tip that he was gonna try to rip you off. That all meant you had somebody in his network."

"It pays to have friends," Byron said, glancing at Spinner.

"Anyway, I didn't actually reach out to you until later," Shade continued, "At the time I was just thankin' that I could get Zerk to meet up since he thought I had his blow."

"How'd you know he'd show in person?" asked Byron.

"He's crazy and paranoid, so there was a chance he'd send somebody else," Shade admitted. "But after that shitshow with his brother, I didn't think he'd trust it to anybody else. Plus, I figured he'd be less wary if he was meetin' up with a female."

"Ya girl," Lord Byron concluded.

"Exactly," Shade said. "It made sense to use her. She seemed to have a reason for wantin' me dead and she didn't want a psychotic drug dealer comin' after her, so on the surface her wantin' to make a deal seemed like sommin' he'd buy. But when I put myself in Zerk's shoes – which ain't fuckin' easy – it didn't feel right. Basically, from the Zerk point of view, there was no guarantee that my girl wasn't workin' with me to set 'im up. If I was him, I'd be lookin' for some kind of insurance, so my girl came up with the idea to give him some if he asked: she'd tell him where my sistas were."

Lord Byron shook is head in disbelief. "Man, that's cold."

"It's called play-actin'," Shade reminded him. "She would just be playin' a role, and givin' up my sistas would convince Zerk that she and I weren't workin' together. It would make her offer sound legit. Then it would be mostly a matter of timin' things so he couldn't be in two places at once – make it so he couldn't personally go after my sistas *and* meet up to get his drugs."

"He had to pick one or the other," Byron surmised.

"Yeah, and my money was on him comin' to collect his product," Shade stated. "That's when I reached out to you and, among other thangs, asked if yo man on Zerk's team could make sure *he* was the one who went after my sistas, if it came to that. After you told me he could, we put the plan in motion."

"So," Byron droned, "ya girl calls Zerk, arranges for him to get his shit and tells him where to find yo sistas."

"Well, technically she called *me*," Spinner chimed in, "since I was holdin' Zerk's phone at the time. Then it was just a matter of negotiatin' a deal I was already in on, then suggestin' to Zerk that he go get the drugs while I scoop up the sistas. After that I left, waited a decent amount of time, then called Zerk and said I had 'em."

"That reminds me," Shade said. "At one point Zerk called you, and there was a voice in the background that was s'posed to be one of my sistas. Who was that?"

Spinner shrugged. "Some hoodrat I handed a twenty to be on standby, just in case. Her job was just to say shit like, 'Leave me the fuck alone' whenever I gave her the high sign."

"That was smart," Shade noted.

"It was necessary," Spinner added. "I mean, I never got the *real* location for yo sistas, so I wudda been up shit creek if Zerk had wanted to talk to one of 'em and there was nobody to put on the phone. Plus, it's not like he knew yo sistas' voices or anythang."

"A'ight, we got that part down," Lord Byron stated. "So what happened next?"

"We had wrapped up some powder in plastic so that it looked like a coupla keys," Shade told him. "We put that in a bag and my girl gave it to Zerk at the meet."

Byron looked at him skeptically. "And he just took that, without testin' it or anythang?"

"He tested it," Shade replied. "But there are chemicals and other shit that can mimic the reaction of narcotics – at least temporarily – and I got an 'A' in chemistry."

"So you fooled his ass into thankin' he had the real deal," Byron concluded. "Then what – he just left?"

"Sommin' like that," Shade answered.

"Bullshit," Spinner offered. "As much grief as Zerk went through over those missin' keys, he was gonna take that out on somebody."

"He did shoot one of his guys on purpose," Shade offered.

"That's classic Zerk," Spinner noted, "but ain't no way he was just gonna walk outta there without gettin' a pound of flesh from *you*."

Shade seemed to consider for a moment. "When Zerk and his niggas came in, I was tied up, but *not* tied up, if you know what I mean. The place we were in was bein' powered by a generator that was low on fuel. In fact, we intentionally made sure there wasn't much in there in order to guarantee that the lights would go out before too long. And they did. When that happened, I took off."

"And ya girl?" Byron inquired.

"She played her role to the end," Shade said. "Told Zerk that they needed to go after me and shit like that. Zerk declined and left. She waited until they drove off, they went out the back where I was waitin' for her. As for Zerk and those fools with him, the cops stopped those muhfuckas as they was drivin' away, and the rest is history."

"What about this plea they got Zerk to take?" Byron asked. "How you set that up?"

"There was this nigga whose teeth Zerk knocked out a few days back," Shade stated. "He didn't look like he was gonna make it, and somebody gave the teeth to me as incentive to, uh, do a certain job."

Byron looked at Spinner, who simply gave a curt nod.

"I put the teeth in the bottom of the bag with the fake blow," Shade continued. "That's practically a smoking gun as far as cops are concerned."

"Damn," Byron intoned. "You cold-blooded."

"The pot callin' the kettle black," Shade muttered, causing Lord Byron to laugh. "Anyway, that's it – end of story. Can I have my money now?"

"For sho'," Byron said, nodding. "You earned it. But just one last question."

"Sure," Shade said in a monotonous tone.

Byron rubbed his chin in thought for a moment, then asked, "You thank I can trust Spinner?"

Somewhat surprised, Shade look from Byron to Spinner – who looked like he'd just stepped on a land mine – then back to Byron.

"Whachu mean?" Shade asked, plainly confused.

"Well, he just turned on his boss Zerk," Byron explained. "We in a cutthroat business – literally – but loyalty gotta count for sommin'."

Shade reflected on that for a moment. "So he s'posed to be workin' for you now?"

"Naw," Byron said, "but we gone be collaboratin' in a coupla areas. I'm just curious if you thank I can trust him."

Shade turned towards Spinner again, who looked like he might be regretting that "Bullshit" comment he'd directed at Shade earlier.

"Zerk's a fuckin' psycho who killed his last two lieutenants," Shade said after a few seconds. "I don't view what Spinner did as disloyalty. That's self-preservation. Loyalty's a two-way street and in Spinner's situation, a nigga's gotta right to survive."

"Fair enough," Byron said, then slid the paper bag over to Shade.

Shade opened the bag and peeked inside. Satisfied, he closed it up again.

"Well," he droned, coming to his feet, "it's been a pleasure doin' business wichu."

"There is one last thing," Lord Byron said. "About Zerk's missin' coke."

"Look," Shade stated, "I don't know why everybody thank I know sommin' 'bout that blow. I don't know shit. I never even seen it."

"I wasn't gone ask you about it," Byron insisted. "Just pass on some info."

"And what's that?" Shade asked.

"From what I hear, that coke came from Bush."

Shade looked at him in surprise. "The dope king? *That* Bush?"

"That's the one."

Shade frowned. "I thought Bush didn't deal with bricks."

"Normally he don't, but I gather this was a special situation. But the point is, whoever got those keys is holdin' shit that belongs to Bush, and that is one nigga you don't wanna get on the wrong side of. He is a *muthafucka*."

Shade seemed to chew on that for a few seconds, then declared, "Then I'm glad I ain't the one with his shit."

THUG LIFE: EMANCIPATED

Chapter 87

After the warning about Bush, Shade paused only long enough for Spinner to tell him that they were square on Gin's debt before quickly leaving Lord Byron's place. He had another appointment that he absolutely could not be late for, and giving Byron a play-by-play recital of what had transpired at the factory had cost him some time. That said, what he had relayed had mostly been the truth. But as he got in his car and started driving, he thought about what had *actually* happened.

Basically, Shade had relented and told Yoni his plan when it appeared that she was about to call Zerk. At that point, it didn't seem like he had any options. In essence, if she couldn't be trusted, she was going to call Zerk whether he told her anything or not. But if there was the slightest chance that telling her could bring her over to his side, he had to take the chance. Ergo, he had rolled the dice, and it had paid off.

"Zerk's my problem child," he had explained to her. "It's *his* drugs, his brother that got killed, and his business that's sufferin'. Plus, he's the one lookin' to put some hurt on me right now, so I need to get rid of his ass."

Initially, Yoni had thought that meant Zerk having some kind of "accident," but Shade disabused her of the notion.

"I already got the cops lookin' at me for a bunch of shit," he'd told her. "Another body is just gonna add fuel to the fire. Plus, I don't need Zerk dead. I just need the muhfucka to go away."

That's when he outlined his plan. Ironically, it was that cop Gummerson who had given him an idea of what to do, but the genesis of his plan could actually be traced back to a news story he'd seen the year before. That was when a TV reporter, talking about the expansion of a new highway, had mentioned the condemnation of the factory where Shade had spent that summer playing with Sally.

Nostalgia had set in then, and Shade decided that he wanted to see the place at least one more time before it got torn down. With that in mind, he'd made a trip to the factory a few weeks later, but when he arrived he found a guy in a hard hat posting signs that stated the placed was now a government facility.

Mr. Hard Hat had told Shade that he couldn't be there – that he was trespassing on government property. In response, Shade had detailed how he'd spent a summer at the factory and just wanted to see the place before it got levelled, at which point Mr. Hard Hat just laughed. He had then explained to Shade the concept of legal condemnation – that the government had simply taken ownership of the factory.

"Eventually they probably *will* tear this place down for the highway to come through," Mr. Hard Hat had told him. "How soon depends on funding, but we're probably talking years at the very least."

Following that encounter, Shade had done a little research and become more familiar with legal condemnation. However, he didn't find much about it in relation to the factory. Apparently condemnation of that sort was only newsworthy when the government was taking someone's home or a thriving business. Abandoned industrial plants in the middle of nowhere didn't merit much attention.

After that, Shade had pretty much forgotten about the factory, but it came to mind again when Detective Gummerson was interrogating him and started talking about conspiracy and government buildings. It was at that point that the real seed was planted.

Of course, by then, Shade had already decided that he needed to deal with Zerk. He had come to that conclusion immediately following their men's room meeting.

THUG LIFE: EMANCIPATED

After Shade's interrogation, things had been hectic, to say the least, but the rudimentary plan had already been outlined in his brain: get Zerk to a government facility (in this case, the factory), alert the cops to his presence there, and then let the boys in blue do their jobs by throwing a stack of federal charges at that nigga. However, getting the police to a secluded site in a timely fashion was obviously a little tricky, and that was one of the sticking points he was trying to mentally iron out when Yoni conked him on the head. However, as he was explaining his plan, she claimed to have a solution.

"I can get the cops to show when we need them," she'd promised. When Shade had asked how, she had responded, "I'll tell I'ma White lady 'bout to get gangbanged by a bunch of niggas."

Shade didn't know if she was joking, but it was at that juncture, after he'd given her the basics of what he had in mind, that she'd untied him. Afterwards, she had watched him a little warily at first, but Shade had stayed on his best behavior, initially thanking her and then saying that he thought he'd need a couple of days to flesh out the rest of the plan.

Yoni, however, had other ideas.

"We're doing this *tonight*," she had told him, in a tone that was clearly non-negotiable. She had also stressed that they stick with the notion of her reaching out to Zerk, like she had threatened to do before Shade told her his plan. Thinking that it might make Zerk lower his guard, Shade had acquiesced.

After that it had been a mad scramble to get everything together. There was a big-box store maybe twenty minutes from the factory, and they had gone there to get the stuff they needed: plastic wrap, baby powder, distilled water, and more.

There had been video cameras in the store (although none in the parking lot), so they'd disguised themselves as best they could. Shade had tied one of his work rags around his head like a filthy bandana and sported a pair of sunglasses, while Yoni wore a hoodie that she had packed, keeping it pulled in tight around her face. Neither was perfect, but if anyone bothered to look at store cameras later, they'd be hard to identify.

Naturally, they had paid cash and then hustled back to the factory. Once there, they had gone to the shower area Shade had previously mentioned and started making *faux* bricks with the plastic wrap and baby powder, trying to match the quantity of actual coke that they had.

"Why we doin' this?" Yoni had asked at one point as she wrapped plastic around powder. "Why can't you just give him the real drugs? If yo plan work, he ain't gettin' far with 'em anyway."

"'Cause if my plan *don't* work," Shade had replied, "Zerk gone make off with a coupla keys, and I'm gone have a pissed-off Lord Byron lookin' to flay my ass. I don't need that, so if Zerk get away with sommin', I want it to be anythang other than actual coke."

"What make you thank he gone show up anyway?"

"'Cause he wants his shit."

"But why not send somebody? That's the benefit of bein' the boss – you don't have to risk yo own neck."

"He's had too many underlings fuck up lately, so I don't think he'll risk it. But we can always try to offer him some kind of guarantee."

"Like what – a promise? You thank he'll take our word for it?"

"Not likely. Zerk's the type who'll just threaten to kill yo family if you set him up."

"Hmmm," Yoni had droned. "Family…"

Following that, they had quickly settled on the idea of using Shade's sisters as "insurance." That in turn had led to the inevitable call to Lord Byron to discuss two things: Shade agreeing to "get rid of" Zerk (for a price), and Lord Byron's contact in Zerk's crew being recruited to "scoop up" Shade's sisters.

Taken as a whole, their plan was something of an elaborate con with several moving parts. For instance, they were trying to con Zerk with respect to Shade's sistas being taken as bargaining chips. They were also trying to trick him into taking possession of fake cocaine instead of the real thing. That second one, of course, involved initiating a switch and had two components that were slightly problematic.

First of all, to pull a switch, they ideally needed to have a second overnight bag that was identical to the one that the coke had originally come in. Given a day or two, Shade could probably have located one, but with their time constraints they had to settle for what they could find at the store they had visited. The one they had ultimately purchased wasn't an exact match, but was close enough to pass a cursory inspection.

Next was the problem of actually pulling off the switch itself. There was no doubt that Zerk was going to test the cocaine when he got it, and – contrary to what he'd told Lord Byron – Shade didn't have a ready method of mimicking the necessary chemical reaction. Ergo, they'd have to give Zerk the real blow initially, then find a way to swap bags.

The answer had come when they were using the distilled water they'd bought to wash up after making the fake bricks. The lights had flickered a couple of times and gone off. That's when Shade had an epiphany: swapping out bags would be easy if the room they were in was dark.

At that juncture, he'd already made the rounds once in terms of going through the factory and siphoning propane from other generators with a hose and bucket he'd found. He had then used the additional fuel to power the warehouse generator. More to the point, having dealt with the warehouse generator a couple of times by then, he had a rough idea of how long a certain amount of propane would keep the lights on. It wouldn't be exact, but he could get it close.

They were almost ready at that point. One of Shade's final tasks before they reached out to Zerk was to drive his car off the factory grounds and park somewhere away from the road. The fact that Yoni hadn't felt the need to go with him said volumes about the level of trust and faith she had in him.

At that point, Shade took on what was probably the most distasteful item on his to-do list. After parking the car (but before heading back to the factory), he took a bloody steak they had bought from the store and smeared it all over his shirt. This was for a two-fold purpose: to hopefully convince anyone looking that Yoni and been roughing his ass up, and - bearing in mind Spinner's comment about Zerk's dislike of blood – hopefully it would make that nigga keep his distance. It didn't mean he wouldn't shoot Shade from across the room, but it was about all he could come up with.

After that, it had taken Shade about fifteen minutes to jog back to the factory warehouse. It had been taxing, but no doubt would help with making him look the part he'd have to play later. At that juncture, Yoni had also insisted on slapping him a few times to make sure his face "was a lil' fucked up."

"You got a bloody shirt, but yo face still all pretty and shit," she had said. "Those two don't go together."

Shade had agreed that it sent a mixed message, but thought Yoni got a little too into it – especially when she punched him one time instead of slapping.

By then, it had been a few hours since Shade had told Yoni his plan. Needless to say, they were both tired but felt it was worthwhile to do a few dry runs, following which Yoni had made the call to Zerk.

Shade had to admit that she'd done a good job on the phone; if he hadn't been in on it, he would have sworn she was being sincere. Asking for the ten kay was a little impromptu on her part, but coming across as a greedy bitch definitely made her seem more credible.

After that, they had settled in to wait, watching until they saw headlights approaching. It was then that Shade had gone to make sure the generator had the proper level of fuel while Yoni made her call to the police. A few minutes later, Shade found himself "tied" to a chair in the warehouse.

Fortunately, no one checked his bindings. Not that nigga who initially came in through the back (tripping all over shit when he was trying to be stealthy); not Zerk when he came in looking all smug. If they had, they would have noticed that he could slip out of that shit at any time.

There were a few touch-and-go moments – like when Zerk shot one of his own gang, and when it looked like he was about to cap Shade – but for the most part things had gone according to plan. In essence, Zerk had tested the drugs and received proof of their authenticity. Then it was just a matter of keeping him preoccupied – and staying alive – until the lights went out.

To that end, the flickering lights had been a heads-up, letting them know the power was about to go out for good. When that happened, Shade had immediately jumped up and intentionally kicked over the table the bag of coke was sitting on, then dashed for the back door. It was a little tricky in the dark, but that's part of the reason they had practiced a few times. After leaving the warehouse area of the building, he had headed to the back door and – upon exiting - made a beeline for the generator.

His job at that point was to pour the rest of the propane into the generator, which would then bring the lights back on. Until he did that, Yoni was going to be stuck inside a pitch-black warehouse with a bunch of nervous niggas with guns, as well as one armed sociopath. Moreover, the longer it was dark in there, the more likely it was that something bad would happen. In fact, he feared the worst when some shots rang out as he was adding propane to the generator. At that point, although it was a deviation from the plan, he had gone back inside in case Yoni was in trouble.

Yoni's main job throughout everything was to stay close to the bag of coke. When the lights went out, she was supposed to grab the bag and toss it into the drawer of a nearby desk. There was always a chance that Zerk would be holding the bag when the power died, but Yoni had insisted she'd be able to improvise and get it away from him. Thankfully, it didn't come to that. She was able to pull off her part without having to do anything crazy. Then, when the lights came back on, she had pointed to the fake bag they had planted earlier.

After Zerk and his people left, Yoni had quickly retrieved the bag of coke from the desk. Next, after using her shirt to wipe off the drawer handle, she had headed for the back warehouse door. However, it opened before she got there as Shade stepped in, having come back to check on her. At that point, they had left and started running for his car.

As they ran, Shade had done a final mental check, trying to make sure he hadn't overlooked anything. They had bought rubber gloves at the store and had worn them almost up until the time that Zerk arrived at the warehouse. In addition, Shade had gone through the place and wiped down every surface they might have touched before getting "tied up," and he watched Yoni use her shirt to wipe off door knobs as they left. Almost everything they had bought from the store (or the trash left from them) was in his car, and when they left the factory he'd also taken the bucket and hose he'd used to siphon propane. About the only thing on the premises of the factory that could possibly show they were there was the shower area where they had put together the fake bricks.

450

However, getting anything useful out of there was a longshot in Shade's opinion.

En route to the car, Shade couldn't help but notice all the flashing lights as Zerk and his crew got stopped. He had smiled then, thinking of all the shit Zerk would be in. If the cops halfway did their jobs, Zerk would be facing a slew of federal charges just based on the fact that he went into the warehouse. The gunfire was a bonus, as it added damaging federal property to his list of crimes. (In truth, Shade merely yanking the sign off the warehouse door was enough for that, but having Zerk charged with more offenses couldn't hurt.)

On top of that, the bag with the fake coke that Zerk had taken was actually the original bag that Shade had found. So again, if the cops were even halfway competent, there was evidence on that bag that would link Zerk to what had happened to Sneak.

But the *coup de gras* was obviously the teeth. With everything going on, Shade had never gotten rid of them – had practically forgotten about them, in fact. But as they were putting the fake drugs into the bag, he'd had a sudden inspiration. Thus, he had retrieved the pouch with the teeth and tucked it into the bottom of the bag, under the plastic-wrapped baby powder. That way, even if the cops completely shit the bed regarding everything else, they'd still have an ironclad case against that nigga Zerk.

Upon reaching the car, they had quickly driven away – initially with the lights out so as to avoid attention. Afterwards, they had found a secluded spot where they quickly changed clothes. Next, they had adopted Shade's earlier methodology and found a few barrel fires and the like where they disposed of various evidentiary items: the clothes they had worn, the remnants of the things they'd bought at the store, all of the related trash…basically anything that could tie them to what had happened at the factory. Actually, Shade had realized that there was still one thing that could place them – or more specifically, *him* – at the scene. There was no way to handle it at that moment, but he'd made a mental note to deal with it later.

****

Reflecting on everything that had happened as he drove to his appointment, Shade had to admit that he was surprised that it had worked. Ordinarily, he would have wanted more time to plan and get everything together. Given the time constraints, among other things, he and Yoni had actually done an admirable job, but it was not how he ordinarily did things. It had been hasty, sloppy and imprecise – the kind of thing his grandfather would have hated. In fact, his grandfather was probably rolling over in his grave. If he were alive, he'd most likely be saying that Shade had simply gotten lucky.

I'd rather be lucky than good, Shade thought, which was actually an adage his grandfather had been fond of saying.

At that point, however, he had no more time to critique his performance at the factory. He had arrived at the location for his appointment.

Concentrating now on what was about to happen, Shade grabbed a tie that was in the front passenger seat and began putting it on. He spent a moment thinking about how his life was about to radically change – and not just because of the bag of cash he'd gotten from Byron, which he had placed it in the trunk. Suddenly feeling nervous, he used the rearview mirror to check out the tie he'd just put on. Then he took a deep breath and stepped out the car.

THUG LIFE: EMANCIPATED

Chapter 88

The hearing was already underway when Gummy slipped into the courtroom. He had initially planned to sit at the back, but there was almost no one present so he moved closer. Ultimately, he ended up sitting on a bench a few rows back from the front, but chose a spot that allowed him to get a good profile view of the guy responsible for this particular court session: Shade.

He was standing in the middle of the courtroom, directly in front of the judge's bench. Dressed in a coat and tie, he looked incredibly professional – more like a college student or an intern than someone straight out the hood. Much to his chagrin, Gummy had to admit that the kid cleaned up nice.

Next to him was his lawyer, that little fireplug Bronwyn DuBose. At the moment, she wasn't speaking (which was probably a first for her, in Gummy's opinion). Instead, she and her client were both listening to the judge, who was sitting at the bench dressed in her formal robe. Gummy leaned forward to hear what the judge was saying.

"…that Peitioner understands what he is asking for," the Judge said. "This is a request that, once granted, can not easily be undone. Moreover, it will wholly, thoroughly, and completely change your life. For instance, many protections that are currently afforded you under the law will be gone. Do you understand this?"

"I do, Your Honor," Shade replied. "I know that my life will fundamentally change in all respects, and I accept that, as well as any possible consequences."

The judge seemed to consider this, then glanced slightly to the side. Following her gaze, Gummy noticed two girls seated on the front row of benches not too far from Shade. He hadn't initially noticed them, but quickly gave them a once-over. One appeared to be in her mid- to late teens, while the other was probably ten or twelve. Both were wearing what his mother would have called "their Sunday best."

"And are you two young ladies willing to live with the decision if I grant this petition?" the judge asked.

Both girls rose, but it was the elder who responded, saying, "Yes, Your Honor. Since our grandfather died our brother has been the person who's taken care of us. He goes to work, pays the bills, makes sure we stay focused on school… I mean, we all missed a couple of days this week because of a stomach bug, but outside of things like that our attendance is stellar, and that's because of our brother. He's essentially the parent in our home."

"Alright," said the judge. Turning her attention to the lawyer, she asked, "Is all the paperwork in order, Counselor?"

"Yes, Your Honor," Bronwyn replied. "You have the petition, all motions, and numerous references from teachers, administrators, and others attesting to my client's fitness of character. There's also a statement from the relevant CPS caseworker saying that she thinks this is in the best interest of the family. Finally, you have two years of income statements showing that my client earns enough to comfortably support himself and his sisters."

The judge had appeared to leaf through some papers on the bench while Bronwyn spoke. She then put them down and gave Shade a hard stare.

"To be honest," the judge said, "I don't like what I'm about to do. I don't think that, in general, it serves a beneficial purpose because it thrust decisions and responsibilities on the most important members of our society – our children – that they may not be ready for. That said, in some cases, it is warranted, and it is my sincere belief that this is such a case. With that in mind, I hereby grant Petitioner's Request for

Emancipation and appoint him guardian of his two younger siblings."

With that she banged her gavel.

****

There was a small degree of pandemonium after the judge's decision, with Shade and his sisters practically cheering. The judge, smiling, had told them to take it outside her courtroom, which they gladly did.

Once outside, Shade spent a few moments talking to his lawyer about some last-minute items. It was then that he noticed Detective Gummerson standing off to the side.

After a few minutes, Bronwyn gave him a hug and then went on her way. At that point, Shade's sisters mobbed him again, plainly excited about the outcome.

"Hey," he said to them after a moment. "I'm parked right outside. Why don't you two go on down and I'll see you in a minute."

Nissa had looked like she wanted to say something, then she noticed the detective. Her demeanor immediately became more somber.

"Come on, Cherry," Nissa said, taking her younger sister's hand and leading her away.

Shade watched them for a moment, then turned to Gummy. "Detective Gummerson. Nice to see you again, sir."

Gummy smiled. "I'm not sure how true that is, but it's nice of you to say so."

"How you took it is how I meant it," Shade replied.

"Hmmm... Now I have to think on how to take *that*," Gummy remarked. "Anyway, we can walk and talk. I wouldn't want to keep you from your family."

"Fine by me," Shade commented as they began meandering down the hallway. "So what brings you here today?"

"Honestly? Curiosity."

"About what?"

"For the most part, I was curious as to why a sixteen-year-old needed a lawyer on retainer."

"You could have asked. I would have told you."

"Now where's the fun in that?" Gummy chided jokingly. "Anyway, I had a friend at the courthouse go through all the filings by the delightful Bronwyn DuBose looking for your name, trying to figure out what she was doing for you. Nothing came up."

"Somehow I get the feeling that didn't stop you."

"No, it didn't, because then I remembered something: they don't enter the names of minors on court documents - only initials. So I had my friend go back and look again, this time for initials Jay and Gee."

"And you hit pay dirt."

"Pretty much."

"Well, I'm sure you were disappointed that she wasn't trying to get some drug charges against me dropped, or have me tried as a minor for assaulting someone, or get me a reduced sentence for carjacking somebody. She was just hired to help me become emancipated so I can hold my family together."

"Just for the record, I never thought it was anything bad. You don't have a rap sheet, so I knew it wasn't anything criminal. I just didn't know what it was initially. But since you bring it up, being emancipated does change how the world views you now. For instance, if you do anything criminal, I can arrest you and have you tried as an adult."

"That's unlikely," Shade told him.

"Oh, really?" Gummy muttered almost in surprise. "You don't think you could be tried as adult?"

"That's not what I'm saying. What I meant was that it's unlikely you'd be the person making the arrest. You see, we're moving."

"Huh?" Gummy said with a frown.

"I said we're moving – out to the 'burbs. So if I do anything bad, it'll be out of your jurisdiction."

"I suppose so," Gummy noted, giving Shade an appraising glance. "But the 'burbs? That's gonna be a little expensive, don't you think?"

"Money's not a problem – especially now that I don't have to fork over a king's ransom every time the lawyer says we need to file something. No, the real problem was that, as a minor, I lacked the legal capacity to contract."

Gummy nodded in understanding. "I get it. As a minor, you can't buy a house, lease a place, get cable TV, and so on. Legally, you couldn't sign a contract. But now…"

"Now I *can*. And actually, my lawyer's been working a deal to help me get a place for a while. Again, it cost me an arm and a leg and I had to put a ton of money into escrow, but it's all working out. Plus, it fulfills a promise to my grandparents – that I'd get my sisters out the hood."

"So where did all this money come from?"

"I won most of it online," Shade said. "Stock-picking contests."

"Stock-picking contests?" Gummy repeated dubiously.

"Yeah," Shade confirmed with a nod. "Apparently there are a lot of brokerages and such vying for America's wallet. To attract people they'll have these stock-picking contests every so often, and I just happened to win a couple of them."

"Hmmm," Gummy droned, now recalling that Shade had a slew of accolades relating to IT and website development. "I don't suppose you happen to member the names of these brokerages."

"Sorry, I forgot," Shade lamented. "But I think most of them shut down."

"You don't say," uttered a dubious Gummy. "That's quite the coinky-dink."

"Not really," Shade assured him. "Most of those brokerages were new and the contests were just gimmicks to attract people. After the contests, they had no staying power, so they folded."

"But they paid out when you won."

"Oh yeah – they were *legit*. They just weren't able to remain viable."

"That's a shame. I would love to check them out."

"If I remember, I'll let you know," Shade told him. "Anyway, I hear congratulations are in order – you closed that triple-homicide you were asking me about."

"I see news travels fast."

"It was in the paper, online and on the six o'clock news. Between all that it wasn't hard to see all the charges against the suspect you arrested, as well as which ones eventually got dropped."

Gummy took all that in with a nod. "To be honest, we've always known how one of the guys in that condemned building died, so it was never a triple-homicide in the sense of all three of them being killed by a fourth person. That said, we got a lot of physical evidence linking our suspect to the scene. But we have a better case against him in a different homicide, and that's the one he pled out on. Still, the D.A., police commissioner and everyone on down think he's the culprit in the triple, so they consider it solved and want it closed."

"Sounds reasonable to me," Shade noted.

"I'm sure it does," Gummy retorted.

Shade gave him an odd look, then said, "Well, this is me."

At that point, they had left the courthouse, and as he finished speaking Shade gestured towards his car. His sisters were already inside, with Nissa having apparently used her key to start the engine.

"Wow," Gummy blurted out, eyeing the car. "Looks really nice."

"Yeah, I just had it completely detailed," Shade told him. "Top to bottom and front to back."

"And are those new tires?" asked Gummy.

"Yeah," Shade confirmed. "I drove through a construction area a few days ago, and it was like someone had dropped a keg of nails in the road – messed up all my tires. They were old anyway, so it seemed like divine providence telling me to get new ones."

"Interesting," Gummy intoned. "You know, that suspect we were talking about got arrested at an old factory. Him and some of his crew had driven a couple of cars up there for some reason we haven't completely figured out yet. But here's the thing: we found a *third* set of tire tracks up there."

"Well, that's interesting," Shade observed.

"Yeah," Gummy agreed. "By the way, what happened to your *old* tires?"

"I tossed them into a dumpster – can't remember exactly where, though. But I got a receipt for the new ones, though, if you'd like to see it."

"That's okay," Gummy assured him.

Shade took that in silently for a moment, then said, "Well, my sisters are waiting, so I should get going. Goodbye, Detective."

"I'm just going to assume that's 'goodye for now,'" Gummy told him. "I'm pretty sure I'll see you again."

THUG LIFE: EMANCIPATED

Chapter 89

Shade celebrated his emancipation with his sisters by getting a late lunch at a fancy restaurant. They were already dressed for it, so it seemed to make sense. It was actually something of a double celebration since, as he'd told that cop Gummerson, they'd be moving soon. They were all so happy with the outcome that Shade didn't mind the fact that he'd had to pay Mrs. Romano from CPS two grand to get with the program. It was worth it not to have to deal with her again.

After the meal, he dropped his sisters off at home while he went to see Yoni. She was currently staying in a fancy hotel downtown. For one of the few times in his life, he actually valeted his car, leaving the key in the ignition and taking a ticket from the attendant as he stepped out. Then he went up to see Yoni, taking the paper bag he'd gotten from Lord Byron.

The hotel was more posh than he expected, with marble tile in the lobby and a magnificent atrium that provided a panoramic view as he rode up in a glass-walled elevator. When he reached the proper floor, he noted plush carpeting in the hallway and elegant art niches that were home to ornate sculptures and paintings. Finally, when he got to Yoni's door, he saw that there was no knocker; there was a doorbell instead.

She was obviously expecting him, because she opened the door just a few seconds after he rang the bell, dressed in a luxury bathrobe. They greeted each other with a slightly awkward hug, and Yoni gave him a kiss on the cheek as well.

They really hadn't spoken since the meet with Zerk. After they drove away from the factory and got rid of all evidence linking them to it, Shade had taken them to a twenty-four hour burger joint, where they had grabbed a quick bite and then slept a few hours in the parking lot. When they woke

461

up, Yoni had asked him to drop her off at a relative's house; after doing so, Shade had gone to meet up with his sisters.

Since then there had only been short text messages and even shorter calls. But the gist of it all was that they'd agreed to meet that day after Shade wrapped up everything else he needed to do. Now that he was here, there was a tension in the room that made him wish he'd put things off a little longer.

"What do you think?" Yoni said, gesturing towards the room in general.

"Pretty swank," Shade said truthfully, noting that they were in the living room of what was presumably a one-bedroom suite. Among other things, the room boasted a high-end sofa-and-loveseat combo, a wet bar, and a seventy-inch television. And the window offered a picturesque view of the city.

"Yeah, it's pretty nice," Yoni agreed as she took a seat on the couch.

Sitting down next to her, Shade said, "So how much is this place?"

"Fuck if I know," Yoni announced with a shrug. "My dad's cousin works here, and she hooked me up with the room. She's the one whose house you dropped me at."

"That's the kind of relative we all need."

"Well, I told her that I couldn't go back to the old apartment – not after two muhfuckas got murdered in there – so she got me this place."

"You kiddin, right?" Shade said, grinning. "You thank this the first time a coupla muhfuckas got shot up in there? Every apartment in that place prolly got a bloody fuckin' history."

"Yeah, but this history don't include *me*," she stressed. "Anyway, you probably heard already, but the cops bought that frame-job you set up at my place."

"Again, I didn't frame anybody, but that does remind me," Shade uttered. "How's ya dad?"

"Fucked in da head," She replied. "On the one hand, he thanks he's a real bad-ass who killed two muhfuckas who tried to jack him while he was dead drunk. On the other, he's freaked that some niggas might have followed him home without him realizing it, and cudda killed him and then done whatever the fuck they wanted to me."

"Does that mean he soberin' up?"

"He tryin'. It didn't hurt that the hospital held his ass until he dried out, and he stayed sober long enough to give the police a statement. 'Course, he ain't have shit to tell 'em 'cause he was blind drunk and don't even remember how the fuck he got home that night."

"What about physically? He good?"

"Doctors say no permanent damage, so he should have a full recovery."

"Cool. And he got yo texts?"

"Yeah. The cops had took his phone, and when he sobered up enough to unnastand what had happened they gave it back. But at that point the police had already looked at it, saw the texts I sent about staying with a friend, and reached out to me. I told 'em I really been stayin' with my boyfriend but I don't want my daddy to find out."

"And they were good with that?"

"They told me they want to interview me, but I said I'm too fucked up and scared right now, so they gone talk to me in a coupla days."

"In the meantime you get to lounge around this palace."

"It *is* pretty nice, even though I just lay around in a robe all day, watchin' TV and orderin' room service."

"Poor you," Shade teased.

"It's not free, though," she shot back. "My cousin's gettin' some kind of ninety-percent employee discount, but she know I'm good for payin' her back."

"Speaking of cash…" Shade began, then handed her the paper bag. "Your half from Lord Byron."

"What about yours?" she asked as she opened the bag and peeked inside.

"Took it out before I came here," he explained. Basically, when he had dropped his sisters off at home, he had made the decision to carry the bag inside and take his cut out before going to meet Yoni.

"I see," Yoni commented as she closed the bag up and set it on a nearby end table.

"You don't wanna count it?" Shade asked.

"No, I trust you," she replied. "Although I'm not sure if you'd say the same about me."

Shade gave her a confused look. "Whachu talkin' 'bout?"

"I'm talkin' 'bout the fact that you separated yo part of the money before comin' here – like maybe I was gone have a nigga waitin' behind the doe' to club yo ass when you walked in, then run off with all the cash."

"It's not *you* I don't trust – it's the fuckin' valets. See, I was just gone bring it all and leave my half in the car, then I thought 'bout *those* muhfuckas. They have yo car keys, and trust me, they go all through yo shit when you park with them."

"Then why not self-park?"

"It's a fuckin' mile away," Shade insisted. "You want me showin' up all hot and sweaty?"

"Maybe I *do*," she said with a coy wink.

"That explains the enthusiastic hug when I came in."

Yoni just stared at him for a second, then let out a sigh. "Look, I'm still tryin' to digest everythang that happened the

464

last few days. I mean, maybe all this shit is old hat for somebody who runs 'errands' all the time, but it's new to me, okay? I'm still tryin' to wrap my head around everythang."

"Meanin' that you still wonderin' if I killed Sneak."

"No," Yoni declared, shaking her head. "I don't thank you killed 'em. But that don't mean you ain't responsible."

"Responsible how?" Shade demanded.

"You knew Sneak – knew how he thought. Did you really believe he could walk past two niggas fuckin' like rabbits and not say anythang?"

"Look, all Sneak had to do was walk past that room. That's it! If he'd done that, he'd prolly still be here today – most likely warnin' me to keep my dick in my pants around his sista."

Yoni snickered at that. "Actually, that do sound like him."

"Look, I know you wanna blame somebody," Shade told her, "but the nigga that shot Sneak is dead. The leader of the muhfuckas that sucked him into the drug game is prolly goin' away for life. Basically, the people that hurt yo brutha are out the picture."

Yoni seemed to think reflect on that for a minute, then said, "I guess you right. So where does that leave *us*?"

"Right where we were before. Like I said, you can trust me."

Her eyes narrowed. "But you don't think you can trust *me*."

"That depends."

"On what?"

"Whether you tell me the truth."

Yoni shrugged. "Regarding…?"

Shade frowned, not liking what he was about say, then just blurted out. "How long you been workin' for the police?"

Yoni stared at him for a moment, then looked down at her hands. "I don't work *for* them. I was working *with* them – trying to figure out who killed my brutha."

Shade shrugged his shoulders indifferently. "Po-TAY-to, Po-TAH-to."

Yoni looked him in the eye. "Look, if I was working for the cops, I would have worn a wire like they wanted me to when we left the police station. But I didn't."

"It wudna done you any good," Shade shot back. "First of all, listenin' devices usually only have a range of a coupla hundred yards. The best ones can transmit about a mile, but that's in open space. So, if you'd been wired, whoever was listenin' wudda had to stick pretty close – followed us all outside the city and shit – and I was watchin' and didn't see nobody."

"It cudda been the type with a recorder attached."

"Still wudna helped," Shade insisted. "Remember that place where we sat and talked – there was an electrical tower nearby?"

Yoni nodded. "Yeah."

"That tower interferes with certain electrical equipment – includin' recordin' devices. You wudda just picked up a ton of fuckin' static."

Yoni was silent for a moment, then asked, "How'd you even know I was dealin' with the cops like that anyway?"

"When they brought me in, they stopped me in front of the room where you and that cop were talkin'," Shade answered. "I think it was s'posed to intimidate me a lil' – make me wonder whachu was tellin' 'em."

"I been talkin' to 'em ever since Sneak got capped. They was tryin' to find out who killed my brutha and I was tryin' to help."

"I didn't know about Sneak bein' yo brutha at that point, but I could tell from yo body language that you wasn't

466

in there under protest. You were all chummy with 'em, crackin' smiles and shit – not distressed like most muhfuckas who in there gettin' interrogated."

"They saw us kiss at school," Yoni explained. "They wanted to let me know that you were a suspect in they investigation and to ask about anythang you might have let slip."

Shade snorted in derision. "They used to muhfuckas braggin' 'bout who they done killed and shit like that."

"But not you. You that silent killer."

"Damn. You make me sound like muhfuckin' high blood pressure."

Yoni burst out laughing. "Oh shit! I completely forgot that's what they call it: high blood pressure – the silent killer."

Shade chuckled as well, then stated, "You know, I like you like this."

"How's that?"

"Happy. Smiling."

She grinned at him. "Well, I like you like this, too."

Shade raised an eyebrow. "Meaning?"

"Funny. Not killin' people for petty cash."

"Well, I guess I'll raise my rates."

That caused another round of laughter that ended with the two of them just looking at each other and smiling.

"Anythang else you wanna ask?" Yoni said.

"Yeah," Shade responded. "How'd you get those cops to respond so fast when we were at the factory? And don't gimme no shit about a gangbang."

Yoni grinned for a second at that, then turned serious. "I called Gummerson while you were parking your car away from the factory. I told him I had info on evidence in his case and a suspect, as well as where to find 'em. But I stressed three things: he needed to stay back and let whoever was heading to the factory get there, that he shouldn't interfere no matter what he heard, and that he needed to arrest them on their way back out 'cause they'd have his evidence."

Shade was pensive for a moment, then uttered, "I'm surprised he went for that."

"He didn't have a choice, 'cause I actually didn't tell him the location until he agreed."

"Man, you a tough negotiator – strong-armin' the cops *and* drug dealers."

"That how real bitches roll, nigga," Yoni playfully boasted, at the same time tapping her chest twice and then throwing up a gang sign.

Shade threw his head back in laughter, and Yoni joined him. It was a fun, lighthearted moment, and when they finally stopped chuckling a few seconds later, they once again found themselves simply staring at each and smiling.

"Fuck it," Yoni finally said, more to herself than to Shade. A second later she had straddled him and was kissing him, deeply and hungrily.

Shade kissed her back with the same fervor, again savoring how sweet her kisses were. At the same time, his hands found their way under her robe. One went immediately to her bosom and started fondling her tits, while the other slid down between her legs and started caressing her pussy, which was already dripping wet. On her part, Yoni moaned in pleasure while at the same time reaching down and stroking his dick, which had immediately started throbbing in his pants.

All of a sudden, an annoying buzzing sound began, like a fly constantly droning around your ear. Both Shade and Yoni tied to ignore it, but it was persistent.

"Shit!" Yoni grumbled after a few seconds. "I better get that."

"Do you have to?" Shade asked frankly.

"Yeah," Yoni insisted as she got off him and reached towards the coffee table where her cell phone was located.

"It's my cousin," she explained. "I gave her a special ring in case she needed to call me about the room, which is why I need to take it."

With that, she answered the phone while Shade turned his attention elsewhere. In essence he took in the room again, while Yoni seemed to give a series or responses that mainly consisted of "Yeah," "Naw," and "Okay."

When she got finally off the phone, there was a slight frown on her face.

"Everythang okay?" Shade inquired.

"Yeah," she answered. "It's just that my cousin thanks she can only keep the room about three more days."

"So what that mean?"

"Basically that I start payin' full freight for this bitch or I get out." She then looked at him, and – seeing his concern – said, "But it's okay – don't worry about it. I'm not wild about goin' back to the apartment, but I can stay there for a while until I figure out sommin' else."

"Hmmm," Shade droned, thinking. "It's prolly not a good idea, but there's always my house."

Yoni gave him a skeptical look. "Don't y'all have rules and shit about people stayin' overnight? I got the impression yo sistas like me, but not enough to have me as a permanent fuckin' houseguest."

"But it wouldn't be like that," Shade insisted. "See, we movin'…"

At that juncture, he explained to Yoni that he and his sisters were headed to the suburbs. That meant their current house would be uninhabited.

"And you're lookin' to rent it?" Yoni asked.

"I was actually thinkin' of sellin' it," Shade admitted. "But I'm open to rentin'. It'll be a lil' odd, though, if we in a relationship."

"Are we *in* a relationship?"

Rather than answer, Shade remarked, "My point is that I'll be your landlord, so you'll have to be cool with me being able to come in and out at any time. Basically, some of the normal boundaries that couples have won't exist."

"Oh, so we a couple now? This shit's movin' fast," she joked, causing Shade to groan in aggravation. Snickering, she added, "Look, I unnastand everythang you sayin', and if we get good on the rent amount and other shit, it may work out."

"Good," Shade stressed.

"Now, about this relationship thang," Yoni went on, "I don't date drug dealers."

"Great, 'cause I ain't one."

"You not a drug dealer? That's fantastic," Yoni said with a slight bit of sarcasm. "So, if you not a drug dealer, tell me what happened to the coke."

Shade was silent for a moment, then said. "I still have it."

Yoni just looked at him for a few seconds, then asked, "You plannin' to sell it?"

"No."

"You gone keep it?"

"Not if I can help it."

"You gone give it away?"

"I don't think that's a good idea."

"So you plannin' to use it?"

"Fuck naw!" Shade blurted out, surprised she would even suggest it.

"Then I'm fuckin' confused," Yoni admitted. "I don't know that there's any other options."

Shade frowned in concentration, and for a moment considered relaying to her what Lord Byron had said about the blow and where it came from, then decided against it – mostly because it was unconfirmed.

"Look," he finally said, "Zerk never paid for that coke, so somebody's owed for it and is prolly lookin' for it right now. So if they show up, I'll be fucked if I don't have it, but I don't like havin' that shit around either. I'm fuckin' stuck."

"Nigga, you sound like one them damn crabs they told us about in class – the kind that reach into a trap for some food and get stuck cause they can't pull they claw out. But all they gotta do to get away is let go of the fuckin' food."

"I get whachu sayin', but it ain't that easy," he stressed.

"And I can appreciate that," Yoni said, "but I don't wanna get caught up in any shit with a drug dealer boyfriend."

Shade gave her a hard look. "Whachu tryin' to say?"

Yoni sighed in resignation. "That it's prolly time for you to go."

With that she stood up. Shade, understanding that the conversation was over, reluctantly got up and began walking to the door. However, just as he reached it, Yoni suddenly slipped in front of him, placing her back to the door.

"You forgettin' my rule," she admonished with a coy look on her face.

Shade shook his head in confusion. "What rule?"

Yoni smiled salaciously. "You have to *cum* before you can *go*."

Shade simply stared at her in confusion for a second, then the light of understanding shined in his eyes and a smile started to form on his lips. (Yoni's robe suddenly falling open was also a hint-and-a-half.)

Shade leaned in to kiss her, only to have Yoni bring his advance to a halt by quickly and firmly putting a finger to his lips.

"Two things," she said. "One, lose the fuckin' coke. And two, don't ever fuckin' lie to me. Got it?"

"Got it," Shade assured her with a nod.

THUG LIFE: EMANCIPATED

"Good," she said as she jumped into his arms. "Now bring that dick home to me."

THE END

THUG LIFE: EMANCIPATED

Thank you for purchasing this book! If you enjoyed it, please feel free to leave a review on the site from which it was purchased.

Also, if you would like to be notified when I release new books, please subscribe to my mailing list via the following link: http://eepurl.com/gShzML

Finally, for those who may be interested, I have included my blog and social media info:

Blog: https://nirvanablaque.blogspot.com/

Facebook: https://www.facebook.com/nirvana.black.3597

Twitter: https://twitter.com/BlaqueNirvana

CPSIA information can be obtained
at www.ICGtesting.com
Printed in the USA
LVHW032251280222
712222LV00001B/54